Taking Stock

Taking Stock

❖❖❖

Confessions of
a City Priest

VICTOR STOCK

HarperCollins*Publishers*

HarperCollins*Publishers*
77–85 Fulham Palace Road, London W6 8JB
www.fireandwater.com

First published in Great Britain in 2001
by HarperCollins*Publishers*

1 3 5 7 9 10 8 6 4 2

A catalogue record for this book is available from the British Library

ISBN 0 00 274069 9

Printed and bound in Great Britain by
Creative Print & Design, Ebbw Vale, Wales

Contents

Acknowledgments

Without my literary agent (as she became), Annette Green, listening to me broadcasting on Greater London Radio, this book would not exist. Nor would it exist without the patient help, slaving over many hot screens, of Dilly Erskine Crum, Vanessa Giles, Ian Burleigh, Paul Ronke, Annie Reyersbach and Graham Phillips, who reduced thirty-two volumes of a diary to a manageable and readable text. It would be invidious to pick out any one friend to dedicate these confessions to; suffice it to say, without my many, dearly-loved friends there would be nothing to read.

Introduction

A literary agent wrote me a letter saying that she had heard me on Greater London Radio's *Drive Time*. She thought these funny radio pieces – about life, truth, the meaning of the universe and what was in the newspapers – might mean I had a book in me. Gratified and encouraged (you do not get letters like that from bishops), I told her that, as a matter of fact, I *had* written a bit of a book – about art. This is surely enough to make the heart of a kind literary agent sink. Similarly, everybody has written a book about gardening. I have written one of those too, although only in my head. It is called *Gardening Twice a Month for Not Very Long and Achieving Spectacular Results, Universally Acclaimed by a Dazzled and Admiring World*. 'Oh, but there is my diary,' I added in a throwaway voice. It was upon this that my encourager seized, and here is the result.

Those of us who keep diaries are slaves to an obsession. Every day since 1976 I have written something. It is seldom about life, truth and the meaning of the universe; more often it is about who I have met, what I have had for dinner or what I have seen and done on holiday. The priest's life is essentially about people and places, and these are recorded in my diaries too (perhaps more interesting to the outsider than snapshots of private holidays). It is also about relating those people and places to the great mythic adventure of Sacred Time. Every week commemorates the journey from Good Friday to Easter Day, with every Sunday being a strange kind of entry into the mystery of the Resurrection of Jesus. At least, this is the theory. At St Mary-le-Bow in the City of London, where nobody lives in the parish, things are a little different because there is no congregation for Sundays, Christmas Day or Easter.

This volume is simply a selection of memories from 14 years out of the 30 I have spent working in London as a priest in the Church of England. I have been based at St Mary-le-Bow since 1986 and my life there has been packed with a mixture of the remarkable and the mundane, the funny and the tragic. I have lunched with well-known figures, taken part in the pomp of Lord Mayor's Day, appeared on television, scrubbed the church floor, felt exhausted, fallen asleep at dinner parties, wondered what God might be and how to talk about it. I have survived visits from royalty, a man who smashed in my front door with an axe, and the daily demands of people in trouble who need a sympathetic ear, a helping hand and a smile.

All this is set within the fantastic, enchanted landscape of London. The city's flats and Underground, parks and cinemas, pubs and museums, dinner tables and classrooms are no less outposts of heaven than the sight which greeted me one night when I arrived in the Holy Land after an exhausting journey. Looking out from the balcony of the theological institute where I was staying, I asked someone smoking a cigarette what the lights were down below us, and was told in an offhand kind of way, 'Oh, that's Bethlehem.'

Banana on the Sideboard

I f you live in a London suburb, you might as well be living in a
 different city altogether. For seven years I was the Rector
of Friern Barnet, an example of the usual, outer London medieval
village, swamped by the expansion of the 1920s and '30s. Yet
Friern Barnet was the bread and butter of Church of England life.
There was a well-attended church in the Victorian, mock-
medieval St James's beside the golf course, and another, less
well-attended, in the freezing cold, dark Pearson masterpiece of
St John's. This was next to the enormous mental hospital, now
demolished, for which Friern Barnet was famous.

I remember visiting rows and rows of similar-looking houses, all
of which seemed to have unused dining rooms with 1930s oak
sideboards, each sporting a cut-glass fruit bowl containing one
rotting banana. This must be an exaggeration of memory, but I
associate a great deal of parochial visiting with the smell of over-
ripe banana in a room seldom used except for the Rector's visits or
funeral teas.

The people were nice, though. Some were sad and lonely, of
course, and those are the ones with whom priests spend a lot of
time. When I gave an old lady a kiss as I left after visiting on a grey
afternoon, I often thought that I was probably the only person to
have kissed that old widow recently, if her children lived far away
and seldom visited.

All this was the pattern for seven years. Then, on Christmas
Eve 1985, the Bishop telephoned not long before Midnight Mass.
Would I be interested in going on to the shortlist for the post of
Rector of St Mary-le-Bow in Cheapside?

Just after Christmas, I went down to the City to be interviewed
in the offices of the Worshipful Company of Grocers, joint
patrons of St Mary-le-Bow with the Archbishop of Canterbury.
The original church was built in 1070 and its Norman crypt is still
in use. Above the crypt is the church rebuilt by Christopher Wren
after the Great Fire, the imposing tower and spire dominating the
Cheapside skyline. It was the major parish church of the western
end of the City and, if you were born within the sound of the

bells, you were deemed a Londoner, a Cockney. Thomas à Becket was born within the parish, in a house on the site of the present Mercers' Hall – the Mercers' Company, like the Grocers, being parishioners. The American state of Virginia was founded by another parishioner, John Smith, and Arthur Phillip, the first Governor of Australia, was baptized here. Trinity, Wall Street, a prestigious Anglican church founded in 1697 which owns large parts of Manhattan, is commanded in its charter 'to do everything according to the use of St Mary-le-Bow'.

Arriving for my interview, I found a group of aristocratic, distinguished men sitting around a table designed to frighten the candidate. 'I am afraid,' said the Chairman, 'I can't shake your hand. The table is too wide.' It was not impossible for him to walk around the table, but it would have spoiled the point. 'This table is a copy of the table in the Cabinet Room in No. 10 Downing Street,' he added.

'Oh, yes,' I said, brightly. I remembered being interviewed at the same sort of table with the same intent to frighten when I was 18 and applying to do Voluntary Service Overseas. It was a helpful precedent.

During this City interview I thought to myself, *If they ask me to do this job, I think I might say 'yes'.* I was quite sure they would not offer the post to me, especially after I told them, 'If you want the Rector to support Mrs Thatcher, it's no good asking me.' (In the mid-1980s Mrs Thatcher was the Supreme Ruler of the Universe, at least to many in the City.) As soon as I got home to Friern Barnet that evening, however, the telephone rang and the Clerk of the Grocers asked me if I would like the job, because they would like to have me.

Thus the Rector of St James and St John, Friern Barnet, came down from the most northerly edge of the diocese to the pulsing heart of the Square Mile and found himself in a 1960s rectory, sandwiched between the magnificent masterpiece of Wren's great tower and the nave of the church of St Mary-le-Bow. The rectory was a depressing place, painted the sort of very pale pink familiar from the mental hospital in Friern Barnet, and with a large, bare roof garden which contained one dead bay tree in a broken pot and a great deal of leftover scaffolding.

I took up my post in the summer of 1986 and eagerly awaited the Induction Service, which would, I hoped, be full of City ceremonial, a rousing start to my new life. My diary records the occasion.

21 July

I looked down to see rows of City dignitaries in fur (it was a very hot evening). Aldermen and Masters of Companies seem to wear fur all the time, even in heat waves. They were all asleep. There is a bit in the Induction Service where the rubric says, 'Here the Bishop will introduce the new Rector,' and I imagined him saying, 'I have known Victor Stock for years. In fact, I ordained him when he was a promising young man and I have admired him ever since and you're jolly lucky to have such a dynamic, exciting, amusing, tender, sympathetic, but, under it all, highly serious priest to look after you. Gosh, I wish I was a member of his congregation, etc. etc.'

In fact, Bishop Graham Leonard stood there and said, 'I present to you the Reverend Victor Stock, formerly Rector of Friern Barnet.' And then, without a pause, 'We are the body of Christ. By the one Spirit we were all baptized into one body. Let us, therefore, endeavour to keep the unity of the Spirit and the bond of peace...'

As I look back at my diary for those first few hectic days, I see that Dr Robert Parks, the Rector of Trinity, Wall Street, had come over from New York for the Induction Service. The main theme that runs through those days is 'clean the crypt, clean the nave, clean the floor'. I was on my hands and knees, not in prayer, but in soapsuds.

St Mary-le-Bow had not been used very much during the previous incumbency, and it had not been open very much either. There had been a Verger, widely regarded as a saint by the people who did not know him, who liked to give lectures on the City. What he did *not* like was people coming into his church, and he kept them out with a will. The church was not opened until 9 a.m., after everybody was safely stuffed into their offices, and it was closed again at 4 p.m., before people came out of work. As a further deterrent, only one door into the church was open.

There were also wonderful, scrawly notices on bits of old cardboard, saying things like, 'Keep out. Service in progress.' Of my two favourite notices, one was inside the grand piano and read, 'If you have lifted this lid, who do you think you are?' The best one of all was in the manky, spidery, hardly used kitchen in the crypt. Hanging over a not-very-clean tea towel was a cardboard notice which announced, 'These tea towels are for VIPs only.' This conjured up a surreal picture of the Governor of the Bank of England, the Chairman of Lloyds, the Lord Mayor and assorted merchant bankers all jostling each other crossly, vying to be the greatest VIP of them all and therefore allowed to wash up the two cracked cups and scarred enamel teapot which constituted the St Mary-le-Bow Entertainment Facility.

The latter half of 1986 was almost entirely spent trying to get the place clean and attempting to turn the ceremonial vestry, where the Church Council met, into a church office. This was deeply resisted by some of the elderly Masons who made up the Church Council but did not come to services. We triumphed eventually, however, and gradually the place turned into a working church. In time the one service a week on Wednesdays at 12.30 was replaced with Morning and Evening Prayer every day and Holy Communion every day at different times to suit different audiences. I shall never forget one of the elderly Masons saying, 'We're not a religious sort of church, Mr Stock.'

12 September

I love being here, especially the physical layout, lightness and space of the church and its openness, now I have unlocked the outside staircase to the back of the crypt. All the pressure of the parochial grind is absent.

Then comes a glimpse of life beyond soapsuds and vestry wranglings.

17 September

I did an LBC Radio recording with Lawrence Spicer. New York rang and asked me there for a week to see how Trinity, Wall Street, is run. They are going to pay.

13 October

Christopher Chavasse, the Clerk of the Grocers' Company, came to lunch. Getting to know people and entertaining them in my sitting room at the top of the Rector's lodgings is going to be part of the job here.

I spent the morning at the Bevis Marks Synagogue, the old Portuguese Synagogue in the City, because it was the Day of Atonement and I wanted to see something of the Orthodox Jewish community. I have always been interested in Judaism and ashamed of my ignorance of it.

In the evening at the Parochial Church Council we abolished the 1662 Communion Service on Wednesdays, nem. con. – amazing. The proposal was put by Harry Oram, Senior Churchwarden, who has taken a shine to me, I am pleased to say, because that helps.

When I arrived, the only service held at St Mary-le-Bow was a 1662 Communion Service at 12.30 on Wednesdays. It was obvious that most of the congregation were at sea. One of the difficulties with the 1662 Prayer Book is that nobody uses it as it is written. So you start at the beginning of the Communion Service and then you leave out several pages, also leaving out some of the things on the pages you are actually using. To deal with this difficulty, I proposed that we left the 1662 service in use on Wednesdays for people who liked it and were used to it, but suggested that on the other days we should use the 1980 Alternative Service Book (ASB) which my generation was used to, as were all the people younger than me – and they were the people I was trying to get into the church. I also suggested that we should have the essential parts of the ASB service printed on laminated cards for Monday, Tuesday, Thursday and Friday, with a separate set of cards for the 1662 service on Wednesdays.

'Oh,' said Mr Oram, 'I think that would be very confusing. I believe, if the Rector wants to have this new service, it would be much more sensible to have the same service every day.' Everybody agreed, simply because he, the chief man, had said it.

I pointed out that this was a decision of great importance and we should, therefore, vote on it. You run a Church Council by not voting if you can help it – most things are done by consensus. It seemed advisable to have the verdict clear on this matter, however, so we duly voted on it. Nobody voted against the proposal. It was reminiscent of old tribal Africa: convert the chief and the whole village follows. The driving force, of course, was not the merits or demerits of one kind of service against another, but the thought, *We like this new chap. He's friendly and the place needs a bit of a*

5

boost, and perhaps he'll do it by ways we might not really like, but on the whole we're going to throw our weight behind him. And it was so, as the Bible says about the creation in the Book of Genesis.

15 October

I talked to the Business Houses Council set up to interest local offices in St Mary-le-Bow. The City is divided into political Wards, which elect Common Council men, and the Wards also have a social function.

Then I talked to the Cordwainer Club, and had old Father Ken White in for a cup of tea. I cooked dinner for Patrick and Jean Mayhew,[1] Wendy Evans, who is a glass expert and curator at the Museum of London, and Bernard and Andrew.[2] We had a wonderfully funny evening with Patrick doing imitations of a pro-hanging lady who wasn't at all interested in why Sir Patrick was against hanging and for the European Community. He had gone to speak at a constituency meeting about the European Community, whereas the only subject that moved the bosom of this lady was hanging.

21 October

I visited the Clerk of the Grocers' Company about the wages for the illiterate young Verger I am teaching to read and write. In the Middle Ages the Grocers sold, not groceries, but en gros, and were in charge of measuring things out. Now they are a big City charity.

---

1 Lord Mayhew was Solicitor General at that time. I came to know Patrick through his wife Jean when I was Chaplain at the University Church of Christ the King, in Bloomsbury's Gordon Square, and gave a series of talks one Lent to the Parliamentary Wives Group at the Houses of Parliament.

2 Bernard Dawson is the family solicitor and Andrew Dunford is an old friend of mine from London University Chaplaincy days. Andrew came from the University Chaplaincy to use a weekend room in the rectory at St James's, Friern Barnet, along with fellow student Martin Smith, now a surgeon. Martin and Andrew had been lively members of the Chaplaincy congregation and were both of great assistance to me when I took over at Friern Barnet. In 1986 Andrew was working as a GP in Tower Hamlets, living just behind the Tower of London and attending services at St Mary-le-Bow.

Later I conducted a huge memorial service, full of the noisy upper classes, *Tatler* types who don't know how to behave in church and make that sort of Ya, ya noise that breaks glasses in South Kensington drawing rooms.

We put the 900th anniversary of St Mary-le-Bow off for a year.

The *Evening Standard* says 'QUEEN IN RUNCIE CRISIS', followed by five pages of complete tripe. Very amusing, but not, I expect, for the Archbishop or for Lindy Runcie.

23 October

At lunchtime, I visited the Mutual Life Assurance Building. I felt a bit like the Queen in *Spitting Image*, being taken around things of unutterable dullness, but saying, 'Oh, how interesting – how long have you lived/worked here?'

Then I came back to see a young wife in a crisis about life, which prevented me going to the Nikaean Club, entertainment for foreign prelates at Lambeth Palace – no great loss.

28 October

Nancy Lambton came to dinner, one of the people I admire unreservedly. She was a diplomat before the Second World War and got stuck in Persia. She had set out, this aristocratic Lambton, to get herself educated. Men went to Eton and girls had governesses, did the Season and married suitably. Nancy didn't want to be married suitably, she wanted to be educated – all this inspired by a great Persian exhibition at the Royal Academy. She managed to matriculate and get into the School of Oriental and African Studies as an undergraduate. There, for the whole of her life, she stayed, becoming Professor of Persian and the author of a number of internationally renowned books on the history of Iran. She now lives, getting on for 90, in a cottage at Kirk Newton near Wooler in the Cheviot Hills, spending her mornings in her library, writing learned oriental articles and brushing up her Arabic on which she is an acknowledged expert, and her afternoons helping the shepherd or felling trees. When I was at the University church, she was a faithful Sunday communicant in her grey pinstripe suit, severe cropped hair and men's shoes. She had a decisive turn of phrase, did not suffer fools gladly and began every morning of her life reading Book of Common Prayer Matins in her flat in Maida Vale, where in the evenings she entertained Arab and Egyptian diplomats and scholars to meat and two veg, with Wine Society claret and fascinating conversation.

8 November

Heavy rain gave way to brilliant sunshine. St Mary-le-Bow looked like something in Rome, all balustrades and flying urns, swags, cupola and obelisk, against the cornflower blue sky. There is a little balcony sticking out from the bell tower ringing room, built by Wren to commemorate the dais from which the king and queen watched jousting in medieval Cheapside. I stood on this and waved at the carriages and floats in the Lord Mayor's Show. This was a frightening experience as the balcony suddenly moved. In fact, Wren designed the balcony to do this, to 'go with the flow', before anybody in the West had heard of Taoism.

I persuaded two teenagers in the crowd by the door from Cheapside to hold the church's Beata Maria de Arcubus banner on the steps. Some of the Aldermen going by in carriages suddenly humanized themselves by producing glove puppets, which waved shyly at the children in the crowd. It couldn't be more different from the suburbs, being here in the heart of the City.

Then I found myself transported to the heart of another city, visiting New York in response to the earlier invitation from Trinity, Wall Street.

9 November

At the airport I met Eric Pavyer, a businessman from Friern Barnet who was on his way to a meeting in New York, and we flew together. We arrived in New York at 2.20 p.m. in torrential rain. Eric had an amazing stretch limo – black windows, with a TV and drinks cabinet – to take us into town.

13 November

I was summoned to a meeting today with Dr Parks, the 'Cardinal Rector', as they call these important clergy here. He has the most extraordinary office, which looks as if it was the great hall of an English Jacobean country house in about 1648 – carried by the hands of angels in the manner of the Holy House of Loretto to Manhattan and put down on the top of the skyscraper which Trinity owns.

14 November

I enjoyed a swim at the Athletic Club on Father Appleyard's card. All the curates belong to old-fashioned gentlemen's gyms – lots of dark woodwork.

Trinity has its own TV studio, makes its own video programmes and has its own radio and cable. I spent some time doing interviews and then went to the Metropolitan Museum's exhibition of artefacts from Israel, which I went to see because they had the stone, recently discovered in Jerusalem, with the Pontius Pilate inscription on it; also a stone from the corner of the Temple where the trumpets were blown. Then I walked through an icy blast across to the Frick for an hour in paradise. This is the heaven of museums – hushed, gently lit, full of fresh flowers, smelling like only very rich people's houses can smell, the unmistakable scent of civilized wealth.

15 November

I walked again in the sunny park along the reservoir and wondered at Cleopatra's Needle from 1000 BC. It is the fellow, or pair, of our Cleopatra's Needle on the Victoria Embankment in London. New York is an extraordinary place, a mixture of the movies and the old world with tiny neighbourhood shops nestling under every skyscraper. Then there is the dirt and the squalor, trash and mess and that strange steam coming up through the pavements, all juxtaposed with elegance, wealth and sophistication, all cheek by jowl, and the whole thing surrounded by the sea, which you are not conscious of in Manhattan until you get to the end of a street and find yourself at it, like Venice.

16 November

Sunday: I got to Trinity during the readings at the 9 a.m. Mass. There was a full High Mass for a congregation of 30, which felt wrong, but an extremely good sermon from Father Dick May, who is buttoned up, highly intelligent and emotionally shut down. Then I attended one of the Christian education classes which go on all the time – something we don't have in England for adults, to our certain impoverishment. I just made it into the vestry in time for the 11.15 High Mass. Dr May gave the same sermon, but with better illustrations. It was a curiously breathless liturgy, with no silences. Everybody was marching about in chasubles and dalmatics and the Rector wore a cope as if he was a bishop.

At the parish lunch I talked to three men from the night shelter, which is the kind of work that makes Trinity bearable. At 1.30 I gave my presentation on St Mary-le-Bow, its past and its opportunities for work in the City of London. I got them all crying with laughter by telling the Clarence House story of me presenting students to the Queen Mother when the person who should have been doing it was suddenly stricken with nerves.

The story was that the Wynant Volunteers come every year from the States to the UK to do some voluntary work, and the Queen Mother has been in the habit of entertaining them because Ambassador Wynant was a friend of hers years ago. One summer evening I found myself standing outside the garden entrance to Clarence House with a group of shy American students, when the door opened and Queen Elizabeth's Comptroller emerged saying, 'Oh, Father Stock, I wonder if you would be so kind as to introduce everyone to Her Majesty. Do the presentations, you know. The chap who was going to do it suddenly doesn't want to.'

As I was stammering, 'Well, I don't know any of their names or anything about them,' we arrived in the garden and found ourselves in the presence of a twinkling, emerald green silk, chiffon and osprey-feathered vision.

The Queen Mother extended a gloved hand. 'Father Stock, how kind of you to find the time.'

Every student was inaudible and scared, so hard to present. 'Your name?' I said to one girl.

'Trixie.'

'Trixie what?'

'Oh, just call me Trixie.'

'Your Majesty, may I present Trixie?'

Then, from nowhere, gin and tonic appeared and the Queen Mother looked at me and said, 'Drink that straight down.'

Later in the party I was suddenly confronted by the Queen Mother with American students on either side of her, practically hanging on her arms, but not quite. It was just after Mr Nixon had been found out for erasing the tapes in the Watergate scandal, and we had seen those wonderful photographs of his secretary showing how she could have erased the tapes accidentally while doing the typing. 'Do you think the President was guilty, Your Majesty?' asked one of the dear young things, at which the attendant duchesses froze in horror and took several paces backwards.

The Queen Mother fixed a gimlet eye on me and said, 'Father Stock will explain the difference between a constitutional monarchy and the presidency of the United States.'

Well, there we were. I gabbled on as best I could but, undeterred, the same interlocutor pressed ahead. 'But do you think he did it?'

The Queen Mother hoiked her handbag further up her arm, clasped her gloved hands, looked into the middle distance and said, 'If I were the President of the United States, I would look in the bag from time to time.'

She then did one of her vanishing-in-a-shimmer-of-emeralds-and-osprey-feathers tricks and was no more. We were left thinking how sage and wise this saintly old woman was, and I have been wondering ever since what on earth she was talking about.

I left New York a day or so later and returned, with some enthusiasm, to Cheapside and the task of forging closer links between church and City. It seemed to involve a great deal of eating.

2 December

I attended a smart lunch at the Mercers' Hall. The Mercers are the number one of the 12 great livery companies. The Grocers are number two in City precedence. We ate lobster soup and lambs' tongues.

Then I visited Alderman Brian Jenkins in his offices at Coopers & Lybrand to persuade him to start coming to church. He's a Churchwarden but doesn't come. I think, if you are firm and pretend not to be frightened, you can get people like this to do things. Anyway, I said it was his duty to come to church, perhaps only once a fortnight or even once a month.

'What time?' he barked.

I told him we were planning to have a service every day. 'What about 7.30 on a Tuesday morning?' I plucked from the air.

'OK, done!'

That was the beginning of Alderman Jenkins's long and loyal association with the worshipping community of St Mary-le-Bow.

12 December

Friday. I recorded another programme for LBC with nice Lawrence Spicer, then went to a pompous Ward Club lunch at Carpenters' Hall. There were 250 people, and I was placed on the top table, next to the Master's wife who felt snubbed by the Lady Mayoress. It's Toy Town all over again.

Later I took food left over from the posh Duff and Potter's shop in Bow Lane to Malcolm's Crypt for the Homeless at St Botolph's Church, Aldgate, and then Andrew Dunford motored me to his cottage in Clare for the weekend.

Wherever a priest is based, taking time off is a problem. How do you take time off if a priest is something you are being rather than a job you are doing? The problem has its own unique angle at St Mary-le-Bow, where there are no services on Sundays. Every single week somebody asks me, 'If you don't have services on Sunday, what do you do?' The common view of a vicar is of someone who takes services on Sundays, and that is basically it. Well, there is rather more to the ministry than that.

The scaffolding of a priest's life is the daily recitation of Morning and Evening Prayer, whether people come or not. At St Mary-le-Bow we now do this at 8.15 every morning and 5.45 every evening, except on Tuesday mornings when (thanks to Brian Jenkins) we have Morning Prayer at 7.30, the Eucharist at 7.45 and breakfast together at 8.15 in the Court of the Arches. Lunchtimes also have a pattern: there is the Healing Group on Mondays, the Dialogues on Tuesdays, Holy Communion on Wednesdays, concerts on Thursdays and Holy Communion upstairs with a Meditation Group downstairs on Fridays. Those are the givens of St Mary-le-Bow. For all weekday festivals – Ascension Day, Corpus Christi, Epiphany, Ash Wednesday, the Annunciation, All Saints, All Souls, St Andrew's Day, St Luke's Day, and every day in Holy Week – there is a sung Mass at lunchtime. This is a High Mass, with three sacred ministers, gorgeous vestments, clouds of incense and splendid music from the choir, be it Haydn, Palestrina, Mozart, Beethoven, Bruckner or Schubert.

I also spend a great deal of time seeing people individually. People make appointments with the secretary, or just come and knock on the door. Woven in and out of all this is what I call 'pastoral shopping': taking posters advertising Dialogues or services round to the butcher's, the fish restaurant Sweetings, the local bars, the Body Shop on Cheapside (where they are always particularly welcoming) and the shirt shop opposite. I am up at 6 a.m., donning my dog collar, opening the church, lighting the lamps so that people can come in and light votive candles in front of the shrine of Our Lady, which they do from 6.30 every morning. Then it is a question of being available, being about, hanging around, being friendly. Father Harry Williams, in his autobiography *Some Day I'll Find You*, says the only thing a priest needs to do is to smile at the congregation.

It is vital for a priest to relocate during hours or days off, because a priest works from home. Here at St Mary-le-Bow, I see people almost all the time in my study on the first floor of the rectory. It has a very unattractive view of the back of the ladies' lavatory at the Yorkshire Bank, but it is full of comfortable armchairs and piles of books. I also see people in my sitting room, and so they bring their troubles, sorrows, personalities and atmospheres up the stairs from the City where they work, through my bedroom floor in the middle of the house, and up to the sitting room floor, the space at the top of the building for eating and entertaining. When people have gone, in a real sense they are still there. Then there is the telephone. So it is essential sometimes to breathe different air, to get out, to get away. People are always surprised that priests have days off, but they are not surprised that they themselves have weekends.

I learned as a child to enjoy museums, visiting the wonders of the Victoria and Albert Museum or the British Museum with my parents. Sometimes, alternating art with nature, we would walk on Wimbledon Common or Putney Heath, or along the embankment from Putney to Hammersmith. On special days we would visit Chiswick House or Hampton Court. For me these were all pathways into the luxuriant world of the imagination, and I am still happiest spending my spare time exploring the countryside, a museum or an art gallery.

London itself is full of places to explore, of course, but Andrew's cottage in Clare provided an ideal bolt hole, away from it all. Ever since Andrew had been one of my lodgers at Friern Barnet, he had let me use his cottage in Suffolk for time off. I do not drive, but once or twice a month he took me up to Clare in his car.

With Christmas fast approaching, there was little time for days off just yet, although I could look forward to a rest after Christmas Eve because the City would be virtually closed for the holidays.

18 December

We had incense in the church for the first time because somebody lent me a thurible. James Watson[3] came and waved it for me, which made the church smell nice before the carol service. The floor looked clean. I have been labouring over it for a very long time, as has Lee, our Cockney Verger, when he is here, and Doll, our cleaner who never cleans anything usually, just moves the dirt about. She always does her 'cleaning' in bedroom slippers and curlers.

---

3 James Watson, an elderly member of the University Church congregation, had become a friend over the years and I greatly valued his advice on matters spiritual.

24 December

My birthday. I am 42 today. The City was quite empty by noon. Uncle Teddy came to lunch in a dirty old mac. He hadn't noticed quite how dirty it was.

At 3.30 I went to the Cathedral carol service. The whole of St Paul's was packed. They had two choirs, one in the West Gallery with dramatic use of lighting, and excellent readings by all the clergy.

I assisted with the chalice at my neighbouring City church, St Vedast's, at the Midnight Mass. It is a refuge for disaffected traditionalists, 'kneelers and turners', i.e. turning east at all the Glorias as well as the Creed, from the collegiate-style, facing-inwards pew arrangement, with the people looking cross. During Mass, the Advent wreath caught fire, which was a jolly distraction. There was a powerful, vintage Anglo-Catholic sermon from dear old Gonville Ffrench Beytagh, a hero since his South African imprisonment.

25 December

Christmas Day. Today felt like being on retreat. I took a walk in Hyde Park and Kensington Gardens under lowering skies. There were lots of people bowling about under the black branches. At last, two years late, I think, David Hutt,[4] Andrew Dunford and I consumed Ruth Watson's[5] Christmas pudding, softened a little by sherry and steamed for three hours.

26 December

Boxing Day. Suddenly, the present from the Squadron Leader,[6] an alarm clock, shrilled its head off at 6.40 a.m., making me the earliest person to wake up in London on St Stephen's Day.

---

4 David Hutt was the Vicar of All Saints, Margaret Street.

5 Ruth had been my cleaner at Friern Barnet and went on to become a kind of housekeeper for me at St Mary-le-Bow.

6 Don Dunford, Andrew's father.

Taking Stock

I dined at All Saints, Margaret Street, lit by candles, with red glass balls on silver spruce on the table. Margarita[7] picked up one of the glass balls and put it down her bosom, breathed in and broke it. This did not go down well with David.

We had all got rather carried away with this dinner party, thinking it would be smart to dress up in dinner jackets. This, of course, was why, to complement the men, Margarita looked so particularly glamorous. David has made the vicarage extremely beautiful and has devised a kind of Gothic dining room entirely lit by candles reflected in black-framed Gothic mirrors. One of the problems with this sort of entertaining is that it can all get a bit tense. The glass ball breaking should have relieved the tension, but it didn't. Ah well.

---

7 Margarita Clover is a beautiful Mexican lady who had been married to one of the Friern Barnet curates, but was now divorced and living near Andrew in Tower Hamlets.

Small Shopkeepers

Christmas 1986 was the first occasion on which, as a priest, I had been without a resident population to look after since my days as a university chaplain in the early 1970s. At St Mary-le-Bow we shut down before Christmas after our big carol service, our equivalent of Christmas Day, and returned to work with everyone else in the City following the New Year break.

The first part of 1987 was all about this continuing adjustment to being a priest without Sundays and learning to relate to people through their work rather than their spare time. In addition, my diary notes much involvement with the campaign to try to prevent Peter Palumbo from pulling down the listed buildings at the end of Cheapside called – confusingly, for there were nine of them – Number One Poultry. Peter Palumbo, the multimillionaire property developer, had been buying up the leases of the properties which formed Number One Poultry and, after many years, his portfolio of leases was complete and he was able to move towards demolition. A group of local shopkeepers, my parishioners, and one or two people interested in conservation matters asked me if I would help them mount a campaign to save the splendid Victorian buildings. Through this initiative, I got to know a great many people in the locality. Later we mounted an exhibition in the church vestibule (which I got Alan Webster, the Dean of St Paul's, to open) about the Palumbo proposals and what they would do to the City skyline. There was also a certain amount of standing in for other people, or filling preaching gaps elsewhere on Sundays.

12 April

Palm Sunday. I crossed the road to preside over the Palm Sunday ceremonies at St Vedast's, Foster Lane, on the other side of Cheapside, a church now without an incumbent. It has a little Sunday congregation, unlike St Mary-le-Bow. We met on the corner of Foster Lane, with the great baroque magnificence of St Paul's Cathedral as background, to bless Palm crosses and had a procession from the pavement into the church for Mass. This building was beautifully restored after the war and has a silver and gold ceiling and panelled walls, and is beautifully High Church in a restrained way.

14 April

Tuesday. I conducted early Matins and Mass at 7.30. I heard some confessions, then had a conversation with a priest who is a counsellor about an American priest he knows, a psychotherapist from New York who needs to find some part-time work. We talked about whether he could work part-time at St Mary-le-Bow, perhaps helping me with St Mary Aldermary down Bow Lane.[1]

I gave a set of keys to Archbishop Ephraim Akboodi, who is to bring his flock to St Mary-le-Bow for their Syrian Orthodox Holy Week.

It took a while to sort out, but eventually the Syrian Orthodox found a lasting home with us on Sundays, when St Mary-le-Bow is not used.

15 April

I attended Evensong at All Saints, Margaret Street, and stayed on to preach at the 6.30 Mass, as I did on Monday and Tuesday. There were more than 40 in the congregation. I stayed for fish and salad with David Hutt, who is beginning to wilt. No wonder, with all these Holy Week services and confessions and the general dramas and excitements of trying to preside over a famous Anglo-Catholic church where people get into the most fearful temper if you change the fringe on a cope.

---

1 The Bishop of London, Dr Graham Leonard, had asked me to add St Mary Aldermary to my responsibilities, and it had a daily lunchtime Mass at the time when I wanted to put things on at St Mary-le-Bow. An extra pair of hands would therefore come in useful.

16 April

Maundy Thursday. A sunny day. At the morning service Jim and Gareth, two young men who work in banks, carried candles wearing their ordinary clothes and dear old James Watson managed the incense (we borrowed the necessary paraphernalia from St Mary Aldermary).

At the end of the Mass we stripped the altar while the congregation said Psalm 22. This lovely liturgy, the first time such ceremonies have been used at St Mary-le-Bow, was followed by a muffled peal from the bell, which brought people from Cheapside into the empty, smoke-laden church.

In the evening I was back at All Saints, Margaret Street, to preach the Maundy Liturgy. There were 200 people in the congregation, but unsuitable Leighton and Bruckner music – too intellectual and too dissonant. The procession moved with extreme slowness from the High Altar down the nave, around the corner and up the Lady Chapel aisle to the Altar of Repose.

A thing I have always liked about Margaret Street in Holy Week is the Sanctuary behind and around the High Altar being hung with black velvet. The fine Turkey carpet is replaced with black felt, so that the altar floats in a kind of dimensionless vacuum against impenetrable black depth.

17 April

Good Friday. I slept the night at All Saints, Margaret Street – Holy Week at St Mary-le-Bow being over and me being on duty at Margaret Street for Good Friday. We had Matins, then an extraordinarily long liturgy for Good Friday, and then the Three Hours, which I preached.[2]

After all this, at about 4 o'clock, I had tea and hot cross buns and then went out for a sunny walk in Regent's Park. It was packed with people, nearly all of whom were totally oblivious of the fact that it was Good Friday so that, as a

---

2 The Three Hours' is a Good Friday sermon or series of meditations, commemorating the three hours Christ hung on the cross.

Christian, I felt I was living in a world hidden away inside those other people's worlds.

On Holy Saturday I attended the evening Easter Vigil liturgy at All Saints, Margaret Street. It was extraordinarily fussy and the priest who read the Gospel turned over the wrong page and read the bit about the hanging of Judas, but no one seemed to notice. On Easter Day I celebrated Mass and preached at St Vedast's, Foster Lane. It was a much jollier service than the previous night's stiff formality at Margaret Street. I had not expected this chore to turn into a new experience of resurrection and life, but it was so.

The new way of looking at life which Easter can bring was illustrated that same week by an excellent talk from the Bishop of California at the University Church of Christ the King, as part of a conference about looking after people with AIDS. In reference to his more appalled Episcopal colleagues who did not know how to begin to deal with the gay community in California, Bishop Bill Swing said, 'God took the risk of becoming human. Why can't you?'

A few days later, in an abrupt change of focus, I found myself in the crypt of St Mary-le-Bow giving a lecture to a group of Japanese businessmen's wives on the history of the Old Testament. Every couple of sentences, what I had said was translated into Japanese, which seemed to take very much longer to say than it did in English. I kept wondering what was happening in the translation. They asked me if I would do a series of lectures, all an hour each, in which I could cover Christianity, Western civilization, the history of England, and pretty much everything else. I thought I would have a go. It offered a different kind of challenge.

1 May

I took a walk in Hyde Park with a colleague I meet sometimes to share priestly difficulties. Walking around the Serpentine certainly clears the air. There is something restorative and confidence-making about the unchanging landscape of Hyde Park, with its uniformed soldiers out riding from the Guards' Barracks at Knightsbridge and children who belong to smart, private schools walking in docile crocodiles.

Later in May I became a Fellow of Sion College, a seventeenth-century library on the Thames. At the College dinner I was put next to a dreadful old priest in his eighties who believed that black South Africans were being stirred up by the BBC and that, if they were left alone and not interfered with by 'pinkoes', they would be terribly happy.

The diary also shows that during May I was busy pursuing my involvement with the Number One Poultry/Palumbo case – holding meetings, writing letters and talking to journalists. In addition I was preparing a number of people for marriage and Confirmation (the church's first adult Confirmation candidates since 1958) and looking after my Uncle Teddy, then in his seventies, for whom I had bought a flat in Earl's Court.

27 May

I travelled to Pinner on the Metropolitan Line – John Betjeman's 'Metro-land' – and struggled through the Pinner Fair, which has been happening around St John the Baptist's Day since the Middle Ages. I did my Title[3] here under Canon David Ritchie, a notable trainer of priests, to whom I owe an enormous amount. I went to Nookie West's flat for her 100th birthday celebrations. She remembers seeing Queen Victoria at Ascot and later going to watch her funeral procession at Windsor. Nookie's father was born in 1823; her grandfather was born in the eighteenth century before the French Revolution.

At 5.30 I was back in St Mary-le-Bow for the Confirmation of the Election of the new Bishop of Oxford, Richard Harries, who was Dean of King's College, London. Before King's he was Vicar of All Saints, Fulham, where I preached for him. Since 1290, people have become bishops in the crypt of St Mary-le-Bow. The legal part of turning into a bishop has three stages: the Confirmation of Election in the crypt; the kissing of hands with the oath administered by the Home Secretary at Buckingham Palace; and then an Enthronement in the appropriate cathedral.

Confirmation in our crypt is a wonderfully dotty ceremony, with legal officers in short and full-bottomed wigs processing

---

3 This is part of a priest's training after ordination as a deacon.

solemnly from the vestry, through the nave of the church and out into the churchyard, to the amazement of commuters hurrying home from their offices to catch the 6 p.m. from Cannon Street or London Bridge. Led by the Verger, the legal officers, the Chaplain (i.e. the Rector of St Mary-le-Bow) and the Bishop Elect descend the concrete post-war stairs into the just-post-Conquest Norman crypt for the litany in the Chapel of the Holy Spirit. Then comes the Confirmation of the Election in the Court of the Arches, the central section of the three-aisled crypt, which makes up the most ancient part of St Mary-le-Bow. The east end of the Court of the Arches contains a piece of Roman wall from AD 100. The Bishop kneels, prays and takes the oath in front of a wall which was built at the same time as St John was completing his Gospel.

29 May

I went over to Grocers' Hall and visited the Master – a bit like visiting the head of an Oxford college – to talk about the Election Service, which is nothing to do with politics but happens for Masters of livery companies once a year.

I also talked to the Master briefly about the line I am taking on Number One Poultry. I was recently taken to lunch by the chief executive of a City company who pointed out that a lot of the shopkeepers on the site – 'small shopkeepers' he said, disdainfully – were Jews. 'You are the Anglican Rector, are you not?' What was I supposed to say? Should I have thrown up my hands in horror over the lobster salad, exclaiming, 'Of course! I hadn't realized that'? A number of City institutions want to pull down their old buildings and their not-so-old buildings and are afraid that, if some of us prevent the pulling down of the listed buildings on so prominent a site as Cheapside, with all the attendant publicity, this might put a spoke in their plans.

I talked to a nun who has an exhibition on in the vestibule, trying to persuade her that the way she has arranged it is ghastly and will prevent people buying her bits and pieces, but this was met with incomprehension.

After the lunchtime Mass at St Mary Aldermary, I talked to Sir Keith Stewart, one of the Churchwardens, and during this conversation somebody came in to say that the boy who sold vegetables on the corner by the church wanted to see me. I went out to find that his baby had just died. Thus began a friendship brought to birth in sorrow and despair.

Early June saw a visit to Warburgs, during which I discovered how a merchant bank operates, and I spent quite a bit of time generally getting to grips with more of the City. These interesting days led up to the General Election, in which I voted for the SDP–Liberal Alliance. On 12 June Mrs Thatcher returned with a landslide majority of 100 seats. The Alliance won 16 seats, with little success for its leaders: Roy Jenkins lost his seat and Shirley Williams and Bill Rodgers failed to get in. I found this deeply depressing. 'Another five years of Mrs Thatcher,' I wrote in my diary with two exclamation marks, followed by the comment, 'Self-interest prevails.'

On the same day I went to see the Dean of St Paul's, who was equally cast down by the election result, and, having got him on my side, collected letters from him about Number One Poultry for publication in *The Times*.

13 June

I am in Amsterdam with David Hutt for a few days off, including a marvellous visit to the Turchinsky Theatre. This Art Nouveau extravaganza has not only films, but architectural tours organized by the staff and conducted by usherettes. We have had a joke ever since I was at school that every Dutch postman and milkman is highly educated compared to the poor old substandard English. David and I, working each other up on this old theme, asked the usherette if she had been to university. Yes, she said, she had done a thesis on religious ecstasy in Minoan vase painting as depicted particularly on pottery seals and wall paintings. Well, beat that. We progressed in a daze of hilarity to the Modern Art Museum. Today's thought-provoking quote from the exhibition was 'Replace metaphysics with anthropology.'

21 June

This afternoon I was preaching at St Paul's Cathedral at the installation of the Archdeacon of London, an Evangelical clergyman from Ulster. At the reception afterwards the congregation, gathered for tea to welcome the Archdeacon, applauded me.

From there I went on to the Procession of the Blessed Sacrament at St Mary's, Bourne Street. The church was heavy with the smell of crushed thyme, rosemary and bay, for the aisles were covered with herbs over which the Blessed Sacrament was carried in its eighteenth-century Spanish monstrance. What a contrast. This is in the same denomination and the same diocese as the scene of the installation of the Evangelical, Northern Ireland, Protestant Archdeacon in St Paul's Cathedral. I love the Church of England.

22 June

The press conference about the Number One Poultry scheme went well. A wide public is interested in this heart of the City – or, as it is called in a famous Victorian painting in the Guildhall, 'Heart of the Empire'. Had a drink afterwards in the little house made out of the stables in which the head of the Foreign Desk at Lambeth, Christopher Hill, works. We were on the same staircase at college and Christopher is a skilled ecclesiastical diplomat. He is bound to become a bishop, for he already has a wife and children, is charming, clever and tactful.[4]

23 June

On the 6 p.m. news we heard that the Planning Committee of the Corporation of London said 'no' to Mr Palumbo by 17 votes to 13, in a closely fought and argued debate from 10.30 a.m. until 1.12 p.m.[5] I gave the conservationists and their supporters wine on the roof.

---

4 Christopher Hill became Bishop of Stafford in 1996.

5 The Corporation of London is the City's local authority.

Then I went off to a reception at the V & A to celebrate the Queen Mother opening the new garden. Roy Strong[6] introduced me to Colin Amery, the *Financial Times* architectural correspondent, which is helpful in the Palumbo area.

And so the summer passed. I ran a series of marriage instruction classes, continued to find my way about the City, worked hard at developing the rectory roof garden into something worthwhile, pursued my involvement with the Palumbo case (he appealed against the Planning Committee's decision), and visited the 94-year-old mother of James Watson. She looked so much like my grandmother in face and hair – a particular Victorian style which has lingered on to the end of this century with some of the very old.

It was, in many ways, a summer of old people. Uncle Teddy was looking ill and depressed. *He can't last much longer,* I thought as I stood by his sister Rose's grave in Brompton Cemetery. Rose died at the age of 36 in the early 1930s, having been engaged to marry my father. My mother, Violet, took pity on my father and married him instead. Eventually, her brother Teddy came to live in our family house in Fulham when he retired as minister of the Congregational Church in Chelsea. I am always moved by the words on Rose's tomb: 'Radiant in glory.' I sat in the cemetery grounds with Uncle Teddy and he told me about his devotion to the Liberal Party, why he had become a Nonconformist minister and how he had saved up to go to university by working for years and years as a fish-buyer in Harrods.

At St Mary Aldermary one day I discovered Dr Gerald Ellison in civvies, on his way to lunch with his son, a broker in the City. Dr Ellison, the last grand Prince Bishop of London of the Erastian School,[7] seemed, like my uncle, to be old and frail and coming to the end.

---

6 Sir Roy Strong was Director of the Victoria and Albert Museum. I first met him when he was Director of the National Portrait Gallery and he gave me lunch at the Athenaeum.

7 Erastianism is the theory that the State should have ascendancy over the Church in ecclesiastical matters. It is named after the Swiss theologian Thomas Erastus (1524–83).

I also spent a memorable evening having dinner in North Finchley with Rabbi Lionel Blue, his aunt, his mother, his partner Jim and a lesbian rabbinic student and her lover. Lionel was just the same as he sounded on *Thought for the Day* on the BBC, but more real – Polish-Russian Jewry washed up in Finchley, changed into the liberal avant-garde.

July continued with some preaching to schoolboys at Stowe. After lunch we made a circuit of the Elysian Fields and all the temples in the rain. The house itself I found overbearing, but I thought the garden was among the most beautiful in England.

I found this comment in my diary for 10 August, from St Augustine: 'God is not known from navigation, but by love.'

On 16 August, Andrew Dunford made the decision to sell his cottage in Clare, where I had spent many happy days off. It was a tiny cottage at the end of a row and he bought it for just £17,000. He was offered £70,000 for it in the end, so it was obvious that he must sell it.

During that summer I also had a period of swimming regularly, almost every day, and recorded in my diary how many lengths I had swum and how much better I felt for the exercise. Some sort of physical activity is essential for a priest, because you live inside the soul and the mind and hardly notice the body – except that it gets fatter and older as time goes by.

It is clear from the diary how much I was enjoying being in the City. Enjoyment is something difficult for priests to manage. If you really enjoy something, you often feel that you should not be enjoying it. The whole weight of the tradition pulls against pleasure and enjoyment.

On 1 September, with summer behind us, I wrote in my diary that I was seriously considering the idea of reviving the Dialogues, which were to become such an enormous feature of life over the subsequent years of my incumbency at St Mary-le-Bow. They had been invented by Joseph McCulloch, the priest who rebuilt the church after the Second World War. He said the Church of England was always talking and never listening, and there should be at least one church in which conversation took place instead of (or as well as) sermons. He therefore had the refurbished church supplied with two pulpits, one on each side of the altar, and invited a variety of people to take part in the Dialogues. It was a tradition I was glad to revive, and the first series got underway later in the autumn. Everybody did them, from Mrs Thatcher to Yehudi Menuhin, and they became a vital feature of church life.

8 September

The Nativity of Mary. Alderman Sir Brian Jenkins talked to me amusingly about my being his Chaplain during his Sheriff's year.[8]

I had a conversation with someone called William Sewell, who was wondering about giving up being an accountant and becoming a cook and would there be any mileage in discussing a restaurant in the crypt of St Mary-le-Bow? It would have to be vegetarian, so I thought probably not much mileage.

10 September

I found Uncle Teddy much worse. I visited him and saw his GP and a social worker.

14 September

Much telephoning resulted in Teddy being visited by another doctor, but during the day I found that he was to go into St Stephen's Hospital at once. I spent two hours at his flat, cleaning his bedroom and the lavatory. I've done this for old people before, so didn't mind at all. I saw an ambulance leaving as I arrived.

The second half of September saw me talking once more to William Sewell about the possibilities of a restaurant in the crypt. The idea was taking hold. How could it be achieved? How should we go about persuading people that it could be achieved?

I attended the opening of a 'SAVE Britain's Heritage' churches exhibition, the people from SAVE being great supporters of our

---

8 Sir Brian was due to become Sheriff of the City of London in 1988. The role of Sheriff's Chaplain could be given to anyone, although it was often given to a City incumbent living in the Alderman's Ward, and Sir Brian, of course, was one of the Churchwardens of St Mary-le-Bow.

campaign *vis-à-vis* Peter Palumbo. There I met the Duke of Gloucester, shy, sensible and friendly, and he told me a funny story about his father, who had been Governor-General of Australia, and a certain grandee. The grandee only went to church when the Governor-General was present, and His Royal Highness found occasion to point out that God was there, even when HRH was not.

Towards the end of September, my uncle got much worse and I spent whole nights sitting with him in the hospital, occasionally going out for a walk along the Embankment when absolutely no one else was about and Chelsea was silent. I would return to the rectory at 5 a.m. for a couple of hours' sleep. This, understandably, began to take its toll.

I was grateful, therefore, when my dear old friends Sven and Mule Fogh came to London from Copenhagen for a visit. Sven Fogh was the medical officer in Kudat in North Borneo when I did my VSO stint as an 18-year-old in 1963–4. His aristocratic wife Mule was the only other European who was friendly. Every few months I came across the District Officer and his wife, an English couple, and the wife would say, 'You must come to tea one day.' It never happened. The Foghs, on the other hand, were marvellous, whizzing me about the jungle roads in their tiny yellow sports car and giving me meals and a place to have a bath when I had no running water during the first few months. Later they came to England and met my parents, and thus began a firm friendship. I made numerous trips to Denmark, staying in their house in Charlottenlund and being told about the latest developments in the study of mosquitoes, on which Sven was an expert.

There was much confusion in the hospital about Uncle Teddy. He was told one day that there was no malignancy to worry about, and another day that he was about to die. There was a tremendous lack of communication, with big decisions being made by junior housemen, and a great deal of what can only be called neglect. This was particularly depressing, because he was obviously dying and, poignantly, he was dying in the old St Stephen's Hospital just behind Limerston Street, where he had been born at the beginning of the century. Even more dreadful was the fact that he was dying in the hospital where for many years he had been the Nonconformist Chaplain, a duty which he had undertaken with self-sacrificial attention, kindness and goodness. Now he was just a neglected old man.

In the midst of all this worry, there was the great excitement of getting the Dialogues going at last. Sir Laurens van der Post had been booked to get the venture off with a bang, but at the last minute he withdrew in order to visit his dying Japanese torturer. I could not compete with that. Sir Patrick Mayhew, who had recently been made Attorney General, offered to find a replacement for me. A series of coded messages were sent via the Ministry of Defence to China, where the Chief of the Defence Staff, General Sir Nigel Bagnall (who had been Patrick's best man at his wedding), was on a visit. The result of all this Evelyn Waugh-type diplomacy was that I received a summons to the MOD on the night the Great Man returned from China. I arrived for my rendezvous and underwent a grilling. Suddenly, during the conversation, the General decided I was all right. He agreed to do our first Dialogue, we became friends and I ended up going to stay with him and his wife Anna.

6 October

The first Dialogue of the new series took place today. The General is terribly deaf and conversation from the two pulpits turned out to be impossible, so we had to descend from on high and stand next to each other in the middle of the nave.

I'd been asked not to mention the Government's policy on nuclear weapons, as the General didn't agree with it, so I steered clear of the subject. At one point, however, he spoke about the pleasure of watching wild flowers unfold and grow through the highly magnified telescopic lenses used in tank turrets, which he had experienced on manoeuvres on Salisbury Plain. Then suddenly he said, with no prompting at all from me, that he didn't agree with first-strike nuclear policy. It was absolutely ridiculous, he said, because, if somebody from the Soviet Union sent a small missile to take out Birmingham, you saw it coming and sent an intercontinental ballistic missile to take out a very large chunk of the Soviet Union, and then – if they were still alive – they sent an even bigger intercontinental nuclear missile and that was the end of everything, quite apart from the damage done by radiation to noncombatant countries.

I looked nervously at the press, but they were all asleep, obviously having had a few drinks at El Vino's.

The first Dialogue has been an important milestone. I shall try to perfect this art, for art it is, and care and patience are required.

7 October

I visited St Paul's Cathedral Choir School, which is in my parish, where the Headmaster asked me to take over the preparation of the boys for Confirmation. This has already been broached by Kenneth Woollcombe, formerly Bishop of Oxford, now Chancellor of St Paul's and one of the Residentiary Canons, and the Very Revd Alan Webster, the Dean, both of whom told me there was nobody on the Cathedral staff interested in children.

11 October

I was told that the proposed operation on Uncle Teddy was permanently postponed and that he would be given a catheter and sent home. How could an old man who is so ill manage on his own with a catheter in a flat in Earl's Court? I lost my temper at both the staff nurse and the houseman.

12 October

Monday. I rang Mr Gilbert the surgeon. He was absolutely sure, was Mr Gilbert, that Teddy was not going home. He is a frail, tired old man, with pneumonia last week and still a chest infection; his heart is too weak for the operation. Why on earth can't they just let him fade away?

I went to Acton to lecture to the Middlesex Hospital medical students about death and breaking bad news. An apposite subject.

13 October

Sir Roy Strong came for the second Dialogue. He suggested improving the screens and general layout of my roof garden and, as he knows about these things, I took some notice.

20 October

I had another telephone conversation with Teddy's surgeon, who agreed with me that Teddy is at the end and all inter- vention must stop. He'll be transferred to a geriatric or med- ical ward. Mr Gilbert also agreed that the case has not been well handled by the juniors and said, 'You can't teach some people, I'm afraid.'

On the morning of 21 October I went to see Teddy, who was lucid but unshaven, although he had marks of blood on his chin. I told him I had come to say goodbye. I read Psalm 23, we said the Lord's Prayer together and prayed for each other. He asked God to bless me in my work. I anointed him on his eyes, ears, lips, nostrils and forehead, making up a prayer for each – 'May your ears, which have heard so much in the world, be open to hear the songs of Zion' – and trying to think of the sort of language an elderly Free Churchman would appreciate. The surgeon told me he thought Teddy could die that week, although the diagnosis was not lethal. In fact, Teddy lived on for a little while longer.

8 November

At 8 o'clock this morning, I went to St Stephen's Hospital to say prayers with Teddy. He wasn't in his usual bed. Had he been moved again? 'Oh,' said his nice neighbour, 'didn't you know? Mr Hawkins died yesterday at 6 a.m.'

Eventually I found a nurse, who went on eating her toast, sitting down. She didn't bother to stand up or even attempt to be polite. 'Has my uncle died?' I asked.

'Oh, didn't they ring you?' She went on with her toast.

I was surprised at how shocked I felt, and alone. I came out, having asked to see the body, and eventually in the morgue I did so. He was white and cold and thin and ghast- ly. So often the dead look worse dead than when living. All that stuff about 'how beautiful he looked in death' has, in my experience of mother, father and uncle, been untrue. I came out in a kind of numb daze and got a taxi to St Mary's, Bourne Street.

Cabbie: 'Do you believe the universe is finite or infinite?'

This was unfortunate for the taxi driver. 'I have just seen the corpse of my last relative,' I said. Silence descended.

At Bourne Street, fittingly, there was a Requiem Mass in black velvet vestments for Remembrance Sunday.

9 November

This was 'sorting out after death' day – visits to the undertakers and the hospital, and the collecting of clothes and papers in bags. I had to go to the Town Hall to sign certificates, and sorted through the contents of the hospital bags, including Teddy's slippers and pyjamas. In cold drizzle, I walked to Limerston Street, where he was born and my mother's family lived for so many years.

10 November

Today at 9.30 a.m. I conducted the funeral of a suicide, the first funeral that has been held in this church for 40 years. The cremation afterwards took place at the City of London Crematorium in Epping.

I came back after that for a Dialogue with Frank Field MP. What an excellent man. His sincerity was appreciated by the City.

11 November

I went to Teddy's flat via two estate agents and had the place valued.

In the evening, the General Synod decided that homosexuals are to repent and 'witness to marriage'. I can't quite see how they can do that, but the Church is never very sensible about sex.

12 November

Funeral day. The private lives of priests are strange things. Before setting off to bury my uncle, I had a meeting with the Registrar of the Bank of England and another of his officials. You carry on doing your ordinary work and smiling and being interested, while nursing in your heart grief, loneliness and exhaustion.

I took myself to the United Reformed Church in Edith Grove, Chelsea. It's a sad little building put up during the 1950s with cheap brick and absolutely no design. It was all the war damage fund could manage – a church suspended above the vast foundations of the Victorian building it replaced. There is a particularly unpleasant flat for the minister, where my uncle, grandmother and aunt lived when Teddy moved from his church in Dagenham to take over the Congregational church in the place where he had been brought up as a child.

The coffin was laid lengthways, north to south, in front of the pulpit, which takes the place of the altar in a Nonconformist church. As officiating minister and preacher, therefore, I was taking the service across the coffin. There were a few elderly Nonconformists who had been part of the congregation when my mother had acted as hostess to my uncle, his wife having died on the first anniversary of their wedding. The poverty, thinness, ugliness, lack of grace, mystery and style of the Nonconformity of my upbringing flooded back. None of the ministerial colleagues of old Uncle Teddy, who had worked for so long on a pittance, bothered to turn up. At Putney Crematorium I cremated the poor, old remains. Nobody was present except Andrew Dunford, with whom I recited Psalm 90.

I took a slow, reflective meander back through Richmond Park, thinking about the closing down of the past and the end of the family. When I was a teenager, I found Uncle Teddy remote and dull and shy. My own exploration of the mysterious musical, architectural, mystical and historical beauties I discovered in the Church of England pained him. But in the years after his retirement when, at my instigation, he came to live with my father and mother in Fulham, I began to appreciate him and the appreciation grew into admiration.

After my father's death in the Charing Cross Hospital, then my mother's death in the same hospital a few years later, and buying Teddy a flat and looking after him for seven years in Earl's Court, I began to recognize his qualities of goodness, integrity, long-suffering and patience. His hobby and abiding passion was to work for the Liberal Party, to canvass for it in hopeless constituencies like Kensington and Chelsea. Once a year he had a holiday in Weston-Super-Mare and watched the cricket. It was always Weston-Super-Mare. When he came back, his holiday shirts were washed, ironed and folded away in the suitcase with his pyjamas and his travelling Bible, all ready for next year at the cricket. He didn't complain. That was a sign of holiness.

14 November

Today we had an 8.30 a.m. Mass in the crypt for the Lord Mayor, and then breakfast in the candlelit crypt of the Guildhall with steak, lobsters, tomato soup and hot punch. The presentation of addresses in the Old Library was like something out of a Victorian oil painting.

Here I was, in the week of Teddy's funeral, being Sheriff's Chaplain – climbing into a coach lent by the royal family and riding off with the Sheriff through cheering crowds as part of the entourage of the Lord Mayor.

The best part of today, I thought, was Colonel Howard, the City Marshall, being trodden on by his horse and shouting, 'F***!' which, in one of those magical moments of silence, re-echoed around the astonished dignitaries and grandees outside Mansion House.

16 November

This morning I put Uncle Teddy's flat on the market and in the evening attended the Lord Mayor's Banquet: state trumpeters, the choir of St Paul's Cathedral singing the Grace, turbot and lobster, roast beef, ginger sauce with roast pheasant, and a chocolate basket of fruits. There were good speeches from the Prime Minister, the Archbishop of Canterbury and the Chancellor. Before the banquet there was an extraordinary kind of *Come Dancing* reception, ever so posh and grand, with people having to walk the gangplank up the Old Library to be presented to the Lord Mayor and Lady Mayoress as if they were an emperor and empress on golden thrones. This is an occasion when British ladies of a certain girth wear deeply frightening frocks and huge tiaras, blazing with ancient diamonds.

The next day my friend Bernard Jenkin, then MP for Colchester North, took me out to dinner and attempted to persuade me that the Tories were proving to be right about everything. This conclusively proved to me that they must be wrong.

19 November

Today was Ruth Watson's 70th birthday party. We had dinner at the Athenaeum. I much enjoyed listening to Ruth's reminiscences of her shoeless childhood in South Shields. Her father pushed her and her sister on a barrow all the way from South Shields to Scotland to try to find work.

I made the 5.45 evening Mass a Requiem for Teddy. The hymn 'Peace, perfect peace, in this dark world of sin' reduced me to tears.

The rest of the month saw me taking my first Confirmation classes at the Cathedral Choir School, swimming at the Oasis, saying Grace at the Retail Traders' Association dinner and getting to know the Syriac Indian priest and his wife from the City church of St Andrew by the Wardrobe. The Syrian Orthodox Church was breaking into two communities on some arcane doctrinal point which was quite beyond me. At St Mary-le-Bow there was a thanksgiving service for the Reed School (which is supported by the Corporation of London), during which the Duke of Devonshire peered at the order of service through some kind of eye instrument.

Early in December an important Parochial Church Council (PCC) meeting happened, during which William Sewell put over his plans for the crypt restaurant. The plans were accepted. Some students from Notre Dame, Indianapolis, came to the church for a visit with old Dr Gordon Huelin, who was teaching them about Anglicanism. Although they were all Roman Catholics, they all received Communion.

On 17 December, we held a carol service attended by 230 people. Some had to stand. My diary records that I preached a sermon against the *Sun* newspaper for attacking lesbian and gay people.

That evening I also went to a lot of trouble to cook venison for someone who needed cheering up, but he refused to eat it because I had used celery and he would eat nothing that had celery in it.

24 December

I am 43 today. I celebrated this momentous occasion by buying an overcoat, a suit and two pairs of shoes. I was given a glass of champagne at the Bow Wine Vaults and, as I walked along the lane, people came out of shops and gave me presents, which I thought was amazing. I had dinner at the romantic, gas-lit Temple in Nigel Seed's chambers.[9] We ate partridge.

Then I went on to Midnight Mass at St Mary's, Bourne Street – eighteenth-century vestments that belonged to Cardinal Mendoza; all very splendid, gorgeous and extreme. I think Midnight Masses in Anglo-Catholic circles do tend to get carried away. Although, I suppose, if you are going to Bourne Street, you must expect everything to be carried away at Christmas.

25 December

Christmas Day. There was a good sung Eucharist at St Paul's Cathedral – Mozart's *Coronation Mass* and the Latin Creed.

At 3.30 I went to Brompton Cemetery bearing Uncle Teddy's ashes, which I poured on Auntie Rose's tomb and on her father's tomb nearby – 'Called home.' On the ashes, I put some flowers from the roof garden: geraniums still in flower, white freesia that had been on my desk in my study, and some cupressus, holly and ivy. The sky was clear blue and still, the ilex oaks black against it. Above Teddy's old school, just outside the gates of the cemetery, a sickle moon glittered in the Christmas sunset. Here his ashes now rest, within half a mile of the place where he was born, the school he went to, the church he worked in, the hospital he so assiduously visited as a chaplain and in which he died,

---

9 Nigel Seed, a barrister, is a member of the congregation at St Mary's, Bourne Street, Chancellor of the Diocese of Leicester and, in 2001, Chancellor of the Diocese of London.

abandoned and neglected. Here, on Christmas Day 1987, he is buried. Nearby is the Russian Quarter, with its moving tombs: 'Born in Petrograd', 'Lady in Waiting to the Tsarina'.

27 December

I went with Andrew Dunford in his car through a sunny morning, which gradually clouded over, to Dover, which we reached by 10.15 and caught the ferry to Holland. We got to the house of Andrew's friends Aad and Wim at Tilburg at a quarter to seven in the evening and had a dinner of smoked chicken and cabbage. Aad, who is tall and handsome to start with, has had his teeth rearranged so that they are gleamingly, photogenically matinée-idol-like in their ivory perfection.

28 December

I was taken by Aad to his bee research institute. He is a world expert on the diseases of the bee, a more important subject than you think, when you reflect for a moment on the process of pollination.

30 December

In Amsterdam I went to the Tropical Museum for an illuminating exhibition about the religions of Indonesia. How impoverished is our Western post-Christian lack of rituals for birth and death. Births happen in hospitals where people don't see them; ditto deaths, no longer at home amongst the family. Then when death comes, what to do? We are in the hands of the undertaker, not in the hands of widely and deeply observed customs.

31 December

The last day of the old year. I got up at 7.30 to find a calm, clear morning. After breakfast, just as dawn came up, I walked down to the Singel Market and staggered back loaded with a tree chrysanthemum, bunches of berries including myrtle, hyacinth bulbs, white, sweet-smelling jasmine and 50 pink and white tulips for a friend's mother who is lonely and needs particularly cheering up.

From Holland I went to stay with Andrew's parents in Norfolk, a peaceful place to experience the first few days of a new year. One sunny weekday morning we went into the little village church and sang Morning Prayer together, to the amazement of the man who was felling trees in the churchyard. He came in to plug in his saw and found two men in jeans singing Matins from the Book of Common Prayer in an otherwise empty Norfolk chancel.

Not Very Much of a Communist

Despite the fact that St Mary-le-Bow had no congregation over the Christmas holidays, I had instigated the practice of having a crib scene in the church to celebrate the Nativity. Before Christmas, after the carol service, the Three Kings, their big plaster camel and its attendants would begin to make their way down the north aisle towards the font. During the Christmas holiday, when everybody was away, they gradually made the journey up and over the organ case – a bit of mountaineering there – to the south aisle. By the time everyone returned to work and we were nearing the Feast of Epiphany (marking the visit of the Magi to the infant Christ) on 6 January, they had almost reached the altar. Children love this kind of thing, and so do I. On my return from Norfolk in the first few days of 1987 I enjoyed shifting the Three Kings to their new positions in preparation for Epiphany. Their travels were obviously on my mind as I wrote up my diary for that day.

6 January

Another journey was announced today by No. 10 Downing Street: the arrival from Chelmsford of its Archdeacon as the new Dean of St Paul's. Eric Evans is a charming, elderly gentleman suffering from acute arthritis, sporting a silk handkerchief in his breast pocket and a rose in his button-hole. He is famous in the Church of England for a speech he made during the General Synod debate (I was present then as a member) on Lord Justice Scarman's Report on Police Behaviour following the Brixton riots. The Archdeacon said, 'In all my years as Archdeacon of Cheltenham, I have never come across a policeman being violent towards a black man.' That is the kind of thing Mrs Thatcher likes to hear, and he has been rewarded.

Life continued to be as varied as it had been in 1986, and once again there seemed to be a good deal of eating and entertaining.

20 January

I went to have supper at Admiralty House in Patrick and Jean Mayhew's flat. This great building, with its iron stove in the hall, with black iron Roman triremes sticking out of it, is divided up into flats of a very ordinary kind. Lord Havers has one, and so does Tom King, Secretary of State for Northern Ireland. The Mayhews have been given the top one, where Leon Brittan lived when he was Home Secretary. In the bottom of the deep freeze we found a very old pheasant, which must have been left behind by the Brittans. As I panted up the stairs, I wondered why people I know well, like Nigel Seed at the Temple, Gillian Williams, my secretary from university days, in Maida Vale, Bernard Dawson in Holland Park, and now the Mayhews in Whitehall, all live at the top of buildings.

5 February

I had lunch with General Eva Burrows at the International Headquarters of the Salvation Army. General Burrows is a small, dapper, focused and impressive woman. 'My job is most like that of the Pope and the Salvation Army as an organization most like the Vatican. I control the whole of Africa, South America and Asia from this desk,' she said, pointing to a number of impressive-looking telephones. We talked over lunch about having liberalism with conviction.

Then I went to dinner at the Honourable Artillery Company with one of the old St Mary-le-Bow Churchwardens, a Lieutenant Colonel of the regiment. I sat next to the Garter King of Arms, Sir Colin Cole, and inserted concepts of truth and justice into my Grace. I intend to put the Graces I say to useful effect.

15 February

There was a memorial service today for Sidney Evans at King's College, London. He was Dean of the College for 30 years. It was a moving occasion for those of us who were deeply influenced by the civilized, awe-inspiring figure he cut for so long in the Church of England. Professor Dennis

Nineham gave a brilliant address. The fact that none of the London bishops were present is indicative of the state of collapse of the Church of England and the ascendancy of reactionary Anglo-Catholicism in London.

17 February

Ash Wednesday. There were 76 communicants at the 12.30 Mass in the crypt, the church being repainted above us. It was lovely to have the crypt absolutely packed, with people standing on the steps down into it, and to hear Palestrina sung a capella.

When Uncle Teddy died, I put the flat I had bought him in Earl's Court on the market and wondered whether to try to buy a flat for myself in London — too expensive, really — or something much cheaper in the country. I had my heart set on Wiltshire. The difficulty with having a house in the country, however, was that I did not drive. Perhaps Andrew, having sold his cottage in Clare, might consider spending some of his time off with me in Wiltshire. On one exploratory expedition, I had been to look at a house on the Stourhead estate (just too expensive) and was making for Salisbury, when, out of the corner of my eye, I saw the ideal house.

20 February

At 4 o'clock, motoring through Wiltshire, I accidentally passed the perfect house in a village called Codford St Peter. Despite a small back garden, proximity to the road and an imminent bypass beyond the water meadows behind the house, this is absolutely IT. Regency stone, big rooms, copper beech trees in front of the house, beautifully kept by a dear old doctor's widow, Mrs Harris, the daughter of a Congregational minister. Comfort, dignity, unpretentious elegance. The front door has a dolphin knocker gleaming from much polishing. A long, narrow conservatory at the back of the house could be enlarged. Upstairs, from a back bedroom, one can see beyond the little garden wall into the great kitchen garden of the Big House behind.

What I was looking at, in fact, was only half a house. The part of Old Wool Cottage not lived in by Mrs Harris had remained empty for many years and was used by the gardener of the Big House – whose dower house this whole building was – as a place where he could wash his hands. I went home fizzing with ideas. Perhaps one day it would be possible to purchase the empty half of the house with the help of friends.

21 February

At 2.30 I set off for Cambridge to take part in a mission to the university. The atmosphere of Emmanuel College was dull and strained – no sense of fun. I walked with Don Cupitt, the Dean, in the Fellows' Garden. After dessert, I went over to Great St Mary's to hear Bishop Trevor Huddleston, a voice of great holiness from the past. Then I headed back to Emmanuel to talk to undergraduates and members of the Christian Union. We discussed fundamentalism versus liberalism, and biblical literalism versus biblical intelligence. How many times have I had this conversation?

31 March

Maundy Thursday. Last year I was at All Saints, Margaret Street, preaching every day in Holy Week. This year, unusually, I have the freedom to go into retreat, so I have come to Oxford, to the Sisters of the Love of God. I arrived just before 5 o'clock at the hermitage of St Mary of Egypt. After a cup of orange juice, I went to the chapel to rehearse the concelebration of the Mass with the Warden, Canon Donald Allchin, for the 5.30 liturgy. Canon Allchin celebrates prayerfully. There is a lovely Altar of Repose with garden moss, little plants and white violets.

Later I went to Compline, with the nuns reciting rather than singing in these most holy days, all by the light and smell of a little wartime oil lamp, in the deep calm of Paul Waterhouse's lovely whitewashed chapel with its mahogany stalls, polished red-tiled floor and alabaster baroque altar.

1 April

Good Friday. I read the Gospel at 2 p.m. at the Solemn Liturgy. Butterbeans, dry bread and hot water were consumed in silence in the refectory. I took a walk along the river to Iffley Bridge and Lock. We had eggs and beans for supper in the hermitage. Compline was at 7 p.m., with bed and Ovaltine following by 8.30.

Today was one of the best Good Fridays I can remember, if not *the* best. It was quiet and unstrained, apart from the world, not half in church and then half on Hampstead Heath at the fair, or half in church and then out for a meal with friends in the evening. It was a day begun in silence and ended in silence and kept in silence, with a walk beside a flowing stream.

2 April

Holy Saturday. I woke at 1.45 a.m. in time to read the Office of Tenebrae with the nuns, and then went back to sleep. I got up again at 6.30 and went to the chapel just after 7.00 for Lauds at 7.20, as yesterday. As yesterday, there was an empty church, the Sacrament House with its door open, just as I left it when removing the Blessed Sacrament for Communion in the Good Friday liturgy.

I had breakfast in the hermitage and then did an hour's reading and writing. Later in the morning, being nearby, I went to visit Michael and Joan Ramsey in St John's Home.[1] They moved there after a fraught retirement in one house after another in Durham and then the unsuccessful experiment of living in a flat at the Archbishop of York's Palace at Bishopsthorpe. On my way to visit them I went into the church nearby, St Mary and St John, Cowley, where cobwebs were floating down from the clerestory in the Holy Saturday sunlight. The empty Tabernacle on the High Altar and the flowers left over from Maundy Thursday's Altar of Repose spoke of that waiting day, in between the times, which is Holy Saturday.

---

1 Michael Ramsey was Archbishop of Canterbury from 1961 to 1974.

I spent from 10 till 12 with the Ramseys, Joan worrying about Michael and hating the 'home' aspect of the place, but looking surprisingly well; Michael, Parkinsonian but amused and amusing. Joan said, 'You're such a tonic for him.'

Bishop Michael and I talked of the Government and the relationship between the Prime Minister and Robert Runcie. Of his own time as Archbishop, he said, 'I enjoyed it all. I didn't get too battered or exhausted until the end and I wrote a few books as well, some of them not too bad, some of them quite good.' He reminisced about Clement Attlee, Harold Macmillan, Ted Heath and Alec Douglas-Home, all of whom he found kind. Of Harold Wilson he said, 'Very, very kind. Very, very kind indeed. I liked him very, very much.' This rather surprised me because he was the Prime Minister I expected Michael to get on with least well.

I said I wondered whether the whole political confrontation mode operating between the Church and the Prime Minister was really new, and Bishop Michael said, yes, in his day government and Primate were not in a permanent state of opposition, whichever party was in power. He said so many interesting things by way of mild rebuke of the present set-up in the Church: 'I always went into retreat with my ordinands and listened with them to the retreat conductor. I found that very helpful indeed. The bishops don't do that now.'

He also told me, 'Donald Allchin has dedicated his new book to me. Very sweet of him. And I've got another little book too.' Out came *Gateway to God*, edited by Lorna Kendell. Bishop Michael took a copy and wrote laboriously in it, 'Victor'. Then he asked me, 'Is that legible?' And then, more laboriously, he wrote, 'With love and blessing. +Michael.'

I was moved by something I found in the book, so I read it to them, a holy moment. The other day, Mervyn Stockwood said in a newspaper article that Michael Ramsey was not such a saint. But Stockwood, enlivening, stimulating, engaging, revolutionary, pompous, egotistical, drunk, important, foolish and useful all mixed up together, was wrong. There was holiness in that small room in the old people's home, a special kind of light that you get with saints. When it was time for me to leave, we kissed each other and I promised to return.

3 April

Easter Sunday, the Queen of Days. There was a bright grey, silvery blue moonlight lying over the convent lawns before the pre-dawn vigil. A foolish nun put on all the lights as soon as the candles had been painstakingly lit in the choir and, of course, the lights were not meant to come on at all, for the dawn would rise during the vigil and fill the chapel with its gentle, natural resurrection.

From 4 a.m. until 6.30 we were in the chapel and then we had a talking breakfast, one of the two which happen in this convent each year. I sang the 10 o'clock Mass and preached at it, and then had sherry with Mother Jane before lunch.

4 April

Bank Holiday Monday. I walked to Brompton Cemetery, where I put daffodils, branches of ilex and horse chestnut blossom on Teddy's grave. His ashes were exactly where I had poured them out at Christmas, still lying there, a grey smudge congealed by snow and rain, not yet integrated into the soil.

7 April

I discovered today that the Chancellor is going to insist upon a Consistory Court meeting over our desire to have a restaurant in the crypt. The Church of England may be exempt from secular planning permission, but any planning matters about alterations to building or change of use have to be heard in the Consistory Court, the ecclesiastical destination for matters concerning planning and doctrine (and goodness knows what else) that fall outside the secular provisions. St Mary-le-Bow is distinguished by having its own Consistory Court in the Norman Court of the Arches. It looks as if we're going to have a case brought against us by the Archdeacon of the Diocese of London, heard by the Chancellor of the Diocese in our own crypt – all because we want to have a restaurant.

Oh dear. We were told this wouldn't happen. Cost and tiresomeness and unnecessary worry at the eleventh hour: it's almost beyond belief.

By early April, a lot had happened in the short space of time since I had first caught sight of Old Wool Cottage in Codford St Peter. I had managed to sell the flat in Earl's Court and my offer on the cottage was accepted by Mrs Harris. She moved out, and all was ready for me to move in on 8 April. Andrew had decided to come in with me – I could at least provide a home for some of his furniture from Clare. I brought other furniture down from my uncle's flat, and from the rectory in Cheapside. It was quite an undertaking, stretched over a number of weeks during April and May, but we got there in the end, despite a certain amount of structural damage to several people's limbs.

8 April

By 10.30 a.m., a group of friends were in Warminster to shop and to help with the unloading at Old Wool Cottage, my new home. Codford Church has six candles on the altar and the Blessed Sacrament and an Easter Vigil. The cottage is even better than I remembered it – a garden full of sun, sweeps of blue anemone *blanda* and daffodils.

Back in London, an *Evening Standard* reporter tried to make me say unkind things about Peter Palumbo. Despite the original decision of the Corporation's Planning Committee to turn down the demolition plans for Number One Poultry, Peter Palumbo, with an enormous financial empire at his disposal, was able to continue the campaign via appeal and public enquiry. He was also able to employ, at vast expense, the very top QC. We were not in quite the same league, but we did our best.

That day's edition of the *Standard* ran the story. I was amused. 'The Revd Victor Stock, a man very careful with his words...' Even funnier was the statement which began, 'In the otherwise peaceful church of St Mary-le-Bow...' Peaceful? St Mary-le-Bow is like Piccadilly Circus in the rush hour most of the time.

It was, as it turned out, a day for being careful with one's words. His Excellency Señor Francisco d'Escoto, the Nicaraguan Ambassador, came for the Tuesday Dialogue and I found myself faced with a rather tricky situation.

19 April

What a day! I had inveigled the Master of the Grocers' Company into having His Excellency to lunch in Grocers' Hall after the Dialogue. The Ambassador, however, decided on the pavement that he had no time for lunch, or at least that he only had time for a sandwich.

I felt I had to talk him out of this, because I could see my street cred with the Grocers' Company running out into the sand. I was forced to think on my feet. 'Ah, Your Excellency,' I said. 'The Grocers' Company have invited you to lunch and you *are* expected there.'

'I can only stay for a quarter of an hour. Enrico, come for me at 2 o'clock,' said His Excellency to his driver – very grand, I thought, for a Communist.

I tried again. 'Your Excellency, I'm sorry, but the Grocers' Company are giving this luncheon in honour of the people of Nicaragua.'

'Enrico: 2.30.'

The idea of the Grocers giving a lunch in honour of the people of Nicaragua was so patently absurd that, if I'd had time, I would have burst out laughing at myself. There was no time, however, for so much as a smirk.

After the Dialogue, His Excellency was taken over to Grocers' Hall where he was wined and dined, given vintage port and thoroughly enjoyed himself, not rising from the table until after 3 p.m.

The next day he sent a box of the very finest cigars to the Master.

I felt I had done my bit for right–left relations. Just before that Dialogue Tuesday, I had met the Master of the Grocers in the street. 'Tell me, Victor,' he had said, 'is the Nicaraguan Ambassador a Communist?'

'Not very much of a Communist, Master,' I had replied, holding my breath. Diplomacy must be such hard work.

Later in April, I scored what I felt was a major diplomatic coup – this time in connection with Australia.

21 April

At 10.45 I went to the Australian High Commission to meet Mr McClennan, the High Commissioner, to invite him to take part in a Dialogue. Doug McClennan is a big Aussie politician, a cross between Edna Everage and Sir Les Patterson. He thinks the former is exactly like at least five women he knows well. He asked me to sign the Visitors' Book, which has Queen Mary and George V in it, and all sorts of universally famous cricketers, none of whom I know anything about, being bored to distraction by cricket.

The High Commissioner was in the process of fixing on St George's, Windsor, St Paul's Cathedral or Westminster Abbey as the laying-up place for the banner of the Order of Australia – a new idea which has replaced the old British Orders of Chivalry. The British members of the Order have to have their banner, of course, and carry on exactly as if they were members of the Order of the Bath or Members of the British Empire.

In a moment of inspiration, I said, 'Why not use St Mary-le-Bow? Arthur Phillip went out from there to be first Governor and founder of the Commonwealth of Australia.'

His Excellency moved into his secretary's doorway, put his head around the door and said, 'That letter you've just written to the Dean of Westminster, Brenda – bin it, dear.'

Thus began the link between Australia and St Mary-le-Bow, with St Mary-le-Bow going on to become the Australian church in London. His Excellency took me right down to the front door afterwards.

I then had to rush back to Cheapside to meet Sir Martin Gilliat, the Queen Mother's Private Secretary, to show him the church and think about the wines we might give the Queen Mother at the Grocers' Hall lunch after her visit to celebrate the church's 900th birthday. The special day was approaching fast. Sir Martin, at 75, was on the ball, utterly charming and authoritative.

That weekend, I set off for a visit to some friends in the Oxford area, head buzzing with the plans for the church's birthday celebrations.

23 April

I am staying with medical friends, John and Jessie Mills – he a doctor working for an international drug firm, she a nurse. I prepared them for Confirmation and marriage and baptized their children. At ten past midnight, the end of dinner, a guest said, 'Oh, we had an old Archbishop of Canterbury die in Oxford today.' Michael Ramsey. I was stunned by this. I rushed out, despite the hour, to ring a friend to see if this was really true. Then on Teletext I saw that it was. I've gone to bed very sad and shaken.

24 April

A fellow guest motored me into Oxford to visit Joan Ramsey. In the bedroom at St John's Home there was sunshine, the crucifix Bishop Michael so loved from the people of Tanzania, and under it, sherry bottles and the announcement of a baby's birth. Joan said, 'He embodied everything he taught. He looked as if he knew that it was true. I also thought he might be going to give God a piece of his mind – in the nicest possible way, of course.' His body had just been taken away.

Joan looked so frail and lost. She put her old head on my chest and we sat side by side on the sofa which had been in both their houses in Durham, with its piles of pink cushions which made it so uncomfortable to sit on. Just before 11, Mother Frances Dominica came to lead Joan to the chapel. Bishop Michael and Joan always walked arm in arm exactly like that. The picture those two women made, Mother Frances replacing Bishop Michael, affected me. I loved Michael Ramsey very much and revered him. In today's *Sunday Times* Owen Chadwick said, 'He was a warm man. He was very close to God. To be near him was to be near Someone above and beyond him.'

From this privately shared grief it was only a few days until St Mary-le-Bow's great public and royal celebration of its 900th birthday. It was an unsettling juxtaposition.

3 May

The great day. The Queen Mother arrived early at the church, worse than arriving late. I presented her to the Archbishop of Canterbury, as one does if one is the incumbent, and said, 'I'm very sorry, Ma'am. You're early. Would you mind engaging the Archbishop in conversation? Tell him a few jokes or something, and I'll be back in a moment.' (I needed to rush in and bring the music to a premature conclusion.)

'Oh, I could think of *lots* of jokes to tell the Archbishop of Canterbury,' she said.

The most splendid thing amongst the many Queen Motherly splendours is her professional ability to enjoy herself. She never goes through a door without looking to left or right to make quite sure that the people holding doors get a smile. It is in this caressing seductiveness that she is so enormously successful. Archbishop Robert Runcie has some of the same grace and charm, so a potentially fraught public occasion can dissolve into pleasure.

At one point during the Archbishop's sermon, the Queen Mother half turned around to me, raised one finger and winked, as if she was enjoying a splendid play. Of course, the great blue-ceilinged, black-and-white floored auditorium which is St Mary-le-Bow, repainted and gleaming, the 22-carat-gold gilding on the Corinthian capitals newly washed and shining, is perfect theatre.

The Queen Mother was kind and interested in everyone. I introduced or presented about 65 people. There was some lovely singing. The Archbishop dwelt in his sermon on uplifting images of spire, bells and the great hanging crucifix from Germany. Everyone looked happy. I got the Queen Mother to sign our register. I suppose royal personages imagine there are always books to sign by doors – doors which are always held open for them by smiling people.

I enjoyed the ride to lunch in the Archbishop's car, and we had a moment to talk about Michael Ramsey's funeral tomorrow.

At Grocers' Hall, I observed Her Majesty having at least part of two glasses of gin and Dubonnet, then some vintage champagne before lunch. She had already drunk a glass of the more modest white wine we offered at St Mary-le-Bow in the vestry. At lunch she had a glass of white Burgundy and then a glass of claret.

A little later the Master, Willy Martineau, said to her, 'Ma'am, as this is such a special occasion, we have a special bottle of Château Yquem.'

Queen Elizabeth fluttered her eyelids, stroked her pearls and said, 'Oh no, I really couldn't drink any more. I'll just have another glass of champagne.' This illuminating exchange revealed that what passes for mineral water in royal circles is champagne.

At the end of the afternoon, the Master, his wife and I finished up some port – Bridget and myself smoking cigarettes, which we had both given up years ago – while Queen Elizabeth, with not one feather out of place, swept away to Clarence House before embarking on the evening G & Ts.

4 May

The funeral of Michael Ramsey took place in Canterbury Cathedral. There was not one bishop present from London, which seemed insulting and perfectly illustrates the strangulated disapproval which permeates Anglo-Catholicism in the London diocese. The nave was not full. I would guess there were about 1,000 people present. An unpleasant psalm tune spoilt an otherwise beautifully arranged Prayer Book funeral service. Six great unbleached candles burned beside the coffin, which had a white mitre and some flowers from Joan lying on it.

We sang 'Praise to the Holiest in the height, and in the depths be praise' with thankful hearts, the music rushing up the great pillars of the nave and crashing against the vaulting. There were candles winking above the High Altar, glimpsed beyond the Pulpitum Screen, and one could just discern the dim outline of Augustine's throne which Michael Ramsey had so graced. There was a very good sermon from the Archbishop of Canterbury.

Joan came down the nave, almost blind, leaning on a stick and Mother Frances Dominica's arm. I had sat in the last chair in the nave and, as she came towards me, I just stepped out into the nave and she said, 'Oh, dear Victor,' and kissed me.

This will be my abiding memory of the funeral: as Bishop Michael's coffin was lifted up the steps and through the West Door, opened to receive it, a shaft of sunlight fell on the coffin which was slowly surrounded by a group of old, black-garbed beadsmen bearing ivory wands of mourning, as in some Elizabethan state portrait. It was an Elizabethan moment. Then the great doors closed and the coffin was gone. I slipped out and waved the coffin away. Joan and Mother Frances turned from the hearse to wave back.

There was a poor attendance, I thought, from the bishops. No one from the political Establishment bothered to come except the Home Secretary.

It has been a sad, sad day. Dear Father Michael, Primate and Metropolitan, a man very close to God. A man not after the fashion of these times. He was very loving to me always.

Tired out by the demands of celebration and funeral, I spent the following weekend at Andrew's cottage in Clare, helping him with the final dismantling before he gave up possession. When all his effects had been removed, the house looked shabby but not sad. We felt it had been, and would remain, a happy place.

Back in the City, I attended my first Court of Assistants meeting at Sion College. I had disliked Sion College when I was a student at King's because of its inaccessibly black and gloomy air. It was a nineteenth-century fantasy evocation of the Gothic Middle Ages – how the Victorians thought a medieval library should look. There was a great deal of black horsehair and indescribably dreary Nonconformist books in black, dusty bindings. We Assistants (as the Fellows who run the College are known) wore academic gowns and hung around our necks silver badges of office with the College's seventeenth-century coat of arms inscribed thereupon, suspended from a purple ribbon – undertakers' purple, which completed the funereal atmosphere. If I were ever to become President of that august body, I reflected, it would be much like becoming the Master of a City livery company.

13 May

Friday 13th – a perfect day for accidents. Tim Auger,[2] Andrew Dunford and I went to Clare to do the very final move out of Andrew's old cottage, with Andrew and Tim dropping iron railings, uprooted from the destroyed back garden, on their legs. Then Andrew dropped the car boot on the bridge of his nose and had to go to Casualty in London to have it glued. This was not a good beginning to the great move, but we arrived at Codford at 6.45 p.m. and by 8.30 we had a pretty sitting room made.

28 May

A weekend visit to the Mayhews. I took the 8 a.m. train to Paddock Wood and then a taxi to Kilndown and Twysden, the rambling, hilltop farmhouse belonging to the Attorney General. A policeman emerged from the rhododendron bushes as the taxi drew up at the stable gate across the drive from the road. I was escorted into the house, down a corridor and out into the garden overlooking parkland. Packed into the little porch seating area were the Home Secretary, Douglas Hurd, and his wife (they came down last night), and Patrick and Jean. I refused breakfast, which they were all having, but took some coffee. We talked about books and gardening in Peking when, long ago, Douglas Hurd was Second Secretary.

I talked with the Home Secretary for about 20 minutes about how boxes are got through, how the job works. And then, when we were far enough away from his police protection officer, I asked him why the Archbishop of Canterbury and the Prime Minister got on so badly. 'The Archbishop is a very witty man and humour is not Margaret's strongest suit,' he said. 'The Primate is the master of the throwaway line. Margaret has never thrown a line away in her life. She doesn't understand the Primate, though she respects him. She doesn't understand his sense of humour. She doesn't understand how a brave man who was awarded the MC in the

---

2 Tim is a publisher friend who was living in Notting Hill at the time.

war has liberal views.' Hurd is civilized, gentle and tough at the same time, reserved, a book-writer. He was at school with John Habgood, the Archbishop of York, and there are similarities – the tall, clever reserve.

A cavalcade of motors and police moved off for a visit to Sissinghurst Castle, where we met Vita Sackville-West's son Nigel Nicolson, then we went back to Twysden for lunch on the edge of the ha-ha. 'What is the point,' I asked, 'of all this security at the front of the house when anybody going along the main road over there on the other side of the field could take out the Home Secretary, the Attorney General and his guests in a burst of machine-gun fire?'

'Oh,' said Douglas Hurd, 'the police must have their lunch.'

I talked with Douglas Hurd about the Princess of Wales, of whom he is extremely pro and thinks highly gifted, sympathetic and intuitive with people.

14 June

Phyllida Stewart-Roberts asked me to help with an 80th birthday Mass for her mother, Veronica Bamfield, who is Richard Hayes's godmother. The Revd Richard Hayes is my neighbour at St Mary Woolnoth by the Mansion House. We were at university together. His mother's was the first English country house I visited – Loppington Hall, absolutely freezing. A whole collection of relationships were made in Shropshire and North Wales with Richard Hayes's friends and relations – the hunting, remote, non-metropolitan upper class, the world of the squires. Amongst them was this formidable and devout godmother of Richard's, Mrs Bamfield. Now, 20 years later, her daughter Phyllida is a member of our congregation at St Mary-le-Bow.

Later the Dean of Westminster, Michael Mayne, came for his Tuesday Dialogue wearing scarlet cassock and the Order of the Bath. I showed his wife and son the roof garden.

After that I went to swim and then had Father George and assorted Mar Toma Syrian Orthodox to see me. I tried to explain to them why using a City church might prove difficult. This was all hopeless. We've got all these City churches that we don't know how to use, but I can think of 8 million legal difficulties which will be put in the way of another congregation trying to use them.

The sharing of church buildings with other denominations is always an awkward and sensitive business, but I found myself anxious to help the Syrian Orthodox if it was at all possible. Unbelievably, in the end it all worked out.

The rest of that week was absorbed by the ongoing Palumbo enquiry. I listened to the Victorian Society giving evidence, and to the beginning of the architectural historian Gavin Stamp's evidence. One afternoon I gave evidence myself, but was tripped up a bit on the surveys. At least I made everybody laugh. The next day I looked in again at the public enquiry and saw the Great Man himself – James Sterling, the architect of the scheme, flown in from Stuttgart. We were told that we must not waste his time because he was a Very Important Person.

20 June

Bunny Hutchinson, now a vicar, came to lunch at the Athenaeum. We haven't met for 18 years. He is still a very nice man. Bunny was an important part of my theological education because he sat in front of me at St Boniface's College, Warminster. He always sat down in a dignified and deliberate way. As he was sitting, I would lean forward and put a copy of the English Hymnal immediately under him so that he would sit on it. The game was to do this at irregular intervals so that he would be lured into a false sense of security and be quite sure there wasn't a book under him, and then, of course, there was. This produced hysterical muffled laughter. Hysterical muffled laughter in church is the best cure going for all sorts of discontents.

22 June

At the 12.30 Mass, St Mary-le-Bow got itself twinned with St Philip's, Sydney, in the presence of 60 or so people. I accepted from Mrs Goldstone-Morris a brass plaque about Governor Arthur Phillip, but where will the Archdeacon allow us to put it?

Maureen Goldstone-Morris has given her life to promoting the work of Arthur Phillip, founder of Sydney and first Governor thereof. She feels acutely that he is not given enough honour around the world, and so she proceeds from country to country on which the Admiral set foot, jollying us all along and making sure that due and proper respect is paid to him. She's quite right.

The jolly Agent General left dustbins of Aussie wine, which came in as handy as anything.

27 June

I was at Westminster Abbey at 11.30 for the memorial service of Michael Ramsey. Pope Paul's ring (the ring he slipped off his own finger and put on Michael's finger at the end of a service outside St Paul-outside-the-Walls and which Michael wore every day ever after) was carried by a girl from the parish primary school in Liverpool where Michael had been a curate. Two schoolgirls from a comprehensive school in Camberwell carried his pectoral cross, the head prefect at Repton, his old school, carried his Canterbury Cap, John Andrew, his Domestic Chaplain, his stole, a graduate of Magdalen College a copy of *Canterbury Pilgrim*, and John Sherborne, who had also been his Chaplain, his wooden pastoral staff. Professor Owen Chadwick preached, evoking Michael and the whole atmosphere of a happier age in the Church of England over which he had presided.

Events far beyond Cheapside opened July. The most important thing was the Moscow Communist Party Conference, at which President Mikhail Gorbachev encouraged debate and argument. For the first time we were seeing debate and argument within Communism *televised*.

14 July

I had a very interesting City day. I visited the Dean of St Paul's, gave John Hughes, our retired administrator, lunch at the Athenaeum, took part in the procession at the Bicentennial Service for Australia at Westminster Abbey and had tea with

Sir Patrick Mayhew in the House of Commons. I met him when I was leaving the Abbey. Then, into the same tea room, came one of my Churchwardens, Andrew Stewart-Roberts, as someone else's guest.

I was back at St Mary-le-Bow at 6 p.m. to hear Archbishop Kyrill of Smolensk. He was allowed out of Moscow this morning to come to England and returns tomorrow for a weekend of talks with Mikhail Gorbachev. Archbishop Kyrill – Metropolitan Kyrill, indeed – is a reforming figure within Russian Orthodoxy. He's a friend to Gorbachev and able to mediate between the emerging political world of *perestroika* and the Russian Church. He also has considerable contacts in the West. Richard Chartres, Gresham Professor of Divinity and a Russian expert, arranged hospitality from the Mercers' Company, who are both parishioners of St Mary-le-Bow and patrons of the Gresham Lectureships. This was a groundbreaking moment in a number of ways and I was honoured to have the Archbishop's lecture in our church.

18 July

I slept, as I am going to for the next few days, at the Grocers' Hall so that I can escape the concrete saw going through the floors of Bow Bells House, which is the most effective of Mitsubishi's torture instruments as they demolish their building next to the church.

At the end of July, Andrew and I left England to visit friends in Amsterdam and then travelled on to various destinations in Germany, Italy and France. On 10 August we passed through Auxerre on our way to Paris and stopped to look round a sadly neglected cathedral. There was broken glass on the floor of the nave, and a crypt full of dusty manuscripts, unpolished chalices, moth-eaten vestments and even a faded stole which had belonged to the seventeenth-century churchman and theologian François de Sales. The contrast with Salisbury or Canterbury was painful. More painful was the news which awaited us in Paris, when we arrived at the home of our friend Jean Louis.

10 August

We went straight from Auxerre to Paris and to Jean Louis's flat. I didn't know its secret electronic code, so Andrew went off to a telephone to ring Jean Louis. In the meantime Jean Louis, seeing me from upstairs, came down. 'Before Andrew comes back,' he said, 'there is bad news for him – his mother has died.'

As always with shock, I could hardly take it in, but decided it was my job, not Jean Louis's, to tell Andrew. Jean Louis found him and brought him back in happy ignorance.

Of course, we had to return to England immediately. It was already quite late, however, so there was no point in trying to set off until the next morning.

11 August

We made the long haul home – Paris, Calais, Dover, Norfolk – travelling from 9 a.m. till 6 in the evening. Andrew's brother Tony and his second wife Carol were at Andrew's father's. It was a quiet evening.

12 August

At 3.30 we went into Norwich to see Kathleen's body. Everyone in this strange, dysfunctional family is being kind to everyone else. At 5 p.m. we motored off to Wiltshire, arriving in Codford at 9.15. Other guests arrived at 11.

18 August

I got the funeral sermon finished and at 2 o'clock in St Mary's, Marlborough, I delivered it and conducted the service. During the funeral, the skies opened. Andrew read 'Death swallowed up in Victory' with confidence.

Then I went with the body to Swindon to the beautiful crematorium and conducted the Committal. In the middle of this: 'Oh, the flowers, the flowers! Quick – the flowers!' shouted Andrew's father Don, and an unnecessary scuffle ensued as people tried to tear them off the coffin before it went through the doors to the flames. Of course, undertakers always take the wreaths off the coffin before the flames consume the body, in order that the flowers should be carefully laid out by the door so that the grieving relatives can see who has sent what. I didn't feel able, in the middle of the liturgy, to explain this. After the flowers had been wrested from the coffin, I continued with the service.

What will happen to Don now, without Kathleen to look after him? I wonder if it would be right to encourage him to come and live at Codford, where he could be looked after by Ruth Watson – thus giving them both a home. Andrew would see much more of his father there than he ever will if Don stays in Norfolk. Perhaps Don and Andrew could find the funds to buy the empty half of the house together. Well, we shall see.

Back in London in September after the summer break, I cleaned out my study and rearranged a crowd of escaped volumes, washing the bookshelves before putting everything back in the right place. Owning such a large number of books is like having an unruly family – they run out of control very easily, making a mess all over the place. I enjoy washing shelves and tidying books, but it happens at extremely rare intervals.

26 September

Father Raymond Avent, my neighbour from St Vedast's, came to lunch. I have decided to go on a Spiritual Director course which he is running for a year. I think I take for granted my ability to help people in this department, and I really know nothing about it at all and would like some more information and input. I would like to know about the spirituality of St Teresa of Avila as opposed to St Thérèse of Lisieux, and what St Benedict really thought about God.

October began with a minor disaster brought about by vanity. In keen anticipation of a visit to St Mary-le-Bow from John Mortimer QC, better known to the world at large as Rumpole of the Bailey, my mind was appropriately fixed upon the law, and I decided to help out the Attorney General one day by taking him some lunch. Patrick, Jean and I had all found ourselves, unusually, in London on a Saturday and I offered to buy some lunch, take it to Admiralty House and prepare it.

Eager to impress, I remembered the existence of Lidgates, my solicitor Bernard Dawson's local butcher in Holland Park. I went there with him and bought some expensive, showing-off meat, then Bernard drove me to Admiralty House with my precious offering. I got out of the car, waved Bernard goodbye, turned towards the portals of the great house – and realized that the meat was still in the car. Under the curious gaze of the guards on duty, I abandoned my air of haughty *savoir-faire* and rushed, waving frantically, into Whitehall in pursuit of the disappearing lunch. It was too late. Chastened, I hurriedly purchased some inferior fare from the nearby Europa Foods store and climbed to the top of Admiralty House with this rather more modest offering. There I discovered the Attorney General about to rush down the stairs, having discovered he was out of tonic water and making for that haven of salvation, Europa Foods.

From Admiralty House I went straight on to Terling in Essex to stay with a Past Master of the Grocers' Company, Charles Roundell and his wife Anne, in order to look after their parish during its interregnum. At church the next morning I had the astonishing experience of seeing Lord Rayleigh and his party from Terling Place enter the chancel, where they sat, leaving at the end of the service by their own private door for the Big House. The nineteenth-century Tractarians exerted a great deal of energy on removing the aristocracy from the chancel seats and replacing them with a choir. This reform had clearly not been achieved in Terling. It was a vignette from a past age.

4 October

Dialogue Tuesday. At 9.15 a.m., John Mortimer rang to ask, 'Is it today? Oh, I *am* sorry, I can't come today, I'm being filmed.'

I rang Bishop Graham Leonard, who was to be in the other pulpit. He was quite sweet about it, so I interviewed him myself. It all went surprisingly well, although on religion he is impossible. He explained why God allows suffering. It was unconvincing and he went on for a very long time until I was forced to say, 'Imagine, Father, that you are just an ordinary parish priest. It's a Monday morning, 8 o'clock, the doorbell rings and it's a woman to say her baby is dead. What would you do? The baby hasn't died of anything interesting and hasn't been ill. What would you say?'

He said, 'I don't know.' For a moment, there was huge intake of breath and people began to be interested and attentive. 'Oh, how terrible. I wouldn't know what to say,' he repeated, just like that, and seemed so human in his purple cassock and glittering gold and jewelled pectoral cross. But then he said, 'I would hurry on to explain the workings of Providence and speak of the Atonement,' and of course he lost us all again.

I interrupted and said, 'I think the Bishop of London has just explained the doctrine Christians call the Incarnation, which is God being beside us, sharing our lives as they are. Thank you so much.'

10 October

I attended a Court of Sion College meeting, leaving no time for lunch because I took the Underground and overground train to Harlesden, to give a lecture to medical students on 'Breaking bad news'. I thought they were unresponsive, but I discovered afterwards that I had traumatized them. The idea of having to speak to people about death – I gave them the exercise of imagining that somebody they knew and loved had just died – silenced the usual medical student ebullience.

11 October

William Rees-Mogg came to do the Dialogue. He said that, as Chairman of the BBC Complaints Council, he had put the Bishop of Peterborough[1] on the committee to represent the views of the man in the public house! Lord Rees-Mogg is kind, very clever, humane and substantial. He was hard to Dialogue with because he was reserved and formidable and

---

1 Bill Westwood, well known for his broadcasts on Radio 4's *Thought for the Day*.

had about him the understated aura of the great and the good embodied. This made me feel trivial, ill-informed and silly, and – unusually – inarticulate.

Afterwards we attended a Grocers' Lunch, presided over by the Master. Suddenly the Master said to Lord Rees-Mogg, 'Aha, I am sure that you have affairs of state to attend to.' Yes, he did actually say this. He went on, 'We have arranged for a taxi to be waiting for you outside and I think the clock is ticking over.' This was clearly said with a mixture of kindness and nervousness.

His Lordship looked enquiringly at me and I said, 'Thank you very much, Master,' and hurried His Lordship away, saying, 'We've got to get in the taxi. It would be kind.'

We did so, waving gratefully to our hosts, and I told the taxi driver to drive around the corner to St Mary-le-Bow – where, of course, His Lordship's chauffeur was waiting to take him away.

19 October

There was a ghastly dinner for the Arbitrators' Company at the Butchers' Hall. 'I am the world expert on aviation arbitration...' Bore, bore, bore. There was a dull but nice old gent on my right with a Malaysian lady. She was wearing nothing except a few sequins and a cigarette. Opposite her sat the silent wife of the aviation bore.

On my left was a man I could get nothing out of at all, except that he lived next to Hyde Park. 'Oh, how wonderful to live next to Hyde Park,' I said. 'You must enjoy it enormously.'

'Never go in it. I hate parks,' he snarled.

23 October

I had some Roman Catholic guests staying for the weekend, so I took them to Downside Abbey for the 10 o'clock Mass. We heard an Evelyn Waugh-like, laconic, clever sermon from an old monk with his arm in a sling. The sun came out and filled the great nave.

In the evening I went to a dinner party in Clapham, where one of the guests was a Roman Catholic who wanted torture

to be reintroduced for heresy. This was matched by an equally horrible, extreme left-wing socialist woman, making dinner
not a pleasure but an endurance test.

30 October

My William IV dining table has gone away to the menders to
have the two halves which have come apart pressed back
together. I bought this table for £9 in Warminster when I was
a theological student. Goodness knows what it is worth now.
It is nice having a proper house, and one of the consequences is that you gradually get your furniture repaired.

There was not much time to enjoy my restored table in the dining
room at Codford during November. On the first day of the month
I had a meeting with the diocesan lawyers Lee Boulton and Lee,
because the Archdeacon of London, as feared, had instructed Sir
John Welch to object to the licence as drafted, seeking permission
to open a restaurant in the crypt. Then I took a train to
Northampton to preach at All Saints' Church on All Saints' Day,
with the Mayor sitting in a marvellously pompous throne, such as
you see in provincial churches in France.

Back in Cheapside, an amusing and unlikely juxtaposition took
place in the rectory one day. The leading opponent of the ordination of women held a meeting in my sitting room with two
priests, whilst in the crypt a German television crew interviewed
Margaret Webster, the doughty leader of the Movement for the
Ordination of Women, about the Bishop of London forbidding
the St Hilda Community from holding a Mass celebrated by
women outside the University Chaplaincy at Westfield College in
the East End. How these two things happened in my house at the
same time, I do not know.

The next day was a public open day for our tower and its
famous bells. Many people came to have a look round. Mark
Regan the steeple-keeper, speaking with pride about England's
most famous bells, said of our City parish, 'Only two people live
here. One is the Rector and the other is the Governor of the Bank
of England.'

'I am the Governor of the Bank of England,' said Mr Robin
Leigh-Pemberton from the midst of the visitors.

6 December

I went with Gillian Williams to hear the *Messiah* at St Paul's. 'Though worms destroy this body, yet in my flesh shall I see God.' In this music and under that dome, God is incarnate. I was moved to tears. St Paul's was absolutely packed with people. I talked to proud parents and excited boys over mince pies afterwards in the Choir School.

Preparation for Christmas continued with a visit from a priest and his wife who were having a difficult life in the Peterborough diocese. We dined at the Athenaeum (Michael Ramsey had made me a member when I was Rector of Friern Barnet) and then they came back with me to stay the night at the rectory. I was trying to give them what the Queen gives her guests at Windsor when they are invited to 'sleep and dine'. At least, that was what Alan Webster and Roy Strong told me. I found that I missed Alan Webster now that he was no longer Dean at St Paul's. He had been the perfect neighbour and it seemed to me that St Paul's was rapidly ceasing to be a refuge for liberal thinkers and openness, having slipped back into a kind of 1662, Masonic, reactionary past.

Then, on 12 December, 35 people were killed in the Clapham Junction train crash. That evening I sat with a man who had to tell someone that her husband had been killed. Deeply distressed at the thought of those suddenly shattered lives, I thought to myself, *You can be quite sure that at Codford the Vicar won't mention the Clapham Junction crash, or Armenia, where an earthquake has killed 100,000, or Mr Gorbachev cutting 500,000 troops in Russia*. The Vicar at Codford never mentioned everyday events in his sermons. He confined himself to entirely religious language, unaffected by what was happening elsewhere. It reminded me of Alan Webster saying that, on the day Airey Neave MP was blown up by the IRA, nobody on the cathedral staff mentioned the fact in any service. It is all too easy for the Church to be completely distanced from what is going on in the world – even when it comes to revolutions, crashes and earthquakes. This has always seemed incredible to me.

14 December

Alan Webster came in to talk, visiting London in his retirement, and the Salvation Army sang carols in the churchyard.
In the afternoon I went with a lot of disabled people from
Camberwell to spend the afternoon and evening at South
Park, a country house in Surrey, for a candlelit carol service
in a sixteenth-century chapel that was once a stable. I took
the service and preached. There were log fires, incense and
holy water. We had dressing up, and in the dressing-up box
was a biretta that had once belonged to Canon Colin
Stevenson. When Canon Colin retired from being the
Administrator of Walsingham, he became Chaplain to
Uvedale Lambert at South Park. It is Uvedale's daughter
Sarah who now presides over this magical, log-fire-scented
place with her handsome, kind husband Tim Goad.

20 December

Robin Leigh-Pemberton called in for a conversation. At
lunchtime I took the Children's Society carol service. In the
address I told them that I am one of their products, being an
adopted baby.

The Grocers' Hall staff came for an impromptu party in my
flat, some of them getting more than drunk. I went to the
Garrick for dinner with Roy Strong. We talked about gardening
and the royal family. He is, apparently, off the royal family, Mrs
Thatcher, the Church and the V & A. When I got home there
were still some late revellers. I persuaded them out into the
street and home in taxis rather than trying to drive.

22 December

Tragically, last night a Pan-Am jumbo fell out of the sky onto
a little Scottish town called Lockerbie. We had something
like 280 people at the parish carol service. I preached on
the *Messiah* text from Job: 'Though worms destroy this
body, yet in my flesh shall I see God.' People sat at my invitation in the Sanctuary and yet, even with all those chairs
taken, some people had to stand. One person had lost a

friend in the Lockerbie crash who had been staying with her last Sunday.

24 December

I was up at 6 a.m. I am 44 today. I watered the roof garden, finished some mega-packing, visited the Blessed Sacrament, said my prayers and fancied, while I prayed, that my mother and family were coming near. It was almost a physical sensation. This was comforting, because their presences were happy.

I set off for Codford, getting there by 11 a.m. The second window we have installed in the dining room has transformed the back of the house. Andrew's father, Bernard and Tim arrived and were given tasks to do – decorations to put up, the tree to prepare, a pasta supper to make – and then we all went for drinks at the Manor House and on to Midnight Mass in the village.

30 December

I had a devout reading and praying morning. The study has become my winter room. It is also my space, into which other people are only invited by me. They can have the run of the rest of the house.

In the afternoon we climbed Clay Hill. It has a marvellous, Netherlandish painterly quality of blue receding distances with smoke curling up from cottages in the valleys.

'Oh No, Oh No,' Said His Grace

We celebrated New Year at Old Wool Cottage for the first time, and I was glad to see my repaired and revitalized William IV dining table being used properly at last. Not only did it accommodate the Christmas guests who came to stay, but also 15 of our village neighbours, whom we invited in for smoked trout rolls and a drink to say goodbye to 1988.

1 January

Sunday. For the first time I celebrated Mass in Codford St Peter. There were 20 people for a said 1662 Communion Service. Stuart, a little boy, served rather uncertainly. I preached, which I discovered afterwards that no one expected. I gave them an idea from Augustine about Jesus freeing us from slavery into childhood.

I then spent a lovely day at home in the front garden, collecting up beech leaves and beginning to deal with the yew hedge, which is completely out of control and I think has been so for a hundred years. Roses, laurel and forsythia are integral to it.

The following Sunday I went to the 10 o'clock Mass at St Mary's, at the other end of the village. St Mary's was a pretty medieval church with a vandalized Norman arcade, hacked out between 1890 and 1908. I noticed that the congregation of elderly brigadiers and respectable old ladies received Communion by intinction – i.e. they each dipped the bread into the wine, rather than sipping from the chalice. *There must be a tremendous fear of AIDS here*, I thought to myself – though not at the other end of the village, where everybody received the chalice in the normal way. Whatever was the matter with people?

Then it was back to Cheapside and the bustle of the City. John Mortimer may have got his Dialogue dates muddled back in the autumn of 1988, but mercifully the Home Secretary was rather more organized at the beginning of the new series in 1989.

17 January

Douglas Hurd stayed to lunch after a very good Dialogue. Phyllida Stewart-Roberts made a wonderful chicken pie and a sprout cream – I didn't know you could make sprouts into something nice. Paul, the butler from the Grocers' Hall, brought some delicious claret over for us. The Home Secretary was affable, funny and quick. Also there for lunch were Wendy Evans from the Museum of London, John Hughes our Administrator, Phyllida and her husband Andrew, and Andrew Dunford. We moved the table into the middle of the room. The detective had his lunch on a tray in the study and left a nice note on it, which I kept. Douglas Hurd didn't arrive until 12.50 and we got through sherry, Dialogue, main course, pudding and coffee and put him in his car by 2.05.

At the Dialogue Douglas Hurd said *Daily Telegraph* things about the Church of England – how much he liked the old Prayer Book and the old hymns, and when he went to church at Christmas and Easter he didn't like having modern hymns. I said it was time he started looking at the inside of religion. Well, in fact *he* said perhaps it was time he started looking at the inside of religion, as his friend Simon Barrington Ward[1] had once advised him. I simply said, 'Yes,' and then there was a silence. I knew that Simon Barrington Ward was at Eton with him, but didn't say I knew they were friends. I like the Home Secretary and hope that one day he may think a bit again about church.

24 January

John Mortimer did come for his Dialogue, with me in the other pulpit rather than the Bishop of London as we had originally intended. He was charming and ease-making, and the church was completely packed. He was very funny about David Jenkins, the Bishop of Durham, saying there was only a cigarette paper between his position and that of John Mortimer's as regards God, and he found this disappointing. He talked about God and suffering as the Bishop of London

---

1 Bishop of Coventry.

and I had talked about God and suffering. Mortimer said
Runcie had explained the meaning of God and suffering to
him once over a Campari soda, but he couldn't remember
what he had said. Laughter from the crowd. Cardinal Hume
had explained the God and suffering business as 'we only
see one side of a tapestry', which he found unconvincing –
though of course, like everybody else, he found Basil Hume
charming. The only person, he said, who had a complete
picture of why God allowed suffering was the Bishop of
London, who had explained it to him in great detail, and he
found this both unconvincing and repellent.

27 January

I took Ruth Watson to Codford. Ruth loved it all and would
like to live in Codford more than anything else. She sees
movement as adventure, which is pretty admirable at 71. We
could look after Ruth and Don and they could look after each
other. Am I able to do all this? Would it work?

7 February

Shrove Tuesday. I spent an hour this morning talking to Gare
Drake, the Registrar of the Bank of England, in his fantastic
room with its signature of Nelson on the wall.

I went to my Spirituality course at St Vedast's, where I got
fed up with the middle-aged Roman Catholic emphasis on
feelings. I would like *information*. I would like to know what
St Teresa of Avila actually did when she was praying, or
thought she was doing when she was trying to pray, instead
of what Sister Patricia rightly described as 'all this subter-
ranean Ignatianism' (i.e. making the Spiritual Exercises of St
Ignatius Loyola the only correct model for the life of prayer).

8 February

Ash Wednesday. About 100 people were at the 12.30 Mass.
The church was sunlit and full of handsome young men and
women in their City suits, not the older ladies and secretaries who came yesterday to hear Canon Roger Royle in

Dialogue. Isn't that fascinating? If 20 of the communicants were Roman Catholics (and we do have a number of RCs who regularly communicate here, despite being told they mustn't by their own Church), that would have left getting on for 80 Anglicans, most of whom were under 40.

I had an apple for breakfast and ate nothing else at all until 8 p.m., when I had beans and tomatoes. The Grocers had a great dinner tonight. How pathetic for a Christian company, at least Christian in origin, to hold such an event on Ash Wednesday. Even more dreadful, the Queen went for lunch at the Guildhall today to celebrate the something-or-other anniversary of the founding of the Mayoralty. To his credit, the Archbishop of Canterbury refused to go because it was Ash Wednesday. The excuse from the Palace was that Ash Wednesday did not appear in the Queen's diary. What she should have done, and what the City should have encouraged her to do, was to have a great banquet for Christian Aid, giving the money they would have spent on today's lunch to the starving and sitting themselves down to a piece of cheese and an apple. It would have made a television moment, bringing people to think about the plight of the hungry, and about Ash Wednesday – not impossible, just imaginative.

Holy days that fall on a weekday, like Ash Wednesday, Ascension Day and Epiphany, have a special quality to them, quite unlike Sundays. A sense of the holy on a weekday: that is what St Mary-le-Bow is for.

13 February

Roger Freeman, the new Health Minister, husband of Jenny Freeman, the architectural historian, came to dinner. Also in the party were the Hon. Bernard and Mrs Anne Jenkin, Gillian Williams and the Hon. George Bruce, the portrait painter. Gillian looked lovely with long pearls and a silk skirt. The Minister left for the House of Commons with his driver to vote on a guillotine motion at 10 p.m. and then came back. Roger looks like a 1950s matinée idol and is the perfect handsome complement to his extraordinarily beautiful wife.

That was the last dinner party I gave in London until Easter. There followed a short period of Lenten abstinence, and there were no more excitements until later in the month.

22 February

I discovered from the *Independent* that I should have been at the Mansion House last night saying Grace. The report says I did, but in fact I was at my Spirituality course and came home to have an apple and some water instead of supper, when I could have been dining off the finest viands. As I was wondering to whom I should apologize, Mr Minshall Fogg, the Clerk of the Arbitrators, rang in a complete rage. Where had I been? They hadn't realized I wasn't there until the Major Domo banged his gavel and said, 'Pray silence for Grace from the Chaplain to the Arbitrators' Company,' and there was an embarrassed silence. Minshall Fogg thought it was because I was so grand, having the Mercers and the Grocers for my parishioners (numbers one and two of the great 12 livery companies), and a newish company like the Arbitrators was so low on my list of importance that I simply ignored them. I started writing letters of apology. This is the sort of thing which people will never forget, all the time I'm in the City.

27 February

I sat in the Headmaster's study at the Choir School seeing each of the candidates for Confirmation one by one. It gave me a chance to do with children what I would do with individual adults concerning the spiritual life, i.e. to discuss the idea of following some kind of rule or discipline – though I did not include the equivalent of confession because I think small boys shouldn't be encouraged into that. It needs a more mature and autonomous adult state, in my view.

I had a Roman Catholic priest friend to supper who needs someone outside his own church to listen to him, where he can be safe.

28 February

Fifteen people came to the 7.30 Mass. Later I sat in on an arbitration tribunal. As Chaplain to the Arbitrators, I thought it would be interesting for me to discover about arbitration. It wasn't interesting.

8 March

I went to supper with Patrick and Jean Mayhew at Admiralty House. When I arrived, a new young policeman insisted on taking me up the main stairs to Tom King's front door – Tom being the Secretary of State for Northern Ireland. As he raised his hand to knock, I whispered, 'No! This isn't the Attorney General's front door.' This would have been jolly for the IRA, but not for Mr King or the Mayhews or the young policeman.

23 March

Maundy Thursday. The *Independent* photographed the foot-washing at our Mass today, which will make a good image for the Christian faith – Ruth Watson representing the elderly, Jim Gough from a nearby bank representing the young, both having their feet washed by the Rector wearing plain white vestments.

24 March

Good Friday in Hemel Hempstead. I got up at 5.15 a.m. and watched at the Altar of Repose until 7.15. This was a real occasion of prayer. I felt myself encouraged because I had made my own confession yesterday and got back into that sense of being holy before God. I can't quite say *with* God, but certainly before God, with the intellectual knowledge of *wanting* to be with God.

But then – oh dear – there was a ghastly procession of 'witness' through the 1960s shopping precinct. A sermon was delivered by a good Salvation Army captain, but my goodness, the content! Did it make any contact at all with the devotees of Sainsbury's?

The Three Hours went well, I think, except for my last address which wasn't connected to the others enough, and the choir – well, it was a brave attempt to sing a 20-minute Bach cantata. I see the picture of yesterday's foot-washing is in today's *Independent*.

With my duties over in Hertfordshire and London for the time being, I crossed to France in time for Easter Sunday, intending to travel on from there for a short holiday in Spain.

26 March

Easter Day. I went to the Anglican Chaplaincy church of St George's, Paris. It was crowded. John Underwood, Peter Palumbo's solicitor, was there at the Easter Mass on his way down to the South of France. John thinks Nicholas Ridley's decision on Number One Poultry may come out this week.[2] It was strange to be talking about the future of listed buildings in my London parish after Easter Mass in Paris. We have had the most wonderful Easter sunshine and opalescent blue sky all day.

From Paris, Andrew and I motored through France and into Spain, visiting Burgos and Segovia after a drive across windswept plains. We visited the resting place of St John of the Cross, which I thought was a place of palpable holiness. By the end of the month we were in Alba de Tormes in the region of Salamanca.

31 March

It was a long drive to Alba de Tormes, where we saw rather than venerated the torn-off arm and withered heart of Teresa of Avila. Here there was no sense of holiness or devotion, nor were we tempted to buy Teresian ashtrays. There is something about ashtrays and Teresa of Avila which doesn't gel. The church had a deathbed waxwork that lit up, apparently to make you feel closer to St Teresa. I have never felt further

---

2 Nicholas Ridley was then Secretary of State for the Environment and was considering the Inspector's Report on Number One Poultry after the public enquiry.

from her. It was all lifeless and deeply unmoving, unlike the tomb and simple church of St John of the Cross at Segovia.

Back in Segovia, we had tapas and beer in the house where Teresa was born and the horribly ugly garden where she played as a little child.

We continued to explore, marvelling at the wonderful library full of Greek, Latin, Arabic and Hebrew manuscripts in the monastery at El Escorial, and brushing the dust from our clothes after we had walked round the uncared-for cathedral at Toledo. Perhaps the high point of the trip was a Mass in the cathedral's Mozarabic chapel. The Mozarabs were Christians in Moorish Spain and the Mass was something like a mixture between our 1662 Prayer Book and the Greek Orthodox liturgy. It gave me a strange and moving sense of connection with a very distant past.

10 April

The end of the holiday. Mrs Flack, the Lord Mayor of Westminster, was getting on the plane just in front of me in Paris. I was working at my desk in Cheapside by 4.30 p.m. Ruth Watson immediately started talking to me while I tried to listen to someone else on the telephone. It's that juxta-position of demand, with both people who want your atten-tion unconscious of the presence of the other, that is so typ-ical of priestly life.

6 May

Today is the anniversary of my mother's death. I miss her still.

Jeremy Davies[3] collected me for dinner in Salisbury and I joined his party after a dull, heavy, Victorian Evensong – the sort of Church of England music I really dislike. At dinner were Sir John and Lady Tooley and Lady Stewart: 'Don't call me Lady Stewart...' I had either forgotten or never knew her Christian name, however, so what *was* I to call her?

---

3 Precentor of Salisbury Cathedral.

Eventually Sir Edward Heath also arrived. He was marvel-
lously funny about Michael Ramsey coming to see him when
Ted was Prime Minister and Michael wanted to resign as
Archbishop of Canterbury.

When got home, I wrote to Sir Edward to tell him why the
Archbishop of Canterbury had acted towards him as he did on
that occasion. I knew, because Bishop Michael had told me.

Sir Edward had told the story like this: 'My secretary came in
and said, "The Archbishop of Canterbury wants to come and see
you," so we cleared the decks for the next afternoon. The next
afternoon His Grace arrived. First there was a great deal of
whistling [here Sir Edward did a brilliant imitation of Michael
Ramsey whistling nervously] and then I offered His Grace tea.

'Eventually I was forced to ask him what it was he'd come to see
me about, to which he replied, "I'm going to resign, resign, resign,
resign. I'm going to resign, resign."

'I said how very sorry we were and how very sorry Parliament
would be, and eventually I said, "Who should I suggest to Her
Majesty as your successor?"

'"Oh no, oh no, oh no, oh no," said His Grace, "that would be
most improper!" And he left.'

Sir Edward had never understood what had gone wrong, but I was
able to tell him. It was a story which Michael Ramsey had loved to
repeat. When Geoffrey Fisher resigned as Archbishop of Canterbury
in 1961, Michael was Archbishop of York and therefore clearly in the
running as a replacement. Fisher went to see the then Prime Minister,
Harold Macmillan, and said, 'I was Michael Ramsey's headmaster at
Repton and I want to tell you that the Archbishop of York would be
a most unsuitable Archbishop of Canterbury. He is a mystic, a
theologian, a writer and a man of prayer.'

Mr Macmillan replied, 'Thank you very much for your kind
advice, Your Grace. You may have been Dr Ramsey's headmaster,
but you were not mine.' This was the button Sir Edward had inadvertently pressed.

19 May

A Mr Surpliss came about being the Verger – too Dickensian to be true.

In the evening I flew to New York with David Hutt for the Historic Churches Conference. This is David's first visit to the US. Eventually, at 11.10 p.m., we got to Fulton Street and Neale House, where guests of Trinity are housed. An intern from England opened the door, interrogated us immediately about the Movement for the Ordination of Women and gave us cranberry tea – not what David wanted at the end of a long journey.

21 May

Trinity Sunday, New York. At High Mass I was put in a cope and given the bishop's place at the end of the procession. Percival Brown, the priest liturgist in charge of all this, and the Head Verger were warm and friendly, but there were no invitations to lunch. The liturgy lasted two hours – not all of it my fault. It was all terribly complicated and breathless, without a moment's silence for recollection: Anglo-Catholicism on speed or over-ripe, wasp-blown fruit. The congregation looked intelligent and multiracial.

From there I went to join David for lunch in a handsome, gloomy Federal House. We had salmon and asparagus, and there was a terrible drama over whether to have knives with the asparagus or not. This is one of those things by which eternal life is given or hell awarded.

22 May

I took the subway to St John the Divine, the great New York Episcopalian cathedral. It is full of ideas and symbols to speak to non-Christians, but oh, what a pickle! It was all conceived and built at the wrong time – time out of time, as if you could re-create the Middle Ages when the twentieth century was well under way. It is an amazing and evocative building, nevertheless. I was encouraged by the attempt to speak religious language to non-Christian people.

24 May

Wednesday, Philadelphia. We received a lecture on political matters from a retired bank chairman and then took a bus ride through north Philadelphia. Utter and contemptible squalor, and in the middle of it a great John the Baptist, Holland Road-like church. We briefly met the Rector at the church's soup kitchen. The most terrible thing was that the men queuing for soup were all thin, the only thin men in America.

27 May

Today we visited St Clement's, Philadelphia – a vast, pitch-dark church. The Rector is Peter Laister, a charming, holy and reactionary Church of England priest originally from Holy Redeemer, Clerkenwell. There were nuns in huge coifs kneeling in the separate Church of St John, which is physically attached to St Clement's. They have their own English Missal, which they print themselves.

'I regard the see as vacant,' said Father Laister cheerfully, as his Bishop was taking part in the consecration of Bishop Barbara Harris.[4] In spite of this attitude (or because of it – *there's* a question), there was a tangible atmosphere of piety and discipline at the church. Father Laister is rake thin, which makes a nice change from the hugely overweight Episcopalian clergymen, full of dinners, who are the norm.

30 May

Back in New York, I had a look round the Trinity Museum and saw the Founding Charter – but couldn't see the bit about 'everything must be done according to the use of St Mary-le-Bow'.

In the evening I visited the retired Rector Dr Bob Parks and his wife Nancy in their apartment – amazingly deluxe. They had a pretty pencil drawing of St Mary-le-Bow done by Peter Luscombe, one of our Churchwardens. They have just returned

---

4 Barbara Harris was African-American, divorced, and the first woman in the US to become a bishop.

from three weeks in Italy on a Metropolitan Museum tour. They looked vital and well, as elderly, rich Americans do.

1 June

Today I had a meeting on the 25th floor of the Trinity building with Dr Dan Matthews, the new Rector. He is attractive, vigorous, voluble, enthusiastic and obsessed with TV. He wants to give moderate Episcopalianism and other mainstream Christian denominations a place on cable TV, but he is fighting against Christians who eat live snakes, walk on water, levitate, roll on the floor and make animal noises. Sung Matins is not really going to grab the American public. I think this is a doomed hope, but he gets full marks for trying.

David Hutt told me he sat next to a Lutheran woman priest at dinner somewhere, and he saw an Episcopalian woman priest celebrating Mass when he went into St James's, Madison Avenue. I think that has helped him with his feelings about the ordination of women. I hope it has.

I was back in London a few days later, picking up where I had left off before my transatlantic trip, and absorbing the shocking news which was soon all over the television and radio bulletins. Like everyone else, I had been following the reports of demonstrations in Tiananmen Square in China, but was not prepared for the scenes of violence which took place there early in June.

4 June

The Ayatollah Khomeini died today. But, most terribly, the Chinese army has fired on and killed students in Beijing.

Bernard Jenkin rang and asked me to be godfather to his son Robert. The other godparents are the Prime Minister's Private Secretary and Bernard's cousin Eleanor.

I watched the dreadful China news at the end of the day. Things may be changing in Russia, but old attitudes towards dissent die hard in Communist China.

6 June

Auberon Waugh, Editor of the *Literary Review*, came to Dialogue. He was charming, diffident, not at all savage – though I was interested that this charming man, so hot on manners, started smoking in my sitting room before he asked if he could. He is, as we know from his journalism, a fanatical pro-smoker.

Then I went to Windsor for a conference organized by the Central Board of Finance about charitable giving, held at St George's House. We went to Evensong in St George's Chapel, with the slow-marching Military Knights. The dear old sausages probably can't march fast any more anyway.

At the Windsor conference I enjoyed chairing a group about the morality of wealth creation, at which the minutes were taken by Caroline Sinclair from 10 Downing Street. She had to rush back to the Prime Minister, leaving me to report back with some difficulty from her notes. The best thing about the conference, however, was meeting Sir Richard O'Brien, the producer of the Church of England report *Faith in the City* and a careful, liberal, concerned man I had long admired.

That evening Michael Brock, the Warden of St George's House, showed us round the chapel. To stand on a vault leading to the remains of Charles I was tremendous. In Queen Victoria's pew, from which she had watched the marriage of the Prince of Wales and Princess Alexandra, the Blessed Sacrament was reserved in a Tabernacle. The Queen Empress would not have been amused, even if she had understood what or who was meant to be inside the Tabernacle.[5]

At St Mary-le-Bow later in June, 50 or 60 people turned up in the Court of the Arches for a meeting of the Smithfield Group, set up by some City bankers. I was delighted to see so many young bankers and lawyers who wanted an alternative to Thatcherite financial policies, and was thrilled that these young and attractive

---

5 Catholics reserve the consecrated Host at Mass in a Tabernacle on or near the altar, to provide a focus for devotion to Jesus Christ and Communion for the sick. Queen Victoria, of course, was a Protestant and would have considered the practice of reserving the Host in a Tabernacle unacceptably popish.

people were using a church in which to voice their concerns. I noted in my diary that I was invited to the pub with them all after the meeting by a jolly woman MP from Redcar called Dr Mo Mowlam.

5 July

I walked to Admiralty House in terrific heat. Patrick's son Henry thinks we should fight for Hong Kong. Patrick thinks Tom King wants to stay in Northern Ireland, and Patrick doesn't want to become Lord Chancellor. Patrick is very much amused by Matthew Parris's article sending him up in *The Times*. All of us were hot and very tired, and I found Patrick asleep with his head on his red boxes when I went to his study to say good night.

14 July

Before going to Codford, I went to George Bruce's studio in Pembroke Way and, over a glass of sherry, parted with £462.50 for the Lambeth Palace preparatory sketch of Michael Ramsey. The sadness of his death and his absence from my life added to the choked feeling of the day.

For some time, many of us who were Anglo-Catholics had been feeling increasingly beleaguered, disapproved of and out of sympathy with the current leadership in the Church of England. The Evangelical or Low Church party was in the ascendancy and the Anglo-Catholic party was in decline because of a determination to oppose the ordination of women, under the vigorous leadership of Bishop Graham Leonard. By contrast, we were quite sure that it was possible to be a full-blooded Anglican Catholic – believing the Church of England to be, not a Protestant denomination, but part of the one Holy Catholic and Apostolic Church – without being against all developments, especially over the issue of women priests.

A number of us began to form friendships and to come together to discuss the situation. One such meeting took place on 19 July at the more liberal end of the Anglican Catholic scale, at St James's, Piccadilly. Among those at the meeting were John Barton of the Student Christian Movement and David Jenkins, the Bishop of Durham, who was seldom out of the headlines. These two could be more accurately described as liberal rather than Catholic and, like the Dean of Liverpool, were very much against forming a new party or initiating any sort of conflict. Without standing up for what we believed, however, we would clearly get nowhere. I found this particular meeting maddening.

I could see, for example, that we needed to get David Hutt of All Saints, Margaret Street, on board. Margaret Street was a flagship of the Catholic movement. When Father Kenneth Ross was Vicar there years ago and came out in favour of union with the Methodists, he made enemies amongst conservative Anglo-Catholics by his courageous embrace of English Nonconformity, welcoming the Methodist Church into a potentially wider Catholicism. At the same time, however, Margaret Street became a beacon of hope to the more adventurous and liberal-minded Anglo-Catholic clergy and laity. Now, I felt, if only we could capture David Hutt for our cause (all we had to do was to convert him to women's ordination), it would be a great encouragement to many.

Others did not see it that way and I was left feeling very frustrated – but frustration turned to excitement after the second meeting of the day.

19 July

At the meeting at St James's, Piccadilly, today I said we needed a name to counterbalance Durham in the Church's mind, i.e. the Vicar of Margaret Street. But the retired Dean of Liverpool said, 'It will all emerge from the group.' I pointed out that the liberal values in Synod and Parliament do not 'emerge from the group'. We got nowhere, really.

Then I went on to the Deanery at Westminster for a meeting of Central Line.[6] We had invited Richard Holloway, Bishop of Edinburgh, to speak to us and it was a heartening experience, quite unlike the dismal meeting at St James's. Here all was transformed by Richard's vigorous, witty honesty. The

---

6 This is a group of clergy who all work, quite simply, along London Underground's Central Line and are therefore able to meet for mutual encouragement and edification.

idea of rescuing Anglican Catholicism has suddenly taken off in a big way. We are to organize a conference in 1990. I have written to Rowan Williams, Lady Margaret Professor of Divinity at Oxford, to seek his support.

30 July

I stood at the font today as godfather to Robert Jenkin. It was a horrible, 1662-to-the-letter service – ludicrous for a Baptism, but Charles Jenkin preached sense.[7]

August was divided between Amsterdam and a baking hot Wiltshire. One day I went to lunch with Sir Edward Heath. There was a police guard at the gate. The other guests were a French musician called Xavier Givelet and his wife, and Sir David and Lady Holden. Sir David was formerly at the Ulster Office. Sir Edward took me for a walk in the garden and showed me the greenhouses, of which he is enormously proud, and his orchid house. We had lunch on the terrace, and when I got home I noted the delicious details in my diary – champagne, quail with red wine, sea bass with white Burgundy, Stilton and port, berries and ice cream, and more champagne. We drank coffee and Cognac in the drawing room, listening to Beethoven and to stories about the Queen, Harold Macmillan and Pope John XXIII, all cleverly told. I teased Sir Edward about women priests and later wrote in my diary, 'He has no private life. His private life is heads of state and musicians.'

Early September is an in-between time in the City. The summer holidays are petering out, but not everyone is back at their desks and it is a little while before life returns to its normal hustle and bustle. By mid-September 1989 the hot summer had passed, and it was back to business as usual.

17 September

Sunday. A cloudy day, but not wet. I walked to St Giles's, Cripplegate, in the Barbican and read the 1662 Communion

---

7 The Revd the Hon. Charles Jenkin, now Rector of Melton Mowbray in Leicestershire, is the brother of Bernard Jenkin MP.

Service for a congregation of nine people and a very noisy baby. The chalice was absolutely filthy and I had to wash it before the service. I walked home for breakfast and then back again for the 10 o'clock Mass. There were 36 people in the congregation for this – 22 communicants. This time I cleaned the chalice with Silvo. St Mary-le-Bow was like this when I arrived.

Then I had a month full of people, from preaching to them in Letchworth to eating with them in Carlyle Square (at the home of society hostess Susan O'Reilly, where we were served by a butler) and Rotherhithe (where I ate with the butler from Grocers' Hall). I took Sylvia Gaskell's funeral in Holborn and her burial in Chatham. Mrs Gaskell had been frail and unable to look after herself for many years and Father John Gaskell, her son and Vicar of St Albans, Holborn, had nursed her selflessly in the Holborn vicarage. Whenever I went for Spiritual Direction or to make my confession to Father Gaskell, I went up to see her in her room. I had buried her husband some years earlier, and Father Gaskell's will said that I was to bury him too.

In addition that month, Hubert Chesshyre, Chester Herald of Arms, came to Dialogue, I did some teaching at Ravenstone Primary School, had some friends to stay at Codford, and discovered that the historian G.M. Trevelyan once said that Edward the Confessor was an imbecile. There was never a dull day.

17 October

Colin Thubron, the writer who has taken us 'Among the Russians', 'Behind the Wall' and 'Up the Hills of Adonis', came to Dialogue and for lunch upstairs afterwards. We discussed conscience and what is really still Confucian China. He is a sympathetic agnostic. Lesley Leader from Goldsmiths' Hall spent the Dialogue gazing up at Mr Thubron in adoration, as were many other ladies, for he is lean and romantic.

25 October

I went to a meeting of the Bow Lane Festival Committee at Anne Craddock's employment office, from which I was hoiked out by my secretary, Dilly Erskine Crum, to be told that Ruth had hurt herself. She had cut her shin and had, with exemplary presence of mind, thrust her leg into a plastic bag. One of our Wardens, Tom Wilmot, and Dilly took her to Bart's Hospital after Evensong while I heard a confession, then I got hold of Andrew and we both went to Bart's – arriving just as she had been taken away for home. Ruth is absolutely fine.

26 October

The Bishop of Edinburgh has sent out a letter to all who responded to his *Church Times* article last week mentioning the proposed conference on Anglican Catholicism and naming Professor Rowan Williams, David Hutt and myself as the organizers. We've done it now.

I took Wim and Aad, who are over from Holland, to Codford. We arrived at 9.45 p.m. to discover that Nigel Lawson, the Chancellor of the Exchequer, has resigned over Professor Alan Waters interfering in monetary policy at Mrs Thatcher's behest. Great excitement. Douglas Hurd goes to the Foreign Office, John Major to the Exchequer and David Waddington to the Home Office. 'Loopy old bag', as one Labour MP called the Supreme Ruler of the Universe. I sniff in the air that Mrs Thatcher at long last may be on the way out.

31 October

Dame Rachel Waterhouse, Chairwoman of the Consumer Council, a sweet, utterly sensible person, came to Dialogue. But we got bogged down in talking about the ordination of women legislation to be debated next week, because yesterday the Bishop of London rallied 1,100 priests against it. His depressing picture dominates today's front pages. Religious people find it easier to be against things than for them.

2 November

All Souls' Day. After Mass, I had Dan and Deanie Matthews to lunch, which was brought over from the Grocers' Hall. Bob and Nancy Parks came to the 5.45 Mass, so we've had both present and past Rectors of Trinity, Wall Street, in church on the same day.

4 November

Saturday. I dined with David Hutt, Harry Bramma[8] and Mervyn Stockwood, the one-time Bishop of Southwark. He's an amazing old monument, clothed from head to food in purple silk. At one point, when Harry and David were out of the room and I was alone with Mervyn, I opened my eyes and realized that I had been fast asleep with him talking at me without noticing – I hope.

The first week of November, as it turned out, brought all sorts of encouraging and exciting events. By some discriminatory old law, Roman Catholics had not been able to have a Mass in the Square Mile of the City of London since the Reformation. As there were unlikely now to be any 'No Popery' riots in the streets if we offered hospitality to the Roman Catholic community in one of our Anglican churches, I was very keen indeed that they should be made to feel welcome again. I was therefore delighted that a possibility arose for such hospitality to be exercised in the Guild Church of St Mary Aldermary within the parish of St Mary-le-Bow. There had been an experimental use of this church by the Roman Catholic community some time in the past, but it had come to grief through a clash of personalities, the usual reason for things hitting the rocks. Now, after the building up of many new friendships, we were ready to start again.

7 November

Nearly 200 Roman Catholics were at St Mary Aldermary today for their first Mass in the building.

Yesterday General Synod voted on the draft legislation for women priests by 2:1 in each house – the bishops 33:17, the clergy 149:85 and the laity 144:78. This is amazingly

---

8 Director of the Royal School of Church Music and organist of All Saints, Margaret Street.

good. Not the special majority required in each house, but a very encouraging step on the way.

Dick Taverne, an ex-Labour Minister, came to the Smithfield Group. I asked, 'What is the Market?'[9] There was no answer to this. I was so encouraged by the women vote that I didn't mind that no one knew what 'the Market' was.

Then international news took over the headlines again, relegating women priests and Cabinet reshuffles to the inside pages, if they featured at all amongst the general excitement. Huge and astonishing changes were afoot in Germany and Eastern Europe.

10 November

It wasn't until the 6.30 a.m. news that the import of the Berlin Wall coming down burst upon us. As I write this, the Wall is being broken into pieces. Last night people partied on it. It is an exorcism and enormously moving. The whole map of Europe will change. As the *Independent* said, 'Europe no longer has an edge.' We may be going back to a pre-1914 world. At the 8.30 Mass we sang 'Praise the Lord, ye heavens adore him' to the German national anthem tune.

In the evening I talked to some students at Holy Cross, Cromer Street, in King's Cross. I went to the pub afterwards with the Vicar, who is upset about women priests. Some people want to stay behind walls.

14 November

John Smith, QC, MP, the Shadow Chancellor of the Exchequer, came for a Dialogue and lunch. He is enormously popular in the City and a thoroughly decent, solid, sensible man. If only he were the Leader of the Labour Party. Before the Dialogue he told me he thought there might never be another Labour Government. There was a packed house for him. He is sharp, but unpompous.

---

9 Mrs Thatcher had said that all financial policy must be driven solely by 'market forces'.

16 November

I went with David Hutt to Oxford – a dazzling but icy day. We had a working lunch with the Bishop of Edinburgh and Professor Rowan Williams in Rowan's rooms next to the cathedral, to plan how to get what we might call 'Mainstream' or 'Affirming Catholicism' going. Rowan lives in fabulous medieval rooms, huge, with eighteenth-century panelling, but full of children's toys to fall over. We got much work done. Rowan is off to Yale in January and doesn't return until April.

I kept a fascinated eye on the news. Since the amazing events in Berlin, everything was beginning to break up and shift in previously battened-down Communist countries. Demonstrations in Prague were broken up by the police.

21 November

The Archbishop of York, John Habgood, came to Dialogue and asked me how I planned my week. He was kindly, but reserved. The church was absolutely full, although it was a more elderly audience than the crowd who came last week for John Smith.

Andrew Stewart-Roberts and Bill Sewell joined us at lunch. The Archbishop warmed up slowly, until he and Andrew Stewart-Roberts discovered they were both at Eton. I thought they would get on because of this, but my non-Etonian naivety miscalculated – they were not in the same house, or something. Things got better when they discovered that through a Colonel Black, who had conducted an evangelical mission to Eton, they had both been introduced to Billy Graham. They both remembered meeting Billy Graham in some room where they had to sit on gold ballroom chairs, and they recalled this as amusing.

I gave the Archbishop a pair of gilt Victorian saucers, which he looked at with some surprise when I suggested that he might like to stand geraniums in them. He went off into Cheapside shyly clutching them, obviously thinking me a lunatic.[10]

---

10 I give all my Dialogue guests a present – usually eighteenth- or nineteenth-century china of some kind.

It was a difficult Dialogue. In the middle of it, he asked me what I thought common sense was. Every shred of common sense fled from me and all I could think of to say was, 'Well, you notice it when it isn't there.' Gulp.

24 November

After Mass, I considered my appearance in the *Church Times* today. Annoyingly, the Editor has written quite a long piece about our Oxford meeting but, of course, omitted any reference to David Hutt as he asked to be omitted. This leaves 'another man', Victor Stock, the Rector of St Mary-le-Bow, London, present, which gives the conservatives ammunition because I am regarded as a hopeless liberal. We needed the title of the Vicar of All Saints, Margaret Street, but David is afraid of disapproval and trouble at his church, where a lot of people are against the ordination of women.

Now Czechoslovakia is free, with 300,000 people on the streets of Prague, and Mr Dubcek back from obscurity in exile addressing the people – 'I love you all' – on the balcony above Wenceslas Square. The whole Central Committee resigned this evening and the army has not moved in. Once the wall was danced on in Berlin, everything erupted.

Meanwhile, at St Mary-le-Bow the Finance Sub-Committee gave me £750 to help with our attempted revival of the Catholic movement in the Church of England. I sat with David Hutt one evening, going over the letters which the Bishop of Edinburgh had been sent after his *Church Times* article. The letters had poured in and were all moving and uplifting. I went on reading them until the small hours. For a change, rather than being against the whole idea, the people who had written to him seemed to be grateful for Richard Holloway's encouragement to be Catholic Anglicans. It was a welcome positive note in those early days of our endeavour.

8 December

I went to the Drapers' Hall to talk to the Lord Mayor and the newly arrived head of Mitsubishi, who recited a whole chunk of John Betjeman's poem on St Mildred's, Bread Street, to everybody's amazement.

In Codford for the weekend, we went duty-bound to see *The Snow Queen* at the Woolstore Theatre. It was simply terrible – amateur dramatics *are* amateur. The costumes, though, were wonderful. John Torrie spent the whole year stitching on sequins.[11] Bernard Dawson behaved so badly he had to leave at half-time.

13 December

I preached at King's College in the Strand today. Brian Horne, Richard Coggins and Gordon Huelin, who all taught me when I was a student at King's in the 1960s, were in the congregation. This time it was me preaching to them, rather than them preaching to me, unlike 25 years ago. Everybody was very nice, which made me feel more secure. Well, I am 45 next week!

Andrew Dunford was 35 yesterday. I gave him some slippers. This is what happens as we get older. Slippers.

17 December

Wiltshire. I celebrated Mass at the High Altar in Edington Priory at 8 a.m., it being only just light – grey space, pale electric bulbs and flickering candlelight, a huge and sacred space.

I preached at the 9 a.m. Parish Communion too. Donald Wright, ex-Prime Minister's Patronage Secretary, was in the congregation, and was appreciative of the sermon. 'Should have been preached at Windsor,' he kindly said. There was a huge wind blowing, whipping my surplice about as he spoke to me in the churchyard under the hill. Last night there was a great storm.

---

11 John Torrie, the owner of the manor house at Codford, was a generous, kind and welcoming neighbour from the day of my arrival in the village.

23 December

We did a quick Warminster shop in a flooding rainstorm.
Patrick Trevor-Roper came to lunch, an old friend of Patrick
Leigh Fermor.[12] He went every year with him to Greece.
Patrick Trevor-Roper rode around the Carpathians in 1938
with a chum. He is thrilled, like me, about the Romanian rev-
olution.

24 December

Today is my 45th birthday. I said the Office, but cut church.
Walking in the rain around Fonthill, I found a tree house and
a whole, intact grotto. We ate pheasants, plucked most
expertly by Andrew, and drank champagne. At Salisbury
Cathedral Midnight Mass I assisted and administered the
Host in the North Choir aisle. The cathedral was packed, and
there was an excellent sermon from the Bishop.

27 December

We went over to Westwood Manor, which of course was shut,
and the church was shut too – the church where I first saw
an Anglican priest say Mass when I was a little boy. I was
staying with my father's cousins at Farleigh Hungerford and
we walked up that magic and romantic lane to the heights of
Westwood and its ancient church, where Father Arthur Taylor
stood at the altar in a green fiddleback chasuble. Well, we
couldn't get in today, so we couldn't look at the marvellous
stained-glass window of Jesus crucified on a Madonna lily,
one of the earliest pieces of perfectly preserved stained
glass in the United Kingdom. What an image – Jesus crucified on a lily.

---

12 Patrick Trevor-Roper is a distinguished eye surgeon and a friend of Andrew
Dunford. Patrick Leigh Fermor is the author of *A Time of Gifts*, the story of his walk
across Europe in the 1930s.

30 December

Andrew made excellent bread rolls last night for our party for the neighbours, and I redid the evergreens in the sitting room. Mrs Tandy, the old householders' cleaner from Cherry Orchard, was the first to arrive. There were 17 of us. Old Brigadier George Goode turned up from next door. By 3 p.m. all the smoked trout had been consumed, the wine drunk, the guests had gone and we were at Stourhead, taking a dignified turn around the lake – duty done.

31 December

New Year's Eve. I read Matins, Evensong and Compline at home, but did not go to church. Sometimes you mustn't go to church if faith is to survive.

Soup at Luncheon

Soon after New Year, the redecoration of the crypt at St Mary-le-Bow began. It was nothing too dramatic – the Court of the Arches and the chapel were painted a conservative off-white just to clean them up – but it meant we had to vacate the crypt for a while. The daily crypt Matins came temporarily upstairs into the nave of the church. This, I felt, was not such a bad thing: if we were not so hidden away below stairs, more people might see that we did begin every day with prayer.

The Palumbo affair also rumbled on. SAVE Britain's Heritage decided to appeal to the High Court against the Secretary of State's decision to overrule the Inspector, who had originally found in our favour – i.e. retaining the nine listed buildings in Cheapside. The process would, of course, cost a great deal of money and we began an appeal for funds. The whole affair caught the imagination of the media because it touched on the vexed question of conservation and heritage versus modernism. Maxwell Hutchinson, at that time President of the Royal Institute of British Architects, had written a book attacking the Prince of Wales for his fuddy-duddy views on architecture and was becoming a popular figure on television. I got to know him as the appeal continued, and he became a Dialogue guest.

11 January

Sarah Mann, who works at the Home Office and is one of the most able people here, happily married with a son of whom she's justly proud, came to talk about prayer and shyly confessed to having an overpowering sense of love in her heart all through last summer when she was praying. This is very unusual in someone who looks perfectly all right – I mean, she's not dotty or peculiar in any way. She couldn't be more on her feet, this woman. I reassured her that everything was all right and read her the last stanza of Dante's *Paradiso* to put her feelings into an intellectual context.

A car came to whisk me off to Wood Lane and the BBC, where Jeffrey Archer and Paul Boateng interviewed me and Max Hutchinson about the Number One Poultry proposals. Max Hutchinson was there as a modernist, very keen on the new architecture, and I, of course, was the old fuddy-duddy resisting change.

I disliked Archer's manner and method immensely. He asked me such a long and complicated question that at the end of it I said, 'I'm afraid I didn't understand what you said,' feeling completely wormlike and inadequate. As I left the chair and walked across the studio after the interview, however, the cameraman gave me the thumbs-up and said, 'Well done, Father!' I didn't see what this meant until later that evening when the clip was repeated on the 9 o'clock news. I realized that my response looked as if I was deliberately insulting Mr Archer and therefore floored him: a triumph out of innocence.

25 January

St Paul's Day. There was a terrific storm during the morning, and I swam in choppy waters at the Oasis. The Underground station closed, traffic seized up and roads were closed off because of flying glass and falling scaffolding. I carefully dodged my way back to Bow Bells in a lurid light. There were telephone calls from PCC members unable to get into or across town. A neighbouring broker noticed our copper cladding on the west-end pediment lifting off. Amazingly, both John Phillips, the architect, and the men working on the crypt were on site and they scrambled up and over to secure the roof.

The next day the *Church Times* used its lead article to report encouragingly on the first steering committee meeting of Affirming Catholicism, during which we had planned our first public day conference. This was to be held at St Alban's, Holborn, which we had chosen because of its pukka Anglo-Catholic credentials. This would, we hoped, encourage even the younger and more extreme Anglo-Catholic clergy to come and listen to Rowan Williams, who would be addressing the conference.

The *Church Times* report was pushed to the back of my mind, however, when Andrew and I drove through storm-lashed countryside to reach Codford for the weekend. The general damage seemed to be extensive, and we approached Codford with misgivings. By then Don Dunford had sold his house in Norfolk and had bought the empty half of Old Wool Cottage in partnership with Andrew. They had also purchased the stable block and courtyard, the apple house and the estate office, so the Dunfords ended up owning about two-thirds of the whole property, while I had the other third. We just hoped that the storm had not wreaked too much havoc with our restoration plans.

26 January

Forty-six people have been killed in the storm and there is huge damage, costing millions. Large parts of the country are without electricity.

I went with Andrew to Codford where all is grim – no electric light and poor Don Dunford unable to find any candles. We set all this to rights, made a cooking hearth from a door-scraper and the coal basket in the dining room, and ate a feast of game stew by candlelight. Rather sadly, the electric light returned at 9.15 just as dinner was ending. I thought this quite a shame.

28 January

Sunday. It was a lovely sunny morning and I celebrated the 9 a.m. Mass and preached at Edington, then preached in the absolutely freezing church at Erlestoke. I talked to an 87-year-old man who had been a shepherd. His father had put tenor and treble sheep bells around the necks of his flock so that he could keep track of them in the fog. Harry thought there might be one or two shepherds right up on the plain still, but I doubt this.

Andrew and I got back at 3.45 to discover that Don had called the police, having not listened, as usual, to us telling him we were out to lunch. Where were we? What had happened? This is all part of the acute depression following his wife Kathleen's death. He is going to need a great deal of care and, what is more difficult to give, patience.

2 February

Candlemas. We blessed candles at the 8.30 Mass in St Mary-le-Bow today. I was absolutely worn out, and then Andrew came in and said, 'Stop! Now we're going to Codford.' And we did. I need somebody to tell me things like that.

Once there, we shopped quickly and then rushed off to the clear blue heights of Longleat. It's lovely to be here on a Friday in the daylight, which is in theory possible with an early morning Mass, because, if I need to, I can leave immediately after it. There were great beeches and oaks down on the estate, but the lime avenue was bursting into crimson haloes of new growth. We pushed open a gate marked 'Secret Garden' and walked in. Inside two elderly gardeners were pruning roses. One of the men tugged his forelock, literally, and told us about the great catalpa tree simply keeling over several days after the last furious gale. It was a perfectly Edwardian scene.

3 February

We had more terrible rain, and the electricity went off again. Andrew motored me to Oxford. Leaving my bag at Magdalen College, where I am preaching tomorrow morning, I walked to St John's Home to have tea with Lady Ramsey, so alone now without Bishop Michael.

On her desk was a pre-publication copy of Michael De-la-Noy's book, *Michael Ramsey – A Portrait*. Affecting nonchalance, I seized it and devoured the references to myself, of which there are too many. Joan said, 'I have a bone to pick with you.' Oh goodness! That could have been about all sorts of things. 'You said we gave you soup at luncheon. We *never* had soup at luncheon.'

'Ah,' I said, 'shades of George V!' and we laughed. George V said that no gentleman ate soup at luncheon. I borrowed the copy to read in bed.

6 February

It was another fraught Cheapside Dialogue day, because the German Ambassador, who was meant to be the star attraction, was suddenly called to Bonn to brief our Foreign Secretary, who is to see the German Chancellor and the Foreign Minister because of the deteriorating state of East Germany. The Embassy sent us the Minister Plenipotentiary instead. In anticipation of the Ambassador the church was packed, of course. Sir Patrick Mayhew and the Master of the Grocers' Company joined us for lunch afterwards and we made the best of an inevitably disappointing occasion.

After lunch, I discovered that Collins had just published *Michael Ramsey – A Portrait,* and I rushed off and got two copies from Grafton Street next to the Medici Gallery.

15 February

Eric James,[1] whom I ran into on the staircase at Sion College, kindly sent me a copy of his *Times* review of the Ramsey books,[2] asking if it was OK. There were fair comments, including some clever criticism of Owen Chadwick. He did, however, say in the review that Robert Runcie succeeded Michael Ramsey. On a postcard I pointed out that he had left out Donald Coggan, which for a historian was a bit of a slip-up!

Later the same day, I flew off to Paris for the weekend. The fish pâté and wine I consumed on the Air France flight were nicer than anything available on British Airways. After an enjoyable couple of days ambling round museums and admiring the great rose windows in Notre Dame, I returned to London to prepare for the start of Lent.

---

1 Canon Eric James is preacher at Gray's Inn, a famous figure both in the pulpit and on the BBC.

2 Professor Owen Chadwick's book, *Michael Ramsey: A Life*, published by Clarendon Press, came out at the same time as Michael De-la-Noy's book mentioned above.

26 February

Today I hung the crypt crucifix above the high altar in place of the 'In the beginning was the Word' panel, to mark the change to Lent.

In the evening I went to the National Theatre for David Hare's play *Racing Demon*. I had a chat with the Archbishop of Canterbury's wife, Lindy Runcie, and saw Jeremy Paxman in jeans and cowboy boots, not looking at all like the presenter of *Newsnight*. The play is brilliantly perceptive about the awfulness of the current Church of England. It is both depressing and very moving. At the end, when the neglectful Vicar says to his wife, 'Shall we go to bed, darling?' she, potting up geraniums, doesn't look up to deliver her devastating clincher, 'It's too late now.'

27 February

Sir Jeffrey Owen, the Editor of the *Financial Times*, is a pet – gentle, big, fair and sensitive at today's Dialogue.

In the evening I went to Lambeth Palace, where I talked to a confused Joan Ramsey and an importunate Mrs Runcie, who asked me to stay to make up the placement at dinner, disarranged by Professor Chadwick's wife not turning up. I said no, being engaged to dine with Andrew Dunford at the Liberal Club. Then the Archbishop pressed me. He had already been warmly affectionate about the De-la-Noy book and said he had enjoyed my bits on the plane home from Pakistan. I declined him also, saying I realized that to refuse the Archbishop's wife, Lady Ramsey and the Archbishop of Canterbury himself was likely to bring my career in the Church of England to a grinding halt.

Then I rushed along the Embankment and was immediately asked for my wallet by a maddened black man. I said I hadn't one, which was a lie, for I had £100 in it. He began lightly, but messily, to cut my face with his cutthroat razor. 'I'm going to kill you,' he said.

Revealing my dog collar and trying to sound calm, I said, 'It would be a very serious thing to kill a priest.' It was just like the movies.

When I thought he wasn't going to lunge any more and had withdrawn the knife from my cheek, I walked slowly on over the bridge to the Liberal Club, angry and shocked, but oddly not frightened.

I went to the lavatory to wash my face, but it was bricked up. This was beginning to get surreal. I went on up to the library, where Andrew was waiting with a couple of Bloody Marys. He was alarmed and upset, took me away to wash up and arranged for me to have a tetanus injection. We had a jolly dinner and the last drink before Lent. What a Shrove Tuesday, eh?

Lent began with the *Independent* carrying my mugging story, because I happened to tell the journalist Andrew Brown about it (he had earlier been a Dialogue guest) and then the diarist on the *Independent* rang me to get the full story. It was very amusingly written and several people telephoned in a concerned way, including the Bishop of Edinburgh. I kept rubbing the scar to make it last.

6 March

Sir Edward Heath was late for his Dialogue today because he was held up by the BBC. Friendly police came with him and Ruth Watson gave the officers tea upstairs. Over 300 people came, with 80 standing at the doors, and afterwards there was an enormous ovation. It was a fascinating journey through European history. I went with Sir Edward in his car to lunch at the Grocers' Hall. There he was not so good at talking to people. The Dialogue experience was deeply and movingly uplifting nevertheless. It made me proud to be a European.

That same week, in the newly painted Court of the Arches, we held the Confirmation of the Election of Bishop Michael Ball as Bishop of Truro. His brother, Peter Ball, was already the Bishop of Lewes, and it was oddly amusing to think that the Church now had two replica bishops. Being identical twins, Michael and Peter are the spitting image of each other. There was a dinner at Grocers' Hall afterwards, where I had a brief conversation with Lord Home, the second ex-Prime Minister I had spoken to within 48 hours.

Some sad news burst the bubble the next day, when I was told that one of my Confirmation candidates, June Judd-Goodwin, had cancer and would have to undergo an operation very soon. It was unlikely, therefore, that she would be confirmed with the others at the service planned for Easter week.

At the end of the week I took myself off to retreat with the Sisters of the Love of God at Fairacres in Oxford, where I am a priest associate and where I had spent the Easter weekend of 1988. I went straight into the library to settle down to some work, and immediately got into hot water with an elderly nun who told me that I had no business to be there. The library was apparently now out of bounds, as was the garden entrance to the chapel. This meant that I could not walk from the hermitage, where I was staying, across the garden to the chapel. Instead I had to go down a miserable passage behind the dustbins, appropriately called 'the rat run'. The Community had evidently decided to tighten up their enclosure regulations and keep their guests firmly out of various areas. Sadly, it made the guests feel distinctly unwelcome.

9 March

Friday at Fairacres. I celebrated the 9.05 Mass and got lost in the Ministry of the Word, partly because I felt so agitated by not being welcomed into the sacristy beforehand, partly because they have a peculiar structure for Mass.

I went to see Sister Jane, once the Reverend Mother General. She is now shrunk, very ill and confined to a chair, but luminous in spirit. The nicest thing about Fairacres is Compline by lamplight and the smell of the little oil light in the Visitors' Chapel, its only illumination – not enough to read or sing by, but enough to be comforting. You just sit in the dark with this little flickering flame, the nuns singing around the corner in their choir, heard but not seen.

13 March

Dame Judi Dench came to Dialogue, and we both laughed for 40 minutes in front of an absolutely packed house. She is the most delightful woman.

When she went to Buckingham Palace to be made a Dame, one of the captains of industry who was there to be knighted asked a courtier, 'May we smoke?'

'No,' replied the courtier, 'but you may play the piano if you wish.' There wasn't one, of course.

Her Majesty complimented Judi on her tapestry, which she said she had seen in Birmingham. Judi was silent, thinking the Queen confused, but afterwards remembered that she *had* made a tapestry. It was on exhibition for an AIDS charity and the Queen really had just seen it in Birmingham and was therefore being really sweet and imaginative.

In the afternoon, when Dame Judi had gone, trailing clouds of glory and leaving an atmosphere of proud pleasure, I had a wedding interview and then went as Anton Cowan's guest to a meeting of the Roman Catholic Deanery.[3] Two smoking and drinking priests started attacking Anglicanism, not knowing there was an Anglican present. I felt so sorry for Anton. Although I stood up and made an amusing joke that I was one of the people being attacked, they didn't stop it. At the meal afterwards, the Italians, Germans and some of the English sat with me. The Irish and the rest of the English sat together and wouldn't talk to this Anglican interloper. Fascinating.

What a contrast with lunch and Judi Dench. Of course, Judi lives in the real world and is a Quaker. Some of these Roman Catholic priests live in a ghetto and are also harried and beset by their own Church, which in consequence they feel they must defend at all costs in as aggressive a way as possible. We Anglicans would behave just as badly given the opportunity.

25 March

I arrived in High Barnet at 8.25 a.m., to be told by the person I had come to meet that it was in fact now 9.45. I had missed the Mass altogether. I didn't know the clocks went on an hour today.

---

3 Father Anton Cowan was the Roman Catholic priest at St Mary Moorfields with whom I had begun to share St Mary Aldermary in Bow Lane.

Jean Mayhew rang to invite me to dinner on Wednesday with the Lord Chancellor, Lord Mackay of Clashfern, and Lady Mackay, plus the Chief Whip, Tim Renton, and his wife Alice. The Rentons are Andrew and Phyllida Stewart-Roberts' neighbours, as it happens.

29 March

It's the day after my dinner with Cabinet Ministers at Admiralty House, where I said I kept a diary and they all said they didn't. Keeping the political theme, I went to the House of Commons today, where I talked to Ken Livingstone before the Smithfield Group dinner. I sat opposite Margaret Beckett, Shadow Chancellor John Smith's number two. She is very good, though a bit shy, which she doesn't look on television in her public persona.

After that I escaped for a weekend in Amsterdam and spent much time in the Rijksmuseum, absorbed in the intricacies of the hand gestures depicted in Buddhist carving. One gesture, with the thumb and forefinger held together, was strongly reminiscent of the way priests used to hold their hands at Mass before the Second Vatican Council reforms. We had been taught that this was a utilitarian practice, to avoid particles of consecrated bread falling to the ground, but after my visit to the museum I decided that it probably had some more powerful and ancient symbolism, long since lost.

1 April

Passion Sunday. In the little brick street behind the Duif, a door stood partly open between a silver birch and a white prunus in full bloom. Both rose from a few bricks' worth of soil planted with purple and yellow pansies. The door opened into the old vestry of the Duif, which is now the Russian Orthodox church. I pushed my way in and came into the middle of a baptism. The baby had just been hauled up out of the bathwater, for Orthodox babies are dumped, naked, beneath the waters of what has to be a bath-sized receptacle to take the whole baby. They are not prissily dripped on by the vicar's hand, as in the Church of England. I crept out again and was followed immediately by two strong men carrying the old sink bath, bereft of its adorning baptismal garment. Very carefully, the men poured the warm water of regeneration into the tiny flowerbeds. No wonder the white prunus, the silver birch tree and the purple and yellow pansies bloom so magnificently. If ever there was a magic door to Narnia, it is the door into the old vestry behind the Duif. This is the way into the mystery of salvation – with a pretty good effect on the gardening too.

7 April

The Choir School Confirmation Service took place at St Paul's. The Bishop of London was sticky and it was the usual awful service. Much more important was the fact that June Judd-Goodwin *did* make it from the hospital to be confirmed. Ivy Clements, Ruth Watson and Wendy Evans turned up to support June and Carol Oppenheimer, our congregation's two candidates. These small numbers of people being prepared for Confirmation are of huge importance to the Kingdom of God – and neither June Judd-Goodwin from her impoverished background, nor Caroline Oppenheimer from her well-off background, have had anything like the culture of support and acceptance of religion that surrounds boys in a privileged place like the Cathedral Choir School.

Later, on the train to Salisbury, I discovered that I was wearing an overcoat that belonged to John Scott, the organist of St Paul's Cathedral.

12 April

Maundy Thursday. Sadly, this was Dilly Erskine Crum's last day in the office. Simon, her husband, is to command Goose Bay in Labrador. Like a lot of wives of men with careers, particularly amongst the politicians I know, wives often feel the struggle of carving out a life for themselves when children are no longer a daily responsibility. Dilly has magnificently made a persona as the perfect personal assistant and doesn't relish at all being the wife of a Commanding Officer without her own career. If I was going to be stuck in the snowy wastes of Goose Bay, however, Dilly is just the person I would like to be stuck there with – excellent at the penguin fritters. Dilly's cousin Vanessa Giles is to join us after Easter as a replacement secretary.

The Aldermen and Common Councillors who are members of the Cordwainer Foundation Charity came to the Maundy Thursday Eucharist. Being the City of London, of course, they came in their robes – rather unsuitable on Maundy Thursday, the day when Jesus laid aside his garments, girded himself with a towel and washed the feet of the disciples. How splendid if the Queen, instead of giving three pennies out to well-deserving old ladies, knelt down in a pinny and washed the feet of some poor people. The Lord Mayor or the Prime Minister could also do this. The trouble with the Christian religion is that it's radical and dynamic, but has been so overlaid with ludicrous pomposity as to kill stone dead what it's really about.

13 April

Good Friday. It has been a strange, disjointed, squally day with driving rain and bitter cold and no real place to belong to, as I wasn't preaching for anyone. I went to Matins and the Litany in St Paul's Cathedral. Allegri's *Miserere* was wonderfully sung; the story of Abraham and the sacrifice of Isaac shocking in its depiction of Abraham's apparent indifference. How un-Greek, I thought – no arguing.

Then I took a taxi to City Road to visit and pray with June Judd-Goodwin in St Mark's Hospital. At 3 p.m. I went to the Liturgy of the Lord's Passion at Westminster Cathedral. There was not a seat to be had in that vast building and hardly any standing space. It was a simple and dignified liturgy, presided over by the tall, kindly figure of Cardinal Hume in a plain white mitre. His homily was a simple one for his multinational congregation. It was about the Christian faith. He didn't mention Catholicism, but spoke of the Protestant Martin Luther King, the Catholic Oscar Romero and Jesus Christ.

18 April

I bought the *Literary Review* and read the reviews of Owen Chadwick's life of Ramsey and Michael De-la-Noy's book. One of my stories is picked up in the review, that of Michael Ramsey and the Duke of Edinburgh and their dislike for each other: 'He thought me very donnish, which I am. I thought him a very great boor, which he is,' said Bishop Michael.

1 May

At his request, I took the Japanese Chairman of Mitsubishi (UK, Europe and Africa) around the City churches. This was after a grand Japanese lunch at which I was served every possible kind of Japanese food and then, at the end, an enormous steak that I had to eat.

In the afternoon we had the Confirmation of the Election of the Bishop of Ely. Unlike all the other bishops, Professor Stephen Sykes wouldn't put a cross before his name on the documents because his old tutor told him, 'Bishops are now putting a + sign in front of their names, whereas in most cases a minus sign would be more appropriate.'

10 May

Today was our memorial service for Joseph McCulloch, the post-war rebuilder of St Mary-le-Bow, and very splendid it all was. There weren't many people from the present, sadly, but we did have the Bishop of Oxford, Julian Glover and Diana Rigg, as well as me taking the part of Edward Carpenter, who rang at 8 a.m. to say he couldn't come – rather typical of the dear old ex-Dean of Westminster. Dame Peggy Ashcroft came, and Bernard Levin, whom I put in my sitting room for an hour at 11, quiet and modest.

Afterwards I couldn't get a taxi for Dame Peggy, so I tapped on the window of a waiting Rolls-Royce and asked the occupant if she would like to take Dame Peggy Ashcroft home. Later it transpired that this surprised member of the public was Madame Helen Spiro, the wife of a banker who lives at No. 1 Belgrave Square. So Hampstead, where Dame

Peggy lives, was hardly next door – but, as I said to Andrew Stewart-Roberts, if you have a Rolls and a driver, you can afford to give a retired actress a lift.

In the evening I went off in my frock coat to dine and say Grace at the Livery Dinner for the Arbitrators' Company at the Barber Surgeons' Hall. There was a nice maritime lawyer who lived for eight years in Holland on my left, and a self-important Thatcherite suitably enough on my right. 'History is of no use or importance because it's over,' declaimed this genius. He told several people this in complete self-confidence.

The best thing about the evening was getting home and taking off my trousers, which are too tight. That's what we all say about our dress trousers when we mean we're getting too fat.

29 May

Jeremy Paxman was a bit aggressive, as he is on television, and hard work at the Dialogue – though he was much more relaxed and forthcoming over lunch. During the Dialogue he suddenly switched into his interviewing-Margaret-Thatcher mode. He asked me if I thought that Colonel Gaddafi and Margaret Thatcher were the same and then asked how I could say such a thing, when I hadn't said anything of the kind. I felt wrong-footed and thrown off track.

I was fascinated that Jeremy Paxman goes occasionally to the early Communion on a Sunday at St John's, Notting Hill. It's an encouragement to think that highly able and intelligent people believe in God, belong to the Church of England and go to Holy Communion.

June began with a bad car accident. Matthias, a doctor friend of Andrew's from East Germany, had come to stay and we were on our way one afternoon to Kew Gardens. Suddenly a car in front of us hit a woman pedestrian, who was flung violently into the air. Andrew slammed on the brakes and leapt out to do what he could to help. The woman had stopped breathing, but miraculously there was a cardiac surgeon in the car behind us and, with him and Andrew working together, she was saved. I just held her legs and said soothing words into the screams, and then went to give some attention to the young boy who had run her down. He had been showing off to his girl passengers.

After that shaky start, the month improved and there were several highlights in amongst the usual collection of humdrum engagements and preoccupations of everyday life.

4 June

I attended a grim Institution for the new Rector of St Margaret's, Lothbury, during which there was a resounding attack on liberalism and the modern world from that scourge of modernism, Graham Leonard, the Bishop of London.

'God,' he said, 'is not unconditional love.'

Well, that's us finished, I thought.

9 June

Today was a very important day: the first one-day conference for Affirming Catholicism. 'We need a new Doctor of the Church,' said Father John Gaskell as he looked across St Alban's, Holborn, at Professor Rowan Williams. In his own address Rowan said, 'We bury our sins in Christ's grave and break bread with him at Emmaus.'

The famous church was packed for this first meeting, and there were tears. Dame Rachel Waterhouse called on us to be proud, this St Columba's Day, at the rebirth of the Catholic movement in the Church of England.

We're always looking for theological leadership, for a great person of intellectual stature and personal holiness, and it was a revelatory moment when John Gaskell said, 'We need a new Doctor of the Church,' and we realized that we *had* a Doctor of the Church sitting with us. It was typical of Rowan Williams's poetry that he summed up the ministry of Jesus Christ in that lovely phrase about burying our sins with him. So many aspects of our Catholic movement are damaged by fear, pride and faithlessness, and we need to bury them in Christ's grave. Today at the Mass, we were breaking bread together in the spirit of that first Easter evening, when those who had walked with the stranger from Jerusalem suddenly recognized him as Jesus Christ during the breaking of the bread. Rowan so cleverly caught that sense of newness today.

I'd said at the beginning of all this work, 'What we need is a Dame,' and in the Chairman of the Consumer Council we certainly had one. She is just the sort of full-blooded Anglo-Catholic laywoman with a highly responsible public post who can speak really well and articulate what so many lay-women and laymen feel about the fearfulness and backward-lookingness of the Anglo-Catholic movement. She was tremendous.

27 June

Michael Kenny[4] produced tickets for the Queen Mum's do at Horse Guards Parade, and it was wonderfully kitsch. The Queen Mother did a lap of honour to the sound of a massed choir singing Parry's 'I Was Glad'. She is 90 now, but behaves and looks like 63. We saw the Royal Horse Artillery, Aberdeen Angus cattle and racehorses, but not somebody carrying a large gin and Dubonnet on a silver tray.

3 July

The Deputy Prime Minister Sir Geoffrey Howe came for the last Dialogue of the season. He was kindly, funny, clear and clever – altogether a charming gentleman. There were armed police, one in the kitchen, one outside my study door, and the church was packed.

During the last week or so of July, my activities centred around Affirming Catholicism. One day I went to talk to a clergy group in Northampton about what we were trying to do. There was some hostility from the anti-ordination of women brigade, but I felt it had been worth making the effort to go.

At the end of the month I flew to Edinburgh with David Hutt for further discussions with Richard Holloway. We worked on Affirming Catholicism all morning, discussing the possibility of a

---

4 Michael is a member of the Church Council at St Mary-le-Bow.

conference with speakers, perhaps at the University of York, to set out the theological platform for Affirming Catholicism (i.e. why we believed the Church of England to be an authentic part of the Catholic Church yet able to make radical and reforming decisions without reference to Rome), and to encourage the many people who were feeling battered and marginalized because they could not be against the ordination of women and were therefore regarded by former friends and colleagues as 'unsound'.

We then spent lunch discussing the news of Archbishop Runcie's replacement as Archbishop of Canterbury. It had been announced that George Carey, the Bishop of Bath and Wells, was to be the next incumbent. What would it mean, we wondered, to have an Evangelical Archbishop of Canterbury? We came to the conclusion that a lot would depend on the kind of friends he had – namely, who would influence him.

In August Andrew and I flew to Williamsburg, Virginia, where I was to act as locum for Dick May, whom I had first met at Trinity, New York. The rectory was a beautifully finished, 1930s mock-up of a colonial house, in every detail just like the set of *I Love Lucy*, the fridge the size of a small English house. This was definitely not sexy, raunchy, cool or violent America. It was the National Trust.

3 August

Friday. I read Matins on the porch. This porch is going to be an important part of the holiday. After a long drive we took a ferry across the wide James River to Jamestown, where there is a copy of the statue of John Smith, the original of which stands in St Mary-le-Bow's churchyard. How odd that somebody should have gone from Cheapside to this remote American coast in the seventeenth century.

There were fireflies in the garden this evening. Iraq has invaded Kuwait.

5 August

At the 7.30 Communion there were 100 people. The 9 o'clock Matins had 200 people. Then I went to the Adult Education class and listened to a girl who has been working in Haiti. It was moving to hear about this poverty and oppression, largely the fault of the US, being discussed here in the very centre of white privilege. I went back to preach at 11 o'clock, a congregation of between 250 and 300. It's self-consciously masculine, this worship – Protestant, straight and tough. There is a huge choir which can't sing, and hardly any young people; lots of retired clergy in the congregation, plus a few generals and naval officers.

7 August

We went up to the national cathedral in Washington. There is no daily Office read there, absolutely no one praying anywhere and no candles to light. There was a horrible gift shop selling a range of items nobody with any intelligence would want to buy. Consequently, they were going like hot cakes.

We retreated to the National Gallery of Art, where I admired the luminous, pearly light of the Perugino *Crucifixion*. I'm sure this is the picture which, in its three-panelled reproduction, went everywhere with Michael Ramsey. As I stood looking at it, Ramsey's words came to mind: 'Good Friday is not a defeat that needs Easter to reverse it. Rather, it is a victory so signal that Easter comes quickly to seal it.'

12 August

In the morning I preached at 7.30, 9 and 11. The whole place, apart from the content of religion during the services, is well organized, alive and vigorous – except that there are no black faces. I asked why this was and was told, 'Well, the blacks have their own church.' I rest my case.

15 August

We drove across to Gloucester County to visit 'King' Carter's church of 1732–4 (Richard King Carter had 1,000 slaves and 300,000 acres, wealth built on misery and exploitation). There was the usual well-arranged visitor centre. The church was well proportioned outside and completely prayerless

inside. What do people do to buildings to take the prayer out?
There's no tradition here of praying in churches in the week.

16 August

We had dinner with some ghastly people on an estate
guarded by police. I sat next to a man called Hagan Wagner,
who said, 'I've just been to Alaska where there are no nig-
gers and no Jews.' I looked around the table to see if this
was a joke and realized to my horror that nobody thought any
of this was strange.

18 August

As a special treat I went for a flight today in a tiny plane, a
three-seater. This was exciting until it seemed to hover for
a moment and I suddenly had vertigo. I was absolutely terrified and in a dead funk I exerted every remaining ounce of will
not to scream, 'Pleasecanwegohome!' We dived and hurtled
about, whizzing up and down so that we could see architecture and rivers. I managed little squeaks of, 'Yes ... Thank you
... I see ... Yes...' It was something to do with the tinyness of
the aircraft. The delightful pilot, Mitch, had no idea what was
going on. To my surprise, I emerged alive.

22 August

I am not sorry to have left the US. All of Williamsburg is replica. I shall never get over people sitting at the 8 o'clock Holy
Communion in Bruton Parish Church wearing farthingales,
frilly bodices, silk stockings, etc. They drive to church in their
Chevrolets, in the costumes they are going to wear all day
behind the counters of Ye Olde Shoppes and Ye Olde
Governor's Palace. They are quite unfazed by coming to
church dressed like that.

Early September saw me returning to the National Theatre for a
second dose of David Hare's play *Racing Demon*. His perspective
on religion was less confident than that of the churchgoers in
Williamsburg. I took Richard Holloway and David Hutt with me,

and the people around us seemed a bit wary at finding a bishop in purple and two priests in black sitting in the audience. Had we escaped from the stage? Once again I found the play bleak but perceptive. Bishop Richard was a bit cast down by it, for it had much to say about hypocrisy, ambition, fright and the second-rateness of bishops – uncomfortable to listen to if you are a bishop.

14 September

I took the train to Paddock Wood, where Jean Mayhew met me and took me back to Twysden – big log fires, candlelight, a dinner of pork chops, fruit and claret, with brandy afterwards. We talked about the Gulf, the War Cabinet (of which Patrick is a member) and America.

15 September

I woke early and read Nigel and Adam Nicolson's book *Two Roads to Dodge City*, with its uncritical description of Williamsburg.

Later on, Jean and I went to Sissinghurst. Suddenly, in the White Garden, we came across Nigel Nicolson picking iceberg roses (apparently they weren't there in his mother Vita's day). We went with him through the house, then Nigel asked me if I would take the secateurs and finish cutting the roses, so I had this rather surreal experience of cutting roses in the White Garden, feeling like a vandal. How strange that I began the day by reading *Two Roads to Dodge City* with no idea that I would end up cutting flowers in the author's garden later the same day.

18 September

The Duke of Kent came to St Mary-le-Bow today, for the service to dedicate a tablet to the members of the Order of Australia. The Bishop of Fulham,[5] standing in for the Bishop of London, is a lump. He didn't know what to say to the Duke of Kent, who arrived early. He doesn't really know what to

---

5 John Klyberg.

say to anybody, except to use bad language, unsuitable in a bishop. He's a large, kind-hearted man out of his depth. The choir was excellent. The Australians made the Lord Mayoral and Aldermanic pomp less stiff and the regal personage gradually melted, though he is shy.

At Australia House afterwards, the High Commissioner said kind things about me and I was put opposite His Royal Highness at a table for 12. I was able to say to the Duke that I was impressed by his equerry having noticed in time that the printed lesson he had to read had a fantastic mistake in it. The whole service was built around the idea that Admiral Arthur Phillip, the first Governor, was a good chap, so we had that bit from St Paul which says, 'Let there be no room for rivalry or ambition among you.' As the Duke mounted the pulpit steps, we realized for the first time, to our horror, that despite endless proof reading the Duke was about to read, 'Let there be room for rivalry...' The magic word 'no' had been omitted at the printers, but the Duke had supplied what was wanting.

'Ah,' he said, 'it wasn't my equerry [a young officer went a bit pink at this point], it was me. I got out my Bible last night to check. I thought it couldn't possibly be right, so I looked it up.' Well, there you are.

23 September

I am at Codford for the weekend. I preached at Erlestoke and visited old Harry the shepherd and Sylvia his wife in their seventeenth-century, very smelly almshouse. Harry has promised to look me out a sheep bell. He said, 'That passage where the sheep know the voice of a shepherd but don't know the voice of a hireling in St John's Gospel always means a lot to me.' Harry gave me a newspaper cutting about Erlestoke House being built on the profits of slavery. This is the sort of thing that keeps England going, that an old shepherd in an almshouse should treasure a bit of journalism that shows us what the grandees were really like.

On the first Tuesday in October we held a Dialogue and service with Rabbi Shafritz from the West London Synagogue. The Lord

Mayor came and I was absolutely delighted that we had done it. After all, as I said to someone at the time, we have enough in common to be able to worship the same God together.

The Bow Lane Festival, which had been going on for a couple of days in the churchyard with all manner of stalls, entertainments and other excitements, ended with an old people's tea in the Bow Wine Vaults and a military parade of the Honourable Artillery Company, with Alderman Brian Jenkins taking the salute. The best thing about the whole occasion occurred right at the end. At 8.45 p.m. I was watching the Punch and Judy people packing up, and I was allowed to hold their crocodile. I have always loved the crocodile in the Punch and Judy show. There's something for a psychologist to tackle.

5 October

I have brought a group to Burford Priory in Oxfordshire for a parish weekend. I was hoping to start with a meeting and then Compline together, but alas, our non-stipendiary minister Dayton Dewey took Jim, Wendy, Joan, Gareth, Vanessa, et al. off to the Mermaid pub, where they simply stayed and I had to go and fetch them like the headmaster. They came back in sixes and sevens without coming to Compline, and I had to stay guarding the door to lock it after them – not a good start.

6 October

Lauds at 7 a.m. in the lovely Jacobean chapel restored my equilibrium. This is a fairy-tale house. Mark Regan said this is the first time St Mary-le-Bow has been together to anything. Father Atwell, the founder of Burford, is a splendid man. The old Reverend Mother who is in charge of the new community pretends to be silly, but isn't.

8 October

Back in Cheapside, the monastic balance, calm, discipline and ascetic atmosphere of Burford has been all too quickly destroyed. It's like blowing on a mandala made of coloured dust – though Buddhists do that deliberately, which gives me pause for thought.

22 October

I went to Cambridge, to the theological college Westcott House, to talk about and commend to the students Affirming Catholicism. My presentation was too aggressive, however, and I had not taken on board the more liberal, 'we're all the same/there are no difficult people in the world/it's all a matter of love' atmosphere of Westcott House, so the idea of Catholicism was itself strange to many of the people there.

24 October

I spoke at the Roman Catholic Society of King's College, London, and talked afterwards to my old friend Derek Jennings, who is now the Roman Catholic University Chaplain. Derek used to take me to stay with his aunt and grandmother in their wonderful country house in South Devon and Libby Jennings has become a friend over the years – a sort of honorary aunt.

28 October

This morning I celebrated Mass at Holy Trinity, Tottenham. There was a memorial service afterwards. I was suddenly moved to make a present of the stole given me at my ordination in 1969 to Elaine Jones, who works here as a Deacon. She is in point of fact the Vicar, but a man has to go in and be the celebrant, as she is not able to be ordained to the priesthood.

2 November

The news on this All Souls' Day is that Sir Geoffrey Howe has resigned from the Government, driven out by Mrs T's anti-Europeanism. Things must unravel now.

6 November

Field Marshal Sir Nigel Bagnall would not wear his deaf aid, was belligerent, sensitive, indiscreet and an absolutely wild success at the Dialogue. He asked me why I had criticized Germany in the last war, when in fact I had asked him a question about the Gulf War. He really doesn't hear very much. He did, however, tell a wonderful story from his time as Chief of Staff, when Mrs Thatcher said to him, 'I suppose silence means agreement.'

He said, 'I have been disagreeing with you about this particular policy for many years, Prime Minister.'

To which Mrs Thatcher replied, 'And you have been wrong for many years, Sir Nigel.'

This brought the house down.

11 November

After Remembrance Day Matins at Offham Church in East Sussex, where I was staying with Andrew and Phyllida Stewart-Roberts, I talked to the Chief Whip, Tim Renton, who said of Mrs Thatcher, 'It's sad to see her come to the end like this.' That seemed to sound the Prime Minister's death knell.

November continued with a great deal of politics in the air. Lord Scarman was wonderful at his Dialogue, although, like the Field Marshal, he was noticeably deaf. He had drafted the Divorce Law Reform with Michael Ramsey and Lord Gardiner and told us how the three of them had sat working in the Archbishop of Canterbury's study, all at the same desk. This was an almost unimaginably remote historical scene for those of us living in the Thatcher–Runcie enmity years.

Meanwhile, in the House of Commons, Geoffrey Howe savaged and mortally wounded the Prime Minister in his resignation speech. Watching her face as Sir Geoffrey stood behind her speaking was a historic moment. The House was stunned. This was no dead sheep, this Prime Minister slayer. He had committed matricide. It was riveting stuff. I celebrated the end of Thatcherism with some friends that evening at the National Liberal Club. Good old Geoffrey Howe.

In the midst of all this political excitement, I found myself increasingly involved in a social project which vividly brought home to me the huge differences which exist side by side in London. Imagining that I knew how to get money out of the City, a group of doctors and nurses had come to me, asking me to help them create a much needed day centre for people with HIV and AIDS in the East End – a less ambitious equivalent of the famous London Lighthouse in Notting Hill Gate. The old Stepney Baths were in a state of terminal ruin and they thought it might be possible to buy the site, keep the shell and rebuild from the inside outwards. It was to be called the Globe Centre.

I was very keen indeed to help with this project and thought it a very useful partnership between the fantastically wealthy Square Mile and the terribly impoverished East End boroughs adjacent to it. With this in mind, I persuaded David Vermont to accompany me on a visit to the site. As Chairman of the Church Committee at the Mercers' Company and a Past Master Mercer, David is a man of great influence and ability, particularly when it comes to getting radical and difficult projects off the ground, because he looks – and is – so eminently respectable and trusted himself.

22 November

I went to Stepney to meet Jonathan Lowe, the social worker in charge of the Globe Centre project for people with HIV and AIDS. I took David Vermont and we climbed about the rubble of the collapsed Baths, the intended site of this centre for people who are in such need and are so disregarded by the City.

We returned to the City thoughtfully, Mr Vermont and I sitting side by side looking at our reflections in the tube train window. He said pensively, 'I suppose that young man needs to wear an earring.' With unwonted tact I said nothing and Mr Vermont continued, ruminating aloud, 'Well, why shouldn't he if he wants to? I must just pull myself together.' This is why I love him.

We got back to Cannon Street Station at 10.30, to hear an extraordinarily excited news vendor shouting, 'Mrs Thatcher has resigned!'

There was an eerie silence in the City. It was Mrs T's day. In the House of Commons she defended her achievements, electric in debate as she replied to Neil Kinnock's vote of no confidence in the Government. Kinnock was feeble and failed to command the House for more than the initial moment. What have the Tories done? It was an inevitable end, but the manner of the going was painful. In defeat, Mrs Thatcher was at her vintage best.

27 November

Today's Dialogue was with Diana Rigg. She was very tense and told me that she had avoided Joseph McCulloch at the end of his ministry here. It was a hard-going Dialogue and I couldn't get her to stop going on about the Church of England in the way that *Daily Telegraph* readers tend to, and we've all heard it before.

In the end, in desperation, I heard myself saying, 'I have always enormously admired your legs, Miss Rigg.'

She asked if I would compliment the Bishop of Oxford on his legs.

I said I didn't know, I hadn't seen them, but he was next week's guest – thinking she was being amusing, as Dame Judi Dench would have been amusing.

But she wasn't amused, she was very, very cross. This seemed a bit unfair, as she had an extremely short black skirt and yards of wonderful, black-stockinged legs.

Then, wildly disregarding Denis Healey's advice that when you are in a hole you should stop digging, I said, 'I have admired your legs ever since I was at school.' How could I have said such a thing? It was panic, I suppose. We didn't really get over that at lunch.

28 November

John Major is the new Prime Minister. As the MP Julian Critchley said, 'When I joined the Tory Party, all the members were called Charlie. Now they're all called Norman.'

Right at the end of November, Andrew and I set off for a week in Prague, where we stayed in a freezing flat jammed under the eaves of a four-storey building. The skies were heavy with snow, the streets ill-lit, the shops sparsely stocked with poor-quality, expensive food. I spent most of the time wandering around the sights of Prague on my own, because Andrew was laid up with a bad back. The crowds on the streets did not talk or smile much. Then I saw some children riding horses at an Advent fair in Tyn Square. They were beside themselves with excitement, and it was lovely to see. Their parents were buying single oranges and bananas from little booths, which reminded me of my own parents at the end of the Second World War. As Christmas approached, they would gradually put aside special treats in the sideboard – dates, prunes, the occasional orange and, if it could be found, a banana. Andrew and I returned, sobered, to London and found the bright lights startling.

13 December

Mary Corbett, Features Editor of the *Tatler*, came to lunch to do an interview with me. During this, Sir Geoffrey Howe rang to ask whether he could quote a letter I'd written him congratulating him on the speech that destroyed Mrs Thatcher. We chatted for 10 minutes. This greatly impressed the *Tatler*. Mary had just asked me how I got to know so many influential people, and I was explaining that it was just part of the job when Geoffrey Howe telephoned. I walked Mary to her car. I had just got back into my study when A.S. Byatt rang and talked for three-quarters of an hour. I suppose it would have been over-egging the pudding for the winner of the Booker Prize to ring up while Mary was in the room.

24 December

I'm in Wiltshire and I have the most awful cough on my birthday. I went back to bed and stayed there all day after saying Matins. I've missed all sorts of drinks parties. Tim and Bernard came and cooked a ham mess for dinner, which I got up for and then went straight back to bed. My lovely birthday present was to discover that I am only 46 and not 47 or 48, which I thought I must be.

I dragged Don, Tim, Bernard and Andrew off to Edington Priory for Midnight Mass – incense, candlelight, careful, quiet, expectant congregation. I was very hot in a flower-powdered eighteenth-century dalmatic, the vestment which the Deacon wears at High Mass on splendid occasions here, but felt less ill at the end of Mass than I did at the beginning.

25 December

Christmas Day. I enjoyed the clean linen, the sparkling silver and much evidence of care at the church at Upton Lovell. St Mary's, Codford, at 10 o'clock, cluttered, ugly and damp. Yet this unattractive church was full – 80 people. I discovered as I began the service that I had left my sermon at Upton Lovell, and this necessitated an extemporary offering. I managed to get the Handel quotes, which were essential to the sermon, in due order from memory.

Tim and Bernard cooked all day. At 5.30 we sat down for an extremely nice Chinese dinner – wood-ear soup, duck pancakes, Mongolian lamb. But, as Bernard was in charge of the kitchen, the whole house was covered with flour and every conceivable pot and pan had been used, including the addition of a primus stove in the middle of the dining room table.

The Queen looked wintry giving her Christmas message. Perhaps she had seen the state of our kitchen.

Eucharistic Apple Sauce

When I returned from Codford to the start of another new year in Cheapside, the newspapers were full of the worsening situation in the Gulf, as the Iraqis continued their offensive in Kuwait and an international force, led by the US, ranged itself against them. During the first week or so back at St Mary-le-Bow, however, my concerns seemed to be rather more light-hearted, until the grim news from the Gulf took over.

7 January

At 12.30 Sir Geoffrey Howe arrived to be photographed with me for Mary Corbett's *Tatler* article, and *Tatler* completely took over the nave from 10 a.m. until 1 p.m. Sir Geoffrey was friendly, jolly and helpful, way beyond the call of acquaintance.

11 January

I see that my story about the Archbishop of Canterbury and Mrs Thatcher getting on so badly, which was told to me by Douglas Hurd when I met him at the Mayhews', is quoted word for word in Adrian Hastings' biography of Runcie. How?

14 January

I went to the reception given by Mowbrays for Adrian Hastings. Who put the Douglas Hurd/Mrs Thatcher/Lord Runcie bit in the Runcie book? I went up to Professor Hastings to get the answer. 'Of course,' he said, 'I must protect my sources.'

Bishop Montefiore said he had thought this was vintage Stock and, whether true or not, perfectly summed up the position at the time between the Church of England and the Government, and he had therefore advised inclusion. I was very puzzled about all of this. Later, of course, I realized that I must have told the story to Robert Runcie himself, and he told the story to his biographer.

15 January

Iraq is intent on war and there is no move for peace.

The German Ambassador and Baroness von Richthofen arrived at 12.30 for the Tuesday Dialogue. He's a charming and diffident aristocrat. She is crisp, sharp and elegant, an author. We had a very jolly lunch – much conversation about Chancellor Kohl and Mrs Thatcher, and Thatcher's unhelpfulness.

17 January

During the night, the war began. Baghdad has been bombed by the Allies. Sadly I prepared my speech for the Mercers' Dinner. War in the desert is ironic today, it being the Feast of St Anthony of Egypt, the Desert Father.

At the dinner I had an opportunity to talk to people about the Globe Project, made possible by the sensitive way David Vermont had arranged the seating.

19 January

In contrast with the Mercers' Dinner, I went on an outing today with the staff of the Grocers' Hall, to the Walthamstow dog-racing track. I loved every minute of it, though I didn't understand how to bet and lost two pounds. I met a woman from the East End who is a tremendous fan of Andrew Dunford and his medical practice there. Working-class culture is still coherent, the 'downstairs' world of friendships and joint pleasures – an exact reverse mirror of the 'upstairs' pleasures of hunting and country life. How strange these livery company worlds are. They still keep intact cultural class patterns of 300 years ago.

28 January

At the Crusaid party in the Grand Committee Room of Westminster Hall this evening, the Princess of Wales was in black velvet mourning for King Olav of Norway. She looks the person she is talking to straight in the eye. She is sexually seductive in an almost virginal way. I said to Anne Blanchard from the Grocers' Company, with whom I attended the party, 'Do you think we could talk to each other instead of both staring with our mouths open at the vision that is the Princess of Wales?'

29 January

I arrived at Westminster Abbey just as Ambassador and Baroness von Richthofen did so. We went in together for the Meissen Agreement service, which I found deeply affecting.[1] There was German singing and reading, and the bell of HMS *Verdun* nearby, which brought the body of the Unknown Warrior to England in 1920. Dean Michael Mayne said a prayer at this most famous of all tombs, as ghosts and memories crowded about us.

At the party afterwards, to which the Ambassador had invited me, I talked to the Archbishop of York about his excellent sermon on the Gulf, and the Archbishop of Canterbury asked me if I had any funny stories for him. I hadn't.

I was so very glad to be asked to this event, about which I'd known absolutely nothing before the German Ambassador came to Dialogue and lunch. Now the Church of England is in communion with Germany. Anglicans and Lutherans are united at the altar, and yet there has been hardly any publicity about it.

30 January

I addressed an amazingly hostile Church Council at St Magnus the Martyr about women's ordination. The Rector, Father Woodgate, said in my defence, 'Father Stock would regard himself as a Catholic.'

'He may regard himself how he likes,' said one old gent, 'but I think he's no better than an Evangelical.'

Rather sweetly afterwards, another old gent came up and said, 'I voted for you [i.e. for the ordination of women – 1 to

---

1 The Meissen Agreement brought the Evangelical Lutheran Church of Germany and the Church of England into full communion.

15 against], not because I believe in it, but because I felt so sorry for you.'

Heavy snow at the beginning of February brought in its wake a bout of flu for the Rector and a Confirmation service that very nearly did not happen. One man asked if he could be confirmed the following week instead, but I had to explain that was really not how it all worked.

Then the IRA fired a mortar bomb from the middle of Whitehall at No. 10 Downing Street, which did not do much damage but must have been a bit of a shake-up for the Cabinet meeting that was taking place at the time. Patrick Mayhew told me later that they had looked out of the window, shrugged their shoulders and said, 'Well, we'd better get on with the meeting.'

A pre-Lent treat was Julian Critchley's Dialogue. He was as wonderfully funny in the flesh as he was in print, a more relaxed, less upper-class version of Auberon Waugh. Despite the snow and cold – and the church had become very, very cold indeed – 87 people came to be enlivened by him.

13 February

Ash Wednesday. The thaw continues. I got up at 6 a.m. and had a lovely Quiet Day. We sang Matins at 8.30 for just six or seven people, then had beautiful music at the lunchtime Mass: Palestrina, Allegri and Bairstow. I did some teaching in the Choir School. These boys are too young, really, but what can be done now? I don't approve of the age they get confirmed. The Cathedral does, though I don't think anybody there really cares enough or thinks very much about these children.

19 February

After the Dialogue, I had General Sir David Ramsbotham,[2] Lady Mayhew, Andrew and Phyllida Stewart-Roberts and Ruth Watson to lunch. Ruth was Sir David's nanny, it has transpired.

---

2 Sir David, a distinguished soldier, was Adjutant General from 1990 to 1993. He went on to become Her Majesty's Chief Inspector of Prisons in 1995.

After that I went off to Docklands to see Anne Craddock, whose husband Frank died this morning.

Then we heard the news that David Hope, who is Bishop of Wakefield and has really only just arrived there from being Vicar of All Saints, Margaret Street (three years), is to be the new Bishop of London.

28 February

I preached tonight about the end of the Gulf War, for at last it's over and Saddam Hussein has withdrawn from Kuwait. David Peck, a nice young American banker, was in the congregation and thought me not pacifist enough, but I'm not a pacifist and can very occasionally see that war is the only way. On this occasion, however, I'm not all that sure. Of course the West was only interested in oil, not really in the fate of the Kuwaitis who'd been invaded, and, after all, the Kuwaitis are hardly a liberal democracy where human rights are observed. Still, the war in the desert is over, although the oil fields which Saddam set alight will pollute the planet for a long time to come.

12 March

A.S. Byatt's Dialogue day was a triumphant experience. The church was absolutely packed and A.S. Byatt, of course, was brilliantly interesting and clever. I knew her years ago at University College, where she taught and where her room looked down into my garden. Now she has won the Booker Prize and is a famous personality, reaping the rewards of assiduous scholarship, a fecund imagination and a deep knowledge of the nineteenth century. We had a very jolly talking lunch until 3 o'clock. I gave her a Victorian Charity plate and she observed, 'How pinched and cross Charity's face is.'

A few days later there was a lovely Mass at which I baptized Christopher Thornton, Peter Jule and Julian Scott, all St Paul's Cathedral Choir School boys due to be confirmed shortly. Sir Geoffrey and Lady Howe came, being Christopher's grandparents, and with them came their attendant police, keeping the IRA at bay.

Talking to me afterwards, Sir Geoffrey commented, 'We don't seem to be in the *Tatler*.' This was embarrassing. I explained that *Tatler* had decided that the whole thing was too serious and that I was too serious – he could not believe this – and had therefore scrapped the entire enterprise.

27 March

Today was a big day: Confirmation of the Election of the Archbishop of Canterbury, George Carey. James Surpliss, our Verger, actually turned up, which made a nice change, but he took the Dean of Canterbury and Dean of St Paul's out at the wrong point. The Archbishop of York was shy and silent. I took *him* to the wrong place. The Bishop of Chichester was silent. The Bishop of Salisbury was very nice, the Bishop of Lincoln unstuffy. The big surprise was Graham Leonard in a funny and jolly mood, as jolly and funny as can be.

For some reason which is quite beyond me, there were 24 Royal Commissioners present, all bishops. The Dean of the Southern Province is meant to preside over the ceremony. Well, the Bishop of London is evidently Dean of the Southern Province, but the Archbishop of York was quite sure that *he* was going to preside over the ceremony, and he did. At the rehearsal this caused tension, and it was nice to see it resolved later.

The church was absolutely packed for the occasion, partly because of the enormous media interest – it went out on the six o'clock news on the BBC and all the other channels – but also because the last few Confirmations of Election took place in St Paul's Cathedral on the excuse that St Mary-le-Bow had been bombed in the war. St Paul's, having once got hold of it (Michael Ramsey's Confirmation of Election, for example, was held in the crypt of St Paul's), was understandably reluctant to relinquish the prize. I, however, in my determination to get St Mary-le-Bow properly on the map, was equally determined that this ancient ceremony, which belonged here in the Court of the Arches, should return to Cheapside – and it was so.

The new Archbishop swore the oaths on my father's Shaftesbury Society Bible. Afterwards he thought I had given it to him and I had to write in it and say I had. A Queen Mary-like incident, which I will later unpick.[3] He mustn't imagine that everything shown to him is a present, or Lambeth Palace will be bursting at the gunwales.

We lunched off silver plates at the Mansion House and this raised eyebrows, but I tried to explain that they had silver plates instead of gold plates for Holy Week – which, believe it or not, is true. We only had one sort of wine and some lobster, so it was really Lenten fare by Mansion House standards. Some of the bishops were offended at the whole idea of being entertained in Holy Week. Some of the best of them, like the Bishop of Salisbury, rather stupidly stayed away from the lunch because they don't understand how to relate to the world as it actually is.

At the beginning of the morning George Carey came in as Bishop of Bath and Wells – chummy, with people talking to him and being friendly. Afterwards, unrobing in the vestry, he was Archbishop of Canterbury and I noticed a wide circle – people kept away from him. He was now the Boss and was on his own. He's going to be good with the Low Church places like parts of Africa and the Bible Belt in America, but I wonder if he will be comfortable in London and the non-Evangelical world?

28 March

St Mary-le-Bow is on the front of the *Independent* today, at the back of the *Guardian* and on the inside of the *Telegraph*, the *Express* and *The Times*. I feel proud of and absorbed by yesterday – the crowds, the history in the making, thoughts of my dead parents, the kindly modesty of the Archbishop as his reign began, and his wife Eileen, unpretentious and friendly.

---

3 Queen Mary was very fond of visiting stately homes and eyeing up *objets d'art*, which she would enquire after and compliment until, through exhaustion, her host would give them to her. You had to be very determined *not* to give Queen Mary your possessions.

29 March

Good Friday. I went off to sunny All Saints, Fulham, to preach
the Three Hours, where a man interrupted and heckled in the
last hour. The Curate got up and tried to move closer to
remove him. The Vicar got up behind the Curate and moved
closer to stop him trying to remove the man, seeing that an
ugly scene would take place. I made the fatal mistake of trying to answer what the man was shouting. When people
shout out in sermons, don't take any notice. There were 100
people in the church for the final hour, including the
Bangladeshi High Commissioner and his wife. At the front
was the sweetest old lady, giving her all in attentiveness and
prayer, and quite unaware of the drama unfolding behind her.

April began with a walk to Queen Charlotte's Cottage in Kew
Gardens in a cold, grey, wet and wintry light. Then I went to the
East End to help Andrew pack up his flat for what I hoped would
be a temporary move into the Rector's lodgings at St Mary-le-Bow.
It would be nice having him there, I knew, but really the place is
too small for anybody to share permanently. There is no other
sitting room, just the one reception room which is both sitting
room and dining room, with a galley kitchen off it, so any lodger
is effectively confined to his bedroom. It was proving very difficult to manage the finances of Codford, however, and if Andrew
could rent or sell his flat, the money from that could go towards
his and his father's parts of the mortgage in Wiltshire. We decided to try it and see what happened. (In fact, the unsatisfactory
arrangement of having Andrew, a doctor on call, poked into the
guest room of the rectory did not last long. He soon sold his old
flat at his practice behind the Royal Mint and moved into a small
flat in the Barbican.)

After a few days' rest in Codford, mostly taken up with gardening (there was bindweed everywhere), I returned to the fray in
London.

15 April

I'm back in the saddle, and had an odd feeling all day –
partly simply being back at work and partly the continual

interruptions of the telephone. I saw a woman in trouble, then a man about faith and marriage, then a woman straight off Cheapside. I also talked to Dominic Zwigler about faith – he's just off to the US to be the Washington correspondent for *The Economist*.

I spent the evening with Bernard Jenkin. He thinks the Tories may lose the next election. Sir Geoffrey and Lady Howe have just spent the weekend with Patrick and Monica, Bernard's parents. They are all absorbed by Mrs Thatcher's demise and Geoffrey's decisive part in that.

19 April

The day of the Archbishop of Canterbury's Enthronement. I watched a videotape of the ceremony at Canterbury. John Habgood, the Archbishop of York, actually smiled. All seemed relaxed as well as dignified. There was a good, straightforward sermon from the new Archbishop, and modern music – quite appropriate. Mr Kinnock was behaving in a rather silly way. Why? Not used to church, I suppose. The new *Te Deum* was tedious, but all in all, the Church of England came over well: quite well rather than very well, I would say.

At least the Archbishop's Enthronement had been planned and practised properly. On 1 May we had the institution service for the new Rector of St Olav's, Hart Street, conducted by the Bishop of Fulham. It was entirely and ridiculously unrehearsed, and there was very little time: preaching and institution were shoehorned into the available half hour only by being rushed through at breakneck speed. Then the lights failed at the Clothworkers' Hall and the reception had to be cancelled. It was not a good start.

4 May

At Codford we finished the main clearing of the room under the chapel (made out of the old apple store) which is to become Andrew's weekend herbal consulting room and surgery. We splashed distemper on the walls just in time for John Tipping, the Vicar, to come and bless the chapel at 12 o'clock. I asked him because it's right to ask the parish priest to do these things and he did it very nicely, using the service I'd devised, which included a reading from Sidney Evans and Don reading from St John. John Torrie brought lovely flowers from the Manor House. The sun shone and we all had lunch, prepared by me and cooked by Don.

7 May

Sir Ralf Dahrendorf, head of the London School of Economics, came at lunchtime for a good, sparking-off Dialogue. Then I took June Judd-Goodwin around the Museum of London. I'm trying to get her to see as much as possible before she becomes completely immobilized. From there I went on to see *Life is Sweet* – a brilliantly funny, moving film by Mike Leigh, with his wife as the ghastly but wonderful heroine. It was the St John's end of Friern Barnet to the life.

David Hutt told me, 'I now know that women must be ordained,' but he's wondering when he should say this to anybody else.

19 May

At teatime I called on George Bright at the vicarage of St John the Baptist, Holland Road. He wasn't in, so I went for a walk around the area, remembering what it was like going to St John the Baptist as a schoolboy, on the back of my friend Rusty's motorbike, for Benediction on a Wednesday evening in the winter. Then I tramped back to the black cavernous spaces of St John's, with hardly anyone at all present except for Father George, one server, the organist and seven others of us making up the congregation for extremely rapidly executed Roman Catholic vespers, a little pause and then Benediction. This strange and rather frightening church exercises a huge fascination for me, somewhere down in the subconscious depths where horror films are made. It is awesome in its dirt and cold.

20 May

I attended a service for the City Parochial Foundation at St Lawrence Jewry, with a direct but somehow lifeless sermon from Dr Tom Butler, the Bishop of Willesden. It sounded all right, but wasn't. I mean, did he believe in what he was saying? It was forceful, but passionless at the same time. There was something odd and wrong about it, just as there is something wrong about St John the Baptist, Holland Road.

The blessing of our chapel at Codford early in May proved, in retrospect, to be a last happy and peaceful moment before everything suddenly changed. I was at the house during the first weekend in June, but Andrew was away at a conference with other herbal practitioners and complementary therapists. I spent Saturday weeding, while Don painted one of the doors in the stableyard. The two of us had tea and read Evensong together, then I passed the evening reading in my study. Later I went on my own to say night prayers in the chapel. I kept thinking I was hearing the washing machine going next door in Don's part of the house, but told myself it must be something else. Anyway, that was Don's space, and it was not for me to fuss or interfere.

2 June

Sunday. I woke at 6.30, had a bath and read Matins. I noticed that Don's curtains were drawn back and thought he must have got up even earlier than me. At 8.15, however, when it was time for me to go in his car to Edington Priory, he hadn't appeared. I called. The door was unlocked. I went up his stairs and found him dead on the floor of his bedroom.

I rang the police. I rang Edington. I rang the Vicar, who came straight round. No one could contact Andrew. He was staying in the house of an MP on the IRA assassination list and the number was ex-directory.

The undertakers came and took Don's body away. I cleaned up the bloodstain on the carpet where he had vomited. He died, so the doctor thought, of an asthma attack and had fallen over onto his asthma machine, which was the noise I had thought was the washing machine. I hoovered and cleaned his room. I put lots of flowers in the rooms and candles in the window, and waited and waited. Just waiting alone almost all day was unbearable. Margarite Maynard came in the morning after church, but apart from her brief visit and that of the Vicar, I was alone.

At 6.45 p.m., Andrew did come. He had a premonition that his father was dead as he drove home, and as soon as he came into the village and saw the candles alight in the windows, he realized what had happened.

Don's dog was distracted, a little white Yorkshire terrier called Tobes. We took him up onto Salisbury Plain and with happy abandon the little dog, which spent a great deal of its life caged up with Don in his sitting room, flew with enormous energy straight into a steaming cowpat. So the day began with me finding Don Dunford's body on the floor of his bedroom, and ended with me scrubbing Don's dog in my garage sink.

3 June

I rang and cancelled my trip to Oxford. Then I cleaned and tidied the house and helped Andrew deal with the consequences of his father's death.

We went up to London, where I had dinner with the Mayhews while Andrew went to see Bernard Dawson. It was the last evening of the Trooping of the Colour, which took place below Patrick's and Jean's sitting room window. At 10.30 the band played 'The day thou gavest, Lord, is ended'. That's the hymn we must have for Don's funeral on Thursday.

Death smashes up the diary.

6 June

It was a sunny day for Don's funeral, which took place at 12.15 in Codford Church. There were about 70 people, including Brigadier Goode and Colonel Elcombe, the Etonian Cochranes alongside Doris and Bill Windsor, the builder and his wife. Also Colin and Ruth, and builders, joiners, electricians. Bernard Dawson and David Hutt came too. I preached the sermon, which I had constructed carefully, and then presided over the cremation at Salisbury Crematorium where we sang 'The day thou gavest, Lord, is ended'. Don would have been proud and touched. John Torrie read the lesson and helped with food and welcome back at Old Wool Cottage.

7 June

I celebrated a Requiem Mass for Don at 7.30 in our own chapel. I felt sad. Don had come to value the chapel, often saying Andrew's simplified form of the Office on his own there.

Very soon, however, I had to wrench my mind away from the sadness of Don's sudden death. Other affairs were pressing. The Affirming Catholicism conference was looming, with all arrangements in place for the first weekend in July. There was much to be done in preparation. Meanwhile, I was grateful for the first diversion which came along, just a few days after Don's funeral.

10 June

I went to Hereford today on an expedition to encourage Andrew Mottram[4] to take on the challenge of All Saints, an almost physically collapsed thirteenth-century church, allied to a new church with all the difficulties a two-church parish has.

The nine-year-old St Barnabas Church has space and height, but is accumulating bits of Anglo-Catholic tat which simply need throwing away. I say 'simply need throwing away', but throwing away something in church is practically impossible because, of course, the particularly nasty statue has been given in memory of Mum, or the badly designed altar frontal has been got off the rack from some ecclesiastical House of Horrors in memory of Dad. Nevertheless, the people of St Barnabas deserve better than its present arrangement.

The overwhelming smell at All Saints is that of second-hand knickers and corsets. Under the western gallery is a

---

4 I had known Andrew Mottram, his wife Annabelle and their three children for some years. Andrew had been looking after a couple of villages in Bedfordshire with tremendous success, but needed a new challenge. All Saints, Hereford, was certainly that.

sort of opened-up church hall, lit by pale electric light, where elderly ladies scrabble amongst a sale of second-hand under-wear. It is not the odour of sanctity. There is something about a pile of second-hand corsets which really does say every-thing about the present state of the Church of England. The sacristy is filled with Anglo-Catholic vestments in various degrees past their sell-by date. Some of the vestments have little patterns of mouse droppings on them. Nevertheless, a vibrant city-centre church could be achieved here. It's a fab-ulous old building.

When we went to the cathedral later, I saw my old chum from University Chaplaincy days, Dr Venetia France, on duty at the *Mappa Mundi* pay desk. She looked at Andrew Mottram and said, 'God, you must be mad to take on All Saints.'

2 July

I am at the University of York for the Affirming Catholicism conference. We made a mess of the registration and the meal queues were absolutely hopeless. The Archbishop of Canterbury arrived after Evensong, dinner was chaos and I couldn't even produce potatoes for His Grace. Nevertheless, he was relaxed as I walked him over to the Sir Jack Lyon Theatre, and his lecture was excellent. He fielded questions honestly and received a thunderous standing ovation. If he goes on like this, he's going to be marvellous. He made some very liberal and open remarks which I don't think his Evangelical constituency will like, however. It will be interest-ing to see what happens to him as the years go by.

Afterwards I stood around talking to people until midnight. The most important thing about this conference is greeting people and meeting them. David Hutt and I made the right decision to stand at the door and say 'hello' to everybody.

I must remember not to be too funny giving out the notices, or it isn't funny.

3 July

There was a very moving homily at the 7.30 Mass from the Bishop of Lancaster. Jeffrey John was brilliant in his lecture this morning, Dr Jack Dominion less so.[5] After lunch, we rehearsed the Eucharist in the Minster and came back to hear Dr Billings[6] – very good – and Professor Rowan Williams – absolutely sensational. Endless talk with delegates until well after midnight.

4 July

Mother Alaine, Mother Superior of St Mary the Virgin, Wantage, spoke very well. Bishop Richard Holloway was brilliant, but then was a bit snappy with a conservative young priest during the questions. I was in the chair and shouldn't have allowed him to do that, but I got Richard to apologize to the priest publicly later on.

The Minster Mass was moving and strong. The Archbishop of York's sermon was worthwhile but uninspiring, though I don't think we could have been inspired any more and perhaps God realized we needed to be underwhelmed. Afterwards the snapped-at conservative priest told me he wasn't going to leave the Church of England when women were made priests, but would bite the bullet.

At dinner I did the whipping-up-funds routine, telling funny stories and making everyone laugh. Carrying around a bucket raked in £1,600 for our funds.

I have been on the verge of tears all week, tears of joy. This is the Church of England as it should be, as it once was, but as it won't be much longer unless some of us get our fingers out.

5 July

The conference over, I have come to the remote and lovely mountain country round Berwick on Tweed, to stay in a little tidy bungalow with a neat garden, sheep outside the dining room window and a library added, where Professor Nancy Lambton has come to retire.

---

5 In 1991 Dr Jeffrey John was Chaplain of Magdalen College, Oxford. Dr Jack Dominion is a Roman Catholic expert on marriage and sexual ethics.

6 In 1991 Dr John Billings was Vice Principal of Rippon College, Oxford.

Nancy drives like Auntie Libby Jennings – very slowly in the middle of the road, with an increasing tail of angry people behind. We motored off to see a hermit, but he was out. A rather eighteenth-century expedition, this. The hermit lives at the top of a hill with breathtaking views.

My guest bedroom smells of upper-class elderly life, with lots of books, a Persian carpet and linen, and the fresh mountain air coming through the open window.

7 July

The 11 o'clock Matins was taken by Nancy at Doddington – 1662 to the letter. Indeed, she read the Office from a William IV Prayer Book and showed it to me: the prayers were for 'the King, His Most Excellent Majesty King William IV, and Queen Adelaide'.

Back in London, City people were winding down for their summer holidays and as usual I gradually found myself with less to do. By the time August began I was really not busy at all. I had no plans to go away just yet, however, and there were some things I needed to do, so I stuck around. London was hot and sticky, somewhere between New York and Rome, but did not have the advantage of being a holiday place for me. All round the church there was digging and demolition. That was quite normal for the City, of course: London is full of noise, dirt and dust all day and all night. It was, however, particularly tiresome and debilitating in the heat.

6 August

The Transfiguration of Our Lord Jesus Christ. I took the Holy Sacrament and some Holy Oil to June Judd-Goodwin in Chalkwell, near Southend. We talked for a long time about this Feast of Jesus, the cloud of darkness and fear. Afterwards I walked back to Leigh-on-Sea. Old Leigh is tiny and estuary-bound. There are fields of corn all the way back to Upminster, and a ruined castle. It's an unspoilt piece of country landscape just beyond the East End. How has it survived?

7 August

The new Bishop of London, David Hope, came to lunch. He slipped alone into the back of the church at 12.45, halfway through Mass, and stayed on his knees till the end. He's so very nice, frank, unpompous, totally funny. He had a glass of wine, though he doesn't usually at lunch. We talked through lunch until 2.15. His driver, Fred, was waiting for him outside in a grey Rover. It felt like the initiation of an era of normality in the diocese.

19 August

I woke to discover that President Gorbachev has been overthrown in Moscow. The terrible old men return to – in Douglas Hurd's words – 'wind back the clock of history'. During the day, however, Boris Yeltsin defied the *coup d'état*. The West is united against the coup, but there is no word of Gorbachev. Is he still alive? The City is quite empty of workers and all day and evening we watched the Russian news, wondering what's going to happen and holding our breath for the newly liberated Eastern European countries.

22 August

Gorbachev is back in Moscow. I watched the incredible sight of him descending the plane steps in a stained, grey jumper. The coup has collapsed due to the heroism of Yeltsin, who is flying the Russian flag over the Kremlin. Gorbachev doesn't seem to understand what has happened. The Industry Minister has committed suicide. Communism is bleeding away.

Early in September, while Russia changed before our eyes, Andrew and I made a quiet journey north into unfamiliar countryside, stopping to visit Lord Curzon's self-conscious display of Tory hardness at Kedleston Hall outside Derby. I dislike these houses made for parade – they are inhuman and speak of the oppression of the poor. We called in at Mount St Bernard Abbey, where a monk was practising on the organ wearing headphones, then skirted Birmingham to see Baron Ash's reproduction Tudor house at Packwood. There we admired the topiary and the bee skeps, and Andrew became enthused with the idea of keeping bees at Codford. I hurried him on through Gloucestershire to Sezincote, the last and most beautiful house we visited – India in Italy, a house to envy.

Life back in London geared up for the autumn as September wore on, and I turned my attention to the forthcoming series of Dialogues. There were some stars to look forward to.

1 October

The tough Arctic explorer Sir Ranulph Twistleton Wickham Fiennes turned out to be an absolute doll at the Dialogue today – witty, humble and kindly. He goes for confession to the Cowley Fathers. 'Sorry I'm a bit quiet,' he said, 'just off a plane from Oman.' *Tatler's* Mary Corbett and Alistair Gossage, whom she is going to marry, came to lunch with him.

8 October

Sir Yehudi Menuhin, lovely, kind and religious, came for today's Dialogue. He is a special person and a great one. The church was absolutely packed.

This evening was the Presentation Dinner at Merchant Taylors' Hall. I said two Graces, including one for the Law Officers, and had a word with the Lord Chancellor.

At breakfast today, after early Mass, we had Alan Webster, who is a Knight Commander of the Royal Victorian Order but as a priest can't use the title, and Brian Jenkins, who is on his way to becoming a knight at the hand of the Lord Chancellor. I teased him about Alan's knighthood being far smarter, i.e. one you can't use.

12 October

I took a train from Euston to Manchester, a journey of 180 miles, to speak about Affirming Catholicism in the well-reordered Church of the Holy Innocents. Then I had dinner in Cheadle with a vicar who was sent 30 pieces of silver for hosting an Affirming Catholicism conference.

13 October

There was a beautifully uncluttered liturgy in Fallowfield, and 90 people who were responsive to the liveliness, if not the content, of what I had to say.

At lunch, Alma, the Deacon at Manchester Polytechnic, told the party stories she'd heard about me, one of which was that I had locked the whole of my theological college in the chapel to give them an experience of the tomb. This sounded extremely funny, but is absolutely and totally legendary.

15 October

I attended a Fabric Advisory Committee meeting at Salisbury Cathedral, well chaired by Sir John Tooley, former Director of Covent Garden.[7] We met in the vestry and walked around looking at the lighting of the Choir, the vestry glass, the lighting in the Trinity Chapel. I later expressed reservations about the lighting and suggested some improvements. It was an enjoyable meeting.

On the train back to London I was offered a drink by a young soldier sitting opposite. I declined, but offered him my *Independent*. I think he'd had one or two bevvies. 'Sorry,' he said, after struggling for a few minutes, 'the *Sun* is more my line.'

On 23 October I flew off to Florence for the weekend, taking Andrew with me. After absorbing as many of the great city sights as we could, we made a trip out to Siena. I loved it.

25 October

Siena is an architectural fairy-tale, a tour de force from start to finish. The central *campo* is breathtaking. All the streets are high, with a kind of brick New York canyon feel, the cathedral like some marine zebra.

---

7 I had been invited onto the Committee by the Very Revd the Hon. Hugh Dickinson.

I tried hard to like the Duccio altarpiece in the cathedral, but was distracted by the guide talking about 'linen cupboards at the Eucharistic event'. And then she mentioned 'Eucharistic apple sauce'. What can she have meant?

I returned to London none the wiser, but all thoughts of apple sauce, Eucharistic or otherwise, left my head on the day that the famous mezzo-soprano Dame Janet Baker came to St Mary-le-Bow. It was a very special Dialogue and is still vivid in my memory even now, nearly a decade later.

29 October

Dame Janet Baker came for the Dialogue. It was an extraordinary, light-filled, grace-bearing occasion, a triumph of the human spirit. She came with Keith Shelley, the husband she is obviously deeply in love with. The Dialogue was as good as that with Yehudi Menuhin, but somehow so much more disciplined, and produced by her. She was in charge. It was a bright, sunny day, but the church had an extra quality, a volume, a dimension of light. I understood, for the first time, the meaning of those ancient writings about the saints as illuminated figures from whom light shone. It was like a physical radiance, except it wasn't physical. I don't know how to describe it at all.

5 November

We had the perfect 5 November Dialogue guest in Lionel Blue, who brought in an audience of 350 people, 100 of whom stood throughout. He said, 'I'm an ungay gay.' He was very funny, and we had a frank conversation following his coming-out article in *The Times*.

Afterwards I heard one old lady say to another, 'He's a lovely man, isn't he?'

'Oh yes, he is, he's a lovely man.'

'I like him so much, don't you?'

'Yes, I like him too.'

'Mind you, I didn't like that what they said about him.'

'No, I didn't like what they said about him, either.'

'You know what I mean?'

'Yes, they said he was "one of those". Horrible, wasn't it?'

'Nasty.'

Well, 'they' hadn't said anything. Lionel had said it himself. But his fans couldn't bear it and turned what they had heard into something they wanted to remember was said *about* him, not said *by* him.

Every November the City holds the great pageant of the Lord Mayor's Show: a carriage procession of the Lord Mayor and Aldermen, using the Lord Mayor's coach (which spends the rest of the year in the Museum of London), with attendant marching regiments, military bands and a huge City carnival. There is a whole complex of ceremonies to mark the installation of the new Lord Mayor. First comes the Lighting Up Dinner, as one Lord Mayor gives way to another, then the Guildhall Silent Ceremony, when the outgoing Lord Mayor hands over to the incoming Lord Mayor in an arcane ceremony conducted entirely in silence. That happens on the Friday, the day before the Lord Mayor's Show. The carriage procession is always rehearsed very early in the morning during the previous week, and this year I was directly involved.

Alderman Brian Jenkins, one of the Churchwardens at St Mary-le-Bow, had been Sheriff a couple of years earlier and I had been his Chaplain. This year he was to become Lord Mayor. He was knighted in the week leading up to the Lord Mayor's Show, and had invited me to be his Chaplain once again. Thus I began a year of attendance on him, which meant saying Graces at government and civic banquets and preaching a number of statutory sermons. The Chaplain to the Lord Mayor, like the Lord Mayor himself, holds the post for one year and is not often able to repeat the performance – though later I was able to do this for Sir Richard Nicholls.

The gorgeous pageantry of the Lord Mayor's Show of 1991 began with Sir Brian Jenkins, his wife, children and the City Sword Bearer coming to a celebration of Holy Communion in the crypt of St Mary-le-Bow, where Sir Brian had been coming to Communion every Tuesday morning. It was a movingly private way to begin a splendid public year, a year when I got to know the ceremonial life of the City from the inside. During that year I greatly enjoyed the consistent, amused, amusing and helpful friendship of the permanent staff of the Mansion House, who see Lord Mayors rise to the dizzy heights of being virtual sovereign of the City, looked after by footmen and chauffeurs, attended by Sword Bearers, Mace Bearers and City Marshals, before returning to do their own shopping in Tesco's a mere 12 months later.

This year the Show coincided with Remembrance Sunday weekend, and the pageantry on the Saturday was immediately followed by the solemnity of Remembrance Sunday, when the Lord Mayor goes in state to St Paul's for Matins and lays a wreath outside the Royal Exchange. All this was followed on the Monday by the Lord Mayor's Banquet, at which the Archbishop of Canterbury, the Chancellor and the Prime Minister always speak, in that order of precedence.

6 November

I was out at 4 a.m., off to Wood Street Police Station for the 4.50 Lord Mayor's rehearsal, and thence to Guildhall Yard where the state coach waited. We got in and clattered past the church and the first bemused commuters, who must have thought they were suffering from a dreadful hangover, to see this great gold coach lumbering through the City before 5 o'clock in the morning.

After Mass, I had an abortive and very annoying trip to Ede and Ravenscroft to get my Geneva gown: it's still being made in Cambridge.

In the evening we had the Guildhall Lighting Up dinner, at which I said Grace. I sat between an Ensign of the Musketeers and a kindly Evangelical Churchwarden from St Margaret's, Lothbury, who told me that being Chaplain to the Lord Mayor is a real job if you wish it to be so, which was helpful.

8 November

I changed into state dress (black cassock, Geneva gown – mine not being ready, I wore my academic gown – black scarf, buckled shoes, tricorne hat, white bands and white gloves) and went to the Guildhall for the Silent Ceremony. This is a most remarkable occasion when the livery, hundreds and hundreds of men and one or two women, pack the Guildhall and the Aldermen sit in a kind of horseshoe before the outgoing and incoming Lord Mayors. The only sound is the scratching of documents as one Lord Mayor takes over from another with much doffing of ostrich-plumed hats – a pool of spotlit activity in the darkened hall that has seen so much history.

9 November

At 9 a.m. I went to Ironmonger Lane (the 'stand-in' Mansion House this year because the real Mansion House is being done up), and then in state for a standing-up breakfast in the Guildhall crypt – everybody in uniform, robes and armour, having hot lobster, spiced wine cup and champagne – before getting into the state coach. Hard work, all that waving.

The Lord Chief Justice made an excellent speech at the Royal Courts of Justice. The crowds who turned out to see us were interestingly East End and suburban and not at all young City. The Lord Mayor was given rum at HMS *Wellington* beside the Thames. It was handed through the carriage window, with a bottle for the Lord Mayor to take home. I had to sit on this, along with the Bible the Dean of St Paul's gave the Lord Mayor. I emerged at Guildhall, clutching both Bible and rum. With the deft assistance of a strategically tactful footman and my voluminous robes, I managed to get the rum into the footman's hands without it all appearing on television.

At the end of the afternoon there were fireworks on the Thames – detonating fireballs and palm trees – and heraldic pennants held by the Thames watermen on the good ship *Nore* as we went upriver from the Tower. There was a Rolls-Royce just for me, to take me back to Cheapside, where we got stuck in the traffic. I felt, after all that drink and waving, like Princess Margaret on a bad day.

10 November

I left Ironmonger Lane in state at 10.20 for St Paul's Cathedral Matins, a dullish, unimaginative service. It was a very long march up the west front steps and nave, all the way to our seats in front of the Lord Mayor's throne in the Quire.

We were absolutely freezing afterwards at the wreath-laying ceremony at the Royal Exchange. I noticed that the pavement is inscribed with the words, 'The Earth is the Lord's and the fullness thereof.'

11 November

I returned to Ironmonger Lane with the Lord Mayor and Sheriffs at 5 p.m. for photographs, and then to the Guildhall for the presentations at 6 p.m. The Archbishop of Canterbury arrived clutching his security pass, of which I relieved him. I said I thought he would be all right. At the banquet I said my 'Atlantic to the Adriatic and London to St Petersburg' Grace, making my point about Europe, standing behind the Prime Minister. The only non-dull speech was the Lord Chancellor's. I fell asleep during the PM's.

Somewhat bleary-eyed, I discarded my finery after the week of pomp and ceremony and returned to rather more prosaic duties (and food) at St Mary-le-Bow. The very next day, however, there was a sad and unexpected epilogue to add to my experiences of the previous week.

12 November

The *Times* journalist Matthew Parris drew 140 people for his Dialogue today. He was rather attacking about Jesus: Jesus wouldn't like all these City churches. This was difficult to answer.

Later I was telephoned by a man to say that he'd been arrested this morning at 7.15. I took a taxi in torrential rain to Hampstead to see him. After that sad interview, I got hold of Bernard Dawson who promised to help. He's a real brick with people who are in trouble. At the Lord Mayor's Banquet yesterday this poor man was confidently speaking of his certainty that he was about to be made a peer of the realm. I wonder if he feels that the banquet yesterday was Belshazzar's Feast: *Mene, mene, tekel, upharsin* – 'You have been tried in the balance and found wanting.'

November continued with a foggy visit to the enormous and viceregal Haileybury School, where I had been invited to preach. Holy Communion in the domed chapel was accompanied by an excellent choir, and all the pupils seemed to be bigger than me. Then I headed north to Edinburgh, to preach and dine with Richard Holloway who was shortly to be made Primus of Scotland. On a tour round Holyrood Palace I was struck by the intense romance of the place.

Then we were into December, and I began Advent by going to High Mass at All Saints, Margaret Street. The silence before Mass was impressive, and there was an excellent sermon from John Simpson, the Dean of Canterbury. Later that day I went to a most invigorating carol service in St Paul's Cathedral. There were thousands of people in the congregation. Very slowly, the choir began to sing in the vast darkness:

> O equal to thy Father thou
> Gird on thy fleshly mantle now
> The weakness of our mortal state
> With deathless might invigorate.[8]

Rows of tiny day boys, Eton-suited, clutched huge candles, goggle-eyed with wonder. As the choir processed around the building, and light gradually pushed back the darkness, St Paul's came alive.

2 December

I went to the Mall Galleries for an exhibition of paintings donated by the artists for our Palumbo campaign. I bought, for £250, an Alan Powers collage of Number One Poultry. I had a talk with Jenny Freeman. Jenny's husband Roger came into the exhibition and whisked me off in his ministerial motor car to the House of Commons for cod and chips in the Police Canteen.

---

8 Words from *Veni Redemptor Gentium* by St Ambrose (340–97).

7 December

At Codford we moved Ruth Watson, tearful, cross and upset, out of the guest bedroom and into her cottage in the old estate office. We have made this cottage for her at vast expense, taking out a second mortgage at goodness knows what personal penury, and now she doesn't want it.

Ruth had been dividing her time between her original home in Friern Barnet and the rectory lodgings in Cheapside, as well as occasionally using a spare bedroom and bathroom in Old Wool Cottage. When Andrew and Don bought the empty half of the property, we decided to do something about housing her permanently in Codford, and went to some trouble to convert the old estate office and attics into a self-contained cottage with its own garden. She had become attached to her room in the main cottage, however, and was at first reluctant to move. Soon, however, she came to value and enjoy her own little home. It was unfortunate that, later on, we could not afford to run the place without help and Ruth's cottage had to be put up for rent. Ruth was duly moved back into the main house. In retrospect, this harrying from pillar to post must have been very unpleasant, but we had set out with the best of intentions and only reluctantly accepted the limitations imposed by our finances.

12 December

At a drinks party at Grocers' Hall given by Phyllida and Andrew Stewart-Roberts for their daughter Lucy's wedding, Sir David Ramsbotham was very funny about how his mother used to shout at Ruth Watson in Welsh. When Ruth was nanny to Sir David, apparently she sometimes drove David's mother mad. When beyond endurance, Mrs Ramsbotham would shout at Ruth in Welsh, to which Ruth would reply, 'It's no good shouting at me in Welsh because I don't know what you're saying.'

14 December

I am in retreat with the nuns at Fairacres. It was cold all night. At dawn there was thick fog and ice, and a newspaper headline announced that Oxford last night was the coldest place in Britain.

At the 9.15 Mass of St John of the Cross we sang this translation by E. Alison Peers:

> O heavenly Truth, that here dost shine
> A light our path to guide
> Set by a hand unseen, Divine
> To all revealed, to none denied
> On high, yet at our side.

I put out the light and watched the grey, twig-shuttered mist darken into night between 4 and 4.20 p.m. I prayed in the chapel for half an hour, using this morning's lovely hymn to go back over my adoption and childhood and up to ordination, full of thankfulness.

17 December

My dear old secretary Helen Lever's funeral took place today at St James's, Friern Barnet, with lots of elderly and very few young people. The casket I clasped in my arms as I carried it to the graveside felt warm and there was a nice, contented feel about it as I poured Helen's ashes into the grave.

24 December

I am 47 today. Wendy Evans gave me a nineteenth-century print of an eighteenth-century parson all got up in state clothes, very fat and pleased with himself, exactly like the Lord Mayor's Chaplain today.

Andrew took me off later to St Anthony's, Nunhead, which I am looking after during its interregnum. It is a huge, gloomy, post-war rebuilt barn housing the reredos from the old St Antholin's, Watling Street, in the City, a church done up after the war by Lawrence King, who was also instrumental in rebuilding St Mary-le-Bow.

25 December

Christmas in London. Sunlight streaming almost too brightly into St Paul's Cathedral. A maundering sermon from the old Dean at Matins, then a very good sermon from the Bishop of London at Mass, at which I adminstered Communion to puzzled Japanese tourists.

Brilliantly decorated dining room at Bernard's flat, and dinner with David, Tim, Paul and Andrew – borscht and roast goose.

The year ended in Amsterdam, where I stayed with Wim. At midnight on New Year's Eve fireworks exploded above the city, so we all went out on the streets, thick with the smell of cordite, and wished 1992 well. The past year had been an important one. Don Dunford had died, of course, but the year had been full of positive things as well as sadness. The USSR had effectively ended, Mrs Thatcher's reign had come to a full stop, the first Affirming Catholicism conference had taken place, I had been made Lord Mayor's Chaplain, and Ruth was now safely installed in her own cottage at Codford. What was in store for 1992?

The Progress of the Spoils

On New Year's Day in Amsterdam we watched more fireworks on the television, as Sky News showed a display exploding over Yeltsin's Kremlin in Moscow. The previous night we had enjoyed listening to a guest playing Telemann, Bach and Purcell on her violin, and the musical theme continued on the first day of 1992. We watched the broadcast of a concert from war-torn Dubrovnik, and I appreciated the beauty of the music in the Oude Church – *'Te Geven Door Herman Van Vliet'*, the lovely 'Faith Shall Light the Lamp of Science' tune by Volckmar. Then duty called me back to London and a fresh year at St Mary-le-Bow.

9 January

I read the Beatitudes to the Court of Common Council this morning at St Lawrence Jewry, at a sort of City 'opening of term' service.

In the evening there was a dinner for members of the local governing bodies in Greater London. I made the first Grace out of the Lord Mayor's article in today's *Evening Standard*. 'Rather political, Padre,' three people said. For the second time, I drank out of the silver goblet given to the Lord Mayor's Chaplain by Bishop Gerald Ellison. How strange that Bishop Gerald, who terrified me when I was a University Chaplain and he was the Lord Bishop of London, should have given to the City a silver goblet for the use of the Lord Mayor's Chaplain on state occasions, and that I of all people should now be in that office, drinking from that cup.

11 January

In the Lord Mayor's car to the Guildhall for the Children's Party. Many of the little mites looked quite overcome. The hokey cokey was rather more lively than 'Scipio'. I think we should come into state banquets doing the hokey cokey instead of having 'Scipio'. There were only two Ninja Turtles among all the children, some Mozarts, a lot of flappers, and two Christmas puddings.

21 January

The Bishop of London, Dr David Hope, arrived at 12.50 for his 1.05 Dialogue, which made me sweat a bit. It's always alarming when guests don't come at 12.30.

In the afternoon I visited St Paul's Cathedral Library and was taken around by Canon Halliburton. The library is a vast, seventeenth-century collection of Bishop Compton's books. 'He was not a scholar,' said John Haliborange (as he's known), 'but a gentleman who bought what a gentleman should.'

28 January

I went to Harrow School, where I was met by James Powell, the Chaplain, and taken first to tea with Ron Swan, the Vicar of St Mary's, in his vast Victorian vicarage absolutely cascading with books. The servants' quarters are now a retreat centre that sleeps 10.

There were 250 fifth- and sixth-formers in chapel going through the coughing routine. I concentrated on getting their attention without saying, 'Will you please stop coughing,' and managed to reduce them to quietness, if not attention. Pleased with myself, I turned to the final page of the sermon and found I had left it in London. I was unable to remember what was on it, so I think the boys won.

February began in fog so thick that the upper part of the drum of St Paul's dome was completely obscured. It ended with me taking Ruth Watson to see the *Making of Saxon Britain* exhibition at the British Museum as a special treat, but when we got there we found that she had left her glasses at home and could not see anything.

The meat of the month was spent dealing with developments which followed the making of an *Everyman* programme for the BBC about the state of the Diocese of London. In the course of the programme I said that the refusal of John Hughes, the Bishop of Kensington, to let women act as Deacons, even though they were ordained Deacons in his area, was illegal. This produced a series of angry letters from the Bishop, demanding a retraction. Timothy Raphael, then Archdeacon of Middlesex, said to me, 'Pity you used the word "illegal". I would have used the word "appalling", but publish and be damned.'

Roger Freeman, now Minister of Transport, came for a Dialogue and lunch afterwards at the Grocers'. He was held up in Whitehall on his way to Cheapside by a bomb scare, and I felt it was appropriate for a Minister of Transport to be delayed by traffic.

As the month wore on, women who had said they would stand by me if push came to shove legally over the Bishop of Kensington gradually faded back into the woodwork – having been advised by families, friends and incumbents that it would not be 'wise' to get involved.

12 February

After teaching in the Choir School, I went in my clerical garb to the Comedy Theatre, where Patricia Routledge had organized a ticket for me to see her in Alan Bennett's *Talking Heads*. It was breathtaking theatre. Patricia introduced me to Alan Bennett afterwards in her dressing room, where we had a glass of Vino Verdi – 'Ladies' tipple, my dear.' Then she took me out to dinner at Café Fish. Derek Jacobi and a stream of others came to congratulate her at the table, including a couple who had come specially from Paris. Everybody was so polite and apologetic for interrupting, but just wanted to say 'thank you'.

23 February

Oxford. I got to Balliol just in time to preach at Evensong. There was a bold, sexy, atheist don's wife at dessert in the Senior Common Room. I escaped by talking with the Chaplain Douglas du Pre and Professor Peter Hinchcliffe, another 'Off-Catholic', as he cleverly put it – like 'off-white'. Peter has been made Professor of Ecclesiastical History and is to live in Rowan's old house at Christchurch, the Lady Margaret Professorship having been frozen.[1]

---

1 Rowan Williams was made Bishop of Monmouth in 1991, later becoming Archbishop of Wales.

I was put to bed in the vast dignity of the Master's Lodge, but was disturbed by an intruder, who jumped through my bathroom window, ran to the bedroom window and jumped out of that. 'Can I help you?' I asked in that feeble English way, addressing his disappearing form. Next the Master arrived, followed by a College servant. As I was wearing only boxer shorts, I didn't feel able to get out of bed to receive these important personages, so I watched this Whitehall farce unfold around me from my bed. Then the police came in, followed by a second visit from the Master. Evidently it's quite common for students to try to break into the Master's Lodge at Balliol.

24 February

To add insult to injury, there was no hot water this morning and a telephone call to the Porter's Lodge produced none. I hope Lord Stockton, Edward Heath, Lord Jenkins of Hillhead and Queen Mary, who all featured in the Visitors' Book in my room, fared better in their day.

3 March

From the stage to the pulpit – Patricia Routledge came to Dialogue. This actress has made a place for herself in people's hearts, and 300 people were in church. Miss Routledge is a Yorkshire woman full of common sense, with the professional actor's careful craftsmanship, allied to the Queen Mother's gracious kindness. The combination is irresistible. Michael Kenny scribbled me a note which said that today was magical and strangely moving. I sent her this in my thank-you letter.

4 March

Ash Wednesday. At lunchtime the William Byrd *Four Part Mass* was exquisitely sung, and there was a marvellous tramp, very devout, at the Communion step amongst all the handsome young.

At 3 o'clock old Edward Carpenter came and prayed over the ashes of Joseph and Betty McCulloch, which I poured into the cavity in front of the crypt chapel altar. Betty's ashes, done in Canada, were big bone shards, like Roman cinerary remains, not Ash Wednesday ash, like Joseph's.

After Joseph McCulloch died in 1990, it had taken some time to come to the decision that St Mary-le-Bow was indeed the right place for the interment of his ashes, together with those of his wife Betty, who died in 1982. Even when the decision had been taken, complex ecclesiastical permissions had to be granted, including a faculty from the Chancellor of the Diocese for the interment of human remains. Witnessing the interment was a small gathering of Joseph's immediate family, and the lady who had looked after him in his old age after Betty's death. The stone marking the spot in front of the crypt altar and the beautiful memorial tablet to Joseph and Betty in the Blessed Sacrament Chapel in the main church were both designed by Kindersley, described by Professor Owen Chadwick as 'that master of epigraphy'. He also designed Michael Ramsey's memorial tablet in Canterbury.

6 March

I spent the morning at Canary Wharf, at the Lifting London conference, which was all about identifying and encouraging leaders of various London groups and communities. On the way there I found myself next to Sir Ralph Dahrendorf on the river bus. He asked me why the Archbishop of Canterbury is not John Habgood. I tried to explain, then tried to lift the gloom by telling my Balliol story, which I thought he would appreciate, being now the Master of an Oxford college himself.

On my way back from the conference I found myself next to Baroness Blackstone, who asked me, 'Why is John Habgood not the Archbishop of Canterbury? He's the most highly regarded of the bishops.' So I again tried to explain.

Isn't this curious? A non-believing Jew and a lapsed Roman Catholic, both hugely admiring of the Archbishop of York and puzzled by the Church of England's inability to give him the top job.

18 March

A limo took me to St Lawrence Jewry for a thanksgiving service for the centenary of the SSAFA.[2] I sat in the row behind the Queen, next to her In-Waitings, who included Lady Susan Hussey. The Queen sang all the hymns with conviction, hardly needing to glance at her order of service.

At the reception, Lady Hussey told me that Her Majesty had said, 'I'm so glad we're going to church this morning.' I asked Lady Hussey who told the Queen unpleasant truths when it was necessary to do so. 'I do,' she said. This was reassuring. Her Majesty was by turn sombre and dignified and then vivacious and girlish. She sipped at a gin and Dubonnet like her Mama, I was surprised to see, having always been told that she only drinks white wine.

25 March

Lady Day. I took a train to Hereford, where Andrew Mottram met me, rushed me off to Evensong in All Saints and then a gin and tonic at the Palace with the Bishop. The Palace is an exquisite house dating back to 1180, with three acres of gardens and a new maze. Merriol Oliver, the Bishop's wife, sitting in her lovely Palace drawing room, said, as you do, 'We must get rid of the Tories.'

I preached at the High Mass in All Saints to encourage the congregation to restore it. Andrew has just had the architect's report on the dire condition of the building. Getting it right is going to cost a very great deal of money. Merriol came to the service. The Bishop didn't because he was chairing an Amnesty International meeting, for which he got full marks and a puff from the preacher.

30 March

At 10 a.m. I went over to the Midland Bank for coffee with the new chairman, Sir Peter Walters. At 10.30 I rose to

---

2 The Soldiers', Sailors' and Airmen's Families Association.

leave, having only been asked for a quarter of an hour, but at 11.05 he was still talking to me. He told me that Mrs Thatcher's downfall was a direct result of Elspeth Howe losing Chevening and Theresa Lawson being asked to leave Dorney Wood and refusing to do so at the beginning of the Lawsons' summer holiday with the children.

Of course, everybody has a theory about Mrs Thatcher's downfall, apart from the obvious one of hubris, i.e. going on believing you are right when very large numbers of your own supporters believe you are wrong. The general election that was about to take place should have come much earlier. It seemed to me that the fascination of Mrs Thatcher's character and public behaviour over Europe had distracted us from the democratic need to go to the polls when the ruling party was so clearly split. As always in public life, there was an intriguing intermingling of personal aggravations (as in the anecdote about the Howes losing Chevening and the Lawsons being asked to leave Dorney Wood), and perfectly proper, though politically destructive, disagreements (in this case over Europe). There were also urgent questions about domestic and financial policy to consider. I was looking forward to election day. There seemed to be a very good chance indeed that the Tories would be out this time.

9 April

General Election Day. I voted Liberal Democrat in the polling station at St Bride's, Fleet Street, and met Sarah Mann on her way to do the same.

I tried to calm down the staff at Ironmonger Lane and to persuade the City Sword Bearer Colonel Tucker not to agree with the Lord Mayor, who is working himself up into a frenzy after reading about some left-wing ecclesiastic. The Lord Mayor suspects a plot from the Bishop of Birmingham to criticize the City at tomorrow's United Guild Service. Well, why *shouldn't* bishops criticize the City?

Then I gave a speech in the hideously vile National Westminster Banking Hall, in which I described a conversation I had this morning with a blind man in Cheapside about his hopes for a change of government. It made for some angry mutterings and, indeed, two walkouts. One of those waited outside and went for me in the street: 'They should help themselves. I gave a lot of money to come to this lunch today, not to hear anti-government rubbish.' This, I confess, rather shook me, as did the faces of wealthy, arrogant anger. Some, however, did applaud.

Back in Cheapside, I heard confessions, celebrated and preached at the 5.45 p.m. Mass, and then dashed off to Ironmonger Lane and the Guildhall for the Prime Wardens' Banquet. I managed a neutral first Grace, but before giving the second I talked the Lord Mayor down again about tomorrow's service in the cathedral, from the advantageous position of standing behind the throne and whispering in his ear.

I sat next to Edna, Lady Healey. She was charming, dignified, in appearance really rather like Queen Mary but more intelligent – a writer, biographer, wife of a statesman, leagues above most of our City ladies in their finery, from a different and better world than many of them.

From the banquet I went on to the Old Bailey and the Sheriff's party. I left at 1.30 a.m. and came home to watch the Labour vote slipping away until 2.30.

10 April

I got up at 5 a.m. and saw Neil Kinnock concede defeat. This was utterly depressing and I found it hard to say Mass at 8.30. The defeat is so unexpected and sad, and then I had to endure the Tory triumph at the United Guild Service in St Paul's. Nevertheless, we had a hard-hitting and intelligent sermon from the Bishop of Birmingham.

At 5.30 p.m. I rang Patrick Mayhew in Kent, where, unsurprisingly, he has been returned for Tunbridge Wells. I talked to both him and Jean, saying, 'It's taken me until 5.30 to be able to talk to *any* of my Tory friends.' Patrick said that I might have more news tomorrow. They're coming up to London.

11 April

Last night a 100-pound bomb demolished St Mary Axe and the Baltic Exchange, killing three people and injuring 90.

I heard the Lord Mayor speak clearly and forcefully on Radio 4, then I put on my dog collar and went over to the Lord Mayor's House, where he was having a mug of tea at his desk. I talked to him for 20 minutes and gave him a blessing. This is where a priest can be useful.

Then I had to rush to get ready for the Confirmation Service in St Paul's. In the vestry the Bishop of London said, 'A certain realism is dawning as far as the Bishop of Kensington is concerned.'

This morning the telephone rang and it was Patrick Mayhew. 'I'm ringing from Downing Street. I need my Chaplain's prayers. The Prime Minister has asked me to go to Northern Ireland and I've accepted.' I'm appalled for his and Jean's safety, but he has the job he's uniquely qualified to do and will do well. The Secretary of State for Northern Ireland has a curious Cabinet post, where in practical effect he runs Northern Ireland as a separate fiefdom, acting both as an old-fashioned Viceroy or Governor General and the Prime Minister of the Province. Jean doesn't fear assassination, but does fear kidnapping. I wouldn't be too keen on assassination, myself.

I spent that evening and the next day worrying about the Mayhews and the City bomb in equal measure. It was astonishing to discover how much collateral damage had been inflicted on buildings quite a long way away from the initial blast. About a quarter of the Square Mile seemed to be out of action – thanks to the way the blast had been directed along the narrow ravines and gullies between the high office blocks. It was a great mercy that the bomb exploded when it did, after most people had gone home, otherwise there would have been considerably greater loss of life. I was away from St Mary-le-Bow when the bomb went off, so did not hear the blast. When I heard the news, my first thought was, 'What has happened to St Mary-le-Bow?' I was mightily relieved to return home and discover the church to be unscathed. With no resident parishioners, there was no one to be comforted or looked after, except for the Lord Mayor, of course. As I was his Chaplain, I tried to do this. Sir Brian is an exemplary man in a crisis, and said exactly the right things on television with the requisite amount of firmness and determination. It was a long time, however, before the City was back to normal.

13 April

The Mayhews appeared on the news in Belfast today, presumably outside Hillsborough or Stormont. Jean's face was held at a funny angle and I tackled her about this later. She said she'd got something the matter with one of her contact lenses, making one eye weep, and she couldn't afford to appear before the population of Northern Ireland at her first public appearance weeping.

17 April

Good Friday. There was a sombre and dignified Matins, beautifully sung with a slow and stately Litany in procession, at 10 a.m. in St Paul's. Afterwards I walked through the horrible 1960s Printers' Buildings around Fetter Lane to make my confession in St Albans', Holborn. Sat in John's Gaskell's study from 12 to 1.30 p.m., reading with a cat on my lap. I stayed on for the 1.30 p.m. liturgy.

I returned to St Paul's Cathedral to preach to about 300 people at Evensong. There weren't enough books for them, only one hymn (and that was unannounced), and tourists were turned away relentlessly. There were no canons present except for Christopher Hill. It was a depressing experience of the unlovedness of the St Paul's set-up, but today in St Alban's, Holborn, I felt the presence of Jesus as Father Gaskell brought in the Blessed Sacrament. It was a curious experience of Real Presence, which I have not had in this way before.

18 April

Holy Saturday. In Wiltshire I said Evensong alone at 10.30 p.m. after supper in Ruth's cottage, then I took her to the Vigil in the parish church at 11.30. There were only 10 people present, including the Vicar's wife at the organ and his daughter. There was no sermon, no explanation, no introduction, no care, no order of service, the whole liturgy hurried through as duty done. This is the peasant religion people must have been used to in eighteenth-century France before the Revolution. There was, however, a strange charm in its hopelessness.

Back in London after Easter, I discovered an invitation from the Mayhews to supper at Admiralty House. On the way there, I walked through Soho trying in vain to find some decent wine for Patrick, but was forced yet again into the Europa Foods store in Trafalgar Square, where I picked up two bottles of 1985 claret.

Patrick was in stockinged feet because of painful new shoes. I sat on the floor and read the Irish and English press cuttings about their first weekend in Ireland, while Patrick talked about unemployment amongst the Roman Catholics and his good opinion of Mary Robinson, the Irish President. They had already called on Cardinal Cahal Brendan Daly, Roman Catholic Archbishop of Armagh, who was surprised by the call and even more surprised to be asked for a blessing. His Eminence was dead set against integrated schools, of course, and also, being a shrewd politician, gave nothing away. Jean had visited a policeman who had his legs blown off, but no nurse would speak to her in the Victoria Hospital. I realized that a great deal of the horror of Northern Ireland was kept from those of us on the mainland. Jessie, the Mayhews' old sheepdog, was suffering from bad breath and Patrick was very funny describing the affectionate bestowal of this upon various Ulster Unionist grandees.

23 April

After a busy morning, I struggled into state robes and just got to Ironmonger Lane in time to get into the Rolls for St Lawrence Jewry, about three feet down the road. Exhausted, I found it an effort today even to read the Bidding Prayer, which is all the Lord Mayor's Chaplain is required to do on the occasion of the Spital Sermon. The Bishop of Chelmsford preached well to the old buffers.

At luncheon, a footman filled all the claret glasses with port. How did he get all round the table without smelling the difference? How, indeed, did nobody else notice the difference?

I cut the Community Service Volunteers' reception at the Foreign Office which I'd said I would drop in on, and made instead for Dover and Calais, arriving in France at 8.15 and reaching Veurne in Belgium just after 9.00 p.m., securing a room in a seventeenth-century hotel on the market square.

After a few days with Wim in Amsterdam, Andrew and I drove south for a great Tilburg church crawl. We marvelled at a selection of extraordinary churches built during the Catholic triumphalism of the early part of the twentieth century when the authorities imagined, having crushed modernist intellectual freedom in Rome, that the educated Dutch would flock towards reactionary Catholic doctrine. It did not work, of course.

I journeyed back, refreshed, to London.

12 May

Dora Boatemah, a tiny and vivacious community project director from Brixton, clung to the edge of her pulpit for our 'Life in Brixton' Dialogue. It was all light years away from the evening with SSAFA at the Guildhall with Prince Michael of Kent, who does look exactly like Czar Nicholas II and stayed too long, so the rest of us couldn't leave. You can't leave before royalty – irritating.

Peter Brooke, whom Patrick has replaced as Secretary of State for Northern Ireland, was very funny about the butler at Hillsborough who retired last year. He had worked at Hillsborough Castle since 1947. When he thought it was time for people to leave, he would go in a stately way round the drawing room, putting out the lights. With a rare attack of self-control, I managed not to say that I knew the Mayhews.

Later on, Sir David Ramsbotham said to the Countess of Limerick, 'Do you want to meet the Duke of Wellington?'

'Not in the least', said Lady L., 'I want to go home like Victor. Come on!'

15 May

I woke at 4.20 this morning to the sound of the front door splintering, in fact being axed in. At first I imagined that Ruth had fallen down the stairs, so I rushed out and was startled, indeed amazed, to discover my splintered front door. The police responded in minutes to my telephone call, but

the man got away down Cheapside. I had left the intercon-
necting door to the vestibule open, so it was my fault.

21 May

I spent from 11.15 a.m. until 1 p.m. in Westminster Abbey
at the dreariest possible service to mark the 150th anniversary of the Diocese of Europe. The whole thing was redolent of
c.1958, with all the lessons from the Authorized Version
of the Bible and Princess Margaret present, straight out of
Spitting Image.

Then I went in the boiling heat to St George in the East to
visit Father Gilhean Craig. He had found a man hanging in his
church and a woman dead in the basement of the Old
Rectory. This church is in Andrew's practice, physically only
one stop on the Docklands Light Railway from my City neighbour St Mary's, Woolnoth, but light years away in all other
senses.

I went to bed thinking about the day's contrasts: the stiff,
unimaginative, unyielding indifference of the ecclesiastical
Establishment at its worst in the Abbey this morning, the
dreary face of the royal personage, bored and lifeless, spoilt
and old; then the terrible deprivation and poverty of the East
End, just on the doorstep of the astonishing wealth, influence and confidence of the Square Mile.

June saw three very different guests appearing at our Tuesday
Dialogues. The famous broadcaster Jonathan Dimbleby was open,
friendly and warm. Elizabeth Hoodless, Director of the
Community Service Volunteers, whom I had thought was a
Methodist, was not and did not like it when I introduced her as
one. Nellie Vahter, the young and very beautiful Latvian chargée
d'affaires, offered us a fascinating glimpse into Baltic politics.

5 June

Our faithful old Churchwarden Harry Oram died recently, and
the memorial service we held for him today went well. The
Lord Mayor's address was personal and warm. The congregation included Lord Stockton, Lord Fitzalan-Howard, five

ex-Lord Mayors and the New Zealand High Commissioner. The bells rang half-muffled.

In the afternoon I went to the Science Museum in South Kensington to have a look at the revamped dinosaurs, which bite and scream. They are so much more exciting than the boring old bones that were there when I was a child, but I noticed that some small children looked, and were, terrified at the similitude.

22 June

In the evening I went to the seventieth birthday party of the Honourable Margaret Fox in Clerkenwell,[3] where I talked to Charles Roundell's sister Lydia about doubt, and to Lord Rayleigh about eternal damnation. I walked home wondering what it is that makes people interested in the idea of eternal damnation. This could have been a nineteenth-century conversation, at a time when orthodox, conservative opinion such as Lord Rayleigh's was outraged by Christians like the forward-thinking theologian F.D. Maurice, who said that God took no pleasure in eternally poking the damned about in hell. There could be damnation, he thought, but not the 'eternal punishment of the wicked'. It's strange how the most perverted religious ideas linger on when both faith and practice have withered. I spend so much of my time, as tonight with Lydia Roundell, saying that doubt is a good thing.

All in all, June was a busy month. I blessed the civil marriage of Eddie Ashton, the manager of the local City branch of the Midland Bank, complete with horse and carriage. Then I held a marriage service in the crypt for a couple who had lived faithfully together for 17 years, so it was not a bad omen that the bride wore black velvet. We also had the funeral of Julia Roberts, one of the great gang of waitresses at the Grocers' Hall. We set out from Cheapside for a crematorium where the tiny chapel was not big enough for all the people, nor did it have enough books. Julia had

---

3 Margaret Fox is the widow of the Venerable George Fox MC, who had been Vicar of St Ethelreda's, Fulham, where I went for a time in my teens. He later became Archdeacon of Wisbech.

an earth burial, and there was much weeping at the graveside. Working-class funerals, I reflected, were more honest about this than middle-class ones and therefore easier.

3 July

Wiltshire. I have been feeling Godless, tired, useless and a bit bored. I couldn't pray at all before Mass in the crypt today, but by the time I got to the country and said Evensong with Andrew in the Codford chapel, things were deepening again. The way forward in these moments of difficulty in religion is to be attentive and meditative in prayer. Trust is the way back. I've been feeling tired and lonely for some time, probably an invitation to retreat.

7 July

This evening I attended the state dinner for the bishops at the Guildhall. The Archbishop of Canterbury made a speech in which he said how marvellous the City was, what good people the Aldermen were, what a marvellous example they all set, and what a privilege it was to be in this historic place. The Aldermen loved this, and purred and stroked their miniver gowns, swelling and exhaling with self-satisfaction. The Archbishop of York, however, rose at 10.45 p.m. and corrected this with a few deft remarks. He was masterly, managing to insert just a little criticism and prick the bubble of complacency. I congratulated him afterwards and asked him if I could have a copy of what he had so carefully said. 'Well,' said he, 'I didn't write it down. I just made a few jottings on my menu.'

I sat next to Dr John Fenwick, one of the Archbishop's advisors on foreign relations. He told me with great confidence that the ordination of women vote will be defeated in November, and the next time too, and the issue will then fade away. This is the kind of rational advice Lambeth Palace is getting.

14 July

The Queen was in St Paul's today for the Order of St Michael and St George service, in amazing blue-mantled splendour with a dazzling diamond tiara, the state carpet on the steps outside. In attendance were lots of ancient and distinguished Knight Commanders, including Lord Carrington. My black preaching scarf came adrift while I was ascending the west steps, forming a train behind me, but a kind Sheriff tidied me up as we stood waiting for Her Majesty inside. It was a gorgeous spectacle, the cathedral sun-filled, and a full orchestra playing: France in 1783, just before the Revolution.

In the afternoon I went off to Miss Cartilage to be manipulated. Isn't it wonderful having a chiropractor called Miss Cartilage?

21 July

The Lord Mayor took me in his official car to Buckingham Palace. It was odd being on the inside of the place – heavily used, battered, impressive but not beautiful, late Regency with a lot of Sèvres china, badly lit à la 1961, and bad studio portraits of Ernest of Hanover and all that crowd. There was a nuclear sun blazing in the garden, which is like a very well kept provincial park with a really horrible municipal herbaceous border of screaming, clashing colours.

One of the great advantages of Adrian Barnes, the City Remembrancer, is that, being so tall, he was able to reach over the heads of people to get me some cake and an iced coffee – the crush being such as to prevent a small person getting anywhere near the food.

I came upon fellow guests Andrew and Phyllida Stewart-Roberts, who stood grandly, foursquare in the middle of the lawn, looking beautiful and receiving the people. 'Have you met Lord Justice Blowfield? This is our friend Victor Stock...' We just escaped the Bishop of Kensington, who was fixing me with a basilisk stare and whose wife, elbowing him savagely, was trying to propel him towards me. Phyllida took me by the arm, said she'd just remembered an appointment, and rushed me away.

I glimpsed the Prince and Princess of Wales actually talking to each other for a change. Strangely, there was absolutely no frisson of excitement about this event. The royals were too far away.

23 July

There was a Central Line meeting at the Deanery at Westminster today. It was wonderfully energized by Sister Lavinia Byrne of the Institute of the Blessed Virgin Mary – or, as the Dean described her Order at the Abbey the other day, the Institute of the British Virgin Mary.

27 July

I took the train from Fenchurch Street to the English seaside world of Chalkwell to see June Judd-Goodwin. Jan Barham, a decent, sensible and kindly person, soon to be ordained Deacon, is the sister in charge at Fairhaven, the hospice of which June is a member. I talked to all the patients, saw everything, talked to the staff, listened to the difficulties and the joys and conducted a meditation on Psalm 139 for everyone. Sister Jan told me about a priest on television who said he almost fell off his chair when Bishop David Hope answered a letter he had written. That was me. It's sobering not to have a more memorable face.

29 July

I have come to Amersham to stay with Field Marshal Sir Nigel Bagnall. He was waiting for me, not in gold epaulettes and spurs, but in a denim shirt and torn jeans. Blackwell Hall Lodge, where he and Anna live, was the gardener's cottage but has grown to twice its original size, as cottages tend to. I had a glass of whisky and a hot bath, then a brief tour of some of the lovely gardens, all made out of rough field and pasture by Nigel over the last 24 years. At 11.45 p.m. Nigel said to me, 'Victor, you look absolutely exhausted. Go to bed,' which is the kind of military command I appreciate.

Then came August, and the holidays began with a train to Utrecht from Amsterdam. At the Caterina Convent there was an absorbing ecclesiastical exhibition which included some film from the 1930s, '40s and '50s, reminding us of the now vanished world of the Princes of the Church. Boggled, we stared at the winter and summer trains, the cloaks and hats, including something called a 'pontifical hat', skull caps, birettas, mitres, whole sets of stockings, gloves, shoes, tunicles and dalmatics, chasubles and copes, chalices, pontifical books, pectoral crosses and a hideous carved oak writing desk, all somehow madly deranged. It was a relief after all that millinery to enter the cool intelligence of St Peter's, the Reformation's Walloon church, with its wonderful crypt dating from 1040, even earlier than ours in Cheapside.

A little later in August, Andrew and I spent a few days visiting Auntie Libby Jennings in Salcombe. She was not a real aunt, of course, but we had known each other long enough to develop an aunt–nephew relationship. Her house was spotless and completely over-run by tiny model animals and even tinier flower vases. One can only take a limited amount of this, and we felt particularly aggrieved by a toy mouse in a basket, which looked coyly up at us whenever we sat at the dinner table. It was begging to be vandalized. Andrew took to hissing, 'Poke the mousy!' at every opportunity.

Carrying this catchphrase with us, we drove on up to North Wales to visit Alun Fon Jones, a teacher at St Paul's Cathedral Choir School who worshipped at St Mary-le-Bow, and his uncle Mickey Burn MC, who had just turned 80 and was a very sweet man, poet, playwright and war hero.

11 August

At Mickey's house, we drank gin and vermouth overlooking the Snowdonia backdrop, or rather, Snowdonia was overlooking us. The house has an extensive and erudite writer's library and good pictures. There is not a single toy mousy and, in contrast to the French polish and glitter of Libby's house, everything here is leaning and crumbling.

12 August

Breakfast was brought to our bedrooms, even though we had said that we would go down for it.

'Will you have eggs?' asked Captain Mickey.

'No, thank you.'

'Boiled?'

And later, 'Have a bath.'

'No, we've had our baths, thank you.'

'Have a bath.'

This has provided the counterpoint for the day. Added to the oft-repeated cries of 'Stroke the mousy!' or 'Poke the mousy!' is the new antiphon, 'Have a bath!'

It was clearly a summer for such sayings. From North Wales, via a preaching engagement at the Edinburgh Festival, we went on to Professor Nancy Lambton's sheep-filled Cheviot Hills. There, at tea in her neat bungalow, we were taken back to the nursery with the question, 'Crust or crumb?' The next day Nancy drove us, extremely slowly, to Lindisfarne, where we listened to a choir from Belfast singing movingly in the church before we drove back, extremely slowly, for more tea and further cries of 'Crust or crumb?' I was rather sorry to return to a catchphrase-free London in the last week of the month, although there were further amusements in store before the autumn season got underway.

22 August

The papers are full of the Duchess of York with her financial advisor sucking her toes. Very Regency. There is a look of Queen Caroline of Brunswick about Fergie.

23 August

I preached at St Paul's Cathedral for the third time this year at a particularly dreary Evensong. At least the sermon was to the satisfaction of the Head Verger and the Canon in Residence.

The *Yorkshire Post* rang to ask what I was going to say about the royal family. 'Not much,' I said, and didn't.

Early in September, Jean Mayhew entertained me with a description of how moving it had been to have the Princess of Wales in Northern Ireland a few days earlier. Women had literally danced in the streets for sheer joy, hugging each other. How much pleasure that woman gave.

Then we had a splendid wedding for Evangelical Christian Eryl O'Day and Jewish Nick Gold, who came from a largely Orthodox family, none of whom had ever been in a church before. I spoke about the God of Abraham, Isaac and Jacob, and about God's love for us which can make us as happy, when we accept it, as those women dancing in the streets in Northern Ireland.

In the middle of September, interest rates went from 2 per cent to 12 per cent, then up to 15 per cent and back down to 12 per cent. Even I recognized that something was going wrong. On 16 September, 'Black Wednesday', the pound was devalued, we left the Exchange Rate Mechanism, and interest rates were cut to 10 per cent.

Other, less worldly, concerns were soon claiming my attention.

22 September

As part of the Decade of Evangelism, a group of Evangelicals came for a vigil from 6 p.m. to 6 a.m. In the event, nobody came who wasn't already a paid-up member of the Evangelical brigade, which is what I think very often happened with Free Church Missions when I was a child. We were all urged to turn to Jesus, but the people who came were people who had already made the turn. I would have judged the impact of such a mission on the area to be zilch. Likewise this evening.

9 October

I went to St Margaret's, Westminster, for the memorial service for Peter Jenkins, once my Dialogue guest and a hero of mine.[4] David Owen was detained in the Balkans, trying to broker peace, but in his place Michael Heseltine came straight from an emergency Cabinet meeting to read Donne's

---

4 Peter Jenkins was Deputy Editor of the *Independent*.

'Ask not for whom the bell tolls, it tolls for thee'. The irony, he said, would not have been lost on Peter. This was history as it happens, for today Heseltine finally came unstuck, taking the blame in the Commons for the disaster of declaring last Wednesday that 30 coal pits would cease production on Friday.

The Editor of the *Independent*, Andreas Whittam Smith, said to me, 'There were no fingerprints on Peter's sources.' Amusingly, at the back of the nave were Sir Bernard Ingham and Sir Charles Powell, the fingerprints.[5]

It was a dramatic occasion, which Peter Jenkins would have relished. His widow, Polly Toynbee, was proud and alone.

28 October

At St Andrew's, Holborn, this afternoon, the Gresham Lecture was given by Ambassador Baron Hermann von Richthofen, utterly splendid and inspiring, pleading for a united Germany in a united Europe. It was just what we wanted and needed. I told him so. The Vicar welcomed the Ambassador in German.

29 October

I stood in for David Burgess to take the First Footing Service at St Lawrence Jewry, blessing the foundations for the new east wing of the Guildhall. Burgess is unwell again. I quoted from Baron von Richthofen's lecture last night – 'deepening and enlarging' – and said generally encouraging things.

That evening, at drinks before the Bankers' Dinner, Alderman Anthony Bull produced a possible Grace: 'Lord, by good interest and less dogma may we be delivered from those who waver in the stresses of life.'

I showed this to the Governor of the Bank of England, who said, 'I would like to use this myself, and if I do so I will pay you royalties, but perhaps you can't quite use it tonight.'

---

5 Sir Bernard Ingham was Chief Press Secretary to the Prime Minister from 1979 to 1990. Sir Charles Powell was Private Secretary to the Prime Minister from 1984 to 1991.

My first Grace was about the common good, but during dinner I fished Bull's Grace out and discussed it with my French banker neighbour. Together, after a few drinks, we turned it into, 'Lord, by good interest and less recession, may prosperity be granted to the public purse.'

A footman was sent to my table after I had said this second Grace. 'Mr Lamont would like to speak to you, sir.'

When I went to his table, the Chancellor of the Exchequer said, 'May I use what you have just said in my speech?' and he opened by congratulating the Lord Mayor on his choice of Chaplain. 'He is clearly a man who understands the impact of recession – unusual among men of the Church.'

On 1 November the *Sunday Times* quoted all this, saying that the speakers at dinner 'were all upstaged by the Chaplain to the Lord Mayor'.

The going proved to be rather stickier at a banquet for the Sultan of Brunei on 4 November. 'The Chaplain has been to Brunei, Your Majesty,' said Prince Edward to the Sultan's wife. 'So that's at least two of us,' he added brightly. Her Majesty said nothing.

'I at least know where it is,' was my inept contribution to this conversation – the sort of helpful thing one inevitably blurts out in front of royalty. Again, Her Majesty said nothing and I began to wonder whether she had the faintest grasp of English.

Mercifully, the state trumpeters came to the rescue with a crashing fanfare. Their George IV uniform – velvet jockey caps, gold-embroidered tabards and mirror-like, thigh-length boots – was quite something and said a lot about George IV. We had cold lobster and slices of turkey for dinner, which was not a success. It was rather like Christmas dinner at the Rotary, trying to be posh.

11 November

The day of the vote on the ordination of women. It went through by two-thirds in the House of Laity. The bishops obviously thought it wasn't going to go through and behaved sourly. The Archbishop said there should be no applause or rejoicing, in the way we Anglicans have of snatching defeat from the jaws of victory. I was amazed and grateful and thought there might be a God after all.

12 November

Sir William Shapland and his secretary came to see me.[6] I was expecting him to give me a large contribution for the Globe Centre project. Instead, he stood in my sitting room and dressed me down for working on such a thing. 'Why are you risking your reputation in the City, when you are very highly regarded, to work with these people? They deserve all they get.' He asked me formally to withdraw my application to Bernard Sunley. 'We wouldn't dream of giving you a penny for these people,' he said.

It was a horrible and depressing interview, but I managed to remain calm and polite. Perhaps, I said, as an accountant he would be prepared to cast his eye over the way we presented our figures? Perhaps we could learn something from his expertise if he would give 20 minutes to doing this for me.

Shocked, I think, by this, he said, 'You don't want chicken feed. I could give you £1,000 from my current account.'

I said, 'Chicken feed would be of very great assistance, Sir William, in the circumstances.' So he pulled out his cheque book and wrote me personally a cheque for £1,000.

13 November

At the Drapers' Hall lunch before the handing over of one Lord Mayor to the next, I talked to HRH the Princess Royal about hot and cold rooms. The royal yacht *Britannia*, said the Princess, is absolutely freezing, 'but when you have 250 people to supper it soon heats up'. Princess Anne is the least awkward and most sensible of the royals – slim, twinkly, dignified and warm. Nevertheless, she lures one into silly conversational responses, which give the impression that one has a yacht too, when one doesn't even have a duck in one's bath.

---

6 Sir William Shapland was the Chairman of the Bernard Sunley Foundation, an enormously wealthy charitable foundation deriving from the property empire of Bernard Sunley, whose mother is commemorated in a tablet on the south side of the nave of St Mary-le-Bow. His secretary, the Revd Anthony Winter, usually dealt with charitable requests for Sir William, and I knew Anthony well. The foundation had made a generous contribution to the post-war rebuilding of St Mary-le-Bow and had always been friendly to me since my arrival in the City.

We then swept away to the Guildhall and the Silent Ceremony. Afterwards, in the Guildhall Yard, HRH walked over to me and said, 'Tell me, why do you have a collar inside your hat?'

'Well, Ma'am,' I replied, 'the Secondary and Under Sheriff changed out of his luncheon collar into his uniform collar and was still holding on to it at the Court of Aldermen. Realizing there was nowhere to put it down, I offered to relieve him of the encumbrance and popped it into my hat. How professional of you to spot that.'

'I have nothing else to do but watch. I spend a lot of my time watching,' said Princess Anne.

In the evening I saw *The Crying Game*. It is the most brilliant movie. It says all that needs to be said about Northern Ireland.

17 November

There were 19 people at early Mass. I was so worried about a man who thought he might discover today that he is HIV positive that, finding myself focusing on him during the celebration, I lost my place in the altar book. Later in the afternoon the man came to say, 'It's bad news.' I had arranged for a close friend of his to be here, who took him out for some champagne whilst I, trying to concentrate, settled down to the next customer, a lawyer from one of our big law firms.

25 November

Outside the Bow Wine Vaults, I was stopped by Sue who works there, because she wanted to talk to me about the vote on the ordination of women. A colleague came and joined her. This subject is interesting people outside the churches. It's not a problem to the people outside the churches at all.

27 November

A farewell Mass took place today for Father Malcolm Johnson, who leaves the City after 19 years. St Botolph's, Aldgate, was packed out – from the down-and-outs and the never-have-beens, to John Underwood, Peter Palumbo's solicitor, and us, the have-beens. There were lots of people with HIV and AIDS. Rabbi Lionel Blue queued for a blessing. If you didn't think the Christian religion was about anything before going to this marvellous affirmation of goodness, the sheer, tangible presence of all that means most would have convinced you utterly.

I sat with the man who has recently been diagnosed as HIV positive and just held him as he wept and wept. At the end of Mass, when we were all choked with emotion, one of the old lags at St Botolph's cried out, 'Anybody got a f***in' tissue?' It would have made a perfect headline.

In his 19 years in the City, Malcolm Johnson had made the crypt work with the homeless – originally a night shelter dealing with 300 people a night, giving them food, medical and social security advice, a chiropodist, a haircut, a friendly ear and somewhere out of the cold – into an amazingly successful Housing Association, with properly managed flats for formerly homeless people. St Botolph's had also become the centre of a Christian ministry to lesbian and gay people. The Lesbian and Gay Christian Movement (LGCM) used a room in the tower as their office for 11 years and many gay and lesbian people, particularly clergy, came to Malcolm for support and advice. It was a ministry requiring an extraordinary amount of both courage and discretion. The annual carol service for the gay community was always absolutely packed. Malcolm also had a significant ministry as pastor and counsellor to the well-heeled, heterosexual City, and was enormously loved and admired.

28 November

There was a lovely *Guardian* article today (not using the old lag's words from yesterday's service) about Malcolm Johnson and his work. The *Guardian* said, 'He is the eye of the storm, this humble man.' Being an out-gay in a happy, stable relationship with Robert all these years, he is disliked by the bishops and will never be given the job in the Church he deserves. The hypocrisy and fearfulness of the Church is sometimes more than can be borne.

1 December

The new Deputy Leader of the Labour Party, Margaret Beckett, was amusing, sensible and responsible at our Dialogue today. There were 150 or so in the audience and very warm applause. She brought her husband Leo, but they had to hurry away without lunch because Margaret was taking John Smith's place at Question Time in the Commons.[7]

Later that week, an overworked Dr Dunford and a tired-out Father Stock travelled to Venice for a sorely needed break. One morning on the Lagoon, our spirits were lifted by the most extraordinary and memorable sight.

5 December

We got to the waterbus to find it cancelled because of 'the Progress of the Spoils'. What could they be? Then, sitting on the top deck of the boat for Murano, we suddenly saw the Spoils progressing, The Spoils turned out to be St Barbara's relics, borne on a naval vessel draped in red velvet, with soldiers and sailors standing to attention and forming an honour guard, red velvet swags flowing in the choppy waters at the stern. Murano was all troops and out-of-tune bands, with the Bishop, the Mayor and the Cardinal Patriarch himself, and women clapping as the foreshortened Barbara, Virgin and Martyr of Nicomedia, was borne along in its crystal coffin. Servers and incense met all this half way, and then outside the church there were speeches from all the old naval and military veterans. It was rather like the British Legion at home in Friern Barnet.

Awestruck by the flamboyant use of so many yards of red velvet, we returned to a grey London. The days were busy, as always in December. In the course of one day I attended Bishop Graham Ellison's memorial service in St Paul's Cathedral, went to Kennington to see a video of my godson Robert Jenkin's Nativity

---

7 John Smith was elected Leader of the Labour Party, replacing Neil Kinnock, in July 1992.

play, and then on to the House of Commons for a birthday dinner. At the Commons I ran into Margaret and Leo Beckett, rather shocked after an attack by robbers at their home in Derby. I was able to introduce them to my Tory friend Bernard Jenkin, and enjoyed effecting such an unlikely meeting between left and right.

23 December

There were 140 people at the Charterhouse carol service, including a boy with the word 'rat' shaved into his hair. I talked about how cool this was in my sermon, to his and his mate's great pleasure.

24 December

I said my prayers in Notre Dame de France behind Leicester Square and arrived in Codford at 7 p.m. after a long, foggy journey over ice. At Edington Priory before Midnight Mass all was quiet and still, and later candlelit and full. I preached about starlight, making the point that we are all made out of the dust of stars. The house was as silent when we returned to it as Edington Priory had been when we arrived at it. There was a hard, glittering white frost, and fog.

25 December

At Upton Lovell this morning chairs filled the aisle. There were 90 people, lots of them young, and a much improved choir, all in this tiny space. During the service I espied a window dedicated to St Barbara. Well. I didn't expect to find a link with Murano and the Procession of the Spoils in a little Anglican parish church in Wiltshire.

Edna Healey and the Lift

After the New Year break, work in London got underway again with a Solemn Mass for Epiphany at lunchtime on 6 January. There were about 90 people in the church. The day was also made special by my dinner guest in the evening, Sir Roy Strong. He brought champagne for us to drink, 'because everything is so awful we need to celebrate something,' and was affectionate and funny. We ate brown shrimps from Holland, duck from Bow Lane and Bonchester cheese from Neal's Yard. It was a splendid Epiphany Feast. Another feast followed the next day, this one full of Tories.

7 January

I went to a dinner party at Anne and Bernard Jenkin's house in Kennington Road, where I sat next to Michael Portillo, the Chief Secretary to the Treasury. I think I understand why he is so attractive to people; he has a lot of sex appeal. At the table there was a collection of the bright Tory right, including a gay couple, one of whom is chairman of Torch, a campaign to make Tories nicer to homosexuals. A triumph of hope over experience.

20 January

I went to St Paul's Cathedral today, where there was to be an Evensong for the endangered St Bartholomew's Hospital – at least, that's what Bart's thought. The old Dean, however, made it clear that this was not to be a demonstration, just a matter of welcoming people who didn't want Bart's Hospital closed to the usual Choral Evensong. There was a Latin anthem, and even the Lord's Prayer was sung so we couldn't join in. It was the set liturgy for the twentieth evening of the month from the 1662 Prayer Book – Evensong in the presence of a vast congregation of people, some with children in pushchairs, young and old, the majority of whom had never set foot inside St Paul's before and certainly wouldn't set foot inside St Paul's again. It was depressing to see the Church of England so nervous and unyielding. The only good thing about it was the presence of the Bishop of London, who gave the Blessing. But he didn't go to the door at the end, nor did anybody else from the Cathedral staff.

21 January

Jean Mayhew took me to the House of Commons to listen to Patrick during Northern Ireland Questions. I stayed for the Prime Minister's Questions, when John Smith, Leader of the Opposition, laid into John Major.

In the evening I took a taxi to the Dorchester for the Australia Day Dinner, arriving to find that the Prime Minister was expected at exactly the same minute. Mr Major came up, extended his hand and asked me who I was. 'I'm Chaplain to the Order of Australia and I saw you in the House this after-noon,' I said. 'You managed to keep going.'

This was not very sensible. He said he'd had a horrible time in the Commons, and of course he had. He asked after Jean and got on to the awfulness of Dennis Skinner. 'I could kill him,' said the Prime Minister. I agreed enthusiastically to join in his murder.

Feeling that the conversation was now getting better, I then said fatuously, 'The Speaker's very good, isn't she?'

'Oh, do you think so?' he said, and that was that. I dis-covered later that he'd been criticized by the Speaker, Betty Boothroyd, before being laid into by the Leader of the Opposition.

This wasn't very good, but the Prime Minister recovered sufficiently after dinner to ask if I'd enjoyed the evening. He had. 'It's lovely to have an evening free of journalists. Yes, I'd be delighted to sign your menu card.' He spoke extra-ordinarily well (more impressive after dinner than at the dis-patch box) and is friendly and pleasant.

February began with a tonic, when the ballerina Dame Beryl Grey came for a Dialogue. She was serious and beautiful, and it was absorbing stuff. She brought her husband, 85-year-old Dr Sven Svenson, to lunch and they stayed until 3.15 p.m.

Unfortunately, Dame Beryl was followed by a maddeningly deluded and self-satisfied man, who did not understand what contribution he had made to the collapse of his marriage. From that I had to go straight into a marriage preparation class with Penny Wright, a doctor at Andrew Dunford's practice, and her fiancé Andrew Neubauer. The juxtaposition of past hopelessness and future hope was a difficult one, and it took me about 20 minutes to change gear.

The following week I was concentrating on hopeful relationships of a different kind.

11 February

I went to Radlett to give my lecture on 'How do we dialogue with other faiths?' in the Roman Catholic church hall. What I said was enthusiastically received. When I said it's sometimes important that our own cherished beliefs should be put on the backburner, e.g. my belief in Jesus Christ, an elderly Jewish gentleman stood up and said, 'Ah yes, Father, but even things on the backburner are still cooking.'

After this, to my tired dismay, I was hauled off to a Chinese restaurant for dinner when I really wanted to go home, but it was nice food and my Jewish and Christian hosts were delightful. They produced both my train fare and a book token for £20, which does not always happen when you do things for the Church.

23 February

After a two-hour meeting at the Globe Centre, I took a restorative walk back through Spitalfields and Bishopsgate to meet John Wilkins, Editor of the *Tablet,* for a Dialogue. He is a charming, open and honest Roman Catholic, once an Anglican – 'Not a convert: I was converted by the Church of England.' That was a kind thing to say in public.

15 March

After a brief visit to Wells Cathedral, where I lit candles for the people I know with AIDS, I gave my talk and tried to enthuse 27 country clergymen about Affirming Catholicism. There were some cross Catholics among them: 'Why not call it Affirming Liberalism?' It transpired, however, that only 20 out of the 260 priests in this diocese are unhappy about the vote last November to ordain women. There was a very impressive man who had rescued Bosnian Muslims, bringing eight coaches back full of refugees. There was also an Evangelical incumbent from Bath who helps a township in South Africa and goes there regularly. He has planted a church in a school hall on a sink estate. These were by far the most impressive people there, and neither of them, of course, were Anglo-Catholics.

The following week I spent a morning at Mile End, clambering around with the works foreman on the Globe Centre site. I also did a piece for Radio London about the ongoing public enquiry into Number One Poultry – SAVE Britain's Heritage having successfully petitioned for a second enquiry. I did the radio piece sitting in an outside broadcast van on Bucklersbury, the road just behind Poultry and part of the area Peter Palumbo was planning to lay waste. Later that same day, I was part of the group in Ironmonger Lane presenting to the Lord Mayor a 6,000-signature petition against the proposed closure of Bucklersbury. Two days later I spoke at the enquiry itself.

25 March

I gave evidence at the Palumbo enquiry today. Lord Colville cross-examined me and was not unbearably rude. I made him laugh a bit – perhaps more a baring of fangs rather than laughter. Dear old Reg Bridges from the United Reformed Church was quite unruffled by the nastiness of his cross-examination, I think because he's too good and decent a person to understand how *nasty* nasty people are. The drama of the morning was George Allen, our Counsel, forcing the Inspector to say that he would have preferred the Corporation of London to have been represented, thereby succeeding in making the City look seedy.

We approached Holy Week through days of freezing rain and a transport strike. Four extra people ended up staying in the rectory. As it only has two and a half bedrooms, this was a triumph.

3 April

In Codford there was freezing rain all day – an odd accompaniment to the discussion on how to proceed in the small walled garden. Eventually the idea of gravel and a hot, low, Mediterranean landscape emerged.

Last night at 12, Bill Sewell rang to say my front door in Cheapside had been smashed in again and Andrew's typewriter and CD player had been stolen. We obviously need a stronger front door. I hope we're not going to have this mad axeman week in, week out. It's so expensive.

5 April

Monday. I went to Margaret Street to make my confession and when I came back I found a man from Chubbs putting in a new front door with double Banham locks. It won't stop mad axe-murderers from attacking the door, but I hope they've got it out of their system for a bit.

I heard some confessions and then took the Allan & Overy's Evangelical service, wearing my Low Church grey suit. There was an absolutely excellent woman speaker and the atmosphere was much improved from last year, less self-conscious and hectoring.

Then I went to St Albans, where I had dinner with the Dean before Compline in the Lady Chapel. My sermon this evening was better than the one I gave at Evensong here yesterday. Afterwards a man asked me if he could come and talk, and I said, 'Yes, tomorrow on the way to the station.'

6 April

Today, at 12.15, I discovered that the weekend robbers had taken the tin box containing all my letters. It's an old Victorian cashbox, but just picking it up you could have felt by the weight and sound that it was full of paper. Perhaps they thought it was full of paper money. It wasn't even locked and hardly closed because it's so full. Some of the letters were from politicians, one or two written when politicians in government committed to paper things that should never be shown to anyone, even a friend. Also, the entire Michael Ramsey archive – all those old, wonderful handwritten letters, including the ones signed 'William Temple's cat', have all gone.

A sympathetic woman detective came to see me. 'Why don't you let all the people who are still alive know that private letters they've written to you have gone?' she asked.

'Well, they would wonder why I'd kept them,' I said. 'They might be anxious that I was going to betray a confidence.'

After my address at St Albans I walked to the station with the man I made the arrangement with yesterday. I sat with him on the platform for an hour, listening as carefully as I could in the cold.

9 April

Good Friday. Lord and Lady Runcie came for the whole Three Hours.

This morning there was a critical article about George Carey in the *Independent*. I warned Lord Runcie about it and said to him, 'It must be maddening to have nothing but praise now, whereas when you were Archbishop it was nothing but opprobrium.'

'Nothing but sh*t,' said Lady Runcie. I like Lady Runcie.

11 April

Easter Day has been grey and cold. I went to Mayfield in Kent to preach. It was lovely to be in a really full church, especially a beautiful medieval Easter church, perfectly kept. Then it was on to see Andrew and Phyllida Stewart-Roberts outside Lewes, where we had tea and a wonderful chocolate cake with one of the Queen's Ladies-in-Waiting.

We motored on along the coast to Portsmouth and thence up to Salisbury and home to Codford, where there were no guests. We celebrated the Queen of Days by having no drinks or supper because we had eaten such a lot at lunch and tea – not because we wanted to spite the Church by fasting on feast days.

May began in Cheapside. At his Dialogue Eddie George, the Governor Designate of the Bank of England, played to a thin house because it was the day after the bank holiday, it was sunny at long last and we had only just got the posters out. On sunny days people prefer to eat their sandwiches in the churchyard rather than sit inside. The attendance was disappointing, but at least the *Financial Times* came, did an article and took a photograph.

12 May

I had lunch at the *Financial Times* and sat on my old friend Gay Firth's right,[1] next to Sandra Howard, Home Secretary Michael Howard's wife. There was much anti-royal talk and, for her sake, less anti-Prime Minister talk. A story was told about Mrs Howard being rebuked for wearing a black dress at Buckingham Palace. 'The Queen is never to see black,' a courtier told her. Why is the Queen never to see black? What is the matter with Buckingham Palace?

On Rogation Sunday in the middle of May I rogated to Hertfordshire and Cambridgeshire. First I enjoyed a jolly, warmly welcoming lunch at Walden Abbots, Sir Michael Graham's country house – a higgledy-piggledy, friendly, cosy, eighteenth-century place full of portraits, including a good one of Sir Michael as Lord Mayor. Then I went on to Cambridge, where I preached too carefully, perhaps too academically, at Downing. The Master was complimentary because I had defended the Church of England, but that is one of my jobs, to go around defending the Church of England – and goodness, it needs defending.

---

1 Gay Firth has been a friend of mine since University Chaplaincy days. In 1993 she was Letters Editor at the *Financial Times*.

18 May

The Lord Mayor opened the Bow Lane Festival after a lack-lustre welcome from me, which was sad because he described me as 'a ball of fire'.

Well, the ball of fire fell in love today – with Edna Healey, who came to Dialogue. Lady Healey said that the Queen is overawed by her mother and the Prince of Wales isn't grown up.

She was also very amusing about our lift, which is apparently even slower than the one Queen Mary put in at Earl's Court and had to be defridged before she could use it. I remembered suddenly after lunch how lame Lady Healey is. She has a malacca cane, and I should have noticed this *before* she climbed all the stairs to my sitting room. I remembered that we had a lift, but also remembered that we had a refrigerator in it. I ran down the stairs and out into the street, collared the first two young men walking past and said, 'I've got Lady Healey at the top of the house and a fridge in my lift, and I need someone to help me get it out.' They came straight in to help.

June turned out to be politically interesting. It began with a journey to Hereford to launch Affirming Catholicism in the diocese at Andrew Mottram's city-centre church of All Saints, now mercifully without its piles of second-hand underwear. Then I was Patrick Mayhew's guest at Admiralty House for the Trooping of the Colour, which I watched from the balcony of the Northern Ireland Office, having first been asked to remove some drinks glasses which had been left on the parapet. 'Her Majesty doesn't like seeing glasses along the parapet.'

I refused an invitation to lunch on that occasion because I was off to see a gym instructor called Darren who was thinking about ordination, and more glamorous than Admiralty House was the chance to visit him in his flat over a brothel in Brewer Street – another experience of contrasts. Indeed, when I got to Darren's rickety old staircase and began my ascent, one of the ladies who worked in the building came out of her room and leered at me. 'Oh, look, he's just my type,' she said, thinking I was dressed up as a vicar. Quite a lot of people think I am merely dressed up as a vicar and not a real one. It has been a problem on more than one occasion.

On 14 June Michael Portillo's office rang to say that he would be unable to make his Dialogue the next day because the Prime Minister wanted to see him. In his place he would send his Parliamentary Private Secretary, David Amess, familiarly known to those outside the Tory Party as 'Basildon Man'.

15 June

David Amess turned out to be a vibrant, charmingly boyish, extremely pro-hanging, anti-Europe Little Englander. He worked himself up into a fearsome peroration denouncing the European Union, which was received by the City audience, interestingly, in silence. It was gratifying that none of the audience left when it was discovered that the guest was not Michael Portillo but his PPS. Nobody clapped, however, when Mr Amess worked everybody up, crying out, 'And I'm proud to be British!' At luncheon Mr Amess was surprised to discover that his fellow guest, the lawyer Mark Williams, was a Labour Councillor for Hackney.

22 June

I went to a 'Support the Labour Party' dinner in Gresham Street as a guest of Charles Cavanagh,[2] and had a conversation with John Smith.

JS: 'Oh, hello. What are you doing here, Victor?'

VS: 'At a meeting in Mayfair just now, I said I was off to a dinner in the City organized by merchant bankers to support the Labour Party, and a man said, "That's almost a metaphysical impossibility."'

JS: 'Victor, you're in the business of metaphysical impossibilities.'

VS: 'If I may say so, John, we both are.'

His speech at the dinner was excellent, but the MP Tony Banks was awful and the atmosphere was relentlessly that

---

2 A devout Roman Catholic, Charles Cavanagh was Head of Fund Management at Kleinwort Benson.

of a night out at the bingo. The Labour Party *en masse* is still depressing and tonight it still felt class-based. If it is to get elected, this must change.

July was distinctly less political. On 9 July I attended another meeting of the Salisbury Cathedral Fabric Advisory Committee which lasted nearly five hours, then staggered off to Sutton Mandeville for the rehearsal of Penny Wright's and Andrew Neubauer's wedding. The sun shone on the happy couple the next day, and the pretty church looked wonderful – all in all, it was a marvellous occasion.

The only cloud was provided by the knowledge that my rectory cat, Pussy Willow, had been moved down to Codford on the advice of the vet. It was painful to think of her being unwell and in a strange place. She had been my much loved companion since I acquired her as a tiny kitten in Friern Barnet.

19 July

Ruth Watson rang from the country to say that Pussy Willow was crapping everywhere, so obviously something's going seriously wrong. I rang back after Matins to say, 'Please find a vet and we'll take the cat in on Saturday. In the meantime, keep her in the garden.'

Later Ruth rang again to say that Mrs Collins, the vet, had called. Pussy Willow has been put down. She was injected in the house and her body taken away. Both Ruth and I shed a tear over the phone. Full marks to Ruth for organizing it so efficiently.

I rang the builder to cancel the cat-flap. When I put the phone down, I discovered that we have lost the Palumbo appeal. I loved Pussy Willow, but I do not love the lawyers of the wealthy.

The Number One Poultry affair had been a long saga of ups and downs, with the advantage going first to one side and then the other. Many people had put in a huge amount of work. Friendships had been made and relationships secured. This, however, was the end of the road. It was a bitter blow, knowing that in the next few years a large section of the parish would be turned first into a demolition site and then into a new building – which Prince Charles was subsequently to describe as 'a 1930s wireless'.

At the end of July I left these troubles behind and went to Paris for the weekend, staying with Jean Louis. Before leaving I was momentarily cheered by the news that the Liberal Democrats had won a by-election in Christchurch by 16,000 votes, overturning the previous Tory majority. Perhaps life was not so bad after all.

After a few days with Wim in Amsterdam, I returned to the coal face in London. The Globe Centre was taking shape, which I was enormously glad about, but further sad news darkened the horizon towards the end of August.

26 August

After a great deal of thought, I told Jonathan Lowe 'yes' to being Globe Appeals Chairman.

At the beginning of the day, though, in a letter from Barbara Lund,[3] came the news that Sven Fogh has died. I rang Denmark and got Mule. I put on a CD of Parry's 'Long Since in Egypt's Plenteous Land' from the oratorio *Judith*, and all day I kept playing it. Gillian Williams called, I told her about Sven and she was kind. In the afternoon I went to the Wallace Collection and sat in front of Poussin's painting *Dance to the Music of Time*. Whenever a friend dies, I look at *Dance to the Music of Time*.

I began September at York University, for the second Affirming Catholicism conference. This conference inspired us, helped by an excellent paper on Anglicanism from Professor Stephen Sykes and a brilliant talk about science and religion from Angela Tilby.[4] The low point was the Sunday Mass in York Minster. As Father Christopher Seville said, 'The bell before the service, the Bishop of Chicago's sermon and the Psalm after the service were the only sensible and attractive things.'

---

3 Barbara was a member of the congregation of the Anglican church of St Alban, Copenhagen, which I had looked after during two University Chaplaincy holidays. Barbara and her husband Preben had subsequently become my friends.

4 Stephen Sykes, Bishop of Ely, later became Principal of St John's College, Durham, and Chairman of the Doctrine Commission. Angela Tilby is a broadcaster and priest, and lecturer at Westcott House, Cambridge.

Then it was all change, as I left the rolling Yorkshire country-side to visit India with Andrew Dunford. We stopped briefly in Delhi, then caught a train for Lucknow and from there went on to the town of Bahraich, where Andrew was due to spend some time visiting hospitals. I had been invited along because the Hospital Director, Dr Manoha Singh, had stayed in my rectory at Friern Barnet some years earlier when he had come to the UK for a course. In Bahraich we were put up in the new guesthouse at the hospital, where there was a Western-style lavatory (hooray!) and the radio was kept under a lace veil like the Blessed Sacrament in the Tabernacle.

13 September

After breakfast, Manoha took us on his ward round. Poor, ragged, thin, bandaged, the patients lay on their iron beds, some already beyond help. There was a baby with a cancerous eye the size of a golf ball. Both eyes, infected, would have to be taken out and the child would probably die, we were told. Relatives and other people waited in the cloisters and corridor, faces pressed to the mosquito netting. A young assistant was told, 'Never turn them away if they say they can't pay. The money will come.'

As we moved on from bed to bed, the tears rolled down my cheeks. This was a ward round conducted by a saint. Manoha himself was so thin, gentle, always quiet. A touch, a word, a decision given. Here in this filthy, two-bit town of no reputation or beauty was a living Buddha, the tangible spirit of Jesus Christ in this Sikh doctor.

15 September

We went into the forest today, where we saw deer, brown and grey monkeys and some crocodiles. On Manoha's round of the villages, we saw a handsome boy of 29 with both eyes destroyed by a stabbing. His old parent was leading him by the hand, hoping Manoha could perform a miracle, but there was nothing left. There was a tribal woman with split, elongated earlobes, completely blind, and a man blinded by the village holy man who had tried to heal him. Patients were passed for an operation tomorrow and an assistant painted a red iodine circle round the eye to be treated.

In the Land Rover, Andrew was surrounded by children on whom he was trying his Hindi. I got them to read to us and one 10-year-old boy read better than one or two of my Cockney bank clerks at St Mary-le-Bow.

A couple of days later we visited a factory where we learned about the intricacies of splitting pulses and husks and processing *neem* oil, and went to eat dinner at the grand house of the factory's owner. The men ate separately and the food was delicious, so when we rose to leave I asked if we could thank the ladies who had prepared the meal. This was regarded as extraordinary and was probably wrong of me, but we were taken politely out to the courtyard, where five or six women were summoned to hear our thanks. The day after that, we took tea with a local policeman and the Chief Inspector. Manoha introduced me by saying, 'This is the Lord Mayor of London.' The funny thing was that this elicted not the faintest degree of surprise.

19 September

There were at least two electricity cuts during the night, with consequent pools of sweat in the suffocating darkness. We got up in time to go to the American Bible Church – it does say the words 'Bible Church' over the porch – for the 9 o'clock service. The stiff Indian mission owner received us in her mansion and gave us tea and sweet cake. The huge, low veranda would have been nice, but 'because of flies' we were made to sit inside with the windows closed.

As we went into the church, I was told that, far from merely saying a few words, I was the preacher. I asked what the lesson was and was told John 1:1–18. During the first part of the service (in Hindi) I tried with the help of my mother's pocket New Testament to find something suitably 'Bible Church' to say, only to be told, as the first lesson was read out, that it was in fact John 8, the passage about the woman taken in adultery. A hasty rethink was required.

The old minister was wearing a Church of North India smocked surplice and black scarf with three red crosses on it. The mission director had sniffed, 'He's a Methodist, but it's better than nothing.' I didn't like her much. The minister was Uncle Teddy-like and holy. He suddenly thrust a brand-new baby into my hands. 'What am I to do with it?' I asked, thinking for one terrified moment that it might be a present, but all I had to do was bless it, so I offered it up towards the east wall as if it were an alms dish. The minister and the flock were not invited back to the big house, a feudal touch I didn't care for.

Later that day we drank whisky with the District Officer in his vast, East India Company house. He was a charming and helpful man, attended by splendid officers in forage caps. He gave me a plaster cast of a Hindu deity which I treasure to this day. It sits on a windowsill in my Cheapside sitting room.

20 September

At 11 we set off for the Nepal frontier, the town of Rapadia and the Pentecostal Mission therein. They were welcoming, charming people, much easier than yesterday, although they were frenzied because of the visit from the Lord Mayor of London. I can't make up my mind whether Manoha is mud-dled or being naughty. Anyway, all the children were lined up in the schoolyard. I was introduced as the Lord Mayor and addressed them as such. Then I made the Headmaster be the Lord Mayor, with me as his Chaplain and three boys as his esquires. Six other children were the horses and Andrew Dunford was the City Marshal, and off we set in procession up and down the cheering ranks. We were showered with paper flowers and home-made cards, and then I answered questions in a classroom.

A boy told me his favourite Bible story was Samson and Delilah, so I ended by telling it and acting it out. I cast the Headmaster's wife as Delilah. I followed this with the para-bles of the Lost Sheep and the Lost Coin to leave a more Christian impression.

All the children at the school are lepers. They have bunnies to teach them to be loving, and they make their own chapattis. At a big lunch party, the women sat at table with the men, marking this place out as Christian. I managed to convince them that, in fact, I had been the Lord Mayor's Chaplain and was not the Lord Mayor. I hope it wasn't too disappointing. I put the correct facts in the visitors' book.

21 September

To Kanpur, the Cawnpore of old. We left at about 8.15 a.m. and drove almost immediately into a torrential, crashing, blinding monsoon. Everyone was driven from the road except us, but there was the most wonderful clean, clear air. From time to time the driver would lean out and mop at the windscreen (no windscreen wipers). Eventually we bumped into Lucknow and were taken round the enormous and rather crude stucco Islamic monuments and the Imambra. We were not allowed into the mosque. We dutifully took off our shoes, however, and looked at the largest unsupported ceiling in the world, though I never quite see why that sort of information means much.

Then we bumped our way to Dr Rhohatgi's house, complete with biogas plant, where Andrew was taken on a tour of some plants which are going to cure HIV. Where have I heard that before? At 5.30, as dusk fell, we set off over the Ganges in Dr Rhohatgi's air-conditioned car – bliss – on and on through Kanpur to visit hospital after hospital. We were dropping with fatigue.

At the last hospital of the evening, everyone was upset because we were so late. Andrew leapt into soothing Lady-in-Waiting mode and we surged off round the operating theatre, accompanied by a reverent multitude of assistants, doctors and nurses.

In the delivery room I went up and down reviewing the babies, enthusing, 'Oh, look at his dear little hands!' and so on, meanwhile muttering urgently to Andrew, 'What shall I do?'

'Oh, bless them,' he said, so I made the sign of the cross over all those Hindu and Muslim babies. It seemed to be all right.

Eventually we were taken to the station to catch the 11 p.m. train, which arrived at 1.15 a.m. The whole place was a chaos of sleeping street children, cockroaches, cows on the platform, filth, excrement and heat. On the train the air-conditioning unit ran water down the wall, soaking clothes, sheets and my diary.

The next morning, having arrived more or less in one piece in Agra, we set off to see the Taj Mahal. We reached it by 8.15, when all was still quiet – a perfect harmony of cloud, water and sacred geometry. The monument was very familiar to me from pictures, of course, but of all the wonders I saw in India this was the most startling in its impact, an intellectual and refined piece of art.

24 September

Either chicken curry or ice cubes in the whisky have laid us low, and poor Andrew has caught viral enteritis of a distressingly weakening nastiness, with a high temperature and the shakes. Andrew couldn't eat any of the breakfast we had sent up and I didn't enjoy mine. Our car turned up and we set off for Delhi. It was a journey of unalloyed hell, with Andrew being really very ill all the way. Diesel fumes, rain, potholes, traffic, heat, a stop at a loathsome bar and a bog beyond endurance, plus elephants, camels and a dancing bear, each animal looking more suicidal than the last.

In Delhi, Devika Singh gave Andrew rice and curds soaked in lime and put him to bed, where he remained. We had a very good talk in the evening about India. 'We don't have the illusion of evolutionary progress and can accommodate evil within our philosophical system,' I was told. I thought this fascinatingly different from our Western way of looking at things and would like to spend some time absorbing the idea. Andrew began to look better, but still with a high temperature. Got up in his new Indian pyjamas, he looked rather dashing in an 'At Death's Door, End of the Victorian Era' kind of way. He came up to dinner, having a little rice.

Very early the next morning the taxi came to take us to the airport, and we set off for what felt, I am afraid, like a journey into freedom. India was a fascinating but difficult place, and I was glad to get home.

12 October

Today 210 people were at the Dialogue with Michael Portillo, the new darling of the Tory right, lauded in the *Sunday Times* as the future Leader of the Tory Party. Michael Portillo is attractive and combative, but when he started on the 'clergy should devote themselves to spiritual things and not interfere with health and housing' kind of Thatcherite line, I got very cross. I think Mr Portillo is the first of my guests at whom I've shouted.

We had four barristers to lunch, including a Treasury Silk. Portillo started off again on how selfish everybody was, including unmarried mothers having children in order to get flats. As the Treasury Silk was an unmarried mother, this was tiresome. She said, 'Well, we've heard your views on that. Let's hear your views on looking after the elderly.'

'People don't look after the elderly, but send them off to homes,' he answered. I said that in all my years as a parish priest I'd never come across people behaving cavalierly about this. It was always a matter of some anguish – not enough room, difficult teenagers, senility, and so on. Then I asked Mr Portillo if he had experience of nursing the elderly himself. The answer was 'no', which was good of him to admit.

When he left for the House of Commons, the Treasury Silk said, 'Could we open another bottle of wine? I don't think I can go back to work.' What we were treated to was not, I think, what Mr Portillo really in his heart of hearts believes, but the very nastiest aspects of Thatcherism – that careless disregard for life as it really is for people.

13 October

Bernard and Anne Jenkin came to Mass, having been at the Dialogue yesterday, and I gave them lunch. Anne was cross with me for giving the impression that it's impossible to be a Conservative and a Christian. Do I think this? I wonder. Bernard, however, thought it had been an artillery battle and enjoyed it.

Later in the month, following his wife's visit to us earlier in the year, my Dialogue guest was Lord Denis Healey – urbane, charming, very interested in the fellow guests at lunch, taking photographs of everybody with his little camera. He was vastly well read, warm and inspiring. The church was absolutely packed, with

80 people standing. Lord Healey told the 'nuzzled by an old ram' story. The expression had been Geoffrey Howe's witty rejoinder to congratulations from Denis on his appointment as Foreign Secretary. Some years before that, when Howe had attacked Healey, he had famously been dismissed with a remark about being 'savaged by a dead sheep'. Denis Healey commented to an amused Dialogue audience, 'I've never been accused of necrophilia.' These exchanges had their origin just after the war, when Winston Churchill said, after an attack by Clement Attlee, that it was 'like being bitten by a pet lamb'.

28 October

I went to Admiralty House at 9 p.m. for supper. Jean and I talked until 10.30, when Patrick came in with his heavy red boxes and asked me to help write his speech for the Women's Ordination Measure debate tomorrow. We sat together at his desk working on this. It is remarkable that he is prepared to put the extra hours necessary into thinking out the arguments for the ordination of women.

He said on the stairs that he has no sense of people praying for him. He knows they do, but can't feel them or the prayer. I must think about this. One of the many things I like about Patrick Mayhew is that he says things that are honest, i.e. what we all feel, but as practising Christians feel we shouldn't.

Following the women's ordination debate, the House of Commons passed the legislation by an overwhelming majority. In 1994 the first women were – at last – ordained as priests.

At the beginning of November, I visited Mule Fogh in Denmark for the first time since Sven's death, taking the tiny train out to Fredensborg, to the village of yellow-brick, single-storey, severe courtyard houses, a settlement for doctors who have worked abroad. In the long, low drawing room, with its glass wall opening on to a light, well planted courtyard garden, we had a good conversation about Sven and the past, about Borneo and all those parts of the Third World where the Foghs had worked to such effect, and about marriage and childhood in Copenhagen.

Back in Copenhagen, I went to the Royal Theatre with Barbara and Preben Lund. Suddenly everyone rose. There was a silence and then the Danish Queen appeared alone in her box next to the stage. She smiled, looked shyly around, and sat down. We sat too, and then conversation broke out. There was no clapping, no formality, just a much respected middle-aged woman watching the ballet for which she, the Queen, had designed the sets and the costumes. What struck me then and remains in my mind is that, as she looked shyly around, she dropped a curtsey to her people.

16 November

Barbara Lund turned up from Copenhagen just as I was washing the cup and saucer present for Prunella Scales, who decided to arrive at 12.15 and ask for her lunch before the Dialogue instead of after it. We managed it, although a bit breathlessly, and the church was packed for the Dialogue – 275 people.

James Osei, who has a very ill-paid job in the parish, came tearfully at the beginning of the day to say he was going to be fired and would I intercede for him with his boss? I did. His boss rang later and sounded sensible.

No sooner had I got to my own desk upstairs than Michael Banner, the Dean of Peterhouse, Cambridge, rang and asked me to consider putting myself forward for the vacancy at Little St Mary's. I talked for half an hour with him and said that, if the papers about it all came, I would give careful consideration and write a considered reply.

It certainly provided food for thought. Peterhouse were patrons of the living, and my name had been suggested to them. I was quite attracted by the idea of a radical move out of London. I had, after all, been based in London since 1969. Perhaps this was to be the trigger for change.

23 November

Sean Hughes, poet and comedian, who seems to be a real idol to the young, was rather thoughtful and kindly at the Dialogue today. I liked him very much.

I conducted a memorial service for an habitué of the local pubs, which went a treat. The church was full of Irish Roman Catholics and there was Guinness to drink at Finsbury Square afterwards with the mourners.

At Andrew's Barbican flat this evening, I met Werner de Pappas, a half-Greek, half-German dancer Andrew had met in Athens.

24 November

This afternoon at Brick Lane, where we are until the Globe Centre is built, I welcomed Danny La Rue, who is an interesting mixture of hard and kind old queen. He did all the right stuff, being warm and kind with the Centre's users. There was a rather smart East End Mayor present who was actually called Snooks. Councillor Snooks.

With the Centre just camping out in an empty building in Brick Lane at the moment, we need the uplift of celebrity visits, not only to help with fundraising, but also simply to keep our spirits up.

The month ended with various unlikely people rallying round the Secretary of State for Northern Ireland when it was discovered that, with enormous courage and at great risk, contact had been made between the IRA and the Government. It gradually emerged that it was being said by the IRA that the war was over, but it did not come out in that form at the time. The leak of these contacts put the Government, the Prime Minister and the Secretary of State in an acutely embarrassing position, and Patrick Mayhew had to go to the House to make a statement. The place was packed. All Patrick needed to do to win the day was to get Ken Livingstone to praise him and Ian Paisley to attack him. All this came to pass, as Matthew Parris later brilliantly wrote in *The Times*: 'Sir Patrick needed his lemons all to come up in a row and one after another they did' – even to the point when the Speaker ejected Ian Paisley from the Commons for calling the Secretary of State a liar.

2 December

I had to go to Lambeth Palace today. The Nikaean Club, who meet to entertain visiting ecclesiastical dignitaries, were having a special celebration attended by the Queen and Prince Philip. First there was the dreariest possible 1662 Evensong, relayed from the crypt chapel up into the state rooms via televisions, around which we stood in a slightly self-conscious way.

Father Len Tyzack, once Michael Ramsey's Domestic Chaplain, said he would present me to the Queen if I stayed talking to some friends in a particular place when Her Majesty came round. Well, we all had quite a lot to drink and were having a jolly time, when suddenly there was Len saying, 'Your Majesty, may I present Victor?'

For some reason, he didn't say 'Victor Stock', or mention what I did, or give any opening at all to Her Majesty, who extended a black-gloved hand. I moved towards it with the sure and certain knowledge that I was going to be sick. It was something to do with the iconic presence of the Queen and suddenly actually speaking to her.

I wasn't sick, and managed to mumble, 'I was Lord Mayor's Chaplain and stood nearby on several occasions, but of course was never introduced.'

'No, one is never introduced, is one?' she said.

I wittered on about the nurses at a party at the Guildhall the other day, when the Princess of Wales hadn't smiled at them, and I said it wasn't possible to smile at 700 people. Why I started talking about the Princess of Wales to the Queen, I can't think.

The Queen said, 'Oh yes, I just smile my way through the room. It's all you can do, really.' She was very bright and pretty, just like Prunella Scales's Queen in Alan Bennett's *A Question of Attribution* – a remarkably pretty woman with her iron-grey hair and her shyness.

I dashed on recklessly. 'Have you been here in Archbishop Carey's time, or is it your first visit?' Fluster, gush.

'Yes, first time since Dr Carey came.'

On I gushed to Robert Runcie. 'Yes, I came then.'

Then I moved on to Michael Ramsey and the teaspoons, telling her that the furniture and belongings of Lambeth are mostly the property of the Church Commissioners and, when an Archbishop retires, they come round to count the spoons.

'Oh, did they really count the spoons?' asked the Queen, falteringly.

This was a clear signal to stop, but I missed it and went on, 'Do you know, when they were counting things they found a statue, I mean a model, of the temple of Jerusalem buried in the rose garden. No one could think where on earth it could have come from.'

The Queen's eyes glazed over and she moved smartly to one side, saying, 'Goodness, it can't have been here since Jerusalem's time, surely!' What she meant was, 'Who is this barking mad clergyman?'

From the first moment, when I felt I was going to be sick, the whole conversation was impossible. I imagine this happens to the Queen all the time. Afterwards she must have got into the car with the Duke of Edinburgh, who was doing the rounds in another room, and said, 'How many mad people did you meet tonight? I met this person from St Mary-le-Bow who was positively dangerous.'

3 December

Yesterday Lambeth, today Downing Street – for a conversation about possible jobs. When I got to the gates at the end of Downing Street the policeman said, 'Good morning, Mr Stock.' He had cleverly consulted the list of the morning's visitors. I walked up Downing Street to the famous front door feeling self-conscious, but affecting to notice the newly planted pansies in a relaxed sort of way. There was another 'Good morning, sir' from the policeman on the door, then I was inside the Red Hall. Another 'Good morning, Mr Stock' came from the doorman, who took my overcoat and invited me to sit on an eighteenth-century hall chair.

The Prime Minister's Appointment Secretary, John Holroyd, came down and took me up via a staircase which was being painted to his green-and-white-striped office with its heavy mahogany furniture. The room is immediately over the front door. He told me that the Bishop of London had rung in and said, 'We both agree about the pattern your ministry's taking.' We talked about Little St Mary's, Cambridge, and other ideas. After three-quarters of an hour I was taken down to the door and seen off into Downing Street.

In the afternoon a postcard came to say that I was going to be interviewed for Little St Mary's.

15 December

Today was the first public occasion at the Globe Centre. In the afternoon I welcomed everyone and thanked, I hope, everyone at this first official visit to the new building. Of course it's still a builder's site/tip/wreck, so the atmosphere was sticky, with people cross that things aren't further forward. It was a relief, in all this, to find a dog wearing a rhinestone collar, which I borrowed from the dog and put on over my clerical dog collar for my speech of welcome to the Mayor, assorted clergymen, volunteers and rent boys.

16 December

I went to the ICA for Centrepoint's AGM in the presence of the Princess of Wales – her last public appearance, she has told us. There was a most brilliant attack on Thatcherite values from a Professor of Criminology, which HRH obviously enjoyed and agreed with. It must have been good, because a Tory MP got up and stalked out in the middle of it. There was also a very good talk from Ken Leech, who started Centrepoint. I didn't have time to stay for lunch and, as I left, found myself facing banks and tiers of paparazzi and a huge crowd waiting for the last glimpse of the Princess.

In the evening I spoke at the Bellringers' Dinner at South Mimms. On the way back from the dinner I asked the Vicar's wife, 'Do people from this council estate we're walking through come to the church?'

She replied, 'Oh yes. Ladies come from our end and invite the lower orders to tea.'

'How does that go down?' I asked.

'Well, Mrs Jones said the other day, "We've just been to one of Mrs Spriggin's tea parties – silly, stuck-up bitch."'

This has been the treat of the week.

21 December

I went to Cambridge to be interviewed for Little St Mary's. The Dean of Peterhouse, Master and Fellows were all friendly and welcoming. The Dean asked, 'Would you support the Bishops' Statement on Human Sexuality?'

I said, 'No. Would you like me to explain why?'[5]

The Bishop of Ely was sitting in the corner, observing. I was also asked the questions we used to be asked when going up to university – 'What books are you reading?' and so on.

There was a very jolly lunch, during which I was taken aside by the Dean. Would I mind discussing my position on the Bishops' Statement with the Bishop of Ely? Would I take the job if it were offered me? I'm not quite sure about the job, but of course I was prepared to talk to the Bishop.

In the Botanical Gardens afterwards, I met the Dean of Downing. 'Oh, do take the job!' he said. 'All the clergy who work at Little St Mary's are pro the ordination of women, and they just need leadership.'

22 December

The Dean of Peterhouse rang to tell me that I am the enthusiastic choice of the Master, Fellows and the Bishop, but am vetoed by the Forward in Faith Warden.[6] He asked if I would be prepared to wait until the New Year and let the Fellows have one more go. I said yes, and went into the church to pray before our carol service, at which we had 300 people and £1,062 in the collection. During the afternoon I heard confessions and in between I held myself as Father Carey SSJE taught, 'gazing steadfastly at God'. So it seems I am going to Cambridge next year, if everybody but one Churchwarden wants me. It seems settled.

---

5 The bishops had issued a document about sexuality which was described as a 'discussion paper' but was in fact used as policy, and in any case only really dealt with homosexuality. It said that sex was OK for laypeople but never for clergy, except inside heterosexual marriage. Faithful, permanent, stable relationships were deemed good for the laity but bad for clergy. There seemed to be a lapse in logic here.

6 Forward in Faith is an organization within the Church of England for people who are still opposed to the ordination of women and take a generally Roman Catholic stance on all ethical and doctrinal matters.

The Wilderness of Zin

After spending New Year in Amsterdam, I returned to Cheapside to await the final verdict on Little St Mary's. In the middle of a busy working morning in the first week of January, the Dean of Peterhouse rang to say it was 'no go'. The Churchwardens had hardened their attitude over Christmas. Thus that little adventure came to a sudden end. I would probably never know what really happened, I thought, or why they reached their negative decision. It was a sad moment. I had been looking forward to making a new life somewhere quite different. There was very little time to brood over this, however, as life at St Mary-le-Bow was non-stop and all-absorbing.

10 January

Jan Barham, the hospice sister at Chalkwell, rang to say that June Judd-Goodwin is in awful pain. I cancelled my attendance at a couple of meetings and took the train out to Chalkwell. There were black, scudding clouds along the windy seafront. I gave June Communion and Unction and sat with her. She can't eat or drink or lie down. It took a long time to get home. I hope it won't take her so long to get to heaven, poor woman.

20 January

At the Australia Day Dinner at the Dorchester I sat between Mrs Richardson and Lady Carrington.[1] As we were opposite Sir Bernard Ingham, Mrs Thatcher's Press Secretary, our remarks about Thatcherism could be partially overheard by him through the flowers and candles. Lady Carrington is

---

1 Sylvia Richardson was the wife of Professor Sam Richardson, a distinguished member of the Order of Australia. She died in 2000. Lady Carrington is the wife of the former Foreign Secretary, Lord Carrington.

patrician, funny, forthright, liberal and humane. Ingham was brilliantly funny as an after-dinner speaker.

At the end of the week, I saw the Richardsons again at their home, the Old Malt House, Wyle, along the valley from Codford. One of the guests from the Ministry of Defence told a marvellous story about the Imperial State Crown (the crown worn every year by the Sovereign at the Opening of Parliament) being too tight. Apparently the Queen complained that the velvet cap inside the crown was too tight, and Ede and Ravenscroft were asked to ease it. The old man at Ede and Ravenscroft who did this specialized work said that he could not do it without the crown itself. An armoured carrier, with soldiers and machine-guns at the ready, took the Imperial State Crown to Ede and Ravenscroft, where it was left for the old man to work on. When he had finished, he decided he could take it back to the Tower on his own without all that fuss, so he just put it in a plastic bag and took it back to the Tower on a bus.

Early in February, the women's ordination issue came to the forefront of things again. David Hutt, the Vicar of All Saints, Margaret Street, issued a statement which included the words, 'No woman will say Mass or give the Absolution.' This created a certain fluttering in the dovecotes, but did not seem to fit with the pro-ordination stance he had recently taken up. I decided he was still afraid of the conservative element at All Saints.

On Ash Wednesday Downing Street announced the creation of two Flying Bishops, who would look after those opposed to the ordination of women. I felt they gave a very bad impression of themselves at the Lambeth press conference, a clip of which was shown on the 6 o'clock news. One was dull, the other aggressive.

I was at Codford for the first Sunday in Lent, where Andrew, Ruth and I had a Quiet Day. We said Matins together at 8 a.m., Mass in the chapel at 11 and the Midday Office at 12.45, but spent the rest of the day in silent prayer or reading. Andrew made polish from our own beeswax, producing a lovely country-house smell. We all noticed that not talking made the day longer and more productive.

21 February

Bernard Jenkin called to tell me he was going to vote for the age of consent for homosexuals to be lowered from 18 to 16, and he was also going to vote against the reintroduction of the death penalty. In the end, though, the lower age of consent failed to get through by 27 votes. Until we get equality for sexual orientation, it will be impossible for people to teach young gay and lesbian teenagers an ethic by which to live.

22 February

The Dean of Peterhouse was on the BBC today, regretting that the age of consent had not been kept at 21. This, I thought, was revealing about what really happened at Little St Mary's. Perhaps it wasn't the Churchwardens who were up in arms about the ordination of women, but the Dean of Peterhouse who was up in arms about my liberal views on homosexuality.

Paul Whitehouse, the Chief Constable of Sussex, was my Dialogue guest today – a wonderful, devout, reforming, liberal Quaker who said that he would have voted for 16 as the age of consent, and also against hanging.

25 February

Andrew's Greek friend Werner has come to stay for the weekend in the country. He is not at all well. It's good that we can use this house for such restorative hospitality.

Werner was just setting up his first flat in London and only had a mattress to sleep on. He had no chairs or table. We were able to fill a van with spare furniture from the stables at Codford and, encouraged by this loot, he set off happily to settle into his new home.

13 March

I preached in Gloucester Cathedral in the morning – blue copes and Communion from a woman. The worship was dignified, in the style of Canterbury Cathedral 40 years ago.

Gloucester Cathedral is a dream of beauty, but the city was vandalized by developers in the 1960s. Later I preached at Evensong in St Luke's, Chelsea – another example on the same day of sensible Anglicanism, with a friendly Rector and lovely singing.

17 March

A lot of time today was spent writing sermons for Holy Week. I also dictated my 'Londoner's Diary' for the *Evening Standard* and faxed it to the Editor. He rang last night asking me to write the Diary for Easter weekend. This should earn me £240. If you do things for anybody except the Church, you get paid *proper* money.

27 March

Palm Sunday. Elaine Jones called for me at 8.30 a.m. to motor me to Brentwood. She has left the parish where she was a Deacon as the Vicar didn't want her to stay for Easter. She is to become a priest very soon, when the first women are ordained in St Paul's Cathedral. On Friday, at the party the church people gave for her, 130 turned up. The congregation only has 60 people in it. She has been interviewed for a German television programme and has addressed the Enfield Rotary Club. That's good preparation for working at St Botolph's, Aldgate, where she is going as Curate.

At Brentwood there was a sensitive liturgy and a very good boys' and men's choir – old-fashioned Church of England, really, at its best, though with new liturgy. Later on I got myself to Westminster Cathedral for Vespers. There were terrible textiles on both altar and priests. A garden table, old mailbags and two bookcases had been pushed under the pulpit. Westminster Cathedral needs looking after – although the plainsong was well sung.

28 March

This evening I watched again *A Question of Attribution*, the play about Sir Anthony Blunt by Alan Bennett. Prunella Scales moved exactly like Her Majesty the Queen. How does she do this? When I asked her, she told me she did it by watching very closely the way the Queen holds her handbag.

3 April

Easter Day. I said the 8 o'clock Mass in St Thomas's, Brentwood, for 33 people and preached, then got my own breakfast. At 10 I preached to 450 people. Andrew Dunford came from London. The Easter liturgy was inspiring and I felt the truth of it all in this sensible, attentive place. At the end of Mass I was warmly thanked and given a cheque for £100 and a bottle of Bollinger – 'You've brought fizz to the parish, Father!'

12 April

I caught the 12.30 train to Great Yarmouth via Norwich for the Chelmsford clergy conference. No one in Great Yarmouth knew where the bus for Caistor went from, but after a trudge I got to the freezing chalets of Holiday Haven, where we were based. I gave my lecture and upset one Evangelical by suggesting that it mattered about ethics. 'Why does it matter about financial ethics,' he asked, 'when God is going to destroy the world by fire?' I was so incensed that I asked if he'd ever been inside a burns unit and seen the effects of fire on anyone. The fact that people like this get ordained in the late twentieth century is outrageous.

A few days after this depressing encounter, my spirits were lifted by Elaine's ordination to the priesthood in St Paul's Cathedral. Now we were seeing the fruit of all those years during which the Movement for the Ordination of Women had met patiently in the vestry of St Mary-le-Bow.

17 April

At Woolwich Dockyard I preached about how to live together after the ordination of women in a church where everybody's in favour of it except the Rector. This went better than I thought possible.

After lunch I went off to St Paul's Cathedral for Elaine's ordination as a priest. There were 4,000 people in the building. The Rt Revd Roy Williamson, Bishop of Southwark, did the ordinations and I laid hands on dear Elaine. Andrew got there straight from Istanbul, bringing a pair of silver earrings he'd bought for Elaine.

In the evening I preached at Elaine's wonderfully humbling, holy and uplifting first Mass, and was given champagne by her and an ovation from the congregation. Elaine did it all so beautifully – confident, prayerful, happy and right. It was a triumph for God and for the human race. I staggered home soaked with sweat, exhausted and happy.

It was a roller coaster of a month, as it turned out, and emotionally debilitating. Shortly after the joy of Elaine's ordination, we were cast down by devastating news about Werner.

22 April

Now we know Werner probably has cancer of the brain. Andrew, who loves him, was too distraught to come to Codford, quite rightly wanting to spend time with him.

Michael Kenny came into the breach to help with our parish weekend, which was very good of him. We had 14 people to dinner, which Michael cooked with me. Ruth, unfortunately, was hopeless. She hadn't remembered to make any bread, but had spent time weeding up the *viticella* clematis which has taken three years to grow through the pear trees and is now no more.

26 April

At least there was bright sunshine today. Today, South Africa begins to vote. An old lady voting in the Church of the Resurrection in Soweto said on television, in such a sweet and dignified voice, 'I've come to cast off the shackles of oppression.'

Tomorrow poor Werner's parents arrive from Greece. Strain and suffering is etched into the faces of the people around me. All a priest can do is be alongside people – what

Michael Ramsey called 'bearing and sharing', allowing your-self to feel something of what others feel without getting in their light or way. It is sometimes literally desperate and God, although intellectually we believe he is in it, is of no comfort at all – at least never to me.

28 April

A Syrian Orthodox delegation came to see me today, seeking a church to use, knowing that Lord Justice Templeman has suggested that some City churches might fall out of Anglican use and, in his famous words, 'become mothballed'. Later I went to talk to Oliver Leigh-Wood from SAVE about the Templeman Report.

I came back to talk through June Judd-Goodwin's funeral arrangements with her local Vicar, should she die, as I'm sure she will, whilst I am in Israel in the summer.

I feel exhausted and worn out by all this suffering, and spent part of the afternoon lying absolutely stock still on my sofa.

Werner has sent his parents away, having got to that stage of terminal illness when he's really too tired to cope with people. It is most difficult for those of us who watch around a deathbed.

May was an extension of the strains of April. Early in May we had the official opening of the Globe Centre at last, with a marvellous talk by Lord Bramwell, the Lord Lieutenant. I was just amazed that we were finally in the new building. Men and women in the East End with HIV now had a safe place where they could seek med-ical, social and human support. Andrew, I noticed, was looking frail with worry about Werner. I rushed back to St Mary-le-Bow to celebrate Mass at 5.45 p.m., then went straight out again to Dillons bookshop for the launch of *Living the Mystery*, our second collection of Affirming Catholicism lectures. After that I had din-ner with an exhausted Rowan Williams and a jolly but talkative Lavinia Byrne, who seemed unaware of how completely flattened Rowan was feeling. That day I was merely thankful to have stayed alive until bedtime.

10 May

I left the Bishop of Edinburgh, who'd stayed the night, having a Court of the Arches breakfast after our 7.30 Matins and Mass, and was just in time to get to the 8.30 Mass at St Michael's, Cornhill, with the Court of Sion College. At the Court meeting afterwards, I was elected President.[2] At the feast in the evening I was invested with the chain of office and we had a warm speech from Sir Brian Jenkins, the principal guest.

12 May

Ascension Day. Sarah Mann rang from the Home Office to tell me that John Smith died at Barts at 9.15 from a massive heart attack. I was devastated, but immediately had the Union Jack flown at half-mast and got Mark Regan to muffle the bells for the peal before High Mass. I was so upset about John Smith's death that it was difficult to celebrate the Eucharist. I watched the House of Commons at 3.30 on television and saw that the Prime Minister, Margaret Beckett, Tony Benn and Neil Kinnock were all deeply moved. The House, silent, was then adjourned.

At St Stephen Walbrook, where I had to preach for the Parish Clerks' Festival, I prefaced my sermon by explaining why I'd had the bells muffled and the flag flown at half-mast. Nobody else had done this in the City, because John Smith wasn't a person who merited such distinctions by rank and the City runs by clockwork, not imagination. This death on Ascension Day has changed the whole British political landscape. It has consequences which we can't yet foresee and is devastating for the Labour Party, who have lost their leader. It's unbearably sad.

At the High Mass at lunchtime, poor June Judd-Goodwin looked like a skull. She can't possibly last long – nor, I think, can Andrew's friend and patient Julius, if he has pneumonia.

---

2 Being President of Sion College was rather like being Master of a livery company. The President's job was to look after the College and preside over the Court meetings for the term of one year.

At 4 o'clock today I planted out the summer bedding plants in the roof garden – one gesture in the direction of new life.

13 May

I caught the 9 o'clock shuttle to Edinburgh. All the papers heaped praise on John Smith – all of them, even the *Sun*. I was met by Father Alan Moses,[3] motored to St Cuthbert's and left there. I briefed the minister, Tom Cuttle, as I'd been invited to, ahead of tomorrow's conference about running a city-centre church with a weekday ministry. St Cuthbert's is enormous and has a solid white marble altar they refer to as 'the Communion table', which strikes me as an inappropriate appellation.

14 May

We held the conference in the peeling, yellow-walled, grey-woodworked church hall for 30 people, from 10.30 till 3, including lunch with the parishioners. I talked for too long about St Mary-le-Bow and didn't get the tone right about renewal in the Church. I had dinner with the newly elected Bishop of Moray, Ross and Caithness and his marvellous wife, who live in a council flat. The priest who was the Registrar of the National Gallery of Scotland and his wife were also there.

During May, my priestly life began to change gear. I was busy making preparations to celebrate the twenty-fifth anniversary of my ordination as Deacon in 1969. This anniversary was the trigger for a sabbatical leave, starting immediately afterwards.

---

3 Father Moses was Rector of Old St Paul's, a famous Scottish Episcopalian Anglo-Catholic church in favour of women's ordination, with a woman priest on the staff. (The ordination of women happened in Scotland and Ireland before it did in England.)

26 May

Most of the day was spent getting ready for my Silver Jubilee of Deaconing. The police rang at 3 o'clock and a detective crept round the church because the Secretary of State for Northern Ireland had signified his intention of attending the service. 'Of course, sir,' the detective said, 'he may not come as he is seeing a certain person at 5 o'clock.' They do actually speak like this.

In the event, Patrick simply told the Prime Minister he had to leave. 'I said to the Prime Minister, "I'm going to church now." The Prime Minster said, "You can't go to church." I said, "Oh yes, Prime Minister. You can manage perfectly well."'

Sir Brian Jenkins stayed well into the party afterwards, as did the Mayhews. In the speeches I made fun of Bernard Jenkin being so anti-Maastricht and right wing, which was rather unkind, and Sir Patrick took pity on Bernard and Anne and gave them a lift back to Parliament, where they were all voting. At least 150 people came. My first Vicar, Canon David Ritchie, came up from Wiltshire and my first Deacon, Bill Croft, was also there.

At Mass I got Elaine Jones to celebrate, both to make the point that I was keeping the festival of my own Deaconing and also wanting to be supportive to women's ordination. This upset Professor Nancy Lambton who, although she has got to the absolute top of her academic tree, is against the ordination of women largely because her greatly admired friend the Bishop of Newcastle is against it. It also upset Father Michael Tompkins, one of the priests who came to me for spiritual direction and over whom I've laboured oft. He was really angry that a woman was celebrating. Then the use of the hymn 'Once to every man and nation' upset Professor Cameron.[4]

Through all this I felt slightly out of it, because Michael Kenny had made such a fuss about me being exhausted just before my sabbatical and overcome by Life, Truth and Reality,

---

4 Professor Averil Cameron is a Byzantine historian, and Warden of Keble College, Oxford.

that he'd forced me to have half of one of his calming pills. This had calmed me down so much that I was only half awake.

Andrew Dunford and Sarah Mann administered chalices at Communion, and John Gaskell preached about humour in the life of the priest, particularly in the life of this priest. 'Laughing makes people see things in a new way,' he said. At the end of Mass, Alan Wilson rushed straight from the organ console to Australia to get married. Waiters from the Grocers' Hall served delicious food and wine at the back of the nave after Mass.

The congregation gave me £1,225 and some new luggage, the Choir School £300, Peter Luscombe a beautiful watercolour of Codford painted from the herb garden and a double-cuffed shirt with blue and white stripes, and Phyllida had organized a silversmith to make me a pair of silver and amethyst cuff links engraved with the date of my ordination: 29.5.69.

My sabbatical leave began in June with a visit to Amsterdam, before I set off for Israel later in the month. At the very end of May I had gone with Andrew to the Lighthouse to see Werner, and his speech had been much worse. Andrew rang me in Amsterdam to tell me what was happening. He was very sad. Werner's dying seemed like a slow, mournful pavane, playing beneath the early days of my sabbatical. Should he have more treatment? This is always an agonizing question for the terminally ill.

I went to the museum in Leiden and came across a collection of Buddhas in the last room. I sat down before them and prayed for Werner and for Andrew, for June, for Julius, and for others I knew who were in trouble and pain. On 11 June I received a telephone message to say that Werner had been given his first dose of morphine.

19 June

London. I went to the Lighthouse at 3.30 p.m. Immediately on pushing the door open, I knew the Angel of Death was in the room. I gave flowers to Werner, holding rosemary, honeysuckle, mint and scented roses for him to smell, and he tried. I blessed him, then left Andrew and the nurses who'd come to turn him, for now he has bedsores. Later Andrew told me they'd talked carefully of death and the funeral. His parents want Werner's body – such a strong, dancer's body – taken back to Greece for burial. In the Lighthouse garden I saw that the Albertine rose was at her most blowsy.

20 June

I flew from Gatwick to Tel Aviv, then shared a taxi to Jerusalem with a New York Jewish family. Arriving through the steep, stony hill country was exciting. There was a limpid, opalescent light. Tantur is on a hill and I arrived in the dark, late, but found that somebody had kept me supper in a kitchen. I took it out on to a balcony and asked a man smoking a cigarette what the lights were below us. 'Oh, that's Bethlehem,' he said.

21 June

The next Christian community beyond Bethlehem in a straight line is Ethiopia.

In the afternoon we went by bus out to the Judean wilderness and the Monastery of St George, then to Bethany, overlooking the Temple Mount. There, in an ecstasy of gazing upon Jerusalem, the loose lens of my prescription sunglasses fell out and smashed into a lot of very tiny pieces. The wife of a Lutheran Bishop (American, of course) carefully picked up the 30 pieces of glass and handed them back. I'm making up that it was 30, but her painstaking collecting of these useless fragments was extraordinarily annoying, more annoying than breaking the glasses.

The first impression, today's impression, is the vastness of the wilderness, where we saw Bedouin sheep and goats and got turned back by soldiers. Soldiers are intensely biblical.

22 June

We heard a brilliant lecture today on the construction of parables and Jesus as a Hebrew theologian. After dinner, Sister

Sheila motored me to the Old City, where we went to the Wailing Wall and I prayed for June Judd-Goodwin, who died on Monday.

The power of the Wall swirls about you. 'If I forget thee, oh Jerusalem, let my tongue cleave to the roof of my mouth.' There were crowds praying and a full moon.

I went briefly into the narthex of the Holy Sepulchre, which brought back memories of Elizabeth Ritchie's death and me coming out here to bury her the day before Christmas Eve all those years ago.[5]

24 June

As I got into the coach for a day at the archaeological site of the City of David, the fax I'd been waiting for came: 'Werner died this morning at 5.45 of pneumonia. He was sweaty and feverish and frightened yesterday morning, but gradually settled into a coma by the afternoon.'

It was difficult going on into the hot, bright day with remorselessly jolly people and no one I could begin to share any of this with. After lunch, our lecturer Dr Jim Fleming took us into a tomb he'd excavated himself. After a couple of years, the bones were collected and put in an urn called an ossuary. 'How odd that would be today,' he said, adding that he didn't think it happened anywhere now. I pulled myself together sufficiently to read out to everyone the second half of Andrew's fax: 'He will be buried in Athens, probably next week. Some of his bones will be exhumed in three years' time to go into a chapel his family will build next to his little house on Mykonos.'

I rang Andrew at 8.15 this evening. He will probably fly out to Athens next week. Werner was a strong young man, a dancer, 26 years old. Andrew nursed him with tender love. I came across this in a book of Persian poetry today: 'At first love is such an easy thing, but oh, the hard awakening.'

---

5 Elizabeth was the daughter of Canon David Ritchie, who was Vicar of Pinner at the time of her death. She had just qualified as a nurse and was killed during a celebratory holiday when her Land Rover plunged down a ravine in the Sinai Desert. I flew out to bury her because her parents were too unwell to travel and I was her father's Curate in Pinner.

25 June

I got the bus to the Jaffa Gate and walked to the Holy Sepulchre. The church must be the worst kept and least devotional place in Christendom, yet, as I kissed the Cross-socket on Calvary and lit candles for June and Werner in this most holy place, I somehow felt the power of God.

The art in the Holy Sepulchre is uniformly gruesome and the people queuing for the tomb wore baseball hats. Because it is all so ugly, tasteless and discordant, it might just be the true site. Indeed, it's very much more likely to be the true site than the Garden Tomb, which is simply making the tomb as American Protestants would like the tomb site to be.

29 June

The Feast of St Peter and St Paul. I read Matins at 6 a.m. in front of their icon. At Arad today we saw the site of the first Israelite fortress from the tenth century BC. Its altar, holy place and holy of holies were all covered over after the reforms in the eighth century when Hezekiah limited sacrifices to Jerusalem. I picked up three shards, and Dr Fleming dated them to the Iron Age, 1200–1000 BC, the time of the Judges, Ruth, Samuel and Saul.

We walked along the Wadi Zohar in the Wilderness of Zin to look at the acacia wood, from which the Ark was made, and the tamarind tree and manna. Some plants have root systems 100 feet deep. I looked at the sand on the wadi's bed and at a Roman fort built on the rock while we listened to the silence. Everywhere is a boiling, blazing, empty beauty.

2 July

On our tour today we visited the Church of the Agony in Gethsemane. This was the most holy and affecting of all the churches here, because it was full of handicapped young French people, who were praying, singing and listening to Scripture in the dark, purple-windowed calm. I think we all prayed here, kneeling at the altar rails around the Rock of the Agony.

The Palestinian leader Yasser Arafat made a historic trip to the West Bank yesterday, so this evening Jerusalem is cut off by 20,000 Jews demonstrating against him.

3 July

We ran into some of the unrest when a march of young right-wing Jews, on their way to harass local Palestinians, surrounded our bus and the resultant detour made us late for Mass at the thirteenth-century Abu Gosh. The liturgy was in French and Latin, conducted with poise and care, with exquisite singing. The music being sung was once heard by the Crusaders.

When I got back to my room this evening I discovered via Andrew that Anne Reyersbach's father has died.[6] Andrew is glad to have been at Werner's funeral. He said he felt my support for the family as a physical reality. Sometimes people make that observation about intercessory prayer.

5 July

At a brilliant lecture this morning on Judaism, I realized how ignorant I am about it and how shameful this is.

We went to the Armenian Cathedral of St James in time for Vespers at 3 p.m. Teenagers from the seminary wore loose, flowing black cassocks. One boy was sitting cross-legged in a high pulpit, reading aloud from a great Bible. The whole church was carpeted with rugs and was indescribably Oriental and ancient in feel, much more so than the Orthodox churches. There was a strange, strong chant, quite different from anything I've heard before.

6 July

John and Steve, who are Roman Catholic seminarians, and Paul, who is an American RC priest, and I went to the Holy Sepulchre at 7 a.m. There we ascended various stone

---

6 Anne Reyersbach had been a schoolgirl in Pinner when I was Curate there. She had become a close friend, and was now a head teacher in South London.

stairways to the Monastery of Abraham where, in the Chapel of the Sacrifice of Isaac, all was laid out and waiting for us to celebrate Mass, candles lit. As I said the words of consecration, some doves flew up in the vault. They'd been rustling there during the liturgy. This sounds pious and pretty, but it's true. I said a Mass of the Resurrection, with the Gospel reading from Holy Saturday about Joseph and the new tomb. Below us was Calvary, and further down the Easter Sepulchre itself. After the distribution of Communion – all the Roman Catholics were happy to receive Anglican Communion – we sat and looked at the frescoes of the cross, the sacrifice of Isaac, and Abraham entertaining angels unawares.

10 July

We left at 7.15 this morning, with our suitcases and a horrible 'sack lunch', an entirely apposite name. The first stop was Caesarea Maritima, full of archaeologists, breaking waves and the welcome smell of the sea. The huge amphitheatre is still in use. At Mount Carmel we had a mountain-top Mass, beautifully celebrated, with children playing in the woods around, limitless views and a very strong wind. Acre is quite the most attractive site – spices, fish, an enormous Crusader wall, vaults and ramparts. It was a long journey into the high Galilee, a marvellous rolling, fertile countryside, quite different from Judea.

11 July

At Nazareth we saw the beautiful 1950 Basilica over the supposed site of Mary's house. There is space, an air of devotion and prayer here. Afterwards we had a hot climb round Megedo. It's odd to think that Pope Paul VI and Israel's President met and spoke here of Armageddon. What was going on? I don't really get this apocalyptic strain that people have. I seem to be immunized against it.

12 July

At the church beside the sea and the synagogue built over the Apostle Peter's house, there was a holy feeling. I said Mass and preached, but it all had to be shouted against a howling wind. You can't be recollected while shouting. One Canadian and one of the Australian priests will still not take Communion with people who are not Roman Catholics. They prefer to glower.

13 July

This whole trip has one big fault – a sense of rush. From Metuloa on the Lebanon border we motored into the fertile mountain country of Banias. Caesarea Philippi is beautiful and so are the Golan Heights, with a view of the great, dominating Crusader castle of Nimrud from the mountain range of Hermon. At one point we were only 25 miles from Damascus. There were tanks everywhere.

16 July

This morning we were on the Temple Mount – calm, ordered, holy Islamic spaces, and a beautiful Byzantine mosaic from the 690s. A magical site.

I spent the evening sitting in the garden, talking with Teddy – an Irish priest working in Chile – about ecumenism, the Provos, Northern Ireland and why the IRA has morality on its side. This was quite difficult to listen to, but it was worthwhile having to make the effort.

18 July

We spent the morning being taken round a Palestinian refugee camp beyond Bethlehem – lovely, intelligent children learning French. The open drains were as intrusive as I felt we were ourselves. These concentration camps have been here for between 20 and 50 years, and the world doesn't really care. There is a curfew, open sewers, water only three days a week, no work, and soldiers beating young people up.

20 July

Our last day in Jerusalem. We spent five hours in the Israeli Museum – separate pavilions, gardens and water, planets away from those refugee camps.

Back at Tantur, Dilly – now based with her husband in Tel Aviv – arrived to collect me in a silver convertible, charming everyone. I left in a rush of glamour and we were in Tel Aviv by 8 p.m., exchanging institutional concrete for the luxurious house of a diplomat.[7] Dilly said, 'It's a bit *House and Garden*,' but oh, the air-conditioned marble space and light, the garden of frangipani, hibiscus, bougainvillea and palm trees, the driver, maid, gardeners and dining table for 24!

23 July

At 10 we left for Haifa and Elizabeth Ritchie's grave. On the headstone was the inscription I'd chosen all those years ago: 'In the morning you shall see the glory of the Lord.' But Elizabeth's is no longer the newest grave. There are four rows now beyond her.

In the evening we went to a huge party at the Defence Attaché's. The American wives, when asked by me what they thought of the refugee camps, said, 'Oh, we're not allowed to go into the Occupied Territories.' Isn't that America all over?

By 26 July, I was back at home in Codford. The garden depressed me, overgrown and vast, the wisteria rampant. When I had bought my half of Old Wool Cottage, the back garden had been quite small. Don and Andrew, buying the other half, had added to this the large walled kitchen garden, the yew garden of the Big House and the stable yard. All this, plus the two joined front gardens, added up to a great deal of work.

Something had to be done. I rang Andrew to say, 'We must sell Codford. It's too big, too far, too much.' Nevertheless, I hung up

---

7 Dilly, who had earlier been my secretary at St Mary-le-Bow, and her husband Simon Erskine Crum had taken up Air Force and diplomatic postings first in Canada and then in Israel.

my Jerusalem icons and burned some incense from Gethsemane in the chapel.

During the first days of August, my sabbatical continued with a trip across the Atlantic. I stayed with friends in New York and Providence, Rhode Island, before going on to the Society of St John the Evangelist in Boston.[8]

8 August

I was driven from Rhode Island to Boston and left at the monastery in Memorial Drive. Later I had an hour's talk with the Primate of Canada, walking along by the Charles River. The Primate is an enthusiastic supporter of Affirming Catholicism. He is humble, open, friendly and normal – not like a clergyman at all, let alone an Archbishop.

9 August

After breakfast I spent some time before the strange, deep silence of the Sacrament in the dark side chapel of the monastery church. The Sacrament is reserved in a green, veiled, domed Tabernacle like a tent, waiting, as in a medieval tapestry, for some beautiful maiden or wondrous knight to emerge. There was a sung Mass in the monastery church with 87 people, lots of them from the university. Drinks were available afterwards in the cloisters, with people invited to stay to dinner. This is a good place – unlike the uptight, parsimonious, shut-down, anxious Church of England.

12 August

I was up at 5.15 a.m. Later I drove off in bright sunshine for my time in the Hermitage, in the grounds of the Society's country estate on the Merrimack River. It is just built, light, spacious and Japanese. There is a log stove and a log fire, mosquito netting everywhere, a veranda, a splendid kitchen and bathroom, tree-surrounded and shaded. I am alone in a

---

8 The SSJE is an Anglican community of monks originally founded in Oxford by Father Benson in the nineteenth century.

wood like the beginning of Dante's *Divine Comedy*. I was shown the canoe and the rowing boats, all of which I can use, and the library, into which I am welcomed – unlike at Fairacres.

14 August

Sunday. Retreatants and three members of the Society of St John the Evangelist danced to lovely, simple rounds, one at the end of Mass to the Shaker song 'It's good to be simple, it's good to be free'. I spent the morning reading a book by Ken Bailey with the aid of a Greek Testament. The most valuable experience of my time in Israel was hearing lectures by Ken Bailey.[9]

15 August

Today I had a drink at the harbourside with Brother James, who felt like going out. I like these monks who feel like going out sometimes. That's the way to be a hermit: stop sometimes. I rowed for a mile or so through silence and water lilies. It's funny how these hermit days can be wonderful and blessed or awkward and pointless, but I'm sure real hermits feel exactly the same.

At some point over the following few days, I slipped a bookmark into my psalm book which had on it this comment from Father Richard Benson SSJE, the founder of the Community: 'There is nothing Divine about hurry, and nothing hurried about the Divine.'

24 August

It's a sunny St Bartholomew's Day. Brother James phoned to say he'd fixed a whale watch for me today. St Bartholomew's whales. From 1.30 to 6.30 p.m. I was out on the open sea. There were humpback whales, nine in all, and they began to blow, showing their great tail fins. The grace and power of these 30–40 foot mammals was mysteriously beautiful, as

---

9 Ken Bailey is a Presbyterian biblical scholar living and teaching in the Middle East.

they rose and turned over from a mill-pond-blue sea under the white sun.

At the end of August I returned temporarily to England, where I caught the news of an important development in Northern Ireland before setting off on the last leg of my sabbatical.

1 September

The IRA ceasefire came into force at midnight. I watched Patrick on television from No. 10 last night, and live at 6.30 this morning from Belfast. God grant that it holds and the Protestants don't kill too many Catholics. Patrick was calming; John Major and Tony Blair, Labour Leader in place of John Smith, were equally good.

Then I set off in the car with Andrew, heading for Cherbourg and France. We motored through the country to Nantes, then stopped for a few days in Toulouse before going on to Nîmes, which we admired for its general elegance and the beautiful Roman arena. Avignon and Orange were next on the list, and by the middle of September we had crossed over the border into Italy, stopping first in Turin to continue our architectural feast.

A short distance away down the River Po was the Superga, the hideously baroque necropolis of the royal House of Savoy. An obese monk slowly and portentously conveyed us down into the Royal Necropolis, and the vampire movie effect was made complete by a terrific thunderstorm, during which lightning struck one of the window embrasures just as we passed it. The walls were decorated with a series of crowned skulls holding marble table napkins – reactionary Bourbon despots trying to demonstrate what nice people they were.

We moved on to Bologna and Ravenna, where the bright mosaics in the Church of San Vitale cut right through the gloomy day and the tawdry eighteenth-century frescoes. Pausing briefly in Modena to admire the lions, centaurs and griffins, we travelled on to Mantua. The town rose, dream-like, from the three lakes, all towers and domes. In the huge and gloomy San Andrea were two phials containing the Holy Blood of Jesus – blood-soaked soil brought from Jerusalem by the centurion Longinus and 'discovered'

in 804. In the Holy Sepulchre was a photograph of the Pope censing these ludicrous fakes.

On the way to Verona the sun came out at last. In the Teatro
Olympico – the world clearly shrinking – we found Japanese
actors rehearsing Euripides. After stopping in Venice to see
friends, we made our way north again, pausing for a day trip round
Lake Lucerne on a paddle steamer. Not one speedboat or plane
came to disturb our peace, and the surrounding landscape was so
perfect it could have been part of a model railway kit. Via
Strasbourg and Brussels, we eventually arrived in Dunkirk. The
port seemed to be on its last legs, and so did the ferry we caught
back to England.

The long sabbatical, with its mixture of architectural discovery,
deeper reflection upon the person, life and meaning of Jesus, and
time of hermitage, study and silence, was of the most immense
and long-term benefit. Before I went, I thought I knew quite a lot
about Jesus Christ, the development of the New Testament, the
history of the Bible and the beginnings of Christianity. After all, I
had been teaching other people about them for years. On my
sabbatical I discovered how little I knew. The Roman arena in
Nîmes, the Metropolitan Museum in New York, the Museum of
Fine Art in Boston, time to read, old friendships renewed and
deepened in America, Holland, France and Italy – these became
the fat to live on in the lean times to come. Such times invariably
come to a priest, through the daily demand of people in need and
in pain, even when the life of ministry is conducted in as magical
and privileged a place as the Square Mile of the City of London.

Early October saw me ensconced once again in that City life.
The first Tuesday Dialogue of the new season was with Bishop
David Jenkins, who was warmly applauded by an audience of 250.
He had been staying with the Queen at Sandringham and
described the family as close-knit and affectionate. Her Majesty
had said to him, 'We have ordinary old-fashioned Matins here. It's
what I can manage best.' This was not an apology, he said, but an
explanation of preference.

13 October

Sir Patrick Mayhew was quite brilliant, as Matthew Parris
wrote, 'dancing on eggs' at the Tory Party Conference. At 10

a.m. came an announcement of a Loyalist ceasefire from midnight. Dancing on worse than eggs has been going on for a long time.

14 October

I walked round Osterley Park and Osterley House, listening to someone traumatized by an HIV diagnosis busily destroying his life piece by piece. I tried to help him see that professional psychiatric help is what he needs. How often really difficult conversations with people are helped by taking them out of the study and into the park, where trees and water have heard it all before. The sunshine and the dazzling yellow of the leaves were beautiful, but people's lives are sometimes unbearable.

18 October

Maureen Lipman was brilliantly good at the Dialogue, and we had 350 people, 100 standing. Marvellous. She wouldn't leave, which was lovely for all of us, but eventually she did, and I got myself to the bulb shop in Covent Garden where I bought bulbs for Andrew's balconies and some for the man with the HIV diagnosis. I'll pot those up and give them to him, for bulbs are a proof that there is a future.

21 October

I went to Ealing to visit Derek Jennings, who has two lovely rooms in St Saviour's Clergy House, where an old friend of his, Andrew Davies, is the Vicar. Derek looks awful, but we enjoyed meeting each other and I stayed for nearly two and a half hours, too long for somebody who's seriously ill.

24 October

Today I was overwhelmed by people, including a group from the Hispanic Church who may want to use St Mary Aldermary, and the new fundraisers from the Globe project. Suddenly I had to get out of the claustrophobic noise of St

Mary-le-Bow. I went to Hyde Park Corner and walked across a dazzlingly sunny park to Lancaster Gate, thinking about what to preach at June Judd-Goodwin's Requiem, postponed because of my long leave.

The church was packed for June's funeral Requiem, with the ashes on a little table before the altar. At the end of Mass, the whole congregation walked out into the dark churchyard, where I had already dug the hole for the ashes. June's ashes spilled a little and made a fine cloud. I breathed some of them in, but reflected that they would do me no harm. Going back into the church, we were caught up in that wonderful verse, 'Till we cast our crowns before Thee, lost in wonder, love and praise.'

30 October

I'm staying at Offham with Phyllida and Andrew. We went to luncheon at the Rentons' and Tim Renton poured boiling *potage cresson* all over the Dowager Lady Hampden. This poor Viscountess, being wedged in, couldn't move, but endured her discomfort with aristocratic fortitude.

June's former hospice nurse, Jan Barham, came to the end of her placement with us as part of her ordination training by acting as Subdeacon at High Mass on the Feast of All Saints. She did it perfectly, being one of those people with a sense of liturgy, how to move, how to be attentive, dignified and prayerful. Not all these are gifts, but are skills that need concentration and practice.

The next day I had the enormous pleasure of spending several hours in Winchester Cathedral at the invitation of the Precentor, Canon Charles Stewart, who had heard from the Salisbury Cathedral Fabric Advisory Committee that I might know something about colour and design. There had been a problem about replacing textiles and vestments, and an enormously expensive Japanese scheme had recently run into the ground. I began by looking at the bones of the building, and asked if I could have the time of a couple of Vergers. Within an hour we had transformed the nave, simply by removing two standard candlesticks from their too-close proximity to the nave altar and repositioning them on either side of the lectern. This, plus the removal of a great many superfluous chairs, created light and space – space to think.

A little later in November Martyn Lewis, the television presenter, came for a Dialogue. He is a man who believes in Good News, rather than Bad News, on television and he is laughed at for this laudable objective. I liked him very much, as I did the *Times* correspondent Ruth Gledhill, who was doing a series on 'best' church services in the paper, visiting churches and awarding points. She gave us good publicity, and publicity is something I am always thinking about at St Mary-le-Bow: how to get the people outside interested in what goes on inside.

We had Lord Justice Templeman to Dialogue, too. As Chairman of the Templeman Commission on the future of the City churches, what he had to say was of particular interest. Sir Samuel Brittan, financial journalist and Leon Brittan's brother, also came. He would not eat a single leaf of the lunchtime salad, saying, 'I'm afraid I don't eat vegetables.' He was the first absolutely anti-vegetarian I had ever met. He went, lunchless, straight from the Dialogue to write his *Financial Times* piece on the budget, for it was indeed Budget Day – rather a coup for St Mary-le-Bow, I thought.

12 November

I caught a train to Ipswich to talk about Affirming Catholicism, and then to Oxford to stay at Keble College before preaching at Magdalen. The Warden's Lodgings are magisterial, and the Fellows have decorated them beautifully – royal portraits from the Ashmolean, pink sofas, space and height, a huge bedroom, bath, tea and a tour of the house.

13 November

I went off with my robes through the grey morning to Magdalen for Schubert's *Mass in G* and my sermon. The chapel was packed. I think the sermon went well, certainly better than the last one I preached here. There was a terrible student lunch of bread and pâté.

18 November

I have come to the convent of St Katherine's in Stepney to give a retreat. I enjoy giving retreats. I know what I'm doing. There are 20 of us and the nuns here *want* their guests. Not all nuns are like that, though they all pretend they are.

19 November

It's grey and grisly. After celebrating a Mass of the Resurrection, I abandoned the retreatants for a breath of fresh air and a walk along Narrow Street, thinking how little I'd like to live here, even with a river view. I spent the day giving addresses and then seeing people in my room. It's a strange business, with the retreatants putting a cross on the list on the door if they want an interview, and a 'C' if they want Confession. There was the usual amount of marriage breakdown and absence of God.

Early in December I enjoyed the pre-Christmas treat of a visit to Brighton on the train, where I walked to Hove for lunch with the author Michael De-la-Noy, Michael's literary agent and the Latvian Ambassadress. There was a howling gale along the front and, as I walked back to Evensong at St Nicholas', pebbles were cast up on the promenade with the force of the wind. I preached at the 8 p.m. Mass and the candlelit church was absolutely full, with a happy, splendidly mixed congregation.

Later in the month, the Children's Society decided not to come to St Mary-le-Bow for their carol service. This was because I refused to support them against the pressure group Outrage if Outrage were to disrupt the service. There had been rumours that this might happen, because of the Children's Society's decision not to permit gay and lesbian foster parents. 'You must use the police under the Public Worship Measure to cast these people out,' they said. I tried to explain to the Society authorities what it would be like if we were to see on the 6 o'clock news, a couple of days before Christmas, a squad of police ejecting gay and lesbian protesters from St Mary-le-Bow over the adoption of children.

21 December

The shortest day, or the longest night, depending on which way you look at it. I went from Liverpool Street to Romford, where I had lunch in a Friern Barnet-style vicarage and then preached to over 500 people at the town carol service. I shook hands with nearly all the 500 at the door, and enjoyed doing so.

23 December

We motored off at 12.15 with a chattering Ruth to Codford through thick fog. Andrew was falling asleep on the way. As he was driving, we had to stop for a bit to let him recover. The house is utterly freezing. Oh, lovely, lovely electric blanket!

24 December

Saturday, Christmas Eve, my fiftieth birthday. We had nine to lunch: Annie Reyersbach, Tim, Bernard, James Watson, Douglas (a friend of Bernard's), Ruth, Jeremy Davies, Andrew and myself. After Evensong, supper and a rest, I went off to Edington to celebrate and preach at Midnight Mass. A hard, glittering, sparkling frost gave way to drizzle and thaw. In the candlelit church, all the Servers were over six foot, apart from one who was a smaller edition of the same gang of brothers. I managed the rite without mishap this year.

26 December

I slept ill because I now have a bad cold. I conducted Matins and Mass for St Stephen's Day in the chapel at 9.30 because James demanded it. 'When is Matins going to be? When is Mass? I want to have a Mass. We should have a Mass today...' Two Greek friends of John Macintosh, the Headmaster of the Oratory School, arrived, so we had another feast squashed around my William IV table.

It's so nice when people leave. It's lovely having them here, but even lovelier when they go away.

Private Eye

I n the first week back after New Year I took myself to the Lambeth Palace library, where we hoped the most important Sion College books would end up. After a great deal of discussion, the Court of Sion College had come to the view that we had no hope of maintaining or restoring the library building. Selling the building, it was decided, would save the books themselves from threat of sale. We were hoping that the historic collection – pre-1840 – would go to Lambeth to complete the collection there, while the post-1840 books would find a home at London University, with the books on both sites remaining available to Sion Readers.

While we were looking round, Dr Richard Parker, the Lambeth Librarian, showed me an annotation which Charles I had written on a letter to Archbishop Laud. Dr Parker and his wife gave me lunch in their house in the old stables, and told me that Archbishop George Carey took a good interest in the fine library.

From the comforts of Lambeth, I went straight to King's Cross to catch a train for Lincoln, where I was due to give a talk about Affirming Catholicism.

10 January

Lincoln Theological College is depressing – room, building and food all vile. I was too aggressive in my presentation to be popular, partly because I was reacting against disliking the place very much. I had a beer in the bar before and after. The principal of the college, a very nice man, appeared to fall asleep during my lecture. I had every sympathy with him.

11 January

Although my room was horrible, the bed was comfortable and I felt secure in it, as in a little monastic cell. We had Matins from the ASB, and a Eucharist where the celebrant wore vestments but did not move his hands or arms. There was a filthy breakfast, uneatable.

I walked on my own around Lincoln Cathedral with my mouth wide open. It is simply enormous. The chairless nave was fantastic, the chapels beautiful. I got into the library, where there was no clutter but also no people working. The cathedral is well signed, except that the High Altar is inaccurately described as 'the Communion Table' because the Dean is a famous Evangelical Low Churchman, locked in endless acrimony with the Sub-Dean.

15 January

At Codford a mouse has had some of the cheese from the butler's pantry and escaped. There was a rather pretty mouse in my bathroom last night, too.

I went with Annie and Ruth to Edington, where I blessed the plough. Then I blessed a choir boy. Edington is perfection. An old couple in the village have acquired a wafer-making device from a convent and have installed it in the medieval crypt at Edington. There they make their own altar breads for the parish from the bread given at Lammas, which, of course, has been made from wheat sown in the furrows ploughed by the plough I blessed today. The liturgical cycle and the natural cycle come perfectly together in this holy place under the White Horse.

23 January

Derek Jennings was meant to come to Cheapside for lunch today. Instead I visited him in Ealing. He was unconscious and morphia was to be administered by a drip later in the day. I judged he'd last perhaps until Thursday or Friday, but I was wrong. Just after I left him, Cardinal Basil Hume arrived and was with him when he died. Derek died at 6.05 this evening as Cardinal Hume said the words of the Gloria over him. It was very Derek to manage this, but so sad – dead at 48 from cancer.

In the afternoon I visited Canon Anthony Harvey at 3 Little Cloisters.[1] I wanted his professional advice, as feelings are

---

1 Anthony Harvey was Canon Theologian at Westminster Abbey and a former theological college principal.

running very high about the future of Sion. He gave me lemon curd and urged the relocation and retention of the Sion College library – don't sell the books, sell the building. I am sure this is what we must do.

24 January

The Secretary of State for Northern Ireland came to Dialogue today. The fullest security was in force and, although the identity of our guest had only been revealed outside the church at 10.30 a.m., there were 230 people in the nave. There was a standing ovation for Patrick at the end. At luncheon in Grocers' Hall the Prime Minister phoned, and then the Home Secretary phoned – the Grocers were very impressed by this. It all worked a treat, and the Master took the bait and invited Alistair Darling, the Labour City man, to lunch. City companies tend only – and short-sightedly – to invite Tories to their luncheons.

27 January

The Archbishop of Canterbury came to Sion Court as a Visitor, bringing his wife with him. We waited for him in the street and met him as he got out of his official car, rather like meeting the Lord Mayor. It fell to me to do the honours as I happen to be President this year. The Archbishop referred to Stephen Gregory's letter in *The Times* and had obviously been sent a copy of it.[2] A nasty moment. Apart from that, all went comparatively smoothly. He is a friendly man, but has a curious way of not quite looking you in the eye – he looks past you.

30 January

I went to Derek Jennings' funeral at the Brompton Oratory – 1,000 or so friends, with Cardinal Hume celebrating Mass.

---

2 Stephen Gregory was our College Librarian. He was adamantly and, from his perspective, quite reasonably, totally opposed to the dispersal of the books to two new sites.

Black Latin chasubles were worn by the concelebrating clergy, except for Monsignor Gilbey who refused to concelebrate and was in his full Vatican rig as a Domestic Prelate to the Holy Father. Many of the great and the good were there. The whole thing was horrible, particularly for Derek's brother Tim – the only family mourner, Auntie Libby not being well enough to come – who, like the rest of us Anglicans, was denied Holy Communion at his own brother's funeral. This is the sort of attitude which makes Roman Catholicism repulsive.

Derek's death has very much upset me, partly because I did not see enough of him in the last years, and felt estranged from him when he became a Roman Catholic because of its explicit rejection of Anglicanism and all that we stand for. We did have a very close and happy relationship as students and I owe him my long friendship with his grandmother and Auntie Libby. It is another chapter closing, as he knew my parents and many other mutual friends who are now dead. We die with the dying.

31 January

Our Dialogue guest today was Professor Ghillean Prance, Director of the Royal Botanical Gardens at Kew, a most sensible and liberal Evangelical. There was something especially holy about today. Ghillean Prance may be a saint. This shy, diffident man is radiant from the inside with the reality of God and therefore the Dialogue was moving and holy. He spoke about the roots of life on this planet being arteries of God – isn't that a wonderful idea? Such a different world from yesterday: evolving, not defensive.

February began with news of bad floods in Holland, and I was concerned for my friends. The television reports said that 250,000 people had been evacuated from their homes. Meanwhile, the Prime Minister made a broadcast to the nation about Northern Ireland after the Unionists leaked the draft peace document to *The Times*.

14 February

St Valentine's Day, and another Dialogue with actress Maureen Lipman. There were 500 people – 200 standing or sitting on the floor. In fact, there were so many people that we couldn't get in, Maureen Lipman and I. In the end I had to go through the vestry and squeeze my way out of the Norwegian Chapel and up the steps of the pulpit to ask people to come and sit on the floor of the Sanctuary, so that my guest could get in through the door by the font. It was quite astonishing.

We did talk about sex and love, but we somehow got on to the Holocaust and Maureen Lipman asked, 'Who would save me now, as a Jew, if it were to happen again?' She felt, with the amount of anti-Semitism that there is in Britain, that this was a possibility.

There was absolute silence, and I said, 'We would have to.' Somehow we were all drawn into the ghastliness of anti-Semitism, our own anxieties, ambiguities and fears revealed and held.

It was a very special occasion, in its way like the day when Dame Janet Baker came and the church was filled with a heavenly light. I have a very great regard for Maureen Lipman.

The day before Maureen Lipman's Dialogue, I had received the sad news that Joan Ramsey had died in Oxford. Since Bishop Michael's death, Joan had continued to be looked after by the nuns at St John's Home, becoming increasingly blind and frail. After her death, I had a long conversation about her with Alan Webster, who was writing her obituary for the *Independent*. Her funeral took place in Canterbury Cathedral a few days later.

17 February

I walked over to the Provost's House on Bankside, which Colin and Edith Slee have opened up and enlarged. Off we went from Southwark together to Canterbury Cathedral for Lady Ramsey's funeral. The cathedral was sun-filled and there were six tall, unbleached candles around Joan's black, brown and red coffin pall. I sat with Edith, Joan's nearest living relation. Colin gave an excellent sermon. Robert and

Lindy Runcie were in the congregation, and former Chaplains John Andrew and Philip Norwood. This was indeed the closing of a book. It was Church of England, dignified, warm, understated, tolerant, devout and holy.

Edith and I walked behind the coffin, carried out down the steps of the Choir as the Russian *Kontakion* was sung. Edith and I were in tears. Professor Owen Chadwick went in the car with us to the crematorium at Charing. The place was smothered in crocuses, and John Andrew said the Committal prayers with great dignity. Back in the cloisters, the chapter-house reception was all packed away, so none of us got even so much as a cup of coffee. We looked instead at Michael Ramsey's monument – 'Scholar, Priest and Friend' – and repaired to a pub for haddock and beer.

A grande dame said to me disapprovingly, 'Who is that woman in the coat of many colours?'

'That is Lady Ramsey's closest relative, Edith Slee,' I replied. 'She is married to the man Lady Ramsey asked to preach the sermon.' I enjoyed saying that so much, and I am utterly sure that Joan enjoyed hearing it.

24 February

At 2 o'clock today a smart chauffeur in a spanking new BMW was waiting patiently outside the church door to motor me to RAF Northolt, launch point for a private visit to Northern Ireland, my first trip to the Province. Here a young airman took my bag into the VIP lounge and tea was produced. Pictures of the Queen and Prince Philip *c.*1955 gave the place a touch of life, but life in the distant past, typical of service accommodation. After a visit from the Air Commodore in charge of the station, complete with gold aiguillettes, we were packed into a tiny plane while Air Force officers saluted smartly on the tarmac – just like an early Pathé newsreel of the royal family leaving for Kenya.

The other people in the plane, apart from the pilot, were Patrick, Jean, me and the secretaries. There was much conversation about what was going to be happening politically over the next few days. I was given a photocopy of Clifford Longley's excellent and supportive article on the present initiatives. Patrick gave me a copy of the Framework Document to read, and Jean gave me 'Biblical Frameworks for Peace and Reconciliation in Northern Ireland', a wonderfully intelligent document drawn up by a group of Evangelical Christians of different denominations, united by their concern for justice.

When we landed, two cars took us very fast indeed to Stormont. Jean had arranged for the Clerk of Stormont, Mr Kennedy, to show me round the Palace. It is only 60 years old, but is a monument of imperial domination. The interior of Stormont is grand, pompous and oppressive – not a place for poor Catholics in any sense. Next door to this is the baronial Gothic of the older castle. Here Patrick worked with his Private Secretary before doing a live Channel 4 programme at 7 p.m., and Jean signed her letters.

Patrick stayed behind at Stormont, but we rushed on to Hillsborough. I was given the Duke of Edinburgh's bedroom – sofas, armchairs and fire, a drinks table and Sèvres porcelain fruit service laid out, with silver knives and forks and a napkin, in case one should be dying for a nectarine in the night. As we were going up the stairs the first guests for the evening's dinner party were assembling in the State Drawing Room.

When I came downstairs after a quick bath, I found in the Drawing Room some women from the Falls Road, a Baptist minister, a caterer aged 24, a young youth worker and a Roman Catholic priest, Nationalists and Unionists and working-class mums. One woman with peroxide hair and a pink angora cardigan was screaming with laughter, sitting with Jean with her feet tucked up, as Jean had tucked hers up, on a Chippendale sofa under a portrait of William III. These are the people Jean describes as her friends, and so they are. One of them said to me that before the Mayhews came, she had never been to Hillsborough and would certainly never have been invited into a place like this.

Dinner was in the small dining room – red silk walls, crystal chandeliers, candlelight, an attentive young butler, Scallops Mornay from Strangford Lough, pheasant casserole and generous amounts of delicious wine. Patrick arrived after we had begun, the jolly RC priest having been invited to say

Grace by Jean. We had general conversation at the dinner table, everybody being drawn in. It was the most marvellous evening, given to the sort of people who don't normally get invited to Governor Generals' palaces, but who should be. I've spent ages in the City trying to get people to see that there is not much to be gained from inviting the same sort of people to state banquets and government hospitality in Mansion House or the Guildhall, but you don't get anywhere.

25 February

Saturday at Hillsborough Castle. I had another dip in the Duke of Edinburgh's bath. He must be very large, or perhaps the upper classes have bigger bath towels than anybody else. After breakfast Jean took me in her car to a monastery some-where on the Armagh border for an ecumenical conference.

We arrived during the worship service, while a lesson was being read, and Jean flopped down on to the floor. At the end of the service the woman minister from Dublin said, 'We had a message that Lady Mayhew was going to make us a visit...' There were murmurs of appreciation and expectation from the assembled people. I interrupted this, in case it got embar-rassing, by pointing to the floor where Jean was still sitting. There was a warm wave of loving applause and Jean and I did a double act: 'He's my spiritual guide and director, and when Patrick's down I send for Victor to make him laugh...'

Then there was a faintly charismatic hymn workshop and we all had to wave our arms and turn in circles. I didn't for a second look at Jean – I couldn't. Afterwards at coffee, peo-ple stood in lines to hug and kiss Jean, Roman Catholics, Protestants, everyone. I listened to lots of people, lots.

Back at the castle, we loaded sandwiches and Patrick into a car, along with George and Marshall (protection officers), and sped for about an hour through the countryside of Northern Ireland. It is surprisingly beautiful. I had no idea what it might be like. We looked across a dazzlingly blue sea to the Mull of Kintyre and snow-covered Scotland while we had a picnic in a field. Then for three hours we climbed, clambered, slithered, slipped, strode and fell across glen and bog, scree and mountain – George, with his gun and telephone, following at a discreet distance. Not one traffic sound came up from coast or glen, only silence.

26 February

Sunday. The Frost programme camera crew turned the State Drawing Room into a television studio this morning, and at 8.15 Patrick addressed the nation. Then came State Matins, awfully dreary, with an atrocious sermon from a Manchester lay evangelist. We sat in the state box, a sort of raised-up gallery overlooking the congregation, all typical of the old ascendancy. As we 'bowed our heads in prayer' – no one knelt down except the Secretary of State, his wife and his guest – I whispered to Patrick, 'How much will you pay me not to indulge in a display of Catholic devotional practices?'

We walked to and from church, although a car followed us, with George on foot and Marshall on a horse in discreet attendance. The Vicar's party came back to the castle for drinks. I poured out the champers, only spilling one bottle. When everybody else had gone away, we ate chicken, cheese and fruit pudding in the private dining room.

Afterwards we got into our walking togs and went off round the park – ice-house, temple, three lakes, lime avenues, the Arcadian works. Jean picked me snowdrops, Patrick picked me snowdrops, then I changed into clericals, had tea in the sitting room, and there was a car at the portico to take me off at 6 p.m.

On the plane was Mr Molyneux, leader of the Ulster Unionist Party, just two seats away. He didn't eat any of the food except the meat and bread, and put the brandy in his pocket. From Heathrow a driver took me to Bow Bells to leave my bag and then on to the Barbican for supper, where I gave Andrew the Hillsborough snowdrops and told him all my tales.

Northern Ireland's viceregal splendours were followed early in March by the equally encouraging acceptance of Sion College Court's proposals that the pre-1840 books should go to Lambeth Palace library and the rest to King's College, London. Now we could indeed save the books by selling the building. Wider acceptance of this, after the enormous hostility from *The Times* and

Private Eye, took longer to achieve. (*Private Eye* said I was a book-hating, coffee-drinking Evangelical. I do drink coffee.) Nevertheless, I was sure we had made the right decision, however unpopular it made me as President, and it did.

I went to visit old Percy Coleman, who had suffered his share of brickbats over the years (once General Secretary of the Church Union, he came to be regarded as 'unsound' because of his support for women's ordination) and was coming to the evening of his days in the quiet of the Charterhouse.[3] Beside his bed I saw the funeral paper for Sister Jane of Fairacres, a funeral I wished I had been able to attend. Her body had been carried from the convent to a rendition of 'Glory, glory, alleluia, the saints go marching on'. The nun who had said she would jump off Doddington Bridge when she was Mother, if she had time, and who had offered us sherry from a bottle she kept inside her green wellies, was most certainly a saint. She had taken a great deal of care of me, and I loved her dearly.

Mindful of Sister Jane's example, I said I would go to Greece to be with Andrew when he visited Werner's grave. I was also looking forward to discovering something of Greece, but first there was our English Holy Week.

9 April

Palm Sunday, Wiltshire. We walked in procession from the village hall to the liturgy at Edington Priory, then ate lunch at the house of Antonia Southern, a member of the congregation at Edington. We had a very amusing conversation about the Bishop of Chichester, Eric Kemp, who is not at all popular in the Southern household because of his opposition to the ordination of women. Antonia's sister told me of a legend which said that, if herons were to nest on the roof of the Bishop's Palace at Chichester, the Bishop would die. 'We have been devising an elaborate apparatus whereby huge bowls of goldfish are constantly hoisted to the roof of the palace by members of the Movement for the Ordination of Women.'

---

3 The medieval Charterhouse in Smithfield houses 'Brethren' who are largely retired priests with some historical connection to the City. Father Coleman had been Rector of St Andrew by the Wardrobe, and also Area Dean.

14 April

Good Friday. I preached my Three Hours in Chelmsford Cathedral. I was moved myself as I told something of a story about a young man with AIDS, but afterwards I was taken aside by an old Canon and told that I must never be so personal in sermons as it would certainly go against me. I was identifying myself too much with people with AIDS and I would never be given a job, he added. It isn't the first time that sort of thing has been said, but was upsetting on Good Friday.

15 April

Holy Saturday. I said Matins in the bare chapel at Codford, all embellishment removed. James Watson came to lunch bringing sweet scallops. I made an icon of Christ as a centrepiece for the dining room mantel and put chocolate eggs inside a real blackbird's nest on it. We had the time and space to treat Easter as we treated last Christmas, important for what will be our final Paschal feast in this house. A great fire in the dining room was lit with a Celtic prayer of blessing.

By this time we had made a firm decision to put Old Wool Cottage on the market. Andrew had his Barbican flat, of course, but I was unsure what my next move might be. Should I consider buying a studio flat somewhere in London? I could not decide what might be best.

16 April

Easter Day. We were up at 3.55 a.m. and there was brilliant moonlight all the way to Salisbury Cathedral. James and I read lessons from the Book of Exodus by the light of the bonfire before the cathedral's great West Front. The Bishop of Salisbury looked splendid in his Thomas à Becket mitre. It was a lovely liturgy, with clouds of incense. Christ rises in heart and mind across the world.

On Easter Monday I flew with Andrew to Mykonos to stay with Werner's German mother and Greek father. We were to have two

Easters, because it was just the start of the Orthodox Holy Week. All the little churches on Mykonos were packed with devout congregations, black lace and silver-thread veils hung over and around the iconastases and black ribbon was threaded through the chandeliers. In contrast to all that black, the sea was the colour of lapis lazuli and everywhere there were splashes of bright flowers.

21 April

Greek Good Friday. We found the procession of the Dead Christ going round the town, thousands of people on balconies and outside the shops, surging along with candles of unbleached orange wax. There were families and young men in leather jackets and tarty girls, unself-conscious and unchurchy. In one church, as people queued to venerate the cross (which in the Greek Orthodox liturgy is a black cloth with an embroidered Christ lying on it, stretched out on a sort of catafalque covered with flowers), some boys roared up on their motorbikes. Jumping off and leaving the engines running, they rushed into the church crossing themselves, then these leather-jacketed toughs came one by one to kiss the dead Christ tenderly.

23 April

Greek Easter Day. A whole goat was cooked over a wood fire. After some time a salad arrived. Then some white wine. Then the first course. Then a tablecloth, and eventually some chairs, all after the first meat had been devoured. Werner's father George and his sister had been to Communion at the midnight liturgy. They're all kind, artistic and completely disorganized.

When we moved on to Athens, we found the Acropolis already crowded by 10 a.m., and heaving by 10.30. I thought the Parthenon was enormously atmospheric, in spite of despoiling, crowding and neglect – what the Hebrews called a 'High Place'. At the Areopagus, where the Apostle Paul preached about the altar 'to an unknown God', I felt aware of the presence of the saint. It was a profoundly moving experience.

26 April

A sunny walk down through the park to the 8.15 coach, and off across Arcadian landscapes to Delphi: the high, hidden, flower-tumbled amphitheatre, stadium and processional way of Apollo's shrine, black cypress verticality, far blue distances, the umber columns of the Doric temple, the Awful Rocks guarding the Castellian spring, giant fennel purple, blood-red poppies, some almost black, apple-green euphorbia, soft grey-green helichrysums, scented purple stocks, yellow daisies in profusion, bay and myrtle and oak, swallows, and a profound silence since last the Apollonian lyre played.

27 April

At the Kaisarini Monastery, where there are frescoes from 1682 in the eleventh-century buildings, I walked with Andrew down the mountainside through wild flowers, cypresses and birdsong, picking olive, fennel, scabious, daisies and pine to put on Werner's grave. We prayed here, Werner's smiling photograph on the white marble cross, a picture taken by Andrew on Delos.

29 April

Eventually we got to London two hours late. At St Mary-le-Bow the study wall is down and chaos reigns. 'Chaos' is an apposite Greek word, but it's still lovely to be home.

Two rooms were being made into one at the rectory and the very English chaos continued well into May, a speaking contrast with the silence of Delphi. The place was bursting with workmen repairing the ravages of the initial destruction. My study was temporarily nonexistent and every single book in my library was filthy.

There was plenty to take me away from the noise and the dust, however. During the first week of May I was a celebrity guest on a panel at the Clothworkers' Hall with the rugby star Cliff Morgan, the racehorse trainer Jenny Pitman, and Maureen

Lipman. It was to raise money for charity, and on the way in Maureen said to me, 'Do you know, I think we're the only people in this entire room who vote Labour.'

I went to listen to David Hutt preach his first sermon at Westminster Abbey after his installation as a Residentiary Canon, and thought his body language proclaimed a happier man. At the second service that morning Dean Michael Mayne, a sensitive and attractive preacher, gave the most wonderful sermon. On the same day, courtesy of Stephanie Cole who had sent me tickets, I went to see *A Passionate Woman* at the Comedy Theatre.

At Sion College we got the necessary vote through an all-day meeting of the Fellows, and the formal go-ahead was given for the sale of the library and relocation of the books. The day culminated in the Presidential Dinner at which, with some relief, I handed over my collar of S's (very similar in design to the collar you see in portraits of Thomas Cromwell and Thomas More) to my successor David Burton, the Rector of St Michael's, Cornhill. It had been a battering year in the chair and I felt distinctly lighter as soon as I had passed on the badge of office.

I also went to preach to the Lutherans in Gresham Street. Thinking that the orchestra had reached the end of the Couperin piece which was to be the signal for my sermon, I dashed into the pulpit and preached – only to discover that I had interrupted the music before it had finished. As I descended the stairs, the violinists picked up their bows again and played the rest of the piece.

Later in the month, at a Confirmation preparation class in my newly restored study, somebody asked with absolute seriousness, 'When should practising members of the Church of England expect union with God?'

Then Mrs Duck had her babies on my roof and Michael Kenny came to rescue them in a cardboard box, decanting them onto the Barbican lake. And thus we came, more or less in one piece, to June.

3 June

It was rainy and grey more or less all day. London is not Greece. In St Faith's Chapel in Westminster Abbey, the Dean celebrated Mass for 21 or so old boys of St Boniface, my old theological college. It felt like reordination, low key, just four hymns accompanied by a piano, a renewal of vows. There has been so much blessing and grace over the years. The men who were in my year seem sensible, strong, worthwhile, the very best of the hard-working Church of England. David made us all Coronation Chicken for lunch afterwards. The party petered out a bit, but perhaps we only needed what we managed – a Mass together again and some lunch.

6 June

John Gladwyn, the Bishop of Guildford, was clever, straight-forward and sensible both at the Dialogue and over lunch. He was Secretary of the Board of Social Responsibility, exactly the sort of man we need on the Bench of Bishops. He and his wife Lydia have 'a place' in London, he says. That's sens-ible; everyone needs a place in London.

His Archdeacon came to talk to him in my sitting room, and I left them there to go and visit Percy Coleman again in the Charterhouse. 'You are my successor,' he said. 'You do all the things I would like to do.' I found this touching, as I respect him enormously. He knows he's dying and asks all his visitors to take a book away to help get things cleared up. He asked me to choose something, so I took Volume Two of *Elizabethan History* by A.L. Rowse.

13 June

At the Dialogue today we had William Waldegrave, Secretary of State for Agriculture, Fisheries and Food, with two offi-cials and a packed church. A descendant of Robert Walpole, the first Prime Minister, he was charming, intelligent and inaudible.

There were screams of laughter over lunch, just the two of us, as we talked over Norman Tebbit, Patrick Jenkin, Mrs Thatcher and the Brussels percentages, and Ted Heath say-ing, typically, to William, 'You're not doing very well.' Susan Hussey is William Waldegrave's sister and is, of course, Lady-in-Waiting to the Queen. Countess Waldegrave said to her son, who was complaining about how nasty people were being about him in the press, 'Not as nasty as they were to Sir Robert Walpole.' His mother also said – I like this very much – of the local Vicar, 'The Vicar is a saint, but also a bit of a bore.'

14 June

At 11.30 we held a Jewish/Christian service in memory of the Shoah, the Holocaust. It was immensely appreciated by the silent and moved congregation. Brian and Ann Jenkins could hardly speak at the end. Brian has recently been made Chairman of the Woolwich. I would not have expected to see him reduced to tearful silence.

15 June

Corpus Christi. After a clergy meeting in my flat, I went to Liverpool Street to catch a train for Stowmarket. At Liverpool Street I picked up *Private Eye* and there was another article about Sion College: 'The flamboyant Father Victor Stock...' Oh dear.

I was met at Stowmarket by the Vicar's wife, a local head teacher, and driven to Bury St Edmunds where we had High Mass, an outdoor procession of the Host and Benediction. The celebrant was a woman, and it was as if women had been ordained for years and years.

5 July

Jean Mayhew has been packing up Hillsborough Castle in the belief that the Government is about to fall. Yesterday, however, Mr Major won the Tory leadership election and a new Cabinet is being formed. Patrick stays on in Northern Ireland, so Jean can stop the packing and unpack again.

At 4.20 His Royal Highness the Duke of Gloucester came to open the Worshipful Company of Architects' watercolour exhibition in our vestibule. I welcomed him, thanked him for coming and showed him the nave and crypt, which he had not seen and asked after. The Duke is nice in that slightly hesitant, awkward, Hanoverian royal way – after all, he is the nephew of George V and Queen Mary.

6 July

The Feast Day of St Thomas More – a difficult saint for Anglicans, as he opposed really everything Anglicans stand for, but nevertheless a man we should honour. Like Roger Freeman, to whom I wrote this morning, More was also once Chancellor of the Duchy of Lancaster.

At the evening Mass I was talking about the collar of S's in Holbein's portrait of Thomas More and saying how like it was to the collar of S's the Lord Mayor wears today, when Brian Jenkins put his hand up, interrupted the sermon and said, 'Not like, but the same.' The Lord Mayor wears the very same collar. It was a wonderful St Mary-le-Bow moment.

19 July

I anointed Alun Fon Jones in the old St Stephen's Hospital, now called the Chelsea and Westminster, a place so much part of my life and where Uncle Teddy died. I don't think Alun can live much longer.

In the afternoon I travelled up to York for the Affirming Catholicism conference.

20 July

The conference got off to a tremendously good start with the Archbishop of York being masterly and inspiring, for which he received a standing ovation that he shyly enjoyed. Dame Rachel Waterhouse, who was chairing the session, introduced him as the Archbishop of Canterbury. There was complete silence, and then hundreds of people burst into wild applause. John Habgood looked astonished and then rather pleased, before raising his hand to silence us. It was very, very funny – there couldn't have been a better start.

In fact, I felt it was not such a good conference as the previous ones had been. This was partly because, without Richard Holloway and Jeffrey John speaking, there was no grit in the oyster.

28 July

I went to Salisbury for a meeting of the Fabric Advisory Committee. From the tower hoist the foundations of the medieval bell tower stand out clearly beneath the parched lawn looking like the logo of English Heritage, as someone cleverly remarked. The Bishop's wife, Sarah Stancliffe, showed me round South Canonry, the Bishop's house now that the Palace is a school. The façade of this Georgian and medieval house is eighteenth-century, but the back is strangely 'suburban prep school', as Sarah rightly said.

The Chaplain is ill, so the Bishop himself took the wheel of the car and took me to Codford. We had wine in the garden and then sat in the chapel together. For dinner I gave the Bishop cold chicken and some curious soup ill-devised by Ruth.

29 July

With 200 other people, I went off to an outdoor dinner at John Torrie's for his sixtieth birthday. John is our neighbour and Lord of the Manor. I sat next to Professor Sam Richardson and the lady organist from Upton Lovell, and talked to the Vicar. The Duchess of Newcastle arrived with her dress on inside out.

August was spent wondering why I ever kept St Mary-le-Bow open at that time of year. It was extremely hot – so hot that I went out and bought myself a tower fan, iced tea and cold noodles.

Abandoning London, I went into retreat with the Sisters of the Love of God at Fairacres and lived in a little hermitage called St Seraphim with the curtains drawn against the heat. Here I had no iced tea or cold noodles, just sliced bread, processed cheese, instant coffee and the poorest of poor tea bags, all provided for me in the little concrete kitchen. In past years there had been home-made biscuits and cakes, but I decided they were going in for a new kind of deprivation. It was not at all attractive. The nuns' wooden bowls had also gone, in favour of white plastic to suit the new dishwasher – another declension. The best thing about being there was sleeping a lot. I was also pleased by the sound of the nuns' spoons on their ice-cream plates beneath the Orthodox chant being played on the record player during refectory dinner. It made for a somehow Tibetan and happy atmosphere.

At the end of the month, Auntie Libby came up from Salcombe to stay for a few days in Codford, spooning out half her jacket potato with a silver teaspoon and taking a very long time indeed to do so. In my diary I noted that on 29 August we had the first cloud since 18 July, but the next day the sun was back with a vengeance. Now it did feel like Greece.

Towards the end of August, John Habgood retired as Archbishop of York. On the way to Paris with Andrew to see Jean Louis for the weekend, I was amused to see that Andrew Brown of the *Independent* had written a piece about Lord Habgood and included my story about Dame Rachel Waterhouse and her 'Archbishop of Canterbury' introduction at the summer conference.

6 September

This evening I listened to Artus Kholl from the Israeli Embassy speaking at the West London Synagogue on the peace process. What he said was plausible but dishonest, and I came out from the synagogue straight into the Middle East – Lebanon on the Edgware Road. The Edgware Road smells of Jerusalem. It's now raining and summer is over.

8 September

Geoff Thomas, our healer who runs the Monday Healing Group, offered me healing today when he came to talk to me in my study. In silence and without touching me, a weight was lifted and I felt clearer, lighter and happier as the day went on. It was strange and inexplicable, but welcome.

Later in September I was invited to give out 200 prizes at Oxted School in Surrey. My speech went down well, the imitations and funny stories literally making people cry with laughter. There is something impossibly difficult about giving out prizes at schools without turning into a caricature of Joyce Grenfell taking off some old Colonel giving out prizes. 'Jolly good', 'Well done', 'Splendid', 'Splendid', 'Jolly good', 'Well done'. You keep saying the same things, pumping the hand of the next terrified or delighted pupil, part of a never-ending stream. You are also standing at some dizzy height above an endless sea of hugely proud faces, parents sweating and beaming with pride. I was given a big cut-glass vase with the school on it – exactly the kind of thing I dislike, but you have to be gracious in the Joyce Grenfell manner on these occasions, and I hope I was.

Soon after that, I was off being gracious on the other side of the Atlantic.

6 October

I flew to New York to be met by Father Edgar Wells at the airport,[4] and was whisked home to his Hammer Horror vicarage by Times Square, then out to an excellent Japanese dinner. I'm not the only important person in New York at the moment: the Pope is here.

7 October

I took a train to the World Trade Center, getting off at Courtland Street and Century 21. Andrew and Bernard are also in New York, on a shopping jag, and they tagged along. I was overwhelmed by misery at all this shopping, a subject which deeply depresses and uninterests me. It was a grey, grizzly day, with the skyscrapers disappearing into cloud and this awful house full of dust.

Evensong lifted things, though, and that's what I've come for. There was a huge congregation in the vast St Mary's, votive lamps twinkling in the darkness, tumbling flowers decorating the white marble expanse of the High Altar, splendid organ and choir music. I preached about the Church being people who are not as we think we should be.

8 October

Sunday. The 11 o'clock High Mass lasted for two and a quarter hours, but it didn't matter. There was a sense of solidity

---

4 Father Edgar was the Vicar of St Mary the Virgin, West 46th Street, and a very old friend of Father John Gaskell.

and seriousness without crossness, bitterness or madness – a trinity you often get at Anglo-Catholic services. There was an appreciative response to my sermon, although there was some cross reaction to my inclusiveness about the ordination of women. I wanted to speak in support of the brave stand Edgar has taken. Everyone expected him, as the leading Anglo-Catholic in New York, to be against the appointment of the woman Assistant Bishop in the diocese and not to welcome her as he has done.

9 October

Outside St Patrick's Roman Catholic Cathedral on Fifth Avenue I saw the nasty-looking Cardinal O'Connor.[5] He really is a sinister-looking man, like the baddie in a movie. He and other hugely overweight Roman Catholic bishops were watching the Columbus Day parade – too much Irish nationalistic populism for me.

I went to dinner at Aquavit, a smart West 50th Street restaurant, with Trinity Rector Dan Matthews and Maria Campbell, a former banker from Mississippi who is now the Rector's Chief of Staff. We had a hard-work talk about Trinity's visit to St Mary-le-Bow next year. I'm not sure what I think of this corporate-type Christianity.

11 October

I tried to go to Matins, but couldn't unlock the church door between the clergy house and the nave, and Edgar had gone to therapy. In the Church of England priests begin the day by going to Matins. In the Episcopal Church they go to therapy.

At Penn Station I booked a ticket for Boston and then went to the enchanting Pierrepoint Morgan Library, the walls hung with deep crimson velvet. There was a Gutenburg Bible and a book from Egypt with a date of 860, a time when I thought there were only scrolls.

---

5 Cardinal John O'Connor was the Roman Catholic Archbishop of New York and a leading conservative.

16 October

I have come to Boston to stay with the monks at the Society of St John the Evangelist, and today went out in the monastery van with Father Martin Smith to the Cavan coast and Crane Beach. Surf, white sand, wind, crashing, clear sea and the Chinese yellow and crimson leaves of Fall.

18 October

At 4.45 I took a mug of tea down to join Lord Runcie, who has been preaching at Harvard. He was having tea with Father Martin, was told that I was here and wanted to say 'hello'.

As soon as I sat down for Evensong, I was ferreted out of the church and sent off to join the party for the circus – lions and huge elephants in the hands of Chipperfield were perhaps not so very different from dogs and cats. It was an entirely Irish and Italian working-class evening, with very few black faces. 'Too expensive for black people,' I was told.

Back in England a few days later, Patricia Routledge came to dinner. She brought a bottle of Famous Grouse and pointed out, as only Hyacinth Bouquet could, that the pigeon was not cooked properly. She was right. Miss Routledge said she had been feeling imprisoned by Hyacinth Bouquet, but was busy breaking out.

I blessed Julia and Tim Brodie in the crypt on the fortieth anniversary of their marriage, in a little ceremony attended by their children. Julia had been a faithful member of our 7.30 a.m. Mass in the crypt for some time. Tim was a distinguished QC, and afterwards I joined a black-tie dinner for the family at his rooms in Lincoln's Inn.

1 November

The Feast of All Saints. This has always been a special day for me, ever since I stayed as a child in Sturry with a spinster aunt of my father's and went on my own into Canterbury Cathedral on a weekday All Saints' Day and heard the King's School singing Matins up in the Choir. I sat in the nave and heard 'For all the saints who from their labours rest', and wondered if God would ever call me to be a priest. I can remember saying to God, as I knelt there in the nave, 'If you want me to be a priest, that is what I would really most want to do.' Then I told my father and he said, 'How ridiculous, you're not intelligent enough to be a priest.'

7 November

The Opposition Chief Whip Donald Dewar didn't turn up for the Dialogue today. At 11 a.m. we heard on the radio that he was at a funeral in Scotland – he had completely forgotten about us. We rang the House of Commons and his secretary found us an MP called Ken Purchiss, a Midlands back-bencher, who was willing to come instead. It was kind of the secretary to do this, but Mr Purchiss wasn't what the audience came for.

The next day I visited the Sisters of Sion in Chepstow Villas, where I lectured with Rabbi Alexandra Wright on the Book of Job. The Roman Catholic Sisters have convents in Jerusalem and Notting Hill and work to further Jewish/Catholic relations. They were a highly educated audience who all knew a great deal more about Job than I did. At home that evening I watched a most moving programme about the Holocaust and Germany in the 1930s, part of a series called *The People's Century*. After lecturing with a Rabbi earlier in the day, it seemed both a wonderful and terrible juxtaposition.

I was also busy preparing a number of adults for Confirmation, and found myself taking a considerable amount of time over one woman, a middle-aged divorced magistrate, radical, left wing and extraordinarily attractive. Time with individuals is what Archbishop Michael Ramsey thought the heart of priestly life is about. At around the same time, the actress Stephanie Cole came for a Dialogue. She talked about God as 'a bend in the river' – that was what God was for her. I thought about that a lot, afterwards.

The highlight of the month was a lunch with Professor Sir Ghillean Prance and his wife Anne at Kew. On the way to their house I went into the gardens and the shop and bought candles, soap, pasta and pot pourri for Christmas presents, and also Sir Ghillean's biography, just out, for him to sign. Also at lunch were the new Vicar of Holy Trinity, Hounslow, and his wife. The Vicar was a member of Affirming Catholicism. Anne Prance gave us home-made tomato soup, home-made quiche, a delicious salad and pears, and every single item of food came from the Director's eighteenth-century vegetable garden.

30 November

At the Church Council this evening there was much hilarity over something called 'Errol', which Ray Duffy, our Electoral Roll Officer, produced with great aplomb as the answer to everything. This is one of the new centralized Church of England's dafter ideas. We are supposed to give everyone who wants to join the Electoral Roll a card which says 'I belong to Jesus' and a little teddy bear. We won't.

1 December

The weather provided a drizzly and gloomy background all day to our third expedition with Ruth Watson's belongings from Codford to her new flat in Dilton Marsh – perfect sheltered accommodation, with her own kitchen, bathroom, sitting room and bedroom.

Our restaurateur and inventor of The Place Below restaurant in the crypt has an article in today's *Financial Times* in which, amusingly, he is described as Brian Sewell. Brian Sewell is, of course, not like Bill Sewell at all in shape or form. Bill Sewell is small, cuddly, funny and kind, and Brian Sewell, the *Evening Standard* art critic, is tall and thin with a fantastically queenly voice, acid, penetrating and caustic.

Very early on in its existence, The Place Below had become 'a wow'. We opened one cold evening in March 1989 with a free dinner, and by the end of the following week the crypt was full for breakfast and lunch every day, with posher dinners on offer on Thursday evenings. It proved well worth the effort of battling through the initial legal wranglings.

2 December

We spent the morning clearing things out of the stables, taking lots of box cuttings to give to people, and cutting holly and ivy to decorate St Mary-le-Bow. It will be good to have sold Old Wool Cottage and packed Wiltshire up into the past.

4 December

At 12.30, as I was listening to Andrew Mottram in my rooftop sitting room in Cheapside, it got abnormally dark, even for this time of year. Vanessa Taylor, our Verger, knocked on the door to say she was sorry to disturb me, but the National Mutual demolition site was on fire and the police had ordered us to evacuate St Mary-le-Bow. A blowtorch had been applied accidentally to the diesel sump in the basement of the building, enveloping Cheapside in thick clouds of toxic fumes. Out we all went until 4 p.m., shivering in the streets.

When nobody was looking, I went back in and climbed up to shut the windows of the clerestory, which I could get at from the roof garden – thus preventing the black, oily smoke from the burning building getting into the nave and ruining the blue and gold ceiling. I was very pleased with myself and there really wasn't any danger, though people were cross with me for doing it.

7 December

The Cordwainer Ward Club lunch was dreary, but there was an excellently pro-European speech from a European Irish Commissioner, completely round like a ball.

In the evening I went to Anne Jenkin's fortieth birthday party. I talked to Michael Portillo, who was more friendly than when he came to lunch. Being Secretary of State for Defence suits him. The Hamiltons and the Aitkens were also there – I didn't want to talk to them.

8 December

I dressed up in a punk outfit provided by Vanessa Taylor from a theatrical costumier and posed for the *Daily Telegraph* in aid of a homeless charity supported by the Charterhouse Bank. They presume this will be an advantage to them and will make more people come to their carol service and give more money to the charity. We shall see. Originally I was asked by the *Daily Telegraph* if I could dress up in Dickensian costume, but I pointed out that clergymen wore Dickensian costume all the time.

The photograph of me as a punk which duly appeared on the City page in the *Telegraph* maddened everyone and was much discussed, but the Charterhouse carol service was absolutely full. Two homeless youths spoke at the service and in the end there was over £500 in the collection plate, so the *Telegraph*'s photograph did some good after all.

24 December

I'm 51. I went to Brompton Cemetery and said a prayer at Uncle Teddy's grave. At 11 p.m. we all went to All Saints, Margaret Street, for the most elaborate High Mass which went on and on for ever. I was acting as Deacon, with Cedric the MC nicely pushing me about. 'Bow to Father, Father,' was the constant refrain. You can't move without bowing to Father, Father at All Saints.

We had a frightening scene on the way home, yobs knocking over rubbish bins immediately in front of the car as we drove through Soho early in the morning. Andrew was cross and got out of the car. One of the yobs produced a baseball bat, which Andrew didn't see, and made for him. I jumped out of the car, mercifully in my cassock. The fact that I was a priest in a cassock saved us from serious damage.

31 December

We went over to Dilton Marsh for lunch with Ruth in her new flat. While we were there, we rearranged all Ruth's furniture and put up her pictures. Back in Codford, we said Evensong in the bare chapel, cleaned out the big kitchen and threw out bags and bags of old food from the pantry and other mouse holes.

Clandeboye

During January we gradually continued to empty the Old Wool Cottage and made a trip to Stockholm, where we enjoyed the snow. The new year started, however, in Amsterdam, where – perhaps surprisingly – a puppet exhibition deepened my understanding of priesthood.

5 January

From Wim's flat in Amsterdam we took a tram to the Tropical Museum and a wonderfully magical exhibition of puppetry in Africa and Asia. In Holland Mr Punch is anarchic. He's against the military, against landowners, against merchants. He's for the poor. Argument is settled by his frying pan. All over the world, the puppet and the puppeteer are being destroyed by television, as television remorselessly destroys local, indigenous and home-made culture. Before this ghastly effect of Western affluence and unbridled capitalism, however, in some countries the puppeteer was also the priest – he mediated the things of the gods.

In Burma the puppeteer is still powerful. In Vietnam puppeteering is done on water. Malaysia, Vietnam, Thailand, Burma, Sri Lanka, India, Turkey, Java, Bali, Sumatra, China and Japan all have puppets. The puppeteer displays the ancient epics, teaches morality, wards off evil, binds communities together – very much like the work of the Rector of St Mary-le-Bow. There were crowds of little children at the live puppet show put on by the Tropical Museum, but in fact, of course, it was an adult experience too.

The puppet tradition in Vietnam and China is 2,000 years old. Originally the performers were always priests, who presided also over the consecration of temples and marriages, and they used the puppets to drive away evil spirits. During the Cultural Revolution in China, puppet theatre became a medium of political propaganda. People virtually stopped going to the theatre, and the qualities of the performances suffered. Later the performers were given more artistic freedom, but by then the young people in the cities were watching television. Nowadays puppeteers have no priestly function.

7 January

At the Historical Museum we saw an exhibition on St Nicholas for children. The Reformers tried to forbid children to 'put out their shoes' for presents on St Nicholas' Day, and any toys left were given to the orphanages. Isn't that typical of the Protestant Reformation at its worst?

23 January

Terry Waite came to Dialogue and attracted a congregation of 330. His story is more striking than his words. He is an impressive man, but a bit formulaic when speaking in public, giving out little encouraging sermons. The fact that Terry Waite exists after the treatment meted out to him in solitary confinement over so long a time is astonishing.

2 February

Candlemas. I went in Annie Reyersbach's car to Hackney Wick for Elaine Jones's Induction as Vicar of St Mary of Eton. The Bishop was not inducting her for political reasons (so as not to upset the anti-women-priests faction, I suppose), so she was inducted by the Archdeacon and presided herself at the Mass. The Anglo-Catholic clergy who were busy packing their bags for Rome stayed away in protest, but the Salvation Army, the Hindus and the Muslims all came. So did the local Roman Catholic parish priest, who kissed Elaine at the Peace and took Communion from her. I was astonished by this and said to him afterwards that Cardinal Ratzinger would be coming round for him with the thumbscrews. 'She is my priest colleague,' he said.

The church was absolutely packed. There must have been about 400 people, from the patron grandees of Eton to the local publican. The church was piercingly, bitterly cold – even colder than St John's, Friern Barnet, without the heating on, and that's saying something.

3 February

At Codford I found that Ruth, dear old housekeeper that she is, had done precisely what I had asked her not to do, which was to pack all the glasses together and empty out the contents of every single drawer and cupboard in both kitchens, pantry and dining room, wrapping everything up in identical pieces of newspaper and packing them into boxes. She had also managed not to get any food, so there was nothing to eat. Every single box and bag had to be unpacked and started all over again, as we had no idea what was in any of them, or to which house or flat they were to be directed.

The following week I spent some days in Exeter, sharing and giving lectures at a conference on preaching. As part of my lecture on the fundamentals of preaching, I gave out six exercises. The results were dispiriting. Nobody could think of anything intelligent or sensible to say at the funeral of a headmistress killed in a car crash, but that is exactly the sort of thing you have to cope with as a parish priest. Back in London, I discovered that Ruth had been all the way to Wales to get a passport. I pointed out that there were nearer places, but when Ruth is determined to do something, she is determined to do it and does it.

Then I flew to Denmark to visit Mule Fogh. The country was covered in snow and from the aeroplane Holland and Denmark looked like a mass of frozen sea, white, blue and grey, and absolutely still. At 82, Mule looked better, smaller, warmer, less cross and prettier than she had done for some time. She had moved into a home for retired doctors and nurses, and we lunched in the communal dining room. The claret was surprisingly good. Upstairs, in her two rooms looking out over the bare trees towards the sea, we had an intimate and trusting conversation. It felt like a holy time to me. She gave me Sven's Dusan beetle box from Borneo, very like a box of my own which I seemed to have lost. I said I would put Sven's box on my desk when I got home.

Our Dialogue guests for February included Donald Dewar, who has stayed in my mind as a person of tremendous integrity, a stooping, beaky heron of a man. At lunch, being Labour's Chief Whip, he asked me if he could fix the business of the House of Commons during the afternoon by using my telephone in order to speak to the 'usual channels'. The 'usual channels' turned out to be Murdo MacLean, the civil servant who was actually running the United Kingdom. I was intrigued that this Mr Fixit conversation took place in my sitting room. Mr Dewar, of course, later became the First Minister for Scotland, having pioneered the Scottish Assembly. When he died in 2000, he left a huge gap and, indeed, an ache in many people's hearts.

John Tusa, the broadcaster who subsequently took over the Barbican, was another Dialogue guest. During our conversation he asked, 'Is religion information or experience?' His words gave me pause for thought during my Lent teaching week at Rugby School.

The Rugby School experience was extraordinarily hard work. It began with me preaching to 700 people at Evensong and included various train trips to and from Euston so that I could fulfil other engagements in between assemblies for the whole school in the morning and talks with the Sixth Form at 10 p.m. I also did some teaching all the way through the school and ate in different houses with different people at every meal. The only thing I can remember now about that chaotic week was how I upset some convinced young Christians by telling them that the Buddhas in the Folk Museum at Leiden were holy.

In amongst all the other demands on my time, I had also started doing Wednesday evening broadcasts on Greater London Radio (GLR). These took the form of live interviews by the presenters of *Drive Time* and had been set up following my notorious appearance in punk gear in the *Telegraph*. I found myself enjoying this weekly expedition into broadcasting, as it gave me a chance to introduce religion in places where it was not usually seen or heard.

9 March

With Ruth chattering all the way in the back of the car, we drove down to Codford for the final clear-out of the house, leaving only a carpet covered with piles of linen, towels and blankets and all those things one inherits from dead relatives and never uses for the OXFAM shop. We went for final prayers in the empty chapel and drove sadly away, depositing Ruth at Dilton Marsh with our old microwave oven.

13 March

In the car being driven to GLR, I heard the presenter saying, 'In a moment the Reverend Victor Stock will be here to give us his comments on Dunblane.' I asked the driver what had happened at Dunblane and discovered from him that 16 five- and six-year-old children and their teacher had been shot. I hadn't heard a news broadcast all day. I was catapulted from this straight into the studio and was on air within minutes. I said, 'We are speechless in the face of such horror and there are no sensible or comforting things to say. Later on, we may be able to ask the right questions.'

On Maundy Thursday, Good Friday and Easter Sunday I preached for Derek Moody at St Nicholas', Brighton. The Easter Sunday liturgy began at 5.30 a.m., but the church was full, as it was for all the services that day. I had lunch with Andrew and Phyllida Stewart-Roberts and some other friends, and was pleased to discover that everyone at the table had been to Communion in the morning. The Church was certainly not dead.

10 April

I took a seemingly endless flight to New York to speak at two dinners. Bishop Herbert Donovan met me and I spent the evening at his amazing 41st-floor flat with its gigantic, expansive views right up downtown to the Empire State Building and across to New Jersey and the Palisades. What a flat – a flat with four bathrooms, can you believe it?

11 April

In the evening at the Hudson River Club I sat between a lawyer and a corporate executive, both little-black-dress women. One had been to tea at St Mary-le-Bow. We ate the most perfectly cooked venison chops. Waldy Malouf, the cook, came and spoke afterwards, and gave us all a copy of the book he had just produced. More things to cart about, I thought ungratefully. One person's speech was far too long, so I cut mine.

21 April

Sunday, St Mary the Virgin. Huge branches of cherry and plum cascade everywhere in this vast church, climbing up, around and over the white marble High Altar. Matins at 8.40 was taken far too fast by a woman seminarian. I enjoyed the 11 o'clock Mass and preaching at it. I had a long talk with a man who had left the Christian religion for Buddhism, and also spoke to his wife and five children. This is quite a common pattern here, people leaving for Buddhism and then coming back – bringing their Buddhism with them, of course, which I think is humanizing for Christianity. The celebrant at the 10 o'clock Mass had a very similar spiritual journey.

I walked off to Central Park, where I helped a wonderfully glamorous young woman who was unsteady on her new skates. She asked if she could hold on to me, with her little son Adrian holding on to the other hand, so I provided a kind of human crash barrier. It was a romantic moment amongst the banks of violets and yellow cornus.

At the beginning of May I preached at Wycombe Abbey School in Buckinghamshire, but got off on the wrong foot by asking the Chaplain to justify public schools for rich children. Even as I began the sentence, I wondered why I had done it.

After chapel I met the people whom the Headmistress had asked to lunch. My message that I was not staying to lunch, but was going to have lunch with the parents of one of the girls – Rachael, the daughter of John and Jessie Mills – had not got through. This caused immense embarrassment and bad feeling which I learned about later on, but it was not my mistake. The Mills motored me to their house in Chobham. I had prepared John and Jessie for Baptism and Confirmation, had baptized their children and had now gone to preach at Rachael's school. I had known them all a long time since John and Jessie were medical students at London University.

This diplomatic disaster was followed by a happier expedition – another visit to the Mayhews in Northern Ireland.

17 May

Friday. At Admiralty House at 7.30 a.m. I climbed into a black Land Rover with Jean Mayhew and some grey-suited police-men. Jean's sister Olivia and Patrick went ahead in another armoured vehicle. At Northolt we were met by Patrick's Private Secretary, Martin, and an RAF officer. We had break-fast and papers on the plane, Martin saying, 'I expect Victor would like the *Guardian*.' Patrick spent the journey working on his boxes and I was given profiles on all the people I was likely to meet during the weekend.

When we touched down, Patrick was immediately whisked off to Stormont. Olivia, Jean and myself were taken for a fast tour of the Falls Road and the Shankhill, and spent the morning with a working-class women's group run by Ruth, a pretty and courageous Presbyterian Deaconess. The women talked about the beatings, intimidation and torture they and their children suffered – inflicted on them by their own side. Across the wall – literally, a wall built at great expense by us – Catholic women and their children suffered harassment, torture, beatings and intimidation from their men. Most of this is drug- and crime-motivated. They were all so pleased to have Jean with them. She is extremely adroit at sitting on the floor.

We went back to the fairy-tale contrast of luncheon in the State Dining Room with 24 guests, including the Nova Scotia Prime Minister, a doctor interested in theology who was at Queen's University, Belfast, as an undergraduate. He and I had our photograph taken by one of his staff, standing in front of the thrones in the Throne Room. I said that really we had better not sit on them because I knew Jean wouldn't like it. She said later that it might have upset the staff.

It was an excellent lunch (watercress soup, fresh salmon and something made of oranges flecked with almonds) and I sat next to the dentist brother-in-law of the Premier. 'We are middle-class Catholics from Belfast,' he said, 'therefore members of a small community.' He now lives in Dublin. At the drinks beforehand I had an interesting conversation with Ken Newall, a Presbyterian minister who is a friend of Gerry Adams. 'Ask David Trimble what his vision is for all the people of Ireland,' he said – a thoughtful and provocative question from a Presbyterian to a fellow Presbyterian, to be asked via a friendly Anglican in London at a Dialogue one Tuesday soon.

In the evening I met Father Jerry Murphy and an English Catholic woman friend. Jerry had come from saying Mass in the Maze prison. It had been suggested that I meet him in Clonnard Monastery, but the police would not let Jean take me there. Father Jerry put his case, an anti-monarchist vision of space for all, with vigour and conviction. While he was talking, Patrick came in behind him at the far end of the room, put down his red boxes and joined us. If I had seen a well-known Republican sitting in my drawing room towards the end of a busy and exhausting day, I wouldn't have put down my red boxes but would have slipped quietly away.

Patrick asked Jerry if he had enough to drink, poured out another Pimms and, after listening for 20 minutes or so, suggested a walk in the grounds. So down the glen to the lake we went, and up the hill to the lime walk and along to the temple. It helped that Father Jerry and I had both visited St Saba outside Jerusalem and had both been treated to the 'return of the body of St Saba' story by the mad American monk there. Patrick, as ever, was patient and kind. Jerry's woman friend was deeply hurt and angry with the British. It was certainly an unlikely quartet of human beings to be strolling through the blossom and birdsong of the residence of the ex-Governor General of Northern Ireland and the present Secretary of State. I sensed that miracles of meeting were in the air.

18 May

In the cathedral at Downpatrick the pews are arranged to make it impossible to kneel down, kneeling down being thought of as popish, but everything was beautifully kept and displayed.

In the evening we went to Clandeboye,[1] Patrick asking me to sit with him in his armoured vehicle. In front were Charlie

---

1 Clandeboye is one of the great houses of Northern Ireland, and is the seat of the Marquess of Dufferin and Ava. The family had a long connection with Burma. One of John Betjeman's poems is called 'In Memory of Basil, Marquess of Dufferin and Ava'.

the driver and George, the detective who'd been sent twice into Belfast to get me a collar stud – twice because the first time he brought back the small stud laymen wear at the back of their collars, not the big stud clergymen wear. There was something very nineteenth century about that little expedition.

Going into Clandeboye, from the porch where the butler shook hands, through various halls and enclosed staircases and up into a great room leading into the library, was like being in Oxford's Pitt Rivers Museum, the V & A and the Natural History Museum rolled into one. There was a rhino on a Mayan altar and a model of a temple in Mandalay – astonishing. Through all this Orientalism we went up and up and on and on, through galleries and arches and rooms, past animals and tusks and temples, gods and carving and bells and gongs. Suddenly we found ourselves in a calf-bound, drink-filled, fire-warmed eighteenth-century library, with Lady Dufferin waiting for us in purple velvet culottes.

Lady Dufferin was thin, bright and direct. At dinner I sat on her left, Patrick on her right. 'I know a lot about you, your public and private life in Dorset,' she said. Well, she had the county wrong and some of the aspects of my private life seem more hair-raising than they in fact are, but it was interesting. At the end of the evening I discovered that Patrick Trevor-Roper was a mutual friend. We ate salmon and sole, pheasant and red cabbage. Lord Sainsbury was tiresome about the beef crisis and Patrick was patient.

19 May

There were 38 people at lunch in the State Dining Room for the farewell to the Lord Lieutenant, Colonel Brownlow. Patrick described him in his speech as a 'parfit gentil knight', which is exactly what Patrick is. I sat next to a Church of Ireland Rector's wife and asked her what differences she'd noticed in the last few years. 'The Catholics used to keep quiet,' she replied. That, I thought, said it all.

Later in the afternoon I went for a walk in the rain with Jean and we both got soaked through. After baths we had a late supper, picking over the leftovers upstairs in the private dining room.

Back home after the excitements of Northern Ireland, I took a long walk round Regent's Park with Elaine Jones. The new Vicar of Hackney Wick told me all about her recent visit to Eton, where she had preached in the chapel and Prince William had stepped out of his pew to thank her personally as she was leaving. I thought that was very sweet. Lots of people thanked her, in fact. She was the guest of honour and sat at the right hand of the Provost at dinner and was very surprised. I was not in the least surprised. She is a complete star and I told her that polite Etonians *should* fall over themselves to make it clear what they think of a person of such calibre.

28 May

Dr Zaki Badawi, the Principal of the Muslim College and a most remarkable man, came for the 1.05 Dialogue, for which he arrived at 1.06 which made life slightly tightrope-walkish. He was amusing, clear, imaginative and courageous and at lunch told me about the death threats he had to live with and his refusal of a police guard. He made the point that if you have a police guard you get shot, but if you travel incognito and go about ordinarily on the Underground, you don't. Well, I take his word for it. He said he was less likely to be murdered on public transport and had advised Salman Rushdie not to go into hiding.

4 June

David Trimble came for his Dialogue, not as an important politician in an armoured vehicle or chauffeur-driven car, but on the Underground. He is clever, funny, foxy, easily roused and astute. I liked him. He talked to me about how he had been a Christian Fundamentalist, but had begun to move on and open up. He's very worried for his four-year-old child and doesn't want to be in politics for ever. He was honest about his likes and dislikes in private conversation about the personalities running Northern Ireland. I think he has enough bravery and intelligence to be of real assistance to the cause of peace. In public, in the pulpit, he was an excellent ambassador for Unionism. In England we never hear the Unionist case put in an attractive or compelling way.

16 June

I took a train from King's Cross out to Letchworth, and two lads talked to me all the way, asking me religious questions. This is the advantage and disadvantage of wearing a dog collar. It's surprising that a couple of rough lads can ask really sensible questions without being nervous of a priest, and I enjoyed trying to give sensible answers.

It's very, very hot. Every day there has been a background of drilling from the demolition of No. 1 Bow Churchyard, and also some other demolition in Bow Lane that goes on all day, all evening and sometimes through the night.

19 June

On GLR I was frank in my views about Westminster City Council refusing to give the freedom of Westminster to Nelson Mandela. They didn't feel that Nelson Mandela was quite up to their moral standards. This is Dame Shirley Porter's Westminster. The Tory Party is deranged in its self-satisfaction and nastiness.

A woman came and asked for Baptism because she wants to get married in Bali in August and had seen the idea in a holiday brochure. I was very nice to her and persuaded her that she didn't really want Christian Baptism. It's hard work, this kind of conversation, without being unkind.

Ian, the brother of my secretary Graham Phillips, came to talk to me. For a boy with two tumours on his lung he looks remarkably fit, but the prognosis is bad.

24 June

I had dinner in the Grand Paradiso with Roy Strong – a lot of waiters bowing and 'Sir Roying'. Roy is going to publish his diaries. Is this wise, I wonder, and how will he do it? He's grown his hair in a long, curly, grey, bouffant wig style. I can remember when – for a period at the V & A – he had very short hair and looked smart. I don't think older people should let their hair get long. If I had any, I wouldn't.

25 June

Today 250 people came to listen to Melvyn Bragg at the Dialogue. Our nice young lawyer Mark Williams came to lunch. Bragg offered to speak for him when Mark stands as a Labour candidate in the next General Election. This was extraordinarily kind, especially as Mark is standing for Shoreham-by-Sea which has a Conservative majority of 28,000 – certainly a triumph of hope over experience.

At 2.45 I anointed Graham's brother Ian. At a drinks party after Evensong I talked to Roger and Jenny Freeman about the prospects for the Government. The most important thing about today, however, was the conversation I had with Ian Phillips about death. I hope this was helpful. It was honest and we've got the subject out into the open. He can't live for very long.

4 July

At Evening Mass our homeless woman, Daphne, who is spending a lot of time in the church at the moment, weed on the floor, having first thoughtfully removed her skirt. It's interesting, when people behave like this in church, to see how calm and collected most of the congregation manage to be.

7 July

I assisted with the chalice at one of the July Masses at St Paul's Cathedral. Beethoven may be brilliant, if you're not sitting immediately under the brass section. I vented my spleen, partly brought on by proximity to the brass section, on the new wandsmen.

'Why do you have no women?' I demanded.

'Women? We don't want women. We don't need them,' they said.

'Well, they have women at Westminster Abbey.'

'Yes, but *we're* St Paul's Cathedral. We don't need women here.'

8 July

At Sadler's Wells today I made the six people who work there stand on the taken-down stage in silence and then each remember and share something about Sadler's Wells which had meant a lot to them. This all came about because a woman I sat next to at a dinner with John Tusa at the Barbican asked me to come and say a blessing over Sadler's Wells before they pulled it down. The Jamaican nightwatchman, she said, was afraid that some ghosts had been released and felt unhappy about being in the building. Could I do something about it?

I thought we could give thanks for Sadler's Wells' founder Lilian Baylis, so I read something she'd written and talked about my first visit when I was 10 years old to see Gounod's *Faust*. We prayed for the dead and then we took up the cover over the well, from which Sadler's Wells gets its name, and sprinkled it and the stage with holy water, using a sprig of rosemary from my roof garden. We shared a bottle of champagne, drinking from plastic cups on the stage. The man in charge of demolition, an athletic giant from New Zealand, was once a dancer himself. Emanuel, who'd been so worried by the spirits, was really happy and I left my supply of holy water with him.

Later in July I was asked to help a Catholic girl and a Jewish boy get married. The Catholic Church had refused to help, and Laura's cousin, a Roman Catholic priest, would not answer her letters. The Jewish Rabbi would not help Will because he was marrying out of the Jewish faith. Thus they ended up in the Church of England, which was quite right. That is what the Church of England is for – to help people other people will not help. We agreed a date for the wedding in July 1997, and I laid plans for some marriage preparation classes for them.

The Jewish/Christian connection continued in August, with a very special day at St Mary-le-Bow.

1 August

Today our shared Jewish/Christian service with Rabbi Hugo Gryn took place. Sir Peter Levine stood in for the Lord Mayor (who usually attends the service), and 130 people came instead of the expected 50. It was a day nobody will forget. Since I last saw Hugo, he has been diagnosed with an inoperable tumour of the brain and has been a patient in the London Clinic. He was, however, determined to come out of hospital for the Dialogue, which we incorporated into the service, and arrived by taxi looking frail and hardly able to walk. He was too weak to climb into the pulpit and came into the church on my arm. We did our Dialogue together sitting side by side on two upright chairs in front of the altar. Hugo was only just able to speak above a whisper.

The attention in the church was phenomenal and, as we walked out down the nave to cello music from Alan Wilson's daughter, I was conscious of people in tears. We stood together in the porch as people came out. The first was a woman who, instead of saying 'How deeply moving', 'How courageous', 'How brave', or even just 'Thank you', attacked us both with, 'Why don't you do something for the Muslims?'

Remembering that I was about to go on holiday and that Hugo was dying, I summoned up the last residue of gentlemanly politeness and replied, 'Well, as a matter of fact we have had a Dialogue with the Muslims and it was useful and helpful. I hope we will be able to have another with Dr Zaki Badawi, the Principal of the Muslim College.'

At this moment an old man in a white knitted skullcap came up and said, 'Excuse me for interrupting, but I must thank you from the bottom of my heart. I am an Imam. I've never been in a church before. I've just come from South Africa and saw that this was happening and had to come. It has been so wonderful and so blessed by God.'

Hugo and I looked at each other and Hugo grasped my hands. 'My dear,' he said, 'there is a God.' The Mayoral party, who now appeared, were still in a state of deeply moved upset at Hugo's bravery, and were puzzled to see the Rabbi and the Rector laughing.

On 9 August, Ian Phillips died. He was just 21. I left immediately after that for a holiday in Italy and Amsterdam, taking my sadness with me. In Positano I saw Michael Ancram, who was then Patrick Mayhew's number two in Northern Ireland, walking up the high street with his family. I spared him from having to talk to us. He surely did not want to be reminded of Northern Ireland or anything else to do with work, so I controlled myself. Later on, Andrew and I spent a memorable day celebrating the Feast of the Assumption of the Virgin Mary the Italian way.

15 August

The Assumption of the ever-glorious Virgo Maria. The Solemn Mass at 9 a.m. was amazingly awful – though convinced, as Andrew said. A huge choir sang *con gusto*. We were entertained by little poppet servers, so young they could only just walk, who spent the entire dreary sermon time running about and talking. Nobody seemed to be in charge of them. At the end we tumbled out to find a brass band tiddley-pomming in front of the church.

Later in the day we returned to see the statue of Our Lady carried out of the church. After a 15-minute delay, she emerged. The people clapped, the police stopped smoking, the Mayor wore a Napoleonic sash, the choir wouldn't sing and the Curate's new sound system – loud speakers on poles – failed entirely and then fell over. The Franciscan friar opened a box of doves, one of which flew straight up into the lintel of the west door and fell down dead onto the head of a surprised *signora*. The other birds took no further part in the proceedings and nobody took any notice of the dead bird. In England everything would have stopped and we would have rushed forward to give artificial respiration to the bird, called the RSPB and made all sorts of fuss, but in Italy nobody took the slightest bit of notice. I expect the bird ended up, much more sensibly, as somebody's dinner.

The crowd clogged the way into town and there was a human traffic jam as tourists came down from the shops and the congregation surged up from the church. Everyone enjoyed themselves, trailing Tom and Jerry and baby ghost balloons, some of which escaped from the hands of their owners and floated away over the sea. The whole thing was a complete scream and the only clergyman in the whole enormous procession to be robed was the parish priest in a very old cope. He had no stole and no biretta and would not have been thought properly dressed at St Mary's, Bourne Street.

After dinner we went down to the crowded beach, onto an overloaded boat and out onto the inky sea. At 12.25, 25 minutes late, fantastic fireworks burst like immense dandelion heads above the bay, their thunder reverberating around the mountains. The boat rocked alarmingly and we all clutched each other in a delicious terror of imminent drowning.

On the way back I went into the church, where Our Lady had been returned to her shrine, and smelled cigarette smoke. Turning round, in my disapproving Anglican middle-class way, I found a lady of the town in platform cork shoes, torn stockings and a minuscule leopardskin miniskirt, with a cigarette in one hand, giving Our Lady a good talking-to. When she'd finished saying whatever it was she wanted to say to the Virgin Mother of God, she transferred her cigarette to the left hand, made the sign of the cross with the right, dropped a tipsy curtsey and went back to work. An image of church life in Italy never to be forgotten.

From Italy I went on to Wim's flat in Amsterdam for a few days and discovered from the newspaper that Rabbi Hugo Gryn had died. His visit to us for that memorable Jewish/Christian act of worship had been practically his last public appearance. When I got back to the UK, I heard that the funeral at Golders Green had been so enormous that the traffic in North London had come to a complete standstill. Before I left Amsterdam, I noticed an exhibition being put together in the Stadelijk Museum. In the massive room at the top of the staircase, in huge black letters on a white background, were the words from St John's Gospel: 'I am the Resurrection and the Life. I am the door.' I was sorry I could not stay to see the finished exhibition.

30 August

I travelled to Carlisle for the marriage of Gillian Williams's daughter Rosalind. When I arrived for tea at Moor House, a lovely 1720 gentleman's residence with Venetian windows and a carriage sweep, Mr Bennett was reading in his study. That is, Michael, Gillian's brother-in-law, was sitting in his study in a wing chair, his back to the door, reading a calf-bound volume. The house was otherwise filled with women, so it was really just like *Pride and Prejudice*.

There was a huge rehearsal in the church with a friendly Vicar. The BBC are filming the whole of the wedding for some documentary about village life. The whole place was swarming with small children called Josh and Timothy and Lucy. Rosalind, Jessica and Gillian went to a trattoria in Carlisle for the hen party, with me attached.

31 August

At 10.30 my old journalist friend Gay Firth arrived in her car, which was stinking of cheeses from France (she's been staying with Geoffrey and Elspeth Howe), and whisked me off to look at Hadrian's Wall. This took an age to find, all the way into Northumberland, but the clear, high air and the remains of the basilica we found were more than worth it.

At the wedding there were 240 people squashed into a church that could really only take 200 at an absolute maximum. All went well, and the BBC filmed it in its entirety. Some people didn't like my reference to the Prince of Wales's divorce in the sermon, and said so at the party, but many more spoke appreciatively of what I'd tried to say. The party was full of weatherbeaten young hill farmers in black tailcoats and gorgeous, strapping women in cartwheel hats. It was all like some atavistic fertility rite – the upper-middle-class hunting, shooting and shagging world. There was wild dancing and undiminished wine, the women's hats were the smartest I've seen for years, and the Etonian younger brothers all wore tailcoats. I danced with a few dowagers *and* with the beautiful bride. Gillian ran the whole shooting match with consummate skill.

I went back to my B & B at 11.30, leaving everyone else dancing the night away. Gay is off to Ireland tomorrow. She is beside herself about Patrick Mayhew and Drumcree. It'll take a long time for us all to know what really went on, when the British Government seemed to be entirely at the mercy of the Unionist bullyboys insisting on their march through a Catholic area, where the Catholics don't want to be marched through at any price. Our police and soldiers seemed unable to prevent what would not be imaginable on mainland Britain. Knowing the little I do about Northern Ireland, I suspect there's a great deal more to be discovered about all this.

1 September

Post-wedding day. At 9.45 a.m. there was a slightly happy-clappy Family Communion with Baptism, all very ordinary but bearable, with a liquorice all-sorts sermon.

Gillian took me for lunch at Snittlegarth, a long, low seventeenth- and eighteenth-century house on the high fells in parkland. There were 50 people for lunch, all in jeans and jumpers. The coach house conversion where Rosalind and Roddy are to live is superb. 'What is it like in the winter, Mrs Green?' I asked my hostess, Rosalind's new mother-in-law.

'An absolute hellhole,' she said.

The high fell farming community with its country pursuits is as far away as can be imagined from life and work in the City of London. I can see why the BBC have got themselves interested in a hill farmer marrying a Kensington advertising girl.

My next expedition out of London was to Northampton, to a working-class council estate with a run-down church and vicarage in which I spent the night after giving an address to re-found an Affirming Catholicism group. I came away filled with admiration for the heroism of the priest and his family who worked and lived in such a place. Again, it was light years away both from the City and the high fells of Cumbria. During one of these journeys, reading on the train, I came across Oscar Wilde's comment, 'Socialism takes up too many evenings.'

23 September

I went to talk to the nuns at Haggerston in the East End, this time about Scripture. I was shocked by a nun who said that, although Jesus had healed people in the past in the Bible, he hadn't healed her mother and she couldn't believe in God any more. I was astonished by this and at a loss about how to progress the conversation.

At the Wallace Collection in October, Roy Strong's history of country life, *Arcadia*, was launched and I popped in on my way to a broadcast at GLR. It was certainly the most sumptuous setting for a party. On my way back from the GLR studios in Marylebone, I had a long conversation with a *Big Issue* seller and reflected once again how amazing London is in its contrasts. On the same day I had mixed with duchesses and art historians, sipping champagne, and now I was sitting on the pavement with a *Big Issue* seller, listening to his story.

November began with Dame Thora Hird in the pulpit for a Dialogue on Guy Fawkes' Day. She was tiny, vivacious, immensely genial and charming, and completely inaudible. The packed church loved her.

Then David Hutt took me to Berlin, which I had last visited when East Germany still existed. I remember, back then, going through Checkpoint Charlie for dinner and having to get back from the East to the West by midnight. Now it was one place and we were able to walk through the Brandenburg Gate. We visited the Hohenzollern Crypt and the Dom, that nineteenth-century cathedral monument to Prussian pomposity, and went to Potsdam to see where Frederick the Great had recently been reburied beside his dogs, where he had always wanted to be. What a strange man he was, cultivated, cruel and tyrannical, but also a friend of Voltaire and a welcomer of refugees from Roman Catholic persecution.

On our last day we found ourselves in the Berlin War Memorial, a bare building with no religious or military symbols, for both religion and the army had let the German people down. One British Legion poppy was placed among the fresh flowers. A victim of the concentration camps is buried there alongside the Unknown Soldier. I found this deeply moving and was struck, when I saw a tape of the Cenotaph service in Whitehall on my return to London, how nostalgic, militaristic and out-of-date our commemoration was, and how Germany certainly seemed to have won the peace.

11 November

At 4.30 I went to Westminster Abbey for John Betjeman's memorial service and the unveiling of the memorial to him in Poet's Corner. I sat next to John Gaskell, opposite Barry Humphries and Auberon Waugh. I spoke to both, and was introduced by Auberon Waugh to his wife, Lady Teresa. Barry Humphries was very, very funny. Standing next to me afterwards by Betjeman's cartouche, he said, 'Cartouche – that's a foreign word, isn't it? Why can't they find a nice English word? Fancy using a foreign word like cartouche.' He said all this with his lips pursed, Dame Edna Everage appearing briefly.

17 November

I went to Guildford in torrential rain to give a sermon at the cathedral. This red-brick cathedral set on a hill outside Guildford is a kind of 1950s post-war folly. Instead of using a well-attended church in the town and making that the cathedral, they started all over again, making this new building in isolation, surrounded by nothing. Inside is very much nicer than outside – white and spacious, with potential.

In my sermon I congratulated the people on having such a courageous, intelligent and imaginative Bishop. John Gladwyn preached last night, amidst enormous controversy, at a service for gay and lesbian Christians in Southwark Cathedral. After the service I discovered a group of old ladies talking to journalists (the journalists, being ill-informed, had crowded to the cathedral to interview the Bishop, imagining that bishops are in their cathedrals every Sunday). When the journalists had gone away, I asked one of the old ladies how the conversation had gone. 'Well,' she said, 'we told them that we have a courageous, intelligent and imaginative Bishop.'

19 November

John Biffen, one of the most independent-minded members of the House of Commons, came to Dialogue today. He turned out to know Anne Hayes, Richard Hayes's mother, and was very amusing about how you canvass for the Tory Party

– what you don't talk about and how you get round the villages in Shropshire. He was enormously amusing, very funny, but wouldn't eat anything. I liked his independence of mind and can quite see what a thorn in the flesh he was to Mrs Thatcher.[2]

The following week Andrew Marr, then the Editor of the *Independent*, came to Dialogue and he was a great success afterwards at lunch with the grandees at Grocers' Hall. They gave him a particularly delicious 1975 claret, but Andrew said he did not drink in November. I thought this was an interesting idea. He explained that he never gave up drink in Lent, but instead gave it up for a couple of months before Christmas when everybody offered you far too much drink at office parties and so on. I felt I would not have the moral fibre to do that.

The beginning of December saw me attending Dr Venetia Newall's annual party.[3] Cleverly, she gathers together all her Jewish and Christian friends, being deeply involved with both communities, and gives a great dinner party for everybody once a year. If I had the means, as Venetia has, I would do the same. It gets all the washing-up out of the way in one go.

The next day Dr Zaki Badawi came for another Dialogue and stayed a long time afterwards over lunch. We had a fascinating conversation about critical study of the Koran and the current state of Algeria. He was against both. He said he believed there would never be any critical study of the Koran. I was sure he was wrong about this, although it would be a long time coming, and it would eventually have the same effect on Islam as nineteenth-century biblical criticism had on Christianity.

With Christmas approaching, a man called Howard Garfield followed me about the church one day, filming me as I got the crib together. It was made that year out of telephone directories, a *Whitaker's Almanack*, a wastepaper basket, two stools, some old curtains and the Baroque cover from the font. With a bit of work, this

---

2 John Biffen was Leader of the House of Commons 1982–7, and Lord Privy Seal 1993–7.

3 Dr Newall, a member of the congregation at St Mary's, Bourne Street, is a folklore scholar and a member of Affirming Catholicism.

was all turned into an eighteenth-century classical temple as background for the sacred figures.

This was on the morning of our carol service, which was being filmed by the BBC. We had a nasty moment when the power failed and we had no light or organ, but, literally at the last minute, there was a reprieve. Annie Reyersbach's choir from Ravenstone School participated, singing beautifully, as did the St Mary-le-Bow singers, who excelled themselves in Poulenc's *Hodie Christus Natus Est*. All of us, people and clergy alike, were moved by the seriousness and conviction of this parish carol service.

24 December

I am 52 years old. Andrew gave me the *Oxford Classical Dictionary* as an amazingly generous birthday present. This is the sort of book which I will get caught in when I should be reading other things.

At 9.45 p.m. I left for Chelsea, walking from Sloane Square to St Luke's through bitter cold weather. I'm looking after St Luke's at Christmas during its interregnum. Midnight Mass in this church was hard work and liturgically illiterate. Although there was a large number of people in the church, only 146 made their Communion. I would describe the churchmanship of St Luke's as 'Low Church Stiff'. No drinks, or even cups of coffee, were offered to the congregation afterwards.

25 December

I spent the night in a freezing bedroom in Gloucester Road as the guest of one of the Churchwardens. In the morning I woke frozen solid and went back to St Luke's to 'celebrate' – and it felt like inverted commas, too – the 1662 Communion Service and preached to 22 people. Later on was the Family Service. Being Low Church Stiff means that family services are more appreciated and better understood than the Eucharist. Then I celebrated 1662 again for 21 people at 12 o'clock and preached my fourth different Christmas sermon.

I went back to the City to find John Gaskell. His life has taken a tremendous battering recently, hence my offering him refuge here. I laid up the cheese and dessert for our peripatetic dinner party tonight and at 4 p.m. we went to Andrew's and Fred's flat in the Barbican.[4] Annie Reyersbach was already there. We ate delicious turkey, following lovely herby scallops; also a wonderful pudding made by Andrew. It was a splendid occasion and afterwards we processed back to Cheapside for cheese (Stilton from Neal's Yard), a Portuguese and Italian dessert and candied fruits.

When everybody had gone home except John, whom I put to bed, I went back upstairs to the sitting room at the top of the house to watch *The Vicar of Dibley* on television. I had a happy birthday yesterday, and a much enjoyed Nativity of Our Lord Jesus Christ today – and none of it as exhausting as entertaining people in Codford.

27 December

I spent a night and a day at Westminster Abbey for the feast of St John the Evangelist. After the 8 o'clock Mass in the Henry VII Chapel, we could see snow fluttering down in emp-tied-feather-pillow fashion beyond the Great West Door, opened onto this winter wonderland. A most Dickensian scene. Just being in the Abbey early in the morning was a magical experience and we had time to look at the High Altar ornaments, the great pavement and the quantities of medieval polychromy on the Sanctuary tombs. Evensong for St John's Day involved copes, processions and a good deal of glory and glamour.

30 December

It has been grey weather in Amsterdam. There is frost on the ground and the canals are like thick, dark green, oily soup where the ice is broken. I walked along the Amstel River to see Theo Visser.[5] I'm so fond of Theo, one of my most

---

4 Frédèric Bomer is a kindly and attractive Frenchman who became Andrew's partner. They both now live in Marseille.

5 Theo is a Dutch friend who was introduced to me in 1972 by Rabbi Lionel Blue.

eccentric friends. He was wearing a Muslim skullcap today and lives the life of an ascetic hermit. His one passion is bicycles, but I was delighted to discover that he'd spent more on the Meissen figurine adorning his bare study than on any of his bicycles. I can't quite get used to the idea of Theo buying a Meissen figurine of any shape or form.

31 December

At the Asian Department of the Rijksmuseum I consigned 1996 to Shiva, asking God to make a new creation out of the ashes of the ending year. From this comforting Hinduism I moved on to St Francis Xavier, to spend an hour before the Blessed Sacrament. All was quiet and still. 'The truth shall make you free.' I stayed for Vespers and Benediction and then spent the evening with Wim and some friends, until it was time for champagne and the fireworks which are always detonated over Amsterdam as the clocks strike 12. Thus we saw the old year, thankfully on my part, out and into history.

Headache and Heartache

T he first weeks of 1997 were characterized for me by a number of serious conversations on religious matters. After preaching one Sunday at St Luke's, Chelsea, I talked to Lady Helen Lever about the Virgin Birth. She said such subjects were never discussed and, although she felt she ought to, she did not believe in the Virgin Birth. I gave my explanation about it not being intended as a gynaecological description but as an honorific for Mary. The following week, a senior partner in a firm of actuaries came to see me about speaking at their annual dinner at the Dorchester, but this business-type conversation led swiftly into an earnest talk about religion.

Later the same day, the Labour MP Clare Short came for a pre-Dialogue drink. Even before she had climbed the stairs she had started questioning me about what 'the sacrifice of Christ' meant, both in the Mass and in relation to a loving God. This went on hammer and tongs in private before the Dialogue, in public during the Dialogue and in private again after the Dialogue. She did not leave until 3.15 and I wrote to her afterwards to try to further the conversation and make some helpful suggestions. The people loved her. I wrote in my diary that I hoped one day, when there was a Labour Government – which I prayed there would be soon – she would be made a Minister. I also noted that I imagined she was regarded by her parliamentary colleagues as something of a wild card, because she had that unusual trait in a politician of speaking the truth.

Towards the end of January I travelled up to Hereford to see Andrew Mottram at his now refurbished medieval church of All Saints. The trip, as it turned out, offered an unexpected bonus.

24 January

At Paddington I spied Sir Roy Strong in the distance. I didn't think he'd want to talk to me all the way to Hereford, so I hung about in the bookshop. We walked into each other when we changed trains at Newport, however, and Roy said, 'If you're free, come over and see the garden tomorrow.[1] Just ring and come for a cup of coffee.' From Newport to Hereford we travelled together after all, and he showed me some of the pages of the proofs he was reading for his soon-to-be-published diaries.

25 January

All Saints now has an open, remade space replacing the underwear-smelling church hall and nave it had when I first came up with Andrew to see it. The kitchen and the vestry are glass ovals, sited on raised platforms. There is a sense of a holy space. People will be eating in the nave at the same time as a Mass is being said in the Lady Chapel. It's an audacious experiment.

Andrew has got to know Sir Roy Strong quite well and Roy has given him plants from the Laskett, but Andrew's wife Annabelle has never been there, so she motored me over to Roy's. The garden in some places is perhaps too crowded, but otherwise it is an Arcadian landscape, elegant, romantic and going on for ever. The mist gradually rose and the sun shone and Roy obviously adores it.

Back in London, our next Dialogue guest was Field Marshal Lord Carver – tiny, birdlike, and wearing a suit of the kind I had not seen since Uncle Teddy went about in shiny blue serge suiting and equally twinkly shoes. Lord Carver appeared to be an extraordinarily bright man and needed no convincing at all about the need to abolish nuclear weapons. If all the top generals thought nuclear weapons should be got rid of, I thought to myself, perhaps in the end the politicians would find the courage to do so.

That evening I went to the Australia Day Dinner at Lincoln's Inn, where I spoke to Betty Boothroyd. 'I've just popped home to put on some polyfiller,' she told me cheerfully. Then she added, 'Patrick Mayhew is a sound man and will be a great loss.' So there it was: Madam Speaker being quite clear that the Government was not long for this world.

---

1 The Laskett, Much Birch, Herefordshire, is the largest private garden to be created in England since the Second World War.

8 February

I conducted a Quiet Day for the people of St Marks, Myddelton Square, and their co-parish, Our Most Holy Redeemer, Exmouth Market. Holy Redeemer is Anglo-Catholic, a wonderful Italianate church. It was put up in the nineteenth century by Anglo-Catholic clergy who thought that, if they made a church look Italian, it would ensnare the Italian Roman Catholics who lived locally. It didn't.

By contrast, the next day I had been invited to the Union Church, Mill Hill, a church belonging to the United Reformed community. Here, in the absence of a minister, I conducted Divine Worship and preached. It was a fascinating experience, for it all smelled of Uncle Teddy and my Nonconformist childhood, thin, poor and unattractive. The people were friendly and grateful, however, and I did enjoy the experience.

12 February

Ash Wednesday. We purposely kept the light dim in the church for the Solemn Mass with music by Brahms.

In the afternoon Andrew brought me three kittens in a basket from the East End, tied onto the front of his bicycle. Terrified little rat babies they were. I'm going call them Ash, Wednesday and Minou. Minou because I'm going to give one of them to Frédèric for the new flat in Highbury Fields – a French name appropriate for a French gentleman.

Lent got underway with a good-humoured and helpful visit from the Diocesan Advisory Committee, who came to look at proposals to build a new vestry and offices, lavatories and a shower for the restaurant workers in the crypt. During this meeting, however, I suddenly remembered that I was meant to be saying a prayer over the time capsule which was to be ceremonially buried in the foundations of the new Sadler's Wells. I jumped immediately into a taxi, leaving the DAC expostulating in the vestibule.

I arrived at the big do just in time. The new Sadler's Wells was still a building site, of course, and everyone was in hard hats, including the Labour leader Tony Blair and his wife Cherie Booth.

There was an opportunity for me to talk to Mr Blair and I said, 'May I wish you God speed and good luck, sir.' I found him to be an attractive man, bigger than he seemed on television, with a firm handshake. The rest of our conversation was short, but to the point.

VS: 'I've just had Clare Short at St Mary-le-Bow and thought her absolutely marvellous.'

TB: 'Oh, you do the Dialogues, of course. I've wondered about doing one of those.'

VS (seeing an opportunity): 'Well, perhaps you may find time when you're Prime Minister.'

Of course, when he did become Prime Minister, I was not at all sure that his minders would let him out. I have not asked him to a Dialogue – yet.

22 February

I stayed with the Chief Constable of Sussex, Paul Whitehouse, in order to look at houses. I need a bolt hole to replace Codford. Lewes is the town. It has its own theatre, music society, bookshops and antique shops to poke about in and buy people presents from. It's seven miles from Brighton and has hills, a river, walks and friends. All this says to me, 'Victor, come to Lewes!' This is clinched by the fact that it's only one hour from Victoria.

27 February

The pussies woke me at 5 a.m. (one being inside the bed), which was helpful as I had to leave at 6.30 for Copenhagen to visit Mule Fogh. By contrast with London, Denmark was all sunshine and blue sky.

On my way through Copenhagen I stopped to look at the closed door of the Russian Orthodox Church, which had an anti-ecumenical notice in several languages on it, fiercely saying that if you weren't Russian Orthodox you weren't allowed to have Holy Communion in that church. The shut door is the perfect metaphor for the shut mind.

1 March

Mule was shrunk, ill and sad, but momentary glimpses of the old fun appeared. I persuaded her to come out on my arm across the park to the church. A coffin came out as we stood watching. She cried and said, 'Take me away.' As we walked unsteadily and very slowly back across the park, I found a tiny group of aconites and the first snowdrops, and got her to enjoy them.

Back in her room, she said over a cup of tea, 'This may be our last meeting.' I fear it may.

We talked of scepticism and faith and the Church. Scepticism has never kept me away, but it has kept her away. So many people think you can't be a Christian believer unless you believe everything all the time.

Mule promised to tell her lawyer to let me know of her death. She wrote this down and I added my telephone number. I told her how much she meant to me in 1963. 'We have been faithful friends,' she said.

Lent proceeded at St Mary-le-Bow. Sue MacGregor, the presenter of Radio 4's *Today* programme, came for a Dialogue. She made the point that you can be a celebrity on radio but still have a private life, because nobody has seen your face – you can get round Sainsbury's without people asking for your autograph. This was a point I had not considered. I had been listening to Sue MacGregor every morning for years and felt she was part of my life.

Later I spoke at the Actuaries' Dinner at the Dorchester. Lord Tebbit spoke first, attacking the Labour Party and supporting the Conservative Government, and generally treating the black-tie audience – which included a number of Germans – as if they were all Conservatives and would vote to keep the Tories in power. His broadsides against Tony Blair's character and ability were received in silence, as was his attack on Germany.

In my own speech I said I remembered, as Lord Mayor's Chaplain, sitting in the Guildhall while the Tory Foreign Secretary gave his annual report on the state of the Government's foreign policy, in the days when the Government *had* a foreign policy. Lord Tebbit leaned forward and said, rather wittily, 'Ah, Father Stock, we have several policies on Europe now.'

'That is why you are going to lose the next election, Lord Tebbit,' I replied crisply. This was received with what can only modestly be described as 'thunderous applause'.

From that moment I knew that Labour would get in, for here was an absolutely rock-solid businessmen's black-tie Dorchester dinner, which should have been full of people hanging onto the Tory Government – but they could not wait to wash their hands of it. I found this fascinating. At the end of the dinner, Robert Owen QC, the Chairman of the Bar Council, said he wanted at least two Blair terms.

The prospect of such change was immensely exciting, but Easter was approaching and I put the forthcoming election campaign out of my mind and concentrated on Holy Week.

16 March

Passion Sunday. I caught the 7.35 a.m. from Victoria out along that Dickensian Dartford-Gillingham-Rochester-Chatham-Faversham-Canterbury estuary and fruit field country, in order to preach in the mother church of the Anglican Communion. I had coffee with Canon Michael Chandler and his wife in the Cathedral Precincts, and then was allowed to go on my own into the empty crypt. Childhood memories flooded back from all those holidays in Sturry, when I wandered round on my own in this enchanted place. The Solemn Eucharist was liturgy at its most wonderful, and the Dean was welcoming.

27 March

Maundy Thursday. At St Mary-le-Bow's lunchtime High Mass the choir belted out Bruckner and parts of Schubert's *German Mass*. So sublime was this Mass music that at the Sanctus I began to cry. The church was packed with sun as well as intelligent young City people – 90 or so of them. I felt penetrated by the love of God, lifted up into him as I stood at the Consecration. I realized at the Offertory that going round the altar with the thurible and censing the altar vigorously was a kind of lovemaking.

From this exalting experience I dashed to Paddington, the weather changing to cold and grey as I got out of the train at

Charlbury and made my way to Burford Priory. I went straight into the chapel, the wooden floor creaking alarmingly. Brother Robert, who we'd all expected to be the first Prior, took me to the guesthouse, where he lives as Guest Brother.

At 6.30 we assembled for a Passover hymn and went in procession to the refectory for a Passover story. There was handwashing, left over from the time of Mother Mary Bernard, who was too arthritic to wash feet, and a meal in silence. Unleavened pitta bread, lamb chops and a bowl of bitter herbs, all from the Exodus story, plus water and fruit. Then we went back to the inner hall for another hymn, 'Israel came out of Egypt', and a Psalm. Somehow we were caught up in the Exodus and took our part in it.

From there to the 8 o'clock Mass. The Blessed Sacrament was carried in procession to the great outer hall, followed by the whole Community. There were branches of blossom, pots of primroses, bowls of narcissi and candles around the improvised Altar of Repose.

28 March

Good Friday. Lauds at 8 a.m., the Office said today, not sung. I had a cup of coffee at 11, but no food until 2 p.m., when we had hot cross buns. On the radio this week Sister Lavinia Byrne said she saw in one shop that they'd been called 'hot happy buns'.

The liturgy today was done with a simple dignity, unaccompanied singing of Taizé and plainsong chants. I felt tearful at the Veneration, and later took Pontius Pilate's part in the reading of the Passion story. Last night, at the end of the Maundy Thursday Mass, there was no stripping of the altars, as is usually the custom, but when we came to Lauds this morning the statues, the Tabernacle itself, the lamps and even the great crucifix behind the altar were all gone, the chapel stark in its emptiness.

29 March

Holy Saturday. In answer to my question, Brother Robert told me in 15 minutes about the events leading up to his non-election as Superior.

The morning was filled with the quiet bustle of Easter preparation – a music and liturgy practice and the usual muddle, I
was delighted to see, about the ceremonies for the Easter Vigil.
Wherever I've been, either as participant or director, I don't
think anyone has ever remembered what they did last year.

The clock is ticking away all too fast towards the time
when 'normal' life will engulf me again. In eight minutes it will
be 7 o'clock, suppertime, then Compline and an early bed –
the alarm clock due to go off at 4.30 a.m.

30 March

Easter Day. We assembled as the first streaks of a pale blue-
green dawn appeared. At 5.30 the fire was lit on the lawn,
the Easter candle lit from it, and we processed from the front
lawn, through the house and up the creaking stairs.

The Easter sunrise was cold and pale. Robert was almost
in tears administering the Easter Host. I'm not the only person who suffers. There is solidarity in this rediscovery. What
I have experienced this Easter has deepened my understanding of that which I know as God.

Leaving Burford, I went to spend a few Eastertide days in Venice,
then returned to the City for the long-planned visitation from our
sister church of Trinity, Wall Street.

10 April

The Vestry, i.e. the Parochial Church Council, of Trinity, Wall
Street, came to Mass at St Mary-le-Bow as part of their ter-
centenary celebrations. They'd already been to dinner with
the Archbishop of Canterbury and were about to go to tea
with the Queen at Windsor. They made our Churchwardens
Honorary Wardens of Wall Street, and then the Grocers' Hall
gave them lunch.

I had a go at the Earl of Inchcape about his view that the
Church of England had gone Communist over this week's
published report on work and unemployment. He got very
cross. The idea that the Church of England is Communist,
when it's full of people like the Earl of Inchcape!

22 April

I went to 8 a.m. Mass in the incomparable splendour of the Henry VIII Chapel of Westminster Abbey, celebrated by David Hutt to mark the end of his year as Sion College President. He's been an excellent President, particularly gifted and able at chairing the Court.

Afterwards we had a wonderful tour of the Library and Muniment Room. In the former was a letter to the Dean about losing the Imperial State Crown just before the 1937 Coronation from an amused, laconic Lord Chamberlain. 'These things happen, you know.'

30 April

The last day of the general election campaign opened with a letter from the Bishop of Ripon. Would I allow my 'hat to be thrown into the ring', as he put it, for the post of Rector of Leeds? I said 'yes', though I don't feel enthusiastic. It's a big job, however, and I must take it seriously.

1 May

Election Day. At the Past Masters' Dinner as the guest of Peter Luscombe, I said Grace, giving thanks for democratic choice. There were scowls at this. Lady Cazelet turned to me and said she hoped I wasn't going to be disappointed: 'It will be too sad for you.'

'Oh no,' I replied, 'I think I'm going to be delighted.'

Then I went off to Gay Firth's party in Holland Park, the house full of young people and politicians of all parties. Down went the disgraced Tories – the Tatton constituency, memorably, to Martin Bell, an independent, by a 12,000 majority, vindicating his courageous stand against Neil Hamilton.

The room erupted in cheers when Ben Bradshaw, the out-gay Labour candidate in Exeter, overthrew the homophobic Tory sitting member by a 10,000 majority. Just before the election, the Church of England cathedral-going Tory doctor had circulated a letter round the constituency saying, 'If you vote for Ben Bradshaw, your children will not be safe.' The stout burghers of Exeter, not exactly left-wing Islington Socialists, decided that enough was enough. Out he went and in came the charming and delightful Ben. That got the biggest cheer of the evening and then, oh wonder of wonders, Michael Portillo went out at Southgate. Stephen Twigg, another out-gay man, young and inexperienced, saw off the future hope of the Tory Party.

I suddenly remembered that standing behind me amidst the cheering multitude was Lord Howe. I turned round and asked Geoffrey how he was feeling about all this. He said, 'We deserved this. I felt once that Labour might harm the economy, but now I don't. If we had won, irreparable damage would have been done to Europe.'

The slaughter went on until I left at 4.30 a.m. British decency had resurfaced.

2 May

After Mass, Tighe, our social worker with the Young People's Project, Graham, Vanessa and I had a drink to toast the Prime Minister and watched his triumphal arrival at No. 10 on television. Labour have 179 seats and the Liberal Democrats 46, which is just as remarkable. Seven Cabinet Ministers have lost their seats. There are no Tories – no, not one – in the whole of Scotland or Wales. John Major, nice John Major, is stepping down as Tory Leader.

Later we discovered that John Major had left a bottle of champagne on a table in No. 10 Downing Street for the incoming Blairs, along with a note saying, 'I hope you will be as happy in this house as we have been.'

10 May

A young man was run over by a bus in Cheapside today as we were collecting for the Red Cross, and he died in the street in front of me. I tried to comfort a Red Cross nurse who was out collecting by the church and had gone over to help him.

Later in the day I travelled to Exeter to preach the annual legal sermon to the judges on the western circuit and their

German and French legal guests. I went first to the Deanery. The Dean of Exeter, Keith Jones, was witty, warm, civilized and welcoming. Then I went on to the Judge's Lodgings, where I met the very nice Mr Justice Tucker. 'I'm left wing,' he said.

A Sheriff's wife confessed that her husband had voted Liberal Democrat. Another woman said, 'We lost because of Swampy. We should have put gas down the hole, or sent in the hounds.'[2]

One of the judges whispered in my ear, 'That's why the Tory Party lost the general election, I'm pleased to say.'

So there we were, Lord Lieutenants, presiding judges and members of the county judiciary, and only one person had voted Tory. What is happening to this country? It's the sensible old mechanism of change.

11 May

I sat with friendly clergy at the 9.45 Eucharist and at 11.00 preached my legal sermon to a cathedral completely full of judges. People said nice things to me afterwards, including the Countess of Morley, who commented, 'First sermon I've heard for years so good. Thank you so much.'

The Dean said to me wryly, 'She's just discovered how to switch on her deaf aid.'

13 May

We had an audience of 340 people today for the Dialogue with Tony Benn. At lunch afterwards he brought back my childhood, Uncle Teddy and my Fulham and Chelsea background.

At one point he was being silly about titles when one of my guests – I think it was Bill Sewell – asked him what it was like giving up his viscountcy.[3] 'Oh, my Dad never took it very seriously,' he said.

---

2 The eco-warrior Swampy, protesting against road-building, had built a series of tunnels under the proposed Winchester bypass.

3 When his father, Lord Stansgate, died in 1960, Tony Benn automatically inherited the peerage and lost his seat in the Commons. He renounced the title and got himself re-elected as soon as he could.

I replied, 'My grandmother knew Lady Stansgate very well. They were old friends.' That put another perspective on history.

The other amusement was that the pussies found the pudding and jumped into it. There was nothing for it but to remove the traces of paw marks with a spoon and hope for the best.

The following week our Dialogue guest was Dr Wesley Carr, the new Dean of Westminster. Only 106 people attended, but those who came were, I felt, given an introduction to a man of integrity, intelligence, honesty and straightforwardness. I was surprised he had got as far as he had done in the Church of England, because he had no side, did not suck up to people, and had clear views about what was wrong with everything. It was quite unusual. Honesty was not always the best policy, as I discovered when I went for my interview for the Leeds Rectorship.

6 June

I arrived in Leeds at 11.30, to walk about what seemed to be a hideously ugly city. I went into Harvey Nicks, the one bright spot, and then into the parish church of Leeds which is, as it were, the cathedral. It was ugly and dead, civic, Masonic and unspiritual, overwhelmed by pitch-black, hideous pine galleries. The entrance to this basilica was through a tea room full of old ladies with white cardigans and tightly permed hairdos, cutting up lettuce and cheese sandwiches of the sort we haven't seen in London since the Second World War.

The candidates on the shortlist were not introduced to each other, but were given sandwiches and orange juice and left to mill about with the interviewing panel – which included a bluff, big, noisy Archdeacon, a woman Headteacher and a very small Area Dean the size of the ladies in the church sandwich shop.

The first question the Bishop asked at my interview was: 'What is your vision for Leeds?' I thought this such a perfectly ridiculous question that I'm afraid I said so. It was hopeless, really, the whole thing. I asked them some questions, most of which they didn't want to answer. I thought the Bishop kindly but ineffective.

The second interview was with a lady Churchwarden from Holy Trinity, one of the daughter churches, and a nice, competent solicitor. He was the only person who really knew what was going on. At this juncture we discovered that there was no chance to see the rectory and that we'd not been sent the Bishop's report on the future of Leeds and the diocese, or the accounts. When I asked, I was told that the house would be shown to the preferred candidate. Then, when I asked when we would meet the other priest members of staff with whom relationships were crucial, I was told that the preferred candidate would be introduced to them. I also commented, as we hadn't seen the accounts, that rumour had it that there was £3 million in the Leeds Church Institute fund. Was that true, and what was going to be done with it? That went down like a lead balloon.

I met Andy Windross, one of the other candidates, for a second look at the church. After that we went for a couple of beers in a pub. As we sat down, we looked at each other and said, 'F***ing hell!'

It was a very rough pub, but all the men put down their beer glasses and stared at us. I had to turn round and say, 'I'm sorry. We're a couple of vicars in a state.'

On the Monday after the interview, the Archdeacon of Leeds telephoned. 'We can't agree,' he said. 'The parish representatives couldn't put their signature to any of the candidates.' I was not surprised.

I soon had other things on my mind. Since Christmas 1988 I had been broadcasting every week on GLR's evening programme *Drive Time*, in a short live interview about my week. Someone at the BBC had heard this and asked if I would like to make some television programmes about relationship problems brought in by members of the public. Later in June I went for my 'audition'. The BBC had never thought of using a priest to deal with people's problems before, and were amazed when I said this was what we did every day.

18 June

I went to film the pilot programme of *Headache and Heartache* – or it may become *What Now?* The studio was full of fascinating people, including Anne Atkins, the right-wing Conservative Evangelical wife of the Vicar of St Dionis, Parsons Green, full of opinions about everything. I made her laugh by laughing at her, which I think spoilt her image as a boot-faced reactionary. She's fun, though, and I don't mind boot-faced reactionaries if they can laugh.

In the end, the BBC decided not to use Ms Atkins, but chose me and Edwina Currie for what became a series of 20 programmes.

Then I had a few days in Wim's Amsterdam flat, discovering the Armenian Church where an ancient Archbishop presided from his throne. It was Jerusalem again in miniature: the curtain drawn across the Sanctuary during the Prayer of Consecration to hide the impious eyes of the laity from the mysteries within, the fans, the ostrich eggs, and all the other paraphernalia of Armenian worship. At the end everyone kissed the Archbishop's hand and so did I. It was a moving experience, bringing William Dalrymple's book *From the Holy Mountain* very much alive. The little cross on the Archbishop's chest had the two-headed eagle of Byzantium on it.

Back home, I discovered in my Rector's Discretionary Fund an unexpected sum of money which I was able to spend on a special magnifying glass for James Watson. He was becoming increasingly blind and was almost unable to read. I went to Chiswick to read to him one day, and it was a case of the halt leading the blind. My arthritic right foot had been diagnosed simply as 'wear and tear'. I forgot about the pain in my foot, however, when we heard the happy news that one of our Churchwardens, Wendy Evans, had been made Director of the Museum at Westminster Abbey. Then Jean Mayhew was awarded a well-deserved OBE. As John Major said, in Jean Northern Ireland had gained a second Secretary of State.

The first excitement of July was the Roman Catholic/Jewish wedding of Laura and Will.

11 July

I'm at the Royal Berkshire Hotel for the wedding. Elderly ladies from Berlin, who just got out in the 1930s, abound. I had tea and champagne and found a chance to talk to Rabbi Dr Sidney Bricktov, who, unlike every other rabbi we approached, said 'yes' to helping with this mixed marriage. He did the Blessing of the Sabbath and the Blessing of the Marriage over dinner.

12 July

The Sabbath. Amongst the early cups of tea put outside the doors for everyone, the *Daily Mail* had an article in it about 'marrying out', written by a Jewish mother in Stamford Hill. She said that if her son married a Christian, she would never speak to him again, or receive him into her home. This was not what my mother would have called 'helpful'.

The wedding was full of black top hats and people sweating rivers. Handel's *Zadok the Priest* was sung by some musical friends of the couple. To a congregation made up almost entirely of either Roman Catholics or Jews, I said in my sermon, 'We've all read that article in the paper this morning and I've been thinking, why can't religious people talk, when they share things, about "marrying in" instead of "marrying out"? This whole occasion is about joining together, sharing and uniting.'

21 July

I was invited to a Temenos reception and party given by the Prince of Wales at St James's Palace.[4] It was my first visit to the interior of this building, which has a Hampton Court-like feel. We sat and listened to Indian court music, sarod and raga, wonderfully executed. His Royal Highness spoke off the cuff, so well about music and spirituality that I hardly recognized him as the hesitant and cuff-link-fingering public figure.

---

4 Temenos is a group founded by the poet Kathleen Raine to explore spiritual truth and philosophy in all the great religions. I belonged and often went to Temenos lectures.

27 July

Today I found 104 Western Road, Lewes – one of a row of small, 1867 workers' cottages on the curve of the road at the top of the town, just before the prison and the Downs and five or six minutes' walk to them. Mrs Gander, the present owner, is a nice old party: Roman Catholic, devout, sitting in front of a television adorned with statues of the Sacred Heart of Jesus and Our Lady of Lourdes. This is going to be it.

I put in an offer for the house at once. By November it was mine and I had moved in by Christmas. Completely different from Codford, 104 Western Road was very small, with a tiny garden, and I had it all to myself.

29 July

I have taken Father John Gaskell to Rome for cheering up as he has been so lonely and depressed since retiring. At Gatwick there was a terrible scene because he'd lost his passport and boarding pass. He went into a complete panic and started hyperventilating. He had both in his hand all the time, but couldn't see them underneath his copy of *The Times*. This, I hope, will not be an earnest of how things are going to be on the holiday.

31 July

We were repulsed from the doors of St Peter's today because I was wearing old-fashioned Victorian khaki, deeply modest shorts. The guardian of faith and morals admitted a woman in very much shorter shorts than mine because she was extraordinarily beautiful. After an unseemly shouting episode, torrents of abuse and a hard push from a uniformed security man, I retired defeated.

I pointed out that this exclusion had not happened at Santa Maria Maggiore, where I'd been let in by the guardians wearing the self-same shorts, but the man told me, 'We do not care about other churches. St Peter's is the centre of the world.' That claim has caused a great deal of difficulty over the last 2,000 years of Christian history.

3 August

At a bus stop we saw three men hurling themselves from a bus, locked in combat. There were cheers from the crowded bus, a swarm of police, blood and general drama. Pickpockets, we presumed. Feeling superior, we boarded the empty bus, only to be attacked ourselves by three youths who tried to pick John Gaskell's pocket. We stout British clergymen saw them off.

Leaving Rome behind, I paid a quick visit to Venice and then headed for Scotland, where I was preaching at Old St Paul's during the Edinburgh Festival. Towards the end of August, I went to stay with the Mayhews at their home in Kent. Patrick, of course, had relinquished the Northern Ireland post when the Conservatives lost the election.

29 August

I took the train to Paddock Wood to be met by Patrick, Jean, their driver, and two protection officers in a back-up armoured vehicle. Patrick is transformed by retirement, is enjoying the House of Lords and is also learning to cook. Jean is finding adjustment from public to private life harder.

31 August

Coming down the stairs for breakfast, I heard Jean call out, 'Diana and Dodi Fayed have been killed in a car crash in Paris!' This is what shock feels like, I thought, the reverberations going off like a slow detonation as I tried to take in what this would mean. How sad it feels that such a gifted life should end this way.

We went to the Parish Communion in Goudhurst. The Vicar was away and a nonstipendiary minister was celebrating the Eucharist. He wore a black stole, but otherwise nothing at all was said except at the beginning of the service. 'Because of the sad news, there will be two minutes' silence before my sermon,' said the minister, and then went on with the service. When he came to the sermon he said, 'Now we're going to have two minutes' silence.'

The woman in the pew in front of us turned to her neighbour and said, 'What for?' Lots of people had come straight to church without hearing the news.

The sermon was about Christian stewardship and how much money we should give to the Church. There was no mention of Diana, or the grief which was beginning to convulse people. The cowardice and sheer unprofessionalism of this display made me blush for the Church of England.

On the way back to London I wondered what we would do about flying the flags at half-mast, as there had been no instructions on the news about Court mourning. Diana had been removed from the royal family, as she had been removed from the state prayers, and so the protocols for royal mourning or a state funeral did not apply. As I crossed the bridge at Blackfriars, however, I saw that the Governor of the Tower of London had already flown his flag at half-mast, and in Cheapside I saw that the Governor of the Bank of England had done the same. Thus fortified, I climbed the tower and lowered our own flag.

I went on to Highbury, where a group of friends were gathering at Andrew's and Fred's flat. Three of them had already been to The Mall. There was no flag over Buckingham Palace because the Royal Standard is never flown when the Queen is absent, and she was still at Balmoral, the Palace bolted and barred, nobody there. The Prince of Wales had flown out to Paris that morning to accompany the body back home. There had been a discussion about whether or not the Royal Standard would be placed on the coffin. As the coffin emerged from the aeroplane, we saw to our relief that it was indeed shrouded in the Standard.

Thus began a week which saw history being made and all of us caught up in the making.

1 September

GLR asked me to do a piece this evening on the radio, so I thought I'd see what the atmosphere was like. I went to

Trafalgar Square, walked to St James's Palace and looked at the crowds in The Mall. People were bringing flowers and leaving them outside the railings of Buckingham Palace and along the pavement around St James's. There were lots of young people. It was extraordinarily quiet.

Someone suggested that we should have a book for people to sign in the church. I was initially resistant, but then thought it would do no harm and went to W.H. Smith's to buy a large account register. By the end of the week we had more than 2,500 entries in five of these books.

I decided to put on a Requiem Mass for the Wednesday lunchtime. It would be the black-vestmented High Mass with music that we usually have on All Souls' Day. I went round the shops with posters and people kept asking for more. The whole parish gradually filled up with these advertisements for the Wednesday Requiem.

3 September

All these days are Diana's days. We sang the Fauré *Requiem* at High Mass at 1.05. I printed 300 orders of service, but we had 450 people inside the church and 500 in the churchyard. There were builders and bankers, secretaries, past Lord Mayors, the staff of the Mansion House, including the City Marshal and the Swordbearer, the Clerk of the Grocers' Company and all the staff. The accountant Danny Feakin was in tears, and rang in the afternoon to thank me. The Clerk delivered a hand-written letter. The church was so full that people stood all round the altar in the Sanctuary. A former Lord Mayor of London in jacket and pinstripe trousers sat on the floor next to a young worker from a building site wearing cement-covered jeans and a torn T-shirt. It was, in a real sense, a social revolution, for there was only the floor left to sit on.

The BBC came to televise the Mass and a clip of it appeared on the 6 o'clock news, including the part of my sermon when I spoke about Diana and AIDS. I wore an AIDS ribbon pinned to my vestments. CNN beamed this clip of the sermon round the United States and Premier Radio put out the whole service at 9 p.m.

I spoke about Diana having the gift of touch, and how the Stuart monarchy went on touching for the King's Evil, thinking they could cure disease through the power given them by sacramental anointing at the Coronation. Diana was able to touch and heal without being crowned, I said, and, although she'd been cast out and rejected, she had been able to do what no one else in her position dared to do. By simply holding the hand of a man dying of AIDS, she had shown people that AIDS was not contagious. She stopped at a stroke the hysterical reaction which had initially swept through America, when people wouldn't drink at the same bar, or eat in the same restaurant, as people with the disease.

4 September

More and more people came to sign the book. Yesterday evening, as I was closing the church, there was a young man of 18 or 19 writing with great effort, his tongue out with the strain. I said, 'I'm very sorry, I've got to lock the church now, but I'll open it again at 6 o'clock in the morning.'

The boy told me he'd never been in a church before. 'I thought of praying,' he said, 'but if I prayed, my prayers would be selfish.' I thought of all the people who pray, who've never got as far as that boy in self-knowledge and tenderness.

When he'd gone and I'd locked the church, I went back to see what he'd written. It was this, not all spelt correctly: 'Diana, I will never forget you. You came to visit my nephew who had a brain tumour in hospital once. Thank you.'

It just went on like this, the things people wrote being a catharsis of suffering and pain. That was her gift – she was a Princess who could help people cry and share and do all those other things we poor, buttoned-up English are so bad at.

6 September

The funeral of Diana, Princess of Wales. I was up at 5.30 a.m. and off to GLR at 6.15. London was utterly deserted. I walked through an empty Oxford Street to Marylebone High Street and took part in the GLR funeral programme from 7.30 till 8.30. Then I stayed to breakfast with the team. We all gathered round the television as Diana's body was taken on its gun carriage from Kensington Palace. Silence in the studio; silence in the street, broken only by one woman's initial hysterical cry of 'Diana!', then nothing but the jingle of harness, so much more moving than military music.

Philip Wright, a friend of mine on his way to the Middle East, came round to the rectory at 10.30 and we watched the superbly moving funeral service on the television, both in tears. There was applause in the Abbey at the end of Charlie Spencer's sermon, but it began in Hyde Park from the crowd watching the service on a huge screen. It travelled from the Park through the streets to the Abbey, up the nave from the west end, into the choir and transepts. Everybody, but everybody, except the royal family, was applauding. At the end of the afternoon, Diana's body was carried to Althorp.

A week later, when things had calmed down a bit, a quiet morning set aside for reading and writing was spoilt by me slipping on the roof garden parapet and casting myself down. My mother would have said, 'Was this really necessary, dear?' I had gone to water a pot plant on the higher parapet of the roof and, jumping back into the roof garden proper, missed my footing and slipped, falling into the fir tree and across the concrete. As I was only wearing shorts and a minimal T-shirt, I covered myself with scratches, cuts and blood.

The doorbell rang insistently. I picked myself up and tumbled downstairs to find the Syrian Orthodox asking for a sacristy key which they had left behind. I sorted this out for them, dripping blood all over the vestry as I did so, but nobody commented or even seemed to notice. Far from asking, 'Are you all right, Father?' or 'What on earth has happened to you? Can we help?' it seemed to be taken as read that the Rector of St Mary-le-Bow would be covered in blood and dripping it everywhere on a Sunday morning. Perhaps they thought I was engaged in some particularly High Church practice.

Still showing the bruises, I went off one sunny September afternoon to visit my old VSO friend Alan Macdonald, who was in King's College Hospital. He had just been diagnosed with cancer of the brain. Sitting with him, I could not decide whether he had taken this in or not. It was a sad day. The first marriage at which I officiated as a young priest was Alan's marriage to Janice, and I am godfather to their son Alexander.

Back in the City, the incoming Lord Mayor gave what is called the Presentation Day Dinner at the Salters' Hall, a lavish affair of vodka, champagne, caviar and partridges. I was going to be his part-time Chaplain, deputizing for that year's real Chaplain, Frank Weston, who had just been made Bishop of Knaresborough.

At St Mary-le-Bow, life continued with its routines, including some very interesting Dialogues. September saw visits from Ben Bradshaw, the new MP for Exeter, Jeremy Vine, the BBC's Southern Africa correspondent, and, at the end of the month, Rabbi David Goldberg.

28 September

Rabbi David Goldberg spoke movingly, sharing his feelings from Westminster Abbey about the Christian idea of consolation, because the Christian God experienced pain in giving up his son. It was a wonderful thing for a Rabbi to share with a Christian audience in a church. As I said, 'Today we are on holy ground.'

4 November

Today our Dialogue guest was Rosie Atkins, the Editor of *Gardens Illustrated*, and two lovely things happened. One was that I was invited to contribute a 'Personal View', which comes out every month on the back page of her magazine, and the other was a marvellous story told at our lunch at the Grocers' Hall. When the Crown Prince of Japan came to Magdalen College, Oxford, the President of Magdalen asked the young man, 'What does your name mean?'

The Prince replied, 'Son of God.'

'Oh,' said the President, 'you'll find quite a few people from very good families here.'

8 November

For the Lord Mayor's Show the Bishop of Knaresborough, being the official Lord Mayor's Chaplain and having not done it before, rode in the coach with the Lord Mayor. I, as the understudy Chaplain, was looked after by the Pageant Master Dominic Reid, riding with him in his Land Rover. This is the most extraordinary way to travel. We led the way before the Blues and Royals down Ludgate Hill, literally the first people in the procession, and along a thronged, happy and sunny Fleet Street. To circumnavigate St Paul's and enter Ludgate like a Caesar was thrilling, a real *Boy's Own* excitement. At one point, as we overtook the cavalry to lead off, Dominic had to restrain my tricorne-hat-waving because I was frightening the horses.

10 November

After Matins, I went off to the rehearsal for the Lord Mayor's Banquet. In the afternoon I changed into state robes and went to the Mansion House, where, at the pre-banquet drinks, Prime Minister Tony Blair came up and shook hands with me. 'How are you?' he asked.

'I don't think you can possibly remember who I am,' I said, 'but it's very kind of you to say you do. The last time we had a conversation was at Sadler's Wells.' And indeed he did remember.

The Prime Minister got a standing ovation after his speech – much deserved.

13 November

I discovered today that last night, walking home from a restaurant in Highbury, Andrew and Fred were mugged. Fred was kicked severely in the face, and both were kept in hospital all night. Two young men walking home together were simply set upon by some thugs in an act of unbridled homophobia.

The wonderful and unlikely part of this story is that, as the boys were being kicked, a group of police were going by in a car. They stopped, jumped out and arrested the louts, so they will be brought to trial. The fact that this kind of thing can happen in the prosperous and comparatively secure part of London that is Highbury says a great deal about the state of our city.

20 November

I helped 'top out' the new Sadler's Wells today. There were lots of press there. Seeing out of the corner of my eye a turbaned Sikh workman wheeling cement, I asked him if he could come over and join me. So we got our photograph taken together with the piece of fir tree that builders put in the cement (and, my goodness, that must be a pre-Christian custom if ever there was one). We stood on the top of Sadler's Wells against an almost black sky. It was a thrilling occasion – *and* I managed to capture the Chief Executive, Ian Albery, for a Dialogue next year.

Back at St Mary-le-Bow, I gave lunch to Alan and Janice. Alan is now clearly unwell.

21 November

Yes, a triumph! The photograph of Father Stock and Mr Singh topping out Sadler's Wells together appeared large as life and twice as lovely in the *Independent*.

25 November

Dr Peter Selby, the new Bishop of Worcester, was my Dialogue guest. He doesn't take the official line of the House of Bishops on human sexuality, and is going to run into trouble being open, honest and practical about these matters.

There was a letter in the *Independent* about Sadler's Wells, attacking me for participating in a pagan ritual when I should have been preaching God's Holy Word. At least, said the angry letter-writer, the Sikh was not a superstitious man. You can't win, can you? The Sikh wouldn't have been in the picture if it hadn't been for me, and the fir twigs were the builders' property, not mine.

Soon we were into Advent, and on 9 December we had our first carol service of the season, for one of the City's homeless charities. The service included a Seventh Day Adventist black rock band, an enormous choir from Manchester, our own rather dainty

St Mary-le-Bow singers, and Her Grace the Duchess of Norfolk reading a lesson. It was a combination beyond parody.

The weeks rushed past, and suddenly it was Christmas and time for a break. I headed down to Lewes for the first Christmas in my new home.

25 December

Christmas Day has been windy, with squalls of rain. I laid the dining room table for dinner and went to the local church for a very good sermon by an elderly priest who had taken trouble over content and presentation.

In the afternoon Andrew and Fred came for a walk through the blustery weather, down to the river and into the ancient church of St Thomas à Becket. It was damp and 1662-ish, but was at least open, which most churches are not on Christmas afternoon. There was a crib all lit up and welcoming in the porch.

Christmas dinner was a triumph: local red mullet followed by fillet of venison.

31 December

New Year's Eve in Amsterdam. I went through the pouring rain to the Rijksmuseum, where I paid another visit to Shiva. With his drum Shiva calls creation into being, and with fire he destroys it – a fruitful thought at the end of one year and the beginning of another.

The Lady Mayoress and the Napkin

As if there had not been enough eating and drinking over the holiday, my first day back at work in January involved a smart City dinner. I managed, inadvertently, to turn the occasion into a memorable one.

6 January

Back to work in Cheapside. In the evening I went in my cassock to the Lord Mayor's Dinner for the Court of Aldermen. This turned out to be a post-Diana modernization – round tables, no white ties or Aldermanic scarlet gowns, but simply dinner jackets, a jazz band from the Guildhall University and an air of happy relaxation. I was placed on the Lady Mayoress's right and next to me on my right was Michael Dicken, Air Vice-Marshal and Private Secretary to the Lord Mayor.

We got deep into conversation and I kept dropping my table napkin. Stiff white damask tends to slide like card off the shiny surface of a cassock. After the third attempt at bending down and picking it up, I decided I'd pick it up without bending down to look, and grabbed hold of the material from under the table. I decided that the way to anchor the napkin was to tuck it into the buttons of my cassock. This I did. As I turned back to Michael Dicken, however, I felt the Lady Mayoress being dragged towards me.

I could see no way out of this embarrassment but to make a joke of it, so I clapped my hands and said, 'My Lord Mayor, Aldermen, Ladies and Gentlemen – may I have your attention for a moment? The Lady Mayoress is suffering from a terrible nightmare. She is imagining that I am trying to put on her dress. Well, I am.'

One of the footmen whispered in my ear later in the evening that there were 'several Lady Mayoresses who wouldn't have found that so funny'.

22 January

Today we had our annual Arthur Phillip service, celebrating our Australian connection in the presence of the Lord Mayor, with the address being given by Professor Sir Ghillean Prance of Kew.

After this I asked the Assistant High Commissioner Rosalind McGovern what she was going to do when she retired. She said, 'There's an old Australian proverb: "Bugger all!"'

Then I asked her, 'How did you get into the Diplomatic Service?'

'It was an act of sheer bloody-mindedness,' she replied. Oh, she's worth a guinea a minute. We're going to miss her.

26 January

At the Australia Day Dinner the Blessed Rosalind McGovern persuaded the manager of Qantas to offer me a ticket to Australia. I couldn't believe this, but it did happen. The next day I rang up to make absolutely sure it was true, and it was.

Early in February I flew to Copenhagen, where I combined a preaching engagement in the Anglican church with my annual visit to Mule Fogh. Astonishingly, she was alive still, though not well.

7 February

Mule is now very ill, depressed, tottery, yellow and shrunken, with cancer of the bone marrow. It took some time to cheer her up, but I managed it eventually, with stories like 'The Napkin, the Cassock and the Lady Mayoress's Frock'.

The comforting discovery of this visit was that the hospice doctor and nurse have established a good relationship with Mule and she trusts them. I know this will be the last visit. Last year I thought it was; this year I know it is. I stayed with her from 11.30 until 3.15. There were no aconites in the park outside and it began to drizzle, a heavy, grey light pressing down. Last year we talked about funerals and death, but this year it was too painful to do that. I went sadly back to Copenhagen.

8 February

At the Anglican church I celebrated the 9 a.m. Mass and preached at the 10.30 Mass. I lunched with some of the young people in the congregation afterwards and was back in Cheapside by evening. Between the Masses I walked along the quayside and looked at the Little Mermaid, whose head has recently been restored after vandalism. There was a brilliant cold sunshine this morning, bells everywhere on the Baltic air and a big Polish ship alongside the quay. I won't go to Copenhagen again while Mule Fogh is alive.

The following week, Andrew Dunford was cycling to the Barbican from his practice in the East End when he was kicked by a group of yobs at the side of the street – kicked just while riding his bicycle. I was so angry about this that I made a programme out of it for GLR, deploring such loutishness, ignorance and violence.

18 February

The Chancellor of Germany, Helmut Kohl, was in London today to receive the Freedom of the City. I said a carefully written prayer about Germany, reconciliation and the giving of the Great Crucifix to St Mary-le-Bow by the people of the Federal Republic after the war. The Chancellor was impressive, a statesman. I spoke to Eddie George, Governor of the Bank of England, and to Edward Heath, who said, 'Get rid of that beard and come to lunch again.'

The Freedom of the City was given to Kohl on the day the Tory right buried Enoch Powell at St Margaret's, Westminster – a perfect irony. Why, I asked, did Enoch Powell lie in St Faith's Chapel at the Abbey overnight, draped in the Union Jack? The answer: because he was promised this as a member of the Abbey family years ago, when he was a Churchwarden of St Margaret's, Westminster. Nobody at the Abbey had the intelligence to think how that would make the white Establishment look. Powell made vile racism respectable, but Chancellor Kohl made peace in Europe a fact. Hugo Young, who was present this evening, wrote beautifully about it all in the *Guardian*.

As the procession left the high table to take the Chancellor upstairs from the crypt, where we had been having supper, the Prime Minister spotted me, came out of his place and thanked me for what I had said. This meant that, as we were leaving informally, I walked with him up the steps. There were so many things I wanted to talk to him about, but I realized that I couldn't use the opportunity. Now was not the right time.

It was also nice seeing John Major, Tony Blair and Chancellor Kohl sitting together at dinner in animated and friendly conversation. The Thatchers cut this occasion, though they had been invited.

In the first week of March I attended a meeting of the Southwark Fabric Advisory Committee. A team from Railtrack came to explain to the Committee why their proposals to rebuild the railway line on its high viaduct right by the cathedral would do us no harm. Not one of this team of PR experts mentioned the word 'cathedral' – a performance staggering in its ineptitude.

5 March

The church was filled with Masonic power brokers from the City for Sir William Shapland's memorial service. There was an excellent address from family member Charles Patatina, over from New York. Emboldened by what he said, I added extemporarily a little piece about Bill Shapland's way of narrowing his eyes, looking very fierce and saying 'no', but then being generous and writing you a cheque. It happened to me over the Globe Centre some years back, of course. When he'd given me that £1,000 cheque from his current account, I took it back to the Globe Centre Trustees and told them, 'If you want to get money out of the City, it's going to be difficult and you'll be treated as I've been treated. But stick to your guns, don't be rude – be gentle but firm, and £1,000 is better than a kick in the teeth.'

Selected parts of this story – with the charity remaining unidentified – went down such a treat with the memorial service congregation that, at the door afterwards, one grandee after another came up and said, 'Oh, thank you for telling that story. I had exactly the same treatment from Bill myself!' or, 'Heavens! You must have been present when Sir William said something very similar to me years ago.'

11 March

I took the bus to Hackney to help Elaine Jones at St Mary of Eton, where she was sorting through heaps of mouldy, smelly, mousy Latin chasubles she had found in the tower. The church was colder than the Arctic. They can't afford to heat it in the winter. Instead they polythene in the baptistry, like a tunnel of lettuces, and have services in there – very depressing and horrible. Elaine is trying to find a way of raising money and we must certainly get the City to help.

We had a beans and chips lunch in the pub opposite the church, where everyone knows Elaine. It was impressive watching her going about the pub in her dog collar, accepted and loved as the local vicar. As I've noticed before, the Irish navvies putting tarmac down in the road dealt with the difficulty of what to call a woman priest by calling her 'Father'.

24 March

I went to King's College in the Strand to interview Dr Andrew Coyle about Sion. We are possibly giving him two grants of £25,000 to enable his research on alternatives to present penal policy.[1] I think this is exactly what we should be doing with the money we have made from selling the building and saving Sion's books.

Then I went on to St James's Palace for a party in aid of the Children's Society, where I met several friends and talked to Fiona Phillips, the presenter from GMTV. She didn't know Patricia Routledge, so I was able to introduce them. In turn I was introduced to the Duchess of Devonshire. In a muddle with too many titles to remember, I managed to call the Duchess of Gloucester 'Your Grace' – although she is a Duchess, she is also a Royal Highness. This would have been a great

---

1 Dr Coyle, Head of the Department of Prison Studies at King's, was formerly Governor of Brixton Prison and is the author of *The Prisons We Deserve*.

moment for Proust. I tried to explain to HRH that Mary-le-Bow is not Marylebone, but this was hard work.

St James's Palace has a decor perilously near that of the average Indian restaurant.

On the eve of Palm Sunday we had 33 people to a Quiet Day. It ended in the crypt, where we imagined we were in the tomb with Christ on Holy Saturday, the most neglected day of Easter. In the afternoon we spent an hour at the *Holy Russia 1400–1600* exhibition at the Royal Academy. There were many pictures of the Harrowing of Hell, about which I had been talking earlier in the day. This is the strange and affecting idea that, between his death on the cross and his resurrection on Easter morning, Christ went down into hell and brought out the just prophets and kings, holy women and holy men from the classical and Hebrew past. In the Russian icons he is often depicted standing on the door he has broken down, helping people out across the wreckage.

5 April

Palm Sunday. In the morning I went to High Mass at All Saints, Margaret Street, where there was an excellent sim-plification of ceremonial, with lay people reading. In the afternoon I walked across to Southwark Cathedral, where I preached my first Holy Week sermon at 3 p.m. Evensong.

I did this same journey backwards and forwards on the Monday, Tuesday and Wednesday of Holy Week, enjoying the walks to and from the cathedral beside the fast-flowing (and dirty) Thames. As I walked, I thought – on Monday about prayer, on Tuesday about penitence, and on Wednesday about worship. In between I heard confessions from clergy who come to St Mary-le-Bow for this pur-pose from all over the country in Holy Week.

Also on my mind was the fact that the Northern Ireland Agreement was due to be signed at the end of the week. I saw Patrick Mayhew and he gave me a beautiful silver pectoral cross from Axum, the holy city of Ethiopia. It opened to reveal painted scenes of the crucifixion and resurrection of Jesus.

9 April

Maundy Thursday. At the 1.05 Mass I said I would be available in the afternoon if anybody else wanted to come to confession outside the advertised times, and two more came. Instead of saying Psalm 22 when the altars were stripped, the congregation knelt and sang 'Abide with me, fast falls the eventide'.

Jonathan Nicholls, the Lord Mayor's son, was there. I had suggested he might come just to see what religion was like. 'Don't join in,' I said, 'just sit at the back by the door and watch.' Well, he rang me to say that not only had he been to the service, but he had made his Communion and had gone out in tears. 'I didn't know religion could be like this.'

After the Mass, a woman said to me, 'I am a Jew. You made me feel as at home as if I had been in a synagogue.' I'd been speaking about heaven.

At Southwark the Provost, Colin Slee, included me in the foot-washing. I've spent years and years washing people's feet on Maundy Thursday, but have never had it done to me. I walked home along the Thames as 'fast falls the eventide'.

It seems that agreement in Northern Ireland is almost here – not by midnight, but during Good Friday. Hope of the breakthrough is the surging undertow of this Holy Week.

10 April

Good Friday. I went down into the empty church to unveil the crucifix and read Morning Prayer on my own. The Good Friday Agreement was expected to be signed between 12 and 1 p.m. – during the Three Hours service at the cathedral, for which I wrote too much material and said too much, the hazard of the three-hour sermon. I like the care that goes into the Southwark liturgy, and the thoughtfulness and attentiveness of the congregation, the sense of waiting. Afterwards we had hot cross buns and tea, then I walked home to say Evensong on my own in the bare St Mary-le-Bow. I spent the evening alone, reading.

11 April

Holy Saturday. The Good Friday Agreement was signed in
Northern Ireland at 5.26 p.m. yesterday. Tony Blair spoke
brilliantly. I rang Patrick, who was full of praise for the Prime
Minister, stunned by it all last evening and so happy. Mo
Mowlam had immediately rung Patrick from Stormont to
thank him for all he'd done – quite right, but generous of her
in the excitement to remember a telephone call which had no
political advantage to it.[2]

This morning's *Financial Times* carried a large article
headed 'Stock in Trade' about me and Bill Sewell. Very
upbeat about St Mary-le-Bow.

The Vigil rehearsal at St Paul's at 5.30 p.m. was chaotic
but relaxed. I stayed on for the Vigil and Confirmation, from
which we walked out at the end carrying candles. I felt proud
and pleased to have Nicholas baptized and Phillipa, Nigel
and Nicholas confirmed from St Mary-le-Bow – further addi-
tions to our small but steady stream of adults coming into
the Church.

12 April

Easter Day. The Syrian Orthodox community gave St Mary-le-
Bow its Easter incense by coming to use the church for their
liturgy.

At 11 a.m. I administered the chalice at the Solemn
Eucharist in St Paul's Cathedral, taking Nigel, Phillipa and
Nicholas there for their first Communion. The wandsmen were
actually welcoming today, for the first time in my entire experience. There was a congregation of 2,500 people, many of
them young, several of them from St Mary-le-Bow – including
Michael O'Sullivan, the man who cooks for the King of Greece.

I went home for soup, then walked to Southwark for my
last sermon in the cathedral. I felt very tired just before and
during Evensong. On my way back, recrossing Southwark
Bridge, I felt deeply depressed. Why, on Easter Day? I think

2 Dr Mo Mowlam had become Secretary of State for Northern Ireland.

because of sudden tiredness and the surfacing of loneliness – my life being part stage and part hermitage at present.

The next few days were spent in Lewes. On Easter Wednesday, Patrick and Jean arrived, having cycled part of the way from Kent followed by their protection officers in the Land Rover. The house filled with gales of laughter as we had tea and toast round the fire. Later we went off in convoy to Brighton to dine at English's. The protection officers went through the kitchens and cellars of the restaurant, then kept a discreet eye on us from just outside, while inside we ate hot jellied eels and sea bass.

23 April

Today was my old Spitalfield friend Donald Findlay's funeral at the Grosvenor Chapel. He and his partner Michael Gillingham lived together for 26 years.[3] Donald was 48 and ill for only two weeks, dying of cancer on Easter Monday. It was a wonderful service, full of friends from the art world, Parliament and the Church of England. John Gaskell preached a beautifully constructed, highly intelligent sermon about the women at the tomb, silent and afraid. This was masterly, for many in that packed congregation from the English architectural establishment will have heard the Christian gospel preached for the first time today.

In the evening there was a diplomatic banquet at Mansion House. I sat between the Ambassadors for Bolivia and Slovenia. I borrowed the German Ambassador's pen and wrote a second Grace during dinner, for I had forgotten until the footman reminded me that there was a second one to say.

Much fun was had with the silver bowl of rosewater, the German Ambassador teasing the Slovenian by dabbing it behind his ears, and the Indian High Commissioner, a charmer, dabbing his eyelids. I put a stop to this. 'Where will the rosewater be by the time we get to Morocco?' I asked.

---

3 Donald and Michael were friends of mine of many years' standing. They were among the first to buy and perfectly restore one of the seventeenth-century houses in Spitalfields.

On the way home, walking up Cheapside in my Chaplain's robes, I met the Master Grocer on the pavement. He was laughing his head off at the plight of his clerk, stuck in the lift at Mercers' Hall. I marched into the Hall to ask if a priest was required.

The fun of this evening was a sharp contrast to the sad obsequies at the Grosvenor Chapel this morning. Poor Donald, faithful, quiet, intelligent and good. Poor Michael.

24 April

I was driven to Wandsworth for the first filming sessions of the BBC's *What Now?* programmes (they decided against calling it *Headache and Heartache*). We listened on the programme to a gay man and two women. One I judged to be a total fantasist. Indeed, I asked her if she was using her real name. Obviously this kind of programme is going to attract people who agree to go on television to talk about their problems as a form of self-advertisement. The saddest was a battered mother of six with a violent nine-year-old, at her wits' end.

Edwina Currie was excellent on the programme. She has worked with the Workers' Educational Association and has been a first-class, concerned MP. Our star working with us today was Fiona Fullerton, an enthusiastic actress who knows Peter Delaney at All Hallows by the Tower.

The Mercedes home was the bit of luxury I most enjoyed. I spend so much of my life travelling up and down England on hopeless trains that don't come or are late. 'This wouldn't have happened in Leeds,' I kept telling myself.

In the second lot of programmes today, filming from 2.30 p.m. till 9, there was an interesting case involving a gambling couple. The husband, financing his gambling habit by burglary, was beginning to take with him his son by his common-law wife. The question was, should they divorce, or should they try and stick it out? He'd been on a rehab programme, but I thought it unlikely he'd ever escape from his gambling addiction and counselled divorce for the sake of the child.

This created a huge wave of hostility to me amongst the studio audience. Edwina, bless her, leaned across the camera and said, 'You're a man of the cloth. How can you possibly advise divorce?'

Well, I was quite clear it was right and, interestingly, the couple came to see me in my dressing room afterwards to thank me. They said they'd never been able to face the fact that they should part until someone in authority had given them permission. They didn't put it like that, but that's what they meant.

We worked with Leslie Grantham for this session – 'Dirty Den' from *EastEnders*. I like him. He's an impressive person. Not least because he's spent 11 years in prison for murder.

May began with a few days in Rome. Outside St Peter's a sludge-coloured canopy had been erected over an altar at which the Pontiff was to make some of his many new saints. Inside St Peter's there were some Japanese girls doing V-signs in front of the High Altar, being photographed by their boyfriends, obviously with no idea what St Peter's was, what an altar was, or what Catholicism was. Equally sad was the state of the sacristy, where I thought all the plate could do with a good dose of Goddard's Silver Polish.

Later that week I returned to London to record further episodes of *What Now?* It seemed to be becoming a custom that I would undertake real priestly pastoral work in my dressing room between filming sessions.

8 May

I flew to Dublin to give a talk about Affirming Catholicism, and was met at the airport by Clive Wiley, the Rector of Tynan. Unfortunately, the talk had been advertised as being in St George's, Belfast, rather than St Anne's, Dublin. Is this Irish, or is this Irish? There were, understandably, only 10 people there. The Vicar said he wouldn't listen – he would stay at the door instead to see if anybody else wanted to come in. And there he sat, right in the porch where he couldn't hear anything.

10 May

In Middletown, one of the churches in the Tynan benefice, there were rows of Orangemen in suits, and beautifully dressed children as if it were England in 1953. Clive is not only the Rector, but also the organist.

Then I rushed off to another village, also like England in the 50s. Clive has asked me to try to remember not to bow to the altar – or table, as it's called in Northern Ireland – but in this church I forgot. The MEP Jim Nicholson was in the congregation and afterwards, in the churchyard, the men surrounded him, finger-wagging over the referendum on the Good Friday Agreement. The women, all of them, were left in another part of the churchyard, where they were discussing cakes for a church bazaar.

After that we rushed off to Tynan, and a very ugly church where the people all sat in the back rows. Here I preached a third sermon and we had the most terrible Matins, with an organist dreadful beyond description. She is also the Treasurer of the local Unionist Party, however, and is going to vote for Mr Trimble and the 'Yes' party. She stood up to the men, who were uniformly against saying 'yes'. This made up for her not being quite so brilliant on the ivories.

In Armagh we called on the Anglican Dean and he showed me his eighteenth-century library, sweetly smelling of calf bindings and overflowing with treasures. I was also told the most wonderful story about Ian Paisley. Clive and a chum went to hear him preach and were treated to a real rant about hell and damnation and all the things that Paisley likes preaching about. The sermon was delivered to rows of old Belfast ladies. At the end the great man shouted, 'And in hell there will be weeping and wailing and gnashing of teeth!'

He repeated this several times, until a little old lady at the front looked up and said, 'But, Dr Paisley, I haven't got no teeth.'

'Teeth will be provided!' shouted the Reverend Doctor.

19 May

I was at St Paul's Cathedral today for the Corporation of the Sons of the Clergy Service.⁴ At the top of the steps just inside the door, the Bishop of London cocked his head meaningfully at me, but I didn't know what he meant. As we were waiting a little further in, he left the Archbishop of Canterbury, came up behind me and whispered, 'Did you get my letter?'

'No,' I replied. As the introductory fanfare continued, I went back to him and said, 'Is it a complaint about my views on television?'

'No,' he said, 'it's my idea that you might go to a new job.'

That gave me something to think about during the magnificent anthem, '*Spem in Alium*', a 40-part motet by Thomas Tallis, from the combined choirs of Rochester, Canterbury and St Paul's.

Then came the great news that Northern Ireland had voted for the Good Friday Agreement by 71 per cent, the Republic voting for it by 94 per cent. I felt it was a triumph for decency – underlined by the fact that Dr Paisley said the whole thing was bribery and fraud.

27 May

We had the Emperor and Empress of Japan to a state banquet at the Guildhall, and the Empress was so terrified that she had to have an injection from her attendant doctor just before she went in the procession from the Print Room to dinner. There were some old prisoners of war protesting outside, led by a member of the Court of Common Council. I felt ashamed of them and ashamed of myself as an Englishman at this discourtesy.

I sat between the wife of the Silver Stick in Waiting of the Royal Household, whatever that might be, and a sensible,

4 This is a great annual City occasion, always attended by the Archbishop of Canterbury and the Lord Mayor. The Corporation of the Sons of the Clergy is an educational charitable foundation.

Japanese-speaking old gentleman who had a business in Japan and goes to church at Wells Cathedral. I kissed Margaret Beckett, the President of the Board of Trade, and reminded her that she had once said there would never be another Labour Government.

June saw more filming for *What Now?* Leslie Grantham joined us again and was very amusing ('I said in Sainsbury's yesterday, "Got any Victor Stock cubes?"') and the next day we filmed in the company of Samantha Fox. The highlight of that day's filming was Samantha showing me the jewel in her pierced navel. One of the cameramen said as I came off the set, 'Millions of men would have given a great deal of money to have that experience, Father!' When our 20 programmes were 'in the can', we celebrated by having an uproarious party at the Groucho Club. Afterwards I found I missed the fun, youth and buzz of the studio, where people had been amazingly welcoming and kind – much nicer than in the Church.

Early in the summer I found myself doing a remarkable amount of travelling around. I went to Headcorn, near Tenterden in Kent, to give a lecture about Affirming Catholicism to an appreciative audience of 60. The next day I preached at an open-air Mass on the green outside St Michael's, Bedford Park, as part of the Bedford Park Festival. Walking round the stalls afterwards, I met a hat-maker who told me the story of his life since he had been a student in the University Church of Christ the King, Gordon Square, when I was Resident Chaplain. Then I got myself back to St Mary-le-Bow, where someone from Northern Ireland who needed a safe house for a bit, literally and most terribly, came to stay. One of the many advantages of St Mary-le-Bow is that there is always room to put someone up. We are a place for safe breaks.

A day or so later, I went to lunch at the House of Commons. It was a very distressing episode. I had been invited by a woman who came sometimes to the Dialogues and had been Michael Portillo's Private Secretary. Two of the guests were Roman Catholics, one a monk in training at Ealing Abbey, and one a young priest. The young monk said, 'All people who have homosexual sex should die as soon as possible.' This is the sentence he actually used. Then the priest said that Pope Pius IX, the man who opposed freedom of conscience, democracy, freedom of religion and modern science in the nineteenth century, should be canonized. Then the monk announced that Pius XII was the perfect Pope as far as the Jews were concerned.[5] At this point I stood up and said, 'I'm sorry, I can't listen to this any longer,' almost in tears. I felt the palpable presence of evil there in the House of Commons. My hostess, poor woman, pursued me out into the corridor, apologizing profusely. It was not her fault.

The next day was rather better. I replied on behalf of the guests at a City dinner at Trinity House, then went straight on to join the end of a dinner party given by the Bishop of London in the Old Deanery for Alan Webster's eightieth birthday. I sat down next to Lady Callaghan just as they finished the pudding. Her husband, the ex-Prime Minister, thought I was the Bishop. I got kissed by Ben Bradshaw, and Bishop Hugh Montefiore was at his most sparklingly witty. As I opened the door into the dining room, the Bishop said, 'Ah! Here comes Victor Stock, jumping out of the cake!'

Early in July Andrew rang to tell me that his and Fred's assailants from the attack in Highbury had each been sent down for two years. The judge, he said, had made a speech deploring homophobia. Andrew also told me that the Pope had just issued an Apostolic Letter saying that it was wrong even to think about the ordination of women, and theologians who did think about it would be punished. I wondered how you could punish theologians for thinking.

9 July

I took Janice Macdonald, who's having a such hard time nursing Alan with his brain tumour, out for a posh lunch. If I had more money, I'd take more people out for nice meals.

In the Court of the Arches we had the Confirmation of the Election of the Bishop of Southwark, Dr Tom Butler. Afterwards I had some fun telling everyone that *Racing Demon* was on at Chichester, as the new Bishop was being given dinner tonight at the Savoy. This passed the Bishop of Southwark by, because he clearly didn't know what *Racing*

---

5 Pope Pius XII has been widely criticized for his silence over the extermination of the Jews. For more information, see John Cornwell's book *Hitler's Pope*, published in 1999.

Demon is about. He must be the only bishop who doesn't. Paul Morris, the Registrar of the diocese, who organized the party at the Savoy, has also not seen *Racing Demon*. He must be the only other person in the Church apart from Dr Butler who hasn't.

We had a private room at the Savoy, and brilliant food and conversation. The Bishop is tough and rough, but likeable. He drank whisky after dinner. Nonetheless, it seemed amazing to me, almost beyond belief, that (a) the new Bishop of Southwark hasn't seen *Racing Demon*, (b) the Registrar hasn't seen it, (c) the Registrar arranged for the dinner party for the new Bishop to be held in the Savoy, when (d) the climactic scene of that devastating play about the current state of the Church of England takes place in the Savoy, around the figure of a fictional Bishop of Southwark. Astonishing, or astonishing?

Later in the month I saw *Copenhagen* at the National Theatre, a brilliant, many-layered play. I came home moved and intrigued by the work, to discover, extraordinarily, a fax from Edwina Currie inviting me to go and see *Copenhagen* with her the following Tuesday. I had enjoyed the evening so much that I immediately agreed to go again. This was against the background of the appalling behaviour of the Lambeth Conference, which seemed to be in the grip of Biblical Fundamentalists wanting to adopt a Southern States Bible Belt/African Evangelical/Diocese of Singapore bigoted line on lesbians and homosexuals. Once you got out of the Church to a play like *Copenhagen*, I reflected, it was possible to breathe a more informed and hopeful air.

Yet *Copenhagen* raised huge moral questions. What really happened during the Second World War about the development of the atom bomb? Who helped or betrayed whom? The Uncertainty Principle was at the heart of everything. When I saw the play for the second time with Edwina Currie (she had managed to get front-row seats, so we were practically on the stage), it was moving in additional and different ways from my first visit. We had dinner afterwards and I discovered that Edwina, who understands a great many things, also understands Physics, which I do not.

Escaping from London in August, I went to Burgundy with David Hutt to stay in the house of some friends near Taizé. The local town was called St Genoux-le-Nationale and in the medieval parish church was an extraordinary arrangement of nineteenth-century stained glass. I enjoyed explaining the iconography to David. Joan of Arc, Margaret Mary Alacoque and King Louis of France were all put in when the nineteenth-century church was trying to prop up absolutism, helped by a recent definition of papal infallibility. The French right during that period was mad and doomed. Not unlike the general line coming out of the Vatican at the moment, I thought.

Taizé itself was not David's scene, so I went alone to the Midday Office. It was moving to be part of that 2,000-strong gathering of young people. A verse from Romans, 'We are not to rely upon ourselves, but on God alone,' was read out in five or six languages, then an 'Alleluia' was sung as a round. We sang a canticle as a round, then were silent for about 15 minutes before singing another round. A prayer was said in many languages, and we sang a final round as the brothers withdrew. It was all a long way from the Lambeth Conference.

I got back to England to find news that Mule Fogh had died. She was to be buried the next day. I wrote something to be read at her funeral, and talked to her faithful friend Helle Sarttrop, who had looked after her for years. As I could not be there, she promised to read out my words at the funeral.

17 August

I walked through Hyde Park to the Albert Hall for a Prom – Handel's 'The King shall rejoice', Bach's *Violin Concerto in E Major*, Handel's *Water Music*. As this was played, I thought of Mule Fogh and of dancing to an old 78rpm record of the *Water Music* on the veranda of the doctor's house in the jungle outside Kudat Saba, Malaysia, in 1963.

In September I did get the chance to visit Copenhagen, where I had been invited to celebrate Mass at the Anglican St Alban's Church.

13 September

I celebrated the 8 a.m. Mass in St Alban's for eight people, including a party of four educated young adults from Washington who didn't join in once, not even saying 'Amen' at the end of prayers. There were 80 communicants at the 10.30 service, at which I preached, and quite a lot of children.

In the evening I took some plants to Helle Sarttrop, Mule's faithful old friend, who lives just by the Charlottenborg Palace. On a table were a few belongings from Mule's old flat: some cards I'd sent to them over the last 20 years, several antique hyacinth glasses like the purple one Mule gave me and which I have at the top of my staircase in Cheapside, a volume of Shakespeare, some pieces of batik from Indonesia, photographs and a little tin of Sven's flies, the remains of his passion for fishing. I declined the glasses as being too difficult to carry, and the Shakespeare as I have two already, and decided on the little tin of beautifully made flies.

We drank some excellent wine and ate strawberries from their summerhouse while we shared the difficulties of Mule: her bad temper, her demandingness, depression and unkindness, as well as her enormous fund of sophistication, fun and intelligence. Her ashes are with Sven's at the school where she was the nurse when he was in the Sixth Form. To my astonishment, Mule left 4,000,000 kroner as a scholarship to help boys travel from the school. She didn't leave anything at all to Helle except a round table and two oil paintings, in spite of everything the woman did for her.

14 September

This morning I sat and read in the Palm House and then, walking in the garden, I met a Professor of Economics from Dublin with his old parents from Cork who were discussing the sermon I preached yesterday. When I got off the plane at Heathrow, a smart woman in a pink silk jacket stopped me and said, 'Oh, you were the preacher yesterday at St Alban's in Copenhagen. We all argued about your sermon over lunch.'

On 24 September I made use of the ticket from Qantas (blessing Rosalind McGovern once again) and flew out to Australia. I stopped *en route* at Singapore to stay with Tim Auger, now Managing Director of a publishing house there. Singapore had changed out of all recognition since my last visit there on my way back from VSO in 1964. It looked like a cleaner and richer New York, gleaming and towering above the old Chinese temples and godowns.

I eventually arrived in Darwin at 4 a.m. on 28 September. We were pitched out and made to buy cups of undrinkable instant coffee, while we were shown opals which nobody wanted to buy. By 8.15, however, we were in beautiful, magical, tropical Queensland, where I was met by a driver and taken to a beach. I spent a few days snorkelling off the Barrier Reef, visiting a rain forest, swimming, reading and making the acquaintance of koala bears, crocodiles and all manner of bird life. On a boat trip along the Daintree River, an emerald-green tree frog hopped onto my hand and sat contentedly, telling me all about his life and beliefs as we passed enormous snakes wriggling out of the trees and trying to frighten us. They didn't, of course.

I reached Sydney late in the afternoon on Saturday 3 October, and discovered that I had left my black shoes in Singapore. Tim is the kind of host who likes you to take your shoes off at the door. I had obeyed and left them in a companionable pool of shoes, where they apparently still languished. To Father Michael, who met me at the airport, I said, 'Please drive me at once to a shoe shop.' He did and I was able, just as it closed, to buy a pair of Romanian shoes, probably made of cardboard, which did me for my official work in church the next day.

4 October

Sunday. We went to Matins at 7 a.m. in the Victorian poor people's church downtown, curiously like a church you might find by the gas works of some industrial city in Victorian England, but dignified with a fresco of saints in subdued browns and greens, ochres and blues.

I preached slightly uneasily to 50 people at the 9 o'clock Mass, because the atmosphere was like the non-replying kind of congregation we used to have at 8 o'clock at Friern

Barnet, where you said, 'The Lord be with you,' and nothing happened.

At 10.30 this was replaced by devotion and responsiveness from 160 people and an absolutely brilliant choir visiting from Melbourne. At Evensong we had Gregorian chant and William Byrd canticles, perfectly sung, and a full church.

Then there was Pontifical Benediction, given by a Bishop who's a Board of Mission chairman and acts as an honorary Curate in the parish. This was bizarre. The Diocese of Sydney forbids church ministers to wear a chasuble: you have to take an oath saying you won't wear one. But Benediction is such an extremely Catholic idea that it didn't cross the minds of the legislators to forbid it, because it didn't cross their minds that *anybody* – let alone a Bishop – would want to do it.

The following week I spoke in the New South Wales Parliament to 70 members of the Australia–Britain Society. I spoke about Arthur Phillip, but sadly forgot to acknowledge the expert on the subject, Maureen Goldstone-Morris. This proved to be a mistake, but it was a pure oversight, if you can have such a thing as pure oversight.

11 October

Sunday. I rang Mrs Goldstone-Morris and left two grovels on the answer-machine. Last night she left the most outraged message for me, saying that she was going to sue me and demanding a public retraction and apology of the most dramatic kind, because I'd used unauthorized information she'd given me about Arthur Phillip in my talk to the New South Wales Parliament. The only thing to do on these occasions is to grovel.

13 October

I left Sydney, being taken to the airport by the Curate in his very smart open sports car. As it was an open car, my second pair of sun goggles sailed away. The first went overboard off Port Douglas on the way to the Barrier Reef.

I arrived in Melbourne in the afternoon. Dr Helen Gronowsky motored me to Trinity College, where she had to attend a Governing Body meeting. Meanwhile, I was put into the freezing cold Senior Common Room. Melbourne is quite a few degrees colder than Sydney. I was given a cup of tea and locked in. Nobody appeared for two hours, because nobody told Helen where I'd been put.

Helen doesn't change. I met her when she came to London to do a PhD (between distinguished headships in Australia) when I was the University Church Chaplain. She's now a priest and in every way larger than life.

16 October

In the University Club at Trinity College, I found myself eating the Australian coat of arms: emu, lamb and kangaroo on the same plate. It was quite nice, in fact, with mustard mash.

The other guests were the Head of Morpeth College, Newcastle, Anne, a theologian from Trinity, Ross, a Roman Catholic editor and journalist, and the team I was to interview after dinner about the future of leadership in the Australian Church. The audience for this included Keith Raynor the Archbishop, who's also the Primate of Australia, and three other bishops. It was rather hard work and I said 'no' to a drink afterwards.

Somebody took me aside and said, 'We realize you're going to be the new Archbishop. You've been flown out from England purposely.' This was very amusing because he was absolutely serious.

I was back in London before the end of the month, checking up on my supply of smart black shoes. There was a very important engagement to fulfil before November began.

31 October

St Mary-le-Bow was filled with flowers and guests for the wedding of the beautiful Helen Gourley to Jonathan Nicholls, the Lord Mayor's son. The Lord Mayor came in morning coat, not state dress.

The sky turned inky black in the middle of the afternoon and a deluge poured down, unfortunately right through the middle of the roof of the nave in a sort of waterspout, onto the precise spot where the bride would stand. I moved her slightly east of the danger, and kept a mop in readiness behind a vase of flowers.

8 November

I made a wet-leaved, watery trudge from Cheapside to St Mark's, Myddelton Square, to say Mass, the Vicar Paul Bagott being away. When I got there, some women were literally fighting over a child's choir robe, calling each other 'slag' and 'cow' and other even more alarming words, at the very top of their shrill, Clerkenwell voices. The Franciscan lay assistant, though much bigger than me and robed in a Franciscan friar's brown habit, was unable to deal with this, so I did. I packed the women off out of the church, the children all crying their eyes out. I calmed the children down and got a semblance of peace going. During Mass, as I was facing the glass west doors across the altar, I could see these women still going at it hammer and tongs outside, getting through a whole packet of cigarettes each.

That week I visited Alan Macdonald in St Thomas's Hospital. He was paralysed on one side by then, and I encouraged him to go into St Christopher's Hospice in Sydenham, at least for a short time. He very much needed the palliative care which the hospice could offer, and Janice and the family needed him to have it too, but the poor man just desperately wanted to go on working. It was dreadful to watch. A week or so later he did move into the hospice, and I trekked out to Sydenham to see him again. We talked and, wonderfully, even laughed about the imminence of death.

Canon Stephen Oliver, the new Canon at St Paul's, came for a Tuesday Dialogue. He had previously been the Rector of Leeds and said to me of that incumbency, 'You're well out of it.'

19 November

I went to be interviewed for the job of Rector of St James's, Piccadilly, at the Bishop of London's house. There I met Mary Robbins, the assistant priest, and Hugh Valentine, the nonstipendiary assistant priest. What, Mary Robbins asked, did I understand by 'radical welcome'? Well, I didn't know and said I was afraid I didn't understand. I discovered later that it was a very specific question about some of the strange things that happen at St James's.

Neither at that interview, nor at the longer interview with the panel, which included the two parish representatives, the Lord Chancellor's Private Secretary for Appointments and the Archdeacon of Charing Cross (representing the Bishop of London), was I really asked any questions at all about myself, or about the Alternative Programme which St James's runs and which is fascinatingly controversial. I couldn't work out what was the matter with this interview until afterwards, when I realized that, in fact, the parish representatives were not interested in me. They'd decided they didn't want me before they met me – a depressing experience.

I left all that behind for the time being, however, and went to catch a train north. I was due to speak about Affirming Catholicism in Durham, but first I stopped in Newcastle, where I was taken to Gateshead for dinner with a group of local clergy. The streets were full of cheerful young people on their way to the clubs. All were dressed in skimpy tops or short-sleeved shirts. It was freezing, but to wear a jacket was clearly social death.

21 November

I was motored to Durham Cathedral, that great Norman fastness, warm and well lit, confident and godly. The lecture and slides I showed went well, though maddeningly, despite my very best intentions, two slides turned out to be upside down. After the lecture, we celebrated Mass at St Cuthbert's tomb behind the High Altar. It was a holy moment, as we stood in a circle around the four great silver candlesticks, under Ninian's gilded tester with its emblazoned image of Christ as a young man, a Greek god, ruling the universe.

30 November

St Andrew's Day. I had an Amsterdam-like Chinese lunch for £6 – soup, mixed bean curd, fish, meat, a bowl of rice and two pots of tea – before visiting Clare Herbert, the Rector of St Anne's, Soho, who's feeling up against it and needs somebody to talk things over with who has a little bit more experience of incumbency. I admire and like her enormously and sat with her for a couple of hours, promising to help as much as I can.

On my way back to the City from a GLR broadcast, I noticed the new statue to Oscar Wilde: 'We are all in the gutter, but some of us look at the stars.' In the taxi home, the driver recognized my voice from GLR and wouldn't take the money.

1 December

A letter came in the post from No. 10 Downing Street and the Lord Chancellor's Ecclesiastical Appointments Assistant Private Secretary. 'We have decided not to offer the appointment to any of the candidates interviewed.'

I trudged off to Sydenham to visit Alan Macdonald in St Christopher's Hospice.

4 December

As I went into the BBC's Broadcasting House today, I wondered how many people entering its portals can translate the Latin inscription – *Deus Omnipotente...* – that blazons forth the BBC's international vocation above the entrance. I recorded a few minutes' talk for a Radio 4 programme which will go out on Christmas Eve after the broadcast of the carol service from King's College, Cambridge.

During the following weeks, I spent more time by the bedside of Alan Macdonald, now home from St Christopher's Hospice and in his house in Streatham. At his bedside one day I found Jane Myles, whom I had not seen for 14 years. (Jane was a close friend in my University Chaplaincy days, now married to the Vicar of

Isleworth and mother of the actress Sophia Myles.) Alan was at that stage of his terminal illness when he was asking the same questions again and again. 'When will I know I'm going to die?' 'When will I know it's time to say goodbye?' Jane brilliantly said, 'Instead of goodbye, it might be hello.'

24 December

Christmas Eve in Lewes. I'm 54 years old, and I went to a special birthday tea for children, including me, at Andrew and Phyllida Stewart-Roberts' house at Mount Harry. Just after the carol service from King's College, Cambridge, to which we were half listening, a telephone call came through from Daniel, Andrew's and Phyllida's son in Budapest. He said he wanted to talk to me, not his parents. 'I was so surprised to hear your voice just now on the BBC,' he said, 'that I cut myself doing up the children's presents. You would have thought Hungary might be a Stock-free zone.'

31 December

Amsterdam. I sat in the Botanical Garden and thought back over the year that's now closing. In the Palm House I pondered over Lewes and 104 Western Road, which I'm coming to love so much. I must tidy up my book room and papers and throw stuff out from St Mary-le-Bow in January. As to the future, I really have no feelings at all. I can't see into the next months at all, except that I know where I'm preaching.

At midnight, champagne glass in hand, I went out onto the Amstel, enjoying the people and the noise and thinking of poor Alan Macdonald and Mule Fogh, one dying and one dead. On the other side of the canal, men and women were dancing, leaping over a bonfire.

Cloud-capped Spires

When I got back to London, Alan Macdonald was very much on my mind. I went to see him on 5 January, and found he was drifting in and out of consciousness. I sat with him for some time and had a good conversation with his son, my godson Alexander.

Meanwhile, the usual routines continued at St Mary-le-Bow. I was not feeling particularly buoyant early in 1999, and on 7 January I wrote in my diary, 'It's odd being back at work. Am I doing anything worthwhile?' Sometimes I do feel that I am not doing anything worthwhile, but just turning the handle of some ancient and creaky machinery. Simply turning the handle does some good, however, and in some religions turning the handle does more than some good – look at the prayer wheels of Tibet. Perhaps my daily round is a sort of Tibetan prayer wheel in Cheapside.

10 January

Janice rang to tell me that Alan died yesterday, and I rang Jane Myles to tell her. Alone in London in the evening, I was tearful about Alan: another link with my parents and past gone. Alan and I had gone out to Borneo to do VSO together as school leavers back in 1963.

During my GLR broadcast today I talked about Alan and his work for the BBC,[1] and my affection and admiration – hoping that Alexander would hear this tribute to the Dad he loved and admired so much.

I am thinking a lot about what to say at Alan's funeral and have decided to use the pictures of the crucifixion from the Gospels of Mark and John as a counterpoint of belief and unbelief: 'My God, my God, why have you forsaken me?' from Mark, and 'It is accomplished' (or, as Professor Peter Hinchcliffe translated it, 'The goal is scored') from John. Alan

---

1 Alan was Head of Development at BBC World.

was an interesting example of the professed unbeliever who was assiduous in his churchgoing for reasons, he would explain, of family solidarity.

19 January

Carrying my robes, I walked down to St Bride's, Fleet Street, for Alan Macdonald's funeral. John Tusa from the Barbican was appreciative afterwards of what I had said. I rewrote my sermon three times and took a great deal of trouble over it. Alan's sons and close friends carried the coffin. It was a terribly sad occasion. Alan was that little bit younger than me.

20 January

At a dinner at the Mansion House this evening, a judge told us in his after-dinner speech that women and roses are just the same – good in bed or up against a wall. I record this because it took my breath away and I am pleased to say there were gasps of dismay. It's not the first time this has happened at a City dinner.

After that, it was something of a relief to escape to the beauties of Venice for a few days. I came back in a more positive frame of mind.

7 February

Sunday. I went to Emmanuel College, Cambridge, to preach on generosity. I was much helped in this by the altar painting of the Prodigal Son behind me. I'd totally failed to register this from previous visits to Emmanuel, but it came in handy tonight. The Master was friendly, and at dinner I met a pretty don called Dr Catherine Pixstone. She is a Radical Theologian, the latest thing much favoured by the Bishop of London. I don't even know what it means yet.

9 February

I told a grandee who was planning his father's memorial service that I couldn't say a prayer about horses, I was afraid, not with a straight face.

Rhatna Gosa, the spiritual director of the Buddhist Centre, was my Dialogue guest. He was a great success and I will ask him again – an Irish Roman Catholic boy who ran away from County Cork to Berlin at the age of 17, where he became a Buddhist – like you do. Reading Buddhist texts before and after our lunch, I was struck by the concept of 'mindfulness'. I could do with some of that.

11 February

Today Minou was photographed for *The Times Book of Church Cats*. A great deal of trouble was taken. She put her paw to a contract and gave several interviews and is now behaving with a new dignity, aware of her forthcoming status as 'supercat'.

The rest of February offered several memorable occasions, most of them positive, one extraordinarily aggravating. At a party in the House of Lords I got into conversation with Rosemary and Norman Lamont, who were both waxing lyrical in praise of General Pinochet. For some reason, General Pinochet was a hero of the Tory right. I found this impossible to put up with, and we ended up not being able to speak to each other at all. As I said, a mass murderer and torturer is a mass murderer and torturer.

On a happier note, Stephanie Cole came for another Dialogue and was excellent, as always. Pat Manley, a Labour Councillor from Dagenham who came to Mass on Tuesday mornings on his way to his job at Tesco's, shared his excitement at being elected Mayor of Dagenham, and I promised to go to his Mayor-making.

I had a splendid evening at a reception given by the Chartered Architects at the Merchant Taylors' Hall, which included an inspection of the thirteenth-century crypt and other glories. I was rather looking forward to becoming Chaplain to the Master Merchant Taylor later in the year. The best thing about that particular reception was that we were served tiny cones of fish and chips, in a perfect mixture of the vulgar and the dainty.

I also spent some more time with Clare Herbert of St Anne's, Soho, and preached for her in her splendidly light, wood-panelled modern church on the First Sunday in Lent. On my way home, I looked in at the back of St Giles in the Fields, Cambridge Circus, where the Rector (who has been there since the Second World War) was taking the 1662 form of Morning Prayer. There were 23 people in the nave and I reckoned that it was all at least 300 years removed from what had been going on in St Anne's just down the road.

2 March

This evening an already cross Diocesan Advisory Council and the Ward Club stood outside St Mary-le-Bow to watch the floodlighting of the tower. It was meant to be the end of the process – the City Corporation revealing, before our astonished and delighted gaze, the triumphant execution of a long-awaited project.

No. The man in charge said things like, 'Well, we'll be half an hour lighting up and then I'll ask you to walk up and down Cheapside and look back every 10 minutes or so and see how things are coming on.'

This so infuriated two of the people that they got into their chauffeur-driven cars and were driven away at once. It was an astonishing exhibition of incompetence, of course, but it did have its funny side. Michael Kenny, who was present, said that watching one of the great and good practically chewing off his moustache with rage was 'too sad, too sad'.

3 March

There was a party at the Athenaeum for Professor Leslie Holden's seventieth birthday. We heard a brilliant speech from Professor Dennis Nineham, who taught with Leslie at King's before becoming Warden of Keble College, Oxford. Professor Nineham's commentary on St Mark is on my desk as I write. There were 100 people, but only one bishop, a new suffragan taught by Leslie. That, I think, says all that needs saying about the honour paid by the bishops to a great and much loved twentieth-century scholar.

11 March

Coming back from the vet's with a bag of 'science plan' cat food, I had a wonderful conversation at the bus stop with an old East End woman who told me how much she owed to the late Father Bartlett, a man long dead of whom I've never heard. 'Oh, that was a priest that was,' she said. 'He was the bee's knees. I can't read the Bible without floods!' Wonderful.

25 March

Annunciation. We had 70 at High Mass today for Britten's *Missa Brevis*, just the right harsh tone. It is a calamitous day: we have begun to bomb Serbia.

In the afternoon I watched videos, biked over to me by the BBC, of a series of Holy Week films called *On the Street* which have been made by James Jones, the Bishop of Liverpool. They're all about the current state of Liverpool and religion in the city. I thought them very good, so struggled over to Broadcasting House at 7.15 to be interviewed about them. I was supportive of the Bishop and what he's trying to do, but had to be firm with the interviewers, who expected me to be squashed. It's very easy to be squashed when you're being interviewed by famous journalists, but I wasn't.

Towards the end of March I went to Bristol University for the Architects' Conference, where I had been asked to give an opening lecture on the subject of welcome. Afterwards I went to see the Roman Catholic cathedral, which turned out to be all pre-stressed concrete, brown carpet and nasty chairs. I was not impressed. The Palm Sunday procession, undertaken in beautiful sunshine, was much more pleasing. We assembled outside the Anglican cathedral and Brendan Clover, the Precentor, sang perfectly. The procession could have done with a band, I felt, but one cannot have everything.

1 April

Maundy Thursday. In the evening I went in bright sunshine to preach at St Mary's, Bourne Street. I stayed at the Altar of

Repose for an hour afterwards and lit candles for many people, including the souls of Mule and Alan. At Bourne Street the urn in which the Blessed Sacrament is reposed for Communion on Good Friday has the word *Resurgam* written across it.

2 April

Good Friday. I met Susan Howatch at Matins at St Paul's Cathedral. Then, walking towards Blackfriars, I bumped into Canon John Halliburton. I told John how Father Skeoch had said to Father Scott at Bourne Street, 'I see you have Victor Stock preaching. I no longer regard St Mary's as a Catholic church.'² I feel very proud to have de-Catholified a famous Anglo-Catholic church by my presence alone.

A few weeks after Easter, I travelled up to Shrewsbury to stay with Richard and Joleen Hayes, having been invited to a party celebrating their twenty-fifth wedding anniversary and Richard's sixtieth birthday.

25 April

The Lord Hill's Hotel, with its terrible furniture, wallpaper and upholstery, was the unlikely setting for 41 distinguished-looking relatives and friends of Richard and Joleen, mostly family. I made the speech proposing their health.

All Richard's sisters looked exactly as they had when I last saw them years ago. Richard's Mama, who is 94, seized upon me immediately, telling me the old story of the nail through Richard's foot at Loppington Hall, and how stupid Richard had been to let it happen. She went on, still at full pitch, 'I had to shout at him, "Get in the car, drive to the hospital, drive to the hospital, will you go!"'

This elderly Shropshire landed gentry world is and always has been remote from London, and hasn't changed since the eighteenth century.

---

2 Canon David Skeoch, one-time Curate at St Mary's, Bourne Street, and Chaplain to Bishop Graham Leonard, is now Vicar of St Saviour's, Pimlico.

27 April

An invitation came this morning to preach at the service which precedes the Winchester and Eton cricket match. I didn't want to give up another Saturday morning when I could be in Lewes, especially as it would be followed by preaching in Chelsea on the Sunday, so I said 'no'. The Chaplain was surprised that I should turn down such a privilege. Well, tough.

May began with some warm days, and Jane and Peter Myles came for lunch in the garden in Lewes. News came through that same afternoon of a bomb explosion in an Old Compton Street pub. At least two people were dead. There had already been a bomb in the Asian-dominated Brick Lane area. Now it was gays. Next week, I thought bleakly, it would be Jews. The following day, I was saddened to hear news of another death as a result of the pub bomb, as well as amputations and people suffering from severe burns. I walked up to the Downs and reflected on the evil, cruelty and malice of the deranged mind which had planned the atrocity.

The next sorrow came at 7.30 a.m. the following Monday, just as I was about to celebrate Mass. Julia Brodie arrived with her son, Alexander, and told me that her husband Tim had died playing polo at Windsor at 5.30 the previous afternoon. She had left a message for me, but I had not been into the office to listen to the anwer-machine.

I was cheered, ridiculously, by a parcel which arrived in the post a day or so later – a grey magic wand with a pink star that made spell-casting sounds, lit up and twinkled when waved. This excellent device came from Jane Myles and it enlivened my whole day. How had I worked in the ministry for 30 years without a magic wand?

10 May

A letter came today from the Bishop of Edmonton, asking me to consider becoming the Vicar of St Pancras, Euston Road. I passed that gloomy pile only yesterday. I've never liked it. Brendan Clover, the last incumbent, was deeply unhappy there and I can see absolutely no attraction to this idea.

11 May

Only 66 people came for Professor Sir Ghillean Prance's Dialogue. Why does this wonderful, holy and fascinating man not draw in a larger crowd? He talked to me over lunch about Evangelicals he likes and Evangelicals 'who just haven't got it'.

Edwina Currie took me to the National Theatre to see *Candide*, an utterly wonderful production. At home in bed at 12.15, I read my old 2/6d. paperback of it to re-read Voltaire's original ending.

13 May

Ascension Day. I got myself to Southwark's Roman Catholic cathedral and the reception for the Dalai Lama, having been invited by the cathedral's architect whom I met at the Bristol conference. The Dalai Lama is a man of palpable holiness, jolly, quick, funny and absolutely human. 'Smile, it shows what is inside.' 'Practise your religion every day.' Not, you notice, 'Practise *my* religion every day.' The Pope wags his finger at the world, but the Dalai Lama blesses and bows and smiles. The young people all lit up in his presence. He gave white scarves to the designers of the Peace Garden, and there was such pleasure on every recipient's face.

17 May

At Bedford Park I chaired and spoke at a lunch in the vicarage for the Kensington area Affirming Catholicism group. Exhausted by all this, I went to Kew and lay flat on the grass for half an hour before going back to Marylebone to broadcast on GLR. I waved my magic wand over the listeners and the switchboard jammed with people asking, 'Where can we get one?'

30 May

Trinity Sunday. The thirtieth anniversary of my ordination. In the empty nave of St Mary-le-Bow I read the 1662 Matins, just as I did before my ordination in 1969. I was made

Deacon by Graham Leonard in St Pancras parish church, then was made priest in St Paul's Cathedral in 1970.

I was in Lewes by the evening. Andrew rang from Nice, remembering the anniversary, which I very much appreciated. Later he rang back to say that Mark Jones was in St Mary's Hospital, Paddington, having had a blood clot which could lead to a pulmonary embolism. I got through to Mark in his room. He said, 'I feel like an inverted hedgehog and have sent all my visitors away,' but I'm glad I got through.[3]

I read Evensong on my own and during supper Jean Mayhew rang. 'I expect St Mary-le-Bow has showered you with gifts and celebrations for your thirtieth anniversary,' she said.

'No,' I told her, 'I don't think anybody there even thought about it.'

'Well, we have,' she said, 'and we want to come and get you tomorrow.'

31 May

The Mayhews did come and get me, and motored me over to Twysden for champagne and quails' eggs, asparagus, claret and smoked chicken – all laid up on the terrace where, so long ago now, we'd had lunch with Douglas and Judy Hurd. This was all prepared by Patrick and was lots of fun.

Both Patrick and Jean said such kind things about my work over the years, and they asked me to say a special Grace. Later Patrick's protection officers took me at breakneck speed to Paddock Wood so I could catch a train for London Bridge. It was an extraordinarily happy and unexpected treat of an anniversary celebration. Patrick has painted me a little picture, 'For Father's Day'.

I returned to St Mary-le-Bow on a wave of gratitude and good feeling. The very next day, however, I found myself feeling rather less than fatherly towards our Dialogue guest.

---

3 Dr Mark Jones, a consultant psychiatrist, is an old friend whom I prepared for Confirmation at St Mary-le-Bow.

1 June

Today's Dialogue guest was Jeffrey Archer, novelist, former Tory Vice Chairman, life peer, millionaire, Big Personality. He arrived at 12.30 saying, 'Why am I here at 12.30? The Dialogue isn't until 1 o'clock. I'm a very busy person. I shall come back in half an hour.'

'Well, Lord Archer,' I said, 'your office arranged for you to come here at 12.30 so that we can try the microphones.'

'I don't need a microphone, I'm a very practised public speaker.'

'I know, Lord Archer, I'm sure you are, but the microphone is for the benefit of those who are hard of hearing. Now, this is what we do...' I gently led him into the church and up into the pulpit. 'Could you say something into the microphone?'

'Yes, I'm going to leave. I shall leave now. This is ridiculous!' He tore the microphone from its socket and broke it. This was quite a difficult thing to do – it needed twisting and wrenching with some force. He threw the pieces on the floor, pushed our secretary Graham out of the way and made for the door.

'If you leave now, Lord Archer,' I said, 'you need not return.' This calmed him down. At the door he said, 'I'm not going to stay to lunch with the Grocers. It's a ridiculous waste of time. When I'm Mayor of London, I'm going to give you a job. I'm going to take you out to a very expensive lunch and talk about it.'

I have met Lord Archer before, so I took him upstairs and calmed him down. He wouldn't have a drink, but he looked at my flat and said, 'Why don't you sell this? You could get millions for it.'

I explained that it wasn't mine and then he said, 'Why have you been ordained? You're an intelligent person; you've thrown your life away. You could have done something useful for people.'

I smiled sweetly, concentrating on the aim of getting him into the pulpit at 1.05 for the Dialogue. Whatever happens, I thought, I mustn't get cross. He was, in fact, excellent at the Dialogue (without the microphone). Then, at the door, he said again, 'I'm not going to the Grocers,' just as I turned to introduce him to the Master Grocer.

We went, of course. I sat in an exhausted heap through lunch and, when His Lordship had swept out, a member of the Court leaned across the table and said, 'I know you never drink port at lunchtime, Victor, but I think you need a large beaker of it.' Then we all discussed what we *really* thought of the Great Man.

Back at St Mary-le-Bow I found a shaking secretary and an outraged administrator. I wrote a letter to His Lordship about his behaviour, saying that he must apologize to the secretary and that I recognized certain aspects of his character in my own, but I tried to control them.

A couple of days later, a handwritten letter of apology and a bottle of champagne were delivered to Graham from the House of Lords, but there was no apology for the rest of us, nor any offer to pay for the new microphone system which we had to have installed. There was rejoicing at St Mary-le-Bow when, just a few weeks later, His Lordship fell from grace and was unable to proceed as a Mayoral candidate.

Later in June, Cardinal Basil Hume died of cancer and the public responded with affection to this fine leader of the Roman Catholic community. The funeral was televised and I watched it all, having held the Cardinal in high esteem.

26 June

There were appreciative articles in the papers today about the Cardinal's funeral. It was imaginative that the Irish and British Prime Ministers both attended and sat next to each other – an excellent symbol. What a pity that protocol and habit prevented the Queen from going. We know she liked and respected Cardinal Hume, and it would have been an excellent signal to the divided loyalties in Northern Ireland that the British sovereign could go to the Catholic Archbishop's funeral. Either this was never suggested, or, if it was, it was vetoed by whoever vetoes anything imaginative. There must be a great many people whose sole task in life is to veto the imaginative.

30 June

The ordination retreat which I am conducting starts tomorrow, and I took the train to Tooting Bec this evening to have supper with the bishops and the ordination candidates. At Tooting Bec station I discovered I was in a zone not covered by my ticket and was fined £10 on the spot. This was enraging because I went straight to the ticket office with the money that was owing – only to be told that I would be fined £10 as well as having to pay the difference. I'd hardly recovered by the time I got to the Bishop's house.

1 July

Wychcroft, where the Southwark ordination retreat is being held, is an Edwardian house on the South Park estate in Surrey, given by Sarah Goad's father to the Diocese of Southwark. It is horrible, spectacularly horrible.

The first lady who came to see me at the end of the evening with her problems found me in bed. I had just decided that nobody else would want to come and see me and that I could get safely into bed. I had to say, 'Just a moment, please,' and put my trousers back on.

2 July

Today, in Surrey heat and sun, I gave addresses and listened to many people's anxieties and heard some confessions. I illustrated each talk on an aspect of the priestly life with a card I'd bought in the Tate Gallery, so that everybody gradually made a collection of cards. One was of an artist's workshop, to help people think about the creativity of priesthood; another was a circle of stones on a green ground, to help them think about time and eternity, the background to everything the priestly life is about.

4 July

Before the ordination service itself in Southwark Cathedral, I said to Bishop Tom Butler as he stood waiting to go in, 'You must be proud to be the new Bishop of such a diocese, where the morale is high and the liturgy beautifully performed.' He looked rather surprised. He took me out to lunch at the Globe Theatre restaurant afterwards, where I teased him. I don't think he's often teased.

14 July

Stephen Lines, President of the Royal Institute of Chartered Surveyors, has asked me to be the principal speaker at the Drapers' Hall Millennium Dinner on 11 November and to 'say something about God'. It has taken 13 years in the City for this invitation to happen – actually to speak *about God* at a dinner. It will require a great deal of care and the right sort of humour, but I am determined to do it.

20 July

At the House of Commons, where I was dining *chez* Bernard and Anne Jenkin (Bernard recently became Shadow Transport Minister), we met Peter Mandelson and Bernard introduced me. This was an interesting moment. Here was a person who exudes power and is only out of office temporarily.[4]

'Who must I write to, to get you to come to St Mary-le-Bow for a Dialogue?' I asked, never wasting an opportunity.

'You must write to me,' he said, in a way that was not an invitation.

I'm sure he hasn't the slightest interest in people who are not going to be of use to him. He said to Bernard in my presence, 'You're a star.'

Bernard, who knows what power is and obviously admires Mandelson, was very impressed, but Anne said, 'Of course he thinks you're a star. You demolished the Deputy PM John Prescott over transport in that debate.'

---

4 Not so long beforehand, Mr Mandelson had been forced to resign as Trade and Industry Secretary over a loan from former Paymaster General Geoffrey Robinson. Later he was made Secretary of State for Northern Ireland, but was again forced to resign in 2001.

On the Members' Terrace some huge 'Old Labour' women were drinking enormous pints of lager – a jolly scene.

29 July

A man came to see me today, deeply disturbed. As he was shouting in my study, I thought that Evangelicals might diagnose demon possession, but I would diagnose schizophrenia. He threatened me with physical violence, raising his fists at me. I told him he didn't frighten me, which he didn't.

In the evening I discovered him at the back of the church, just before Mass, doing a fine imitation of the creature from the black lagoon, writhing, shaking, screaming and foaming. This put off some of the people who were coming into Holy Communion, so I gradually encouraged him outside to sit on a step in the fresh air. During the service, however, he came back in doing his monster act – arms upraised and claws outstretched, but silently this time. Slowly and threateningly, he made his way up the nave towards me. Most people didn't see him until he got near the front, as the congregation here have been bullied into sitting near the altar.

By this time I was sitting down, as someone else was reading from the lectern. He came round the altar and knelt in front of me, then threw himself at my feet, clutching onto one of my hands and crying, 'Sorry, Father! Sorry, Father!' Two of the young men in the congregation got up and headed towards him to save me from physical assault, but I motioned them to desist and, of course, he was fine. The funny bit was that some people hadn't seen him arrive behind the altar at all. It was only later, when he popped up behind it, that they saw this apparition for the first time. Poor Ivy Clements' eyes were out on stalks. Poor fellow.

Then it was time for a holiday. Umbria in August was glorious, as were the paintings in Perugia's National Gallery. I was particularly struck by Fra Angelico's John the Baptist, who was wearing a lavender silk cloak over his usual camel-hair outfit and looked rather disapproving about such a poncy adornment. In St Sepulcro we were inspired by Piero's *Resurrection*, Christ in the act of stepping out of the tomb, grave, human and majestic.

A surprise awaited me after Assisi, on the day I took a group of friends there to see the restored church, which had been badly damaged in an earthquake. We were having dinner at a restaurant that evening when a man came over from one of the other tables and asked me if I was the 'Rocking Rev' from GLR. 'I recognized your voice and then heard you being called Victor,' he said. 'I hope you don't mind me speaking to you.' This impressed everyone, including me. In the manner of great personages, I went over to his table and graciously sat down for a chat.

8 September

St Mary-le-Bow. We had a sung Mass at which Bishop Michael Marshall confirmed, standing in for the Bishop of London. It was boiling hot and the Bishop sat over lunch till 3.30, letting his hair down. Then Professor Nancy Lambton came to visit, looking 68 when she is in fact 87. She's come down from Northumberland for a conference on theology at King's.

Earlier on, the Dean of Westminster rang on his mobile from a train *en route* to Oxford, to ask me what I was doing next Lent.

'Which Sunday?' I asked.

'Oh, I'd like you to come and preach at Westminster Abbey every Sunday morning in Lent 2000.'

So excited was I by this invitation that I at once broke my resolution not to work on consecutive Sundays.

14 September

Holy Cross Day. I visited Ivy Clements in her tower block. She was very down and sad, but I anointed her and made her laugh. If all the Sacraments made people laugh, we'd be much happier.

22 September

I travelled to Norwich to speak about Affirming Catholicism, then spent an afternoon being shown round disused church-es. At 4.30 I was met by a jolly and kind Reader and taken off to her house, with its serried rows of perfect vegetables, to be given venison casserole. Then I went with her and Canon Michael Stag to East Dereham – in the pouring rain – for Mass. There was a small group of only 17, but I gave my talk entitled 'Is religion absolutely fabulous?' and then fielded questions. After that I was taken off to stay the night at Bilney House, a Regency Gothic rectory, where we had smoked salmon sandwiches and a bottle of red wine.

After the luxuries of Bilney (the house had an open-air heated pool), it was quite a contrast to pay a visit to the chaos, dirt and general disorder of St Mary-le-Bow's single homeless project at Shadwell. Two of our young gentlemen, Tim and Jason, had done a runner with £50 belonging to Jemal (a really worthwhile boy with a future), the fridge, the TV, the iron and the washing machine. All this, of course, was for drug money. I thought once again what an extraordinary man Michael Kenny was to manage all this so patiently.

The autumn Dialogue season got underway with visits from Professor David Rhind, the new City University Vice Chancellor, theatre director Nicholas Hytner, who had to rush off to rehearse Maggie Smith in Alan Bennett's *The Woman in the Van*, and Dr Alan Borg, Director of the V & A.

It is always the famous names that interest people when I talk about the Tuesday Dialogues, but for me Tuesdays are much more dominated by the preparatory ritual of laying the table, making sure there is fresh orange juice and a bottle of white wine in the fridge, and checking the lunch details with the crypt restaurant (we have had one or two spectacular nonappearances of lunch over the years). Then there is the anxious pacing up and down, waiting for the guest to arrive, out in the vestibule scanning the street and looking at my watch. When they do arrive, I am concentrating on trying out the microphones before we climb to the top of the house for a pre-lunch drink. After lunch I am concerned with ensuring that the guest takes his or her present away. This does not always happen, which means that I have to trundle off to some theatre, the BBC or the Houses of Parliament later in the week, bearing gifts. Then there is the washing-up. The famous names often pass me by in something of a blur.

8 October

At 7 a.m. Bernard Jenkin rang, anxious about viewing the burnt-out carriage at Ladbroke Grove after the disaster two days ago, when 26 people were killed in a train crash. He was worried about what to say. As Shadow Transport Minister, this is how his day begins, poor man. Yesterday's *Independent* praised him for his bipartisan stand and his refusal to attack John Prescott over the matter, and I'm proud of him too. This is how politicians must behave if they are to regain respect, but the temptation to make party political capital out of such a tragedy must be almost overwhelming.

11 October

I had a telephone conversation today with Ian Albery, Chief Executive and Producer of Sadler's Wells, who asked me to go on stage at the end of *La Traviata* tomorrow to bless the house on the occasion of its first anniversary.

12 October

During the day I wrote a speech for Sadler's Wells, and prayers, and thought most carefully about what could be said to an audience who would be surprised to see a clergyman suddenly appearing behind the footlights. There would, I knew, be many people there who weren't religious at all, and some who were quite definitely anti-religious. It would be extremely easy to press the wrong button.

At Sadler's Wells in the evening, Verdi's opera was beautifully sung, but my nervous state was increasing all the time. At the curtain call I was rushed straight down with Ian Albery and onto the stage, in the wake of an enormous first-anniversary cake. I'd cut my little speech in half already and managed, at least outwardly, to be calm. It was odd speaking to 1,500 people I couldn't see because of the blazing footlights. I hope I did some good in what I said, which centred on Lilian Baylis and bringing theatre to working people.

15 October

I preached to 2,000 people in St Paul's Cathedral at the Triennial celebration for the Merchant Taylors' schools. I could hear that vast audience listening. God immediately cut me down to size, however, because at the tea afterwards I was attacked by a Lutheran Forward in Faith pastor, who tried to help me become a Fundamentalist. After 10 minutes, I said, 'We live in different universes. Why don't you go and talk to other people and allow me to do the same, before we get very cross indeed with each other.'

The next day I took a coach to Bristol, where I stayed with Canon Brendan Clover before preaching at the Legal Service in the cathedral the day after.

17 October

I was given a lift to the cathedral with the wife of the canon next door. She was actually called Mrs Bile. There was an excellent Eucharist and sermon in the Lady Chapel at 10 a.m., to which I listened attentively. At 11.15 the Legal Service began – trumpets, Red Judges,[5] and lawyers from Ghent, Rotterdam, Amsterdam, Paris and Germany.

At drinks in the Council House afterwards, the presiding Judge Mr Justice Butterworth said nice things about my sermon in his speech and another judge, who had heard me at the Exeter Legal Service, was complimentary about the fact that I'd preached on the doctrine of the incarnation and its relevance to the law. Mr Justice Toulson said, in the course of a long conversation, 'The whole business of prison is barbaric and useless.' It was one of the subtexts in my sermon, so I'd struck a sympathetic note.

On 22 October, John Gaskell rang to tell me that Michael Gillingham had died that morning. I phoned Andrew, whose

---

5 High Court judges wear red robes and are known as 'Red Judges'. Roman Catholic judges go every year to Westminster Cathedral for the 'Red Mass', named after these robes.

patient Michael had been. It was very sad news, coming so soon after Donald Findlay's death in 1998.

29 October

Friday. Michael Gillingham's funeral took place at St Andrew's, Holborn. For some reason the family wanted it there, not at his own church, the Grosvenor Chapel. Graham Phillips, who knew Michael through the Grosvenor Chapel, carried the cross and Canon Roger Greenacre preached the sermon. He didn't quite strike the right note, but it was intelligent and worthwhile all the same. Michael's Evangelical Plymouth Brethren family were ill at ease with the incense and music by Byrd.

In the afternoon I went off to Lewes for Andrew and Phyllida Stewart-Roberts' private view of the Rodin exhibition (including his infamous sculpture *The Kiss*), for which Phyllida has been instrumental in raising the money.

Lady Edna Healey put my Lewes address in her bosom, having asked for it, just before Phyllida came up to ask her if she would like to join the 'Putting Victor Stock in his Place Society'.

'Edna,' I said, 'tell Phyllida where you've put my address...'

1 November

All Saints' Day. As well as High Mass at lunchtime, we had a Service of Light at 7 p.m., attended by the City Corporation, the local Ward Club, the Chief Commoner and the congregation. After that we processed into the churchyard and the Lady Mayoress, Wendy Levene, switched on the tower illumination. Immediately she started speaking, however, poor Lady Levene was drowned out by the bells.

There was a story behind this, of course – crossed wires between the Corporation and the bell-ringers. The time of the ringing had been changed, but the bell-ringers had not been told. Very sweetly, three or four people in the audience pretended they could hear the Lady Mayoress when they couldn't, and made appreciative gestures. Wendy Levene was very good tempered about this – not everybody was.

2 November

We had Herbert Howells' *Requiem* at the lunchtime Mass, and afterwards Michael O'Sullivan and his parents took me out for fishcakes at Sweetings. In the evening I went to the Grosvenor Chapel where I celebrated yet another Mass, the priest being on holiday, but when I got there nothing – vestments, books, chalice – was ready.

From there I walked to the Bag O'Nails in Victoria and talked to the 'Holy Joes' – very nice, mostly ex-Evangelical young brought together by the Revd Dave Tomlinson. This post-modern – post-Evangelical – meeting in the upstairs room of a pub certainly had authentic notes of the early Church and was hugely enjoyable.

11 November

In the evening I talked at the Drapers' Hall to 280 Chartered Surveyors about Jesus and the Millennium, just as Stephen Lines had asked me to do. At the end there was standing applause. I was, I must say, relieved and went home very happy, thinking, as David Jenkins has taught us, 'God is. God is as he is in Jesus. Therefore we have hope.' Even Chartered Surveyors.

15 November

At St Martin-in-the-Fields today I chaired a colloquium on the relationship between Church and State. I enjoyed this once it started, though I felt nervous about my responsibilities, there being members of both Houses of Parliament in the audience. Professor Averil Cameron, made a CBE last Friday, was speaking for the Establishment, and Bishop Colin Buchanan was speaking against it. Both made worthwhile points. The silly Bishop of Winchester was there and was predictably silly.[6]

---

6 The Rt Revd Michael Scott-Joynt, Prelate of the Order of the Garter. He was defending the Establishment of the Church of England as if the changes of the twentieth century had not taken place in English society.

16 November

Dr Indarjit Singh, the Editor of *The Sikh Messenger*, came to Dialogue and it was slightly hard going, for he was gentle, shy and unforthcoming.

Afterwards, however, he told me he'd been to lunch with the Queen and apparently Her Majesty hates bus lanes – never having used a bus, of course – and recommends coat hangers for opening car doors, something she heard from a security officer. 'Conversation was kept at a low level,' he said. 'Prince Philip used colourful language at the corgis.' Dr Singh's comment could have come straight from Michael Ramsey; he used exactly the same tone of voice.

At the Mansion House the other day, Lady Thatcher leaned across to Dr Singh and said, 'You have your religion and I have mine.' 'She seemed nonplussed,' said Dr Singh, 'when I pointed to shared beliefs, and she turned away.' I like Dr Singh.

Later in November, I came across something quite unexpected when I visited the headquarters of the Children's Society about their proposed carol service. While I was being taken round the building and introduced to people, I found myself standing in front of the cabinet in which details of all the Society's children are kept – including my own as an adopted baby. This made me feel quite wobbly, but I kept it to myself. It was an odd moment.

26 November

The Dean of Westminster organized a meeting with the new Director of Music, James O'Donnell (former organist of Westminster Cathedral), and myself to think about how to integrate liturgy and preaching for my Lent series next year. Unique in my experience, my host thought it would be a good idea to link the liturgy music and the preaching together. Would I also, he said, please produce my sermon titles because they wanted to put posters up in Parliament Square. This gives me much food for thought. I shall have to look at those posters all through Lent and before, and wonder what I meant by the titles.

29 November

I worked on the titles for the Abbey, producing: 12 March, 'The Word in the Desert'; 19 March, 'Fasting and Finding'; 26 March, 'Upsetting the Tables'; 2 April, 'The Intolerable Shirt of Flame'; and 9 April, 'Greeks at the Festival'. I shall link my examinations of each Sunday's scriptural readings with paintings, particularly in the National Gallery and the Tate, which visitors might like to look at – anticipating the fact that very large numbers of tourists will be present in Westminster Abbey on any given Sunday, and many of them will want to get inside one or two of the major London art galleries as part of their holiday itinerary.

December began with the unexpected pleasure of discovering at the dentist that all my teeth were all right, even after an x-ray for suspected decay. I was so childishly happy at this news that I went straight into El Vino's in the Strand and bought a case of a wine called Du Reverend. In the evening I went to St Paul's to listen to the splendid Mary McAleese, President of Eire, speak on 'Blessed are the Peacemakers'. As Northern Ireland was due to get devolved government at midnight that very night, the lecture could not have been more timely.

6 December

The Feast of St Nicholas. The day on which children in Holland get their Christmas presents. As I went downstairs to Matins and Mass in the crypt, I thought about Masses being the staple diet of priestly life. I tried, as I stood in the chapel, to offer the day to God in association with the offering of Christ to his Father. Offering something to God is the origin of sacrifice. It is the act of offering which makes it holy, so at the altar we stand with Christ in his self-offering, bringing a diocese on the other side of the world, a parish in the East End, a member of the congregation who is sick, to the holy table and placing them in Christ's Presence. The more eucharistically, i.e. thankfully, we begin the day, the more open, available and attentive we may be to the demands others make on us. I often think, as I begin the celebration of the Eucharist, that

I don't have any idea what the day will bring, despite the numerous appointments in the diary.

Today those appointments included recording something for a BBC broadcast about religion and legal language, which was being recorded in the crypt because of the Court of the Arches. As soon as the BBC team left, a television crew from CNN came, making a programme about Cockneys, and they stayed to film our Charterhouse carol service. From there I went off to Broadcasting House to record a slot on a Radio 4 programme, due to go out at 9 a.m. on Christmas morning.

The next day, Mike Thompson came to record a piece from me for use on the *Today* programme. 'Rather a lot of wireless, dear,' my mother would have said.

Later I preached at the Children's Society carol service in support of their controversial and courageous decision to lift the ban on gay and lesbian adoptions. I was moved when the director, from the pulpit, thanked me for the support I had given them on this issue. Then we had the Architects' carol service, the Arbitrators' carol service and the Mercers' carol service, also attended by the Masons' Company, the Cooks' Company and the Broiderers' Company. You can have too many companies, I decided, as well as too many carols.

21 December

Our parish carol service produced £540 in the collection for our homeless project. The service had a rather dreary beginning – it needs a jollier start, and there was too much 'First Noel'. I must re-read this bit of my diary before planning the carol service for 2000.

Listening to the readings, I was struck by how tenderly and beautifully Andrew Dunford read – so much so that it brought tears to my eyes.

I took Bernard Jenkin out to dinner. He needs cheering up: the poor man is not only Shadow Transport Secretary, but also Shadow London Spokesman, and he has his hands full.

22 December

Yesterday I made my last live broadcast of the twentieth century and this morning I celebrated Mass for the last time this century. A man said to me, 'This is my first visit here, and I've a son called Eli and I've worshipped for six years at Trinity, Wall Street in New York. You mentioned Eli *and* you mentioned Trinity in your sermon.'

24 December

Christmas Eve in Lewes. I'm 55. I woke early and listened to the storm. Michael Kenny has given me some wonderful early editions, including T.S. Eliot's *The Four Quartets*. I read Matins and was thankful. I had a fire in the sitting room and King's College carols in the background, as on so many Christmas Eves past.

I went to supper with Paul and Elizabeth Whitehouse, but Paul was busy evacuating the population from Pevensey. At the other end of Sussex, the coastline beyond Chichester is on red alert for floods.

Paul Ronke[7] came and motored me to St Bartholomew's, Brighton. It was a physical battle through the storm. I enjoyed the great dark nave – the tallest in Europe – and Paul, a non-churchman, joined in with the carols. The Vicar said we were safe tonight inside the ark, but Paul leaned over and said, 'This ark's leaking.'

29 December

London, and time to start preparing for the Millennium celebrations. I laid the table, putting out interesting stones with histories, old coins, a piece of gold tessellation that fell off the roof of St Paul's Cathedral, greenery from the roof garden and various bits of treasure that mean something to me – all as a great centrepiece on the table. Michael O'Sullivan is going to produce the most wonderful food for our New Year's Eve feast.

---

7 Paul is a Dutch friend, an equities editor at UBS Warburg.

30 December

In the evening I went to Holland Park for dinner with Gay Firth, who had two French guests. They told us a story of German persecution, parents hidden by brave peasants, all others in the family taken to the death camps, a Mother Superior saving 90 Jewish children and being herself hidden from the Gestapo in a forest. What a story with which to end the twentieth century. Gay and I sat there in tears.

31 December

President Boris Yeltsin resigned today on this, the last day of the twentieth century. I walked through gathering crowds – damp and uncertain – along the Embankment, past the City of London School, seeing the Tate Modern on Bankside getting ready for the opening next May.

I met Colin Slee outside the Provost's House and he told me that the Queen is going to the Crisis at Christmas shelter after visiting Southwark Cathedral for a service tonight. It's taken two years to persuade officials this might be a good idea. Then I walked into Colin Buchanan-Dunlop, the Clerk of the Goldsmiths' Company, and his party. 'I carry about a sermon you preached at St Paul's, Knightsbridge, two years ago,' a posh woman told me.

I went home for tea and a snooze until Evensong at 5 p.m. in St Paul's Cathedral. I should think there were 700 people there. A deep silence, a sense of waiting, beautifully executed prayers.

Back at the ranch, Michael O'Sullivan took over the kitchen and at 9 p.m. a group of us ate caviar, chopped red onions and teal. By 11.30 there were 120 or so, mostly young people, in the church whom I'd never seen before, but Gay Firth and Gillian Williams were there. There was hardly anyone at all from St Mary-le-Bow's usual congregations. After 10 minutes of readings, including John Donne's 'I have a sin of fear' and Psalm 90, we climbed the tower.

As midnight struck, the low clouds and drizzle forced smoke and cordite lower and lower as the fireworks burst above a city transformed backwards into the Middle Ages.

The modern buildings strangely vanished, leaving only the cloud-capped spires and towers of the churches, sharply black against the incandescent scarlet, white and golden trees, flowers, sunbursts and stars of fire.

I went down the stairs and stood in the street. It was full of people, wandering back from the river. A stranger – a young man – came up and kissed me, then women and men of all ages came up and kissed me as I stood on the steps in my cassock. People shouted out, 'Thank you for the Dialogues!' 'Thanks for GLR!' 'Thank you for having the church open!' 'Happy New Year!' One man pressed a £10 note into my hand. People swirled in and out of the church and sat, knelt or lit candles. I had to keep replacing candles. Sikhs and Hindus came into the church too. 'Thank you, thank you for keeping it open.'

I realized that the street owned St Mary-le-Bow – for, although there is no resident population here, St Mary-le-Bow's congregation is London and far beyond. It was an astonishing beginning to a new era.